CW00524285

THE APOCALYPSE SCROLL

STEPHEN JACOBS

Copyright © 2023 by Stephen Jacobs

All rights reserved.

No part of this book may be reproduced in any form or by any electronic or mechanical means, including information storage and retrieval systems, without written permission from the author, except for the use of brief quotations in a book review.

Cover design by Bookconsilio

www.bookconsilio.com

Back cover image credit: (reversed and coloured) Israel Defence Forces

For my daughters, Tilda and Flo

ACKNOWLEDGMENTS

I owe my greatest debt of gratitude for this book to a long-dead soldier, religious philosopher, priest, politician and historian, without whose voluminous writings I would have had no source material for my story of the siege and subsequent destruction of Jerusalem in 70 CE. Flavius Josephus's accounts of the Jewish War in his *Bellum Judaicum* and *Antiquities of the Jews* are the only surviving Jewish historical texts from late first century Palestine and I plundered them unashamedly for context and historical detail.

It will come as no surprise that, for dramatic purposes, I have taken many liberties with Josephus's accounts and any historical or factual errors are entirely mine. I sincerely hope that the many scholars specialising in this period will forgive me my occasional flights of fancy.

My heartfelt thanks also to Adam Preston, my endlessly patient editor, without whom this book would never have seen the light of day. Thank you for your wise counsel, Adam.

I would also like to thank all those who read various drafts and provided me with valuable advice and insights, especially Tamsin Meddings, Francesca and Simon Hood, Adam Wakeley, Nick Kettlewell, Sarah Billyard and my daughters Matilda and Florence.

PROLOGUE
15 YEARS AGO

IT HAD BEEN A TOUGH NEGOTIATION, but a great outcome.

It wasn't every day you cleared three hundred grand with the promise of more to come. So they were on a real high as they wound their way home through the Sussex countryside. Unaware that a good week would end very badly very soon.

Sometimes you're already dead and don't even know it.

They barely noticed the Volvo semi-trailer truck parked half-on and half-off the grass verge as they sped by, its lights off, the driver scarcely visible in his cab in the gathering gloom. They registered it unconsciously, as you do most things when you're on autopilot on familiar roads. Your mind drifting, half alert to hazards, the other half lazily cycling through the events of the day. Had they been paying closer attention, they might have taken a moment to wonder why a huge cab over truck, with no load, should have been parked by a quiet country lane in the damp dusk of an early April evening.

As it was, they rounded a bend and didn't notice as the truck pulled out behind them. Nor were they aware, as they turned onto the even narrower lane that led, after a couple of miles, to their home, of the truck driver taking the same turning,

1

then halting and quickly dismounting from his cab and placing a diversion sign at the mouth of the lane before resuming his pursuit, accelerating fast.

"Maybe at last we get that trip to Bhutan," mused Geoff. His wife smiled, her head lolling on the passenger headrest, sleepy after their celebratory lunch. "Maybe. And maybe we can put the boys into a decent school and give the house a makeover."

It was his turn to smile. He knew she'd win the argument, as she usually did. And that was okay, because she was the smart one, always had been. Without her, the business would never have got off the ground, for all his expertise and academic brilliance. He'd always relied on her judgment and it had served them well. Which was why he'd been especially proud of himself when, against the odds, it had been he who'd picked up their new client and almost single-handedly landed the deal that was to transform their lives.

He looked across at her. Her eyes were closed, the ghost of a smile still playing on her lips as a lock of dark hair fell loosely across her forehead. In her mid-forties but still striking, still turning heads. He was a lucky man and he knew it. He'd been with Connie since university and even after all these years he still didn't understand why her eye had alighted on him. Why she, the clever, beautiful philosophy student, had fallen for the geeky archaeologist. But they'd made a good team and built a modestly successful business together – never quite breaking into the first division of their profession, but doing well enough and always living in hope of better times.

Now perhaps she would get the future she deserved.

They were in no particular hurry, luxuriating in their good fortune and dreaming their respective dreams as the Audi swung lazily through the curves on the final leg of their journey, its automatic headlights blooming as they entered a wooded

2

stretch, startling a hare that sat bolt upright in the middle of the road before recovering its wits and darting into the hedgerow.

They crested a hill and the trees fell behind as the landscape opened up and the road led down a shallow incline between low hedgerows towards a bridge over the River Arun. Perhaps because he was tired and his mind was elsewhere, perhaps because the setting sun was now in his eyes, or because the truck had no headlights, or perhaps a combination of all three - whatever the reason, Geoff only knew they were in trouble when a shadow abruptly loomed in his rear-view mirror. A split-second later they were flung back against their seats from the force of a powerful shunt from behind. The car slithered from side to side for a second or two and then regained traction as he instinctively hit the accelerator and the rear wheels recovered their grip, driving the car forward.

"What the hell!"

His wife was instantly wide awake and turning around, straining against her seatbelt, and he saw her neck snap sideways as the truck surged forward and rammed them again. She screamed and grabbed for him, her nails clawing at his shoulder as he fought to regain control of the car, which was now at a forty-five-degree angle to the road with the truck's bull-nose tight against the offside corner of its rear bumper. He'd seen all the movies, in which the hero manages again and again to recover control of a flailing vehicle as it is tossed from side to side by the villain's monster truck. But in real life there was no control, just the swiftly dawning realisation that, no matter how expert a driver you are, the laws of physics prevail.

The one movie trope that did hold true, he thought, as the car slid sideways with the front of the truck now jammed against the driver's door, was that in these situations time really did slow down. With crystal clarity he saw his wife's eyes widening, terror etched into her face. He saw the speedometer smoothly zeroing, as the car lost traction and gave way to the lateral force of the truck. He saw every detail of the front grille of the enormous semi-trailer complete with the ticked circle of its Volvo logo, and he took in the dim features of a pale face behind the truck's windscreen just as the driver stamped on the brakes and the huge vehicle abruptly stopped.

He had time to register the rapidly approaching low parapet wall of a bridge a split-second before the front nearside bumper of the car, which was still sliding downhill at speed on the rain-slicked Tarmac, clipped the leading edge of the stonework. The Audi pivoted violently and its rear wheels caught a thick tangle of blackthorn on the bank to the right of the parapet. The truck reversed and then launched its final assault, forcing them off the road completely with astonishing violence. The vehicle turned almost lazily as it rolled down the steep slope, flattening and ripping at bushes and shrubs as it plunged towards the river below.

To add to their disorientation both air bags deployed and the car was filled with the stink of explosives and gas. Somehow, the car landed right-way-up on the bank just a couple of feet short of the fast-flowing water. The squeal of metal and thrashing of branches abruptly gave way to a cloying silence, broken only by the ticking of the cooling engine and the sound of the river.

Geoff was, to his amazement, still fully conscious as he turned to his wife. Her eyes were tightly shut, her fists gripping the sides of her seat. "It's okay, darling," he said. "We're okay." He reached across and put his hand on hers, squeezing it before looking out of the car windscreen, now latticed with cracks. He marvelled at how close they'd come to disaster. The relief washed over him in waves, the adrenalin still pounding through his veins and his heart thrashing in his chest. A few feet more and they'd have been in the river, which at this point was not far off a raging torrent after the heavy spring rain. His mind raced, his synapses snatching at disconnected thoughts and shreds of memory. For some reason they coalesced around a song, *Give me just another day*, appropriately enough by The Miracles, and for a hysterical moment he thought he was going to laugh at the absurdity.

He quickly flexed his arms and legs and found nothing broken, just the promise of a few bruises. His side window was gone and he was covered in a thousand small chunks of shattered glass. The passenger window was still intact. He pulled on his door handle and pushed at the door with his shoulder, but it was jammed shut from the combined impact of the truck and the fall. He gave Connie's hand another squeeze and she opened her eyes, slowly focusing on his face. "Wh– what....?"

"It's okay. It was an accident, some maniac in a monster lorry driving too fast. And God knows what he was doing on this road. But we're alright. It's alright. Can you try your door, darling? Just try opening your door." She hesitated, as if confused by his request, then slowly complied, pulling on the handle, but it was in vain. "It's stuck," she said, "I can't..."

"It's okay, darling. Don't worry. Let's just catch our breath and then we'll figure it out. We can get out through the window." He slumped back against his seat and closed his eyes for a moment.

When he opened them again, he was startled by the sight of a figure standing beside the car. He couldn't see much in the deepening gloom, but enough to make out the body of a tall, well-built man – young, he thought – dressed in overalls and a baseball cap. There was some kind of logo on it. "Thank God!" he shouted through his open window. "Please help us. We were driven off the road. Some maniac –" The words died in his throat as the man's head tilted slightly and revealed the words beneath the logo: 'BRS Transport.'

Everything fell into place. The truck on the side of the road, the violent collision. "It was you," he breathed. "You bloody idiot! You could have killed us!"

The man didn't move, just stood there with his hands by his sides, staring at him through the passenger window. "For God's sake, help us get out!" But still the man didn't move. He just stood there, his head cocked, almost appraisingly. And then he stepped sideways, out of view, moving towards the back of the Audi.

Craning his neck round to follow him, Geoff yanked at his seat belt but it, like the door, seemed to be jammed tight. His wife tried again to pull at the door handle, but still to no avail. At least she managed to release her seat belt and reached across to grasp her husband's shoulders. "He did it deliberately," she sobbed. "He drove us off the road. We've got to get out of here. Please Geoff, get us out!"

It was at this moment that her husband noticed the pungent, cloying stench of petrol which, now he was aware of it, seemed to grow stronger by the second. He redoubled his efforts to get the door open, but it was stuck fast. As he yanked helplessly at the handle, he saw the man return to stand beside his door. To his astonishment, he calmly took a pack of cigarettes out of the top pocket of his overalls and stuck one in his mouth. Pulling out a box of matches, he struck one, cupped his hand over the cigarette and lit it, drawing the smoke deeply into his lungs. In the light of the match and the glow of the cigarette Geoff could make out a fleshy young face and a pair of deep-set eyes, glinting redly with the reflection of the flame.

He had time to register that the man had not extinguished the match. An instant later, he understood why. Pulling a piece of paper out of an inside pocket, the man held it to the match flame and all three of them watched as it flared to life. His face once again illuminated, the man and woman in the car watched in disbelief as the man grinned at them, before casually dropping the flaming piece of paper to the ground and stepping quickly back.

The moment the burning paper hit the ground there was a simultaneous bass thump and a whoosh as flames leapt up beside and beneath the car, hungrily consuming the petrol which continued to pour from the severed fuel line. Both passengers became aware of a searing heat beneath their feet as they frantically threw themselves against their doors in a desperate effort to escape the flames, which swiftly climbed the door panels and were drawn into the car through the open window. The man stood calmly watching, smoking his cigarette, as the occupants of the car thrashed from side to side.

As their skin began to blister and the smoke and flame forced their way down their throats, a silently screaming husband and wife gripped each other's hands and stared at one another with seared, bewildered eyes.

––––––

The man, now standing at a safe distance, smoked the last of his cigarette and ground the stub underfoot before picking it up and putting it in his pocket. As he walked back to his truck, he thought he heard faint music coming from the undergrowth up near the road and, curious, he clambered up to what he thought was the source and saw a faint glow in the undergrowth. Reaching in, he pulled out the ringing phone, which must have been thrown clear of the car through the open window when it tumbled down the slope. Who used disco music as a ringtone, for fuck's sake? he thought as he gazed at the screen. Incoming call from home.

Well, no one would be answering that call anytime soon, he thought, and depressed the power button. When the screen went blank, he dropped the phone in his pocket and continued on his way.

He looked around him at the darkening landscape, as unfamiliar to his city eyes as a rain forest to a Bedouin, and shivered involuntarily. The sooner he was back on familiar turf in London, the happier he'd be. This place gave him the willies. He was not a superstitious man and put it down to an overactive imagination.

It was, after all, his first time.

CHAPTER 1
TODAY

FATHER ANGELOS BARTHOLOMAIOS walked slowly through the gardens of the 1,700-year-old monastery with its thriving olive grove and cypress trees and marvelled, not for the first time, at how remarkable it was that such a beautiful, lush retreat could survive and flourish in the arid wastes of the Judaean desert. It was, he supposed, a blessing from God, but He had had some modest assistance from the sophisticated irrigation network that kept the garden regularly watered from the wadi below.

Father Angelos had much to reflect on as he sat and rested for a few minutes on one of the stone benches. Above him towered the imposing edifice of the Monastery of Saints John and George of Choziba, his home for the last twenty-five years, which clung to the sheer limestone cliff like a nest of barnacles to a ship's hull. Even by contemporary standards it was a remarkable feat of construction.

Founded in the fifth century, it is one of only five surviving monasteries in the Judaean desert and is home to a mere handful of monks. It is located in the Israeli-occupied West Bank in the deep, narrow gorge of the Wadi Qelt, which threads its way through the desert for 35 kilometres, roughly parallel

9

with the highway from Jerusalem to Jericho, along the route of the original Roman road. Many believe that the wadi is the original 'valley of the shadow of death' made famous by the Biblical psalm.

The monastery can only be accessed by a bridge across the wadi, which is reached via a steep winding path. Unlike in previous centuries, when its remoteness guaranteed solitude, today the monastery is a popular tourist destination, as well as an important retreat for Greek Orthodox pilgrims from all over the world.

It has many attractions, including two churches and a fine sixth century mosaic floor. One tradition associates a cave above the main settlement with Joachim, father of the Virgin Mary, who is said to have stopped here to lament the barrenness of his wife Anne, until an angel appeared to him and announced the news of Mary's conception. An even more ancient tradition links the site with the prophet Elijah, who supposedly rested here on his way to the Sinai desert and was fed by ravens.

It was upon this latter tradition that Father Angelos was now reflecting as he watched the sun set over the rim of the wadi. It was in a narrow escape tunnel, leading from the cave-church of St Elijah inside the monastery to the top of the mountain, that he had made his discovery. He had no idea whether the legend of Elijah's visit to the site was authentic, and was profoundly sceptical about the raven story, but he did believe that the monastery held many secrets, which was inevitable given its history stretching back over the millennia. Hence, he was not really surprised when he realised he had unearthed something which centuries of monks, visitors, archaeologists and pilgrims had missed.

It was the daily practice of Father Angelos and his tiny coterie of fellow monks to spend their nights in vigil and prayer, then eat a light breakfast and rest for three hours before beginning work at about 8 a.m., but for the last couple of years Father

Angelos had been finding it more and more difficult to sleep. He struggled with an increasingly elusive faith, which had begun to desert him shortly after his twin brother had suffered a painful death from liver cancer three years before. Although he and his brother had taken very different paths – Andreas had been a successful lawyer in Athens – they had been as close as twins could ever hope to be, and Andreas's death at the age of just fifty-five had shaken Angelos to the core. No amount of prayer and reflection had been able to restore the purity of the faith he had enjoyed before his brother's passing. On the contrary, as the months went by, he found himself becoming angrier and angrier at the God who had inflicted this unwarranted suffering.

So it was that, two days before, Angelos was once again wide awake after wrestling all night with yet another paradox. How could it be, he pondered, that one part of the New Testament argued that someone is justified by faith, not by works, while somewhere else it asserted that a person is justified by works and not by faith alone? It was one of a host of contradictions that Father Angelos increasingly struggled with as his faith ebbed away.

After finally giving up on sleep, he found himself leaving his cell and, on a whim, mounting the stairs from the inner court of the monastery to St Elijah's cave-church, deep in thought, planning to make his way to the top of the mountain and once again give God an opportunity to reveal Himself in His wisdom, as the sun rose on a new day.

Father Angelos had not been in this tunnel for many years, neither had his fellow monks or anyone else. It was accessed from a narrow, gated opening behind the altar and was tricky to negotiate for someone of Father Angelos's bulky form, especially in his heavy robes. But after picking up one of the lit lanterns which were always left burning in the cave, he managed to squeeze through and began to make his way up the steeply inclined tunnel towards the surface.

He had gone no more than a hundred metres before he found his path blocked by rubble. Part of the roof and left wall of the tunnel had collapsed, completely sealing it off. Alarmed and concerned that there might be another rockfall, this one trapping him underground, Father Angelos quickly decided to retrace his steps, but just as he was turning around, he caught sight in the lamplight of an opening in the wall that was too symmetrical to have been caused by the collapse. Examining it more closely, he realised that it was a small aperture, perhaps a foot square, which had evidently been concealed somehow in the wall, but was now exposed by the rockfall. He peered into the darkness, then lifted the lantern and shone it inside.

Deep inside the recess he saw two clay jars, both about forty centimetres in height. Reaching inside, he grasped one of the jars, drew it out and examined it. It was intact. He placed it carefully on the ground and reached inside the recess for the other jar which also appeared to be undamaged. Both were sealed with what looked like a mixture of wax and pitch. Hefting them under each arm, he turned and hurriedly made his way back to the cave, where he set the jars on the ground and for many minutes sat silently thinking. Eventually, with a decisive grunt, he picked up the jars once again and made his way back to his cell, where he placed them under his cot and lay down to try and sleep.

The following day was busy with the monthly delivery and storage of the monastery's provisions, so it was not until after dinner that Father Angelos was able to retire to his cell and withdraw the jars. Turning them over in his hands and finding no identifying markings of any kind on either one, he drew out his small penknife and used it to try and prise open the seal on the first. After a short struggle with the rock-hard pitch, the seal cracked and there was low hiss of escaping air. With growing curiosity, the monk reached inside the jar and his hand encountered what felt like rolls of stiff paper. Grasping one between his fingers, he pulled out a tightly-rolled piece of parchment.

There were six rolls in all in the first jar and another six in the second. They were clearly very old. Parts of the parchment were brittle with age and he was reluctant to try and unroll them for fear of damaging them beyond repair. However, he did lift the edge of one just enough to be able to identify what looked to his trained eye like antiquated Byzantine script. He couldn't deduce the contents and had no idea how to go about safely opening them, so he returned them to the jars, replaced the seals as best he could and returned them to their hiding place beneath his cot.

By the following day, Father Angelos had made his decision. As he sat on the bench and watched the sun disappear behind the top of the gorge, he knew exactly what he must do. If God could not give him closure over his brother's death, then he would have to provide that closure for himself. As the shadows lengthened across the wadi, he shivered involuntarily. It was as if something malevolent had crept across his skin as he contemplated the pending betrayal of his fellow monks, but his resolve was solid and he rose from the bench with a deep sigh and returned to his cell.

The following morning, during working hours, when all his fellow monks were busy with their allotted tasks, Father Angelos made his way across the narrow bridge and up the steep winding path to the top of the wadi and from there to the highway, where he flagged down a passing truck carrying fruit to the market in Jericho and begged a lift into the city. He placed his knapsack on the floor between his legs, holding it firmly so as not to damage the carefully-wrapped jars inside, and settled back for the short journey, engaging in superficial conversation with the polite Palestinian driver who appeared somewhat in awe of his distinguished passenger. If only you knew, thought Father Angelos.

On their arrival in Jericho, Father Angelos made his way directly to the offices of an antiquarian dealer he had identified the day before, through an online search in the monastery library. Among the many untrustworthy reprobates in this arcane trade, the proprietor, Mustafa Rafa, appeared from his online profile and comments from his customers to be a reputable operator, although Father Angelos assumed – rightly, as it turned out – that no one in this trade was above bending the rules a little when it suited them.

Father Angelos made it clear to Rafa that the jars and their contents were to be sent directly to London for expert identification and sale. He would not quibble with any commission that Rafa felt it appropriate to take, but he expected to receive a legitimate copy of the bill of sale and instructed that the proceeds should be deposited in his personal account, details of which he provided. He had taken a number of photos with his mobile phone before leaving the monastery, as proof of the merchandise he was selling, and demanded and obtained a receipt from Rafa with a detailed description of the items being offered for sale. Negotiations completed, Father Angelos made his way back to the main road and waited patiently for another kind driver to return him to the monastery.

Father Angelos had no idea what the manuscripts might be worth and was not given to speculation. Whatever the proceeds, they would be put to good use, distributed to reputable cancer charities. If the sum were sufficient, he hoped that perhaps he could endow a medical facility back in Athens in his brother's name. Just as long as some way could be found for Andreas's memory to be honoured.

The monk's instincts and motives may have been selfless and benevolent, but he could have had no way of knowing, as he knelt once more during Vespers that afternoon, the fatal and potentially catastrophic chain of events that his actions that day were to set in motion.

CHAPTER 2

MICHAEL CARTER WAS in reflective mood as he walked from the station that evening to his rented cottage just outside the Hampshire village of Whitchurch. He felt disappointed and frustrated that his investigations had borne so little fruit, but he had to admit that he was no sleuth. Pretty good at research and analysis, sure, but he would never make a gumshoe.

He was in his early thirties, handsome in a preppy kind of way, with short blond hair, blue eyes and a ready smile. At a little over five feet ten, slightly built and with an ascetic demeanour, Michael's sartorial tastes ran to corduroy jackets and checked shirts with velvet waistcoats. He looked for all the world as if he'd just stepped out of a Cambridge college. Which, given that he spoke five languages fluently, including Arabic and Farsi, he could well have, if he'd chosen that path. But his career had taken him in a different direction.

It was late and he was tired, looking forward to a drink and a bowl of pasta before he settled down with his notes to try and make sense of what he'd discovered. The passing of the years hadn't so much numbed his grief as smothered it. And every now and again, it muscled its way back to the surface and demanded attention. Which was how he'd come to be quizzing a hotel manager in west London a few days ago, hoisting red flags in all the wrong places.

He was so deep in thought as he trudged along the darkened lane, untroubled by any form of street lighting, that he became aware of footsteps behind him only a second or two before the bag was thrust over his head. He was so completely surprised that it took him a few moments to react, gagging on the reek of some farmyard filth in the sacking, struggling against the wiry hands that had taken a firm grip on both his arms and were propelling him forward, virtually lifting him off his feet as he stumbled over the uneven ground. His assailants made no sound, even when he lashed out with one foot and landed what felt like a satisfying kick to one of their shins.

"Who the hell are you?! What do you want?"

Nothing. Just the sound of their footsteps and then, at last a voice. In Arabic, guttural, which Michael recognised as Iraqi dialect: "Get him in the trunk!" Michael redoubled his efforts to pull free, but to no avail. The grip on both his arms was tighter than ever. He was being dragged now, the toes of his shoes scraping the surface of the road.

It was just as he was being lifted off his feet, presumably as a prelude to being stuffed into the boot of the vehicle, that he heard the sound of a powerful diesel engine roar past and the screech of tyres ahead of him. The grip on his arms relaxed and he wrenched himself free, falling to the ground, winded. Tearing the hood from his head, he was astounded to see three black-clad figures leap from the back of a van, two of them brandishing what looked like baseball bats and charging at the men who had just released him and were now standing frozen in surprise behind the open boot of a BMW saloon. Within seconds his assailants had succumbed to the bats and were writhing on the ground. And then, once again, he felt strong hands pick him up and carry him bodily, this time towards the back of the van. He was unceremoniously dumped on the uncovered metal floor, one of the men climbed in behind him and the doors were slammed shut. Almost immediately he felt the van lurch as it accelerated away.

"One of these days you're going to get yourself into real trouble, Michael," said a female voice beside him. He turned towards the figure who had climbed in beside him and could just make out a familiar smile in the gloom of the interior. "Next time, take a taxi, hmm?"

CHAPTER 3

THE PALESTINIAN DEPARTMENT OF ANTIQUITIES AND CULTURAL HERITAGE was created in 1994. Its predecessor, the Department of Antiquities of Palestine, had been established in 1920 under the British Mandate, but was terminated when the State of Israel was created in 1948. Following its abolition, responsibility for archaeological finds in the West Bank was assumed by Jordan and those in Gaza by Egypt. The reinstatement of the body as DACH greatly simplified matters by reassigning responsibility for all artefacts discovered in Palestine to the Palestinian Authority and, in these days of widespread antiquities smuggling, the Authority took this responsibility very seriously indeed.

It was precisely this organisation's clutches out of which Rafa was determined to keep the two clay jars and their contents. Were they to be appropriated by DACH, they would not see the light of day for months or possibly even years. And there would certainly be no payday for him.

So it was that, as Father Angelos settled back into the monastic routine and resumed his struggles with his faith, the jars made their way by a circuitous route out of Jericho and through one of the Palestinians' underground smuggling routes into Gaza, where they passed into the hands of a courier in Khan Yunis. He in turn arranged for them to be taken through one of the tunnels from southern Gaza into Egypt and driven to Alexandria, where they were concealed in a consignment of avocados and crossed the Mediterranean in the hold of a container ship, travelling up the west coast of Spain and France and into Plymouth harbour in Devon.

Six weeks after leaving Jericho, the jars were sitting on the worktable of a manuscript conservator in his workroom round the corner from the British Museum in London.

CHAPTER 4

"THESE ARE UNBELIEVABLY WELL PRESERVED," said the conservator excitedly to the antiquarian dealer who had brought him the rolled manuscripts. A stick-thin grey little man in his early 60s, cursed with a slight lisp and a propensity to twitch when nervous, Geoffrey Parminter was one of Britain's foremost authorities on Byzantine manuscripts, an archaeological enthusiast, a chemist by training and, as it happened, a prodigious gambler. Which was why the dealer, Tom Washbrook, had brought the scrolls to him in the first place. Parminter was reliable, informed, well connected and – above all – discreet. His habit ensured that, with the right level of remuneration, word of the discovery would never find its way out of the tight-knit circles in which he and Washbrook moved.

Washbrook was young, ambitious and bereft of scruples. Just short of five feet five inches tall, with thinning sandy hair and a growing paunch, Washbrook knew he was never going to be anyone's matinee idol, but he was smart and he was determined. Ever since leaving Birmingham University ten years before, with an indifferent degree in anthropology, he had survived on sheer cunning and single-mindedness, building a niche for himself in smuggled manuscripts, starting with a couple of pages from a Russian Orthodox illuminated codex which netted him a few hundred pounds, then moving on to progressively more valuable books and documents, all of them traded under the table through a growing network of professional contacts disinclined to ask too many questions. At the tender age of thirty-two, Washbrook was already a wealthy man, and fully intended to make himself wealthier still.

"I'll need time, of course – unrolling these precious objects is a painstakingly meticulous task – but given their exceptional condition it will be easier than any I've worked on before. Where did they come from?"

"Better you don't know," replied Washbrook. "What you don't know can't hurt you," and, longing against the worktable, he winked conspiratorially at the conservator. "Suffice to say they come from a very reliable source."

"Mmm," muttered Parminter distractedly. "A week to cut the rolls, another to reassemble them, another few weeks to decipher them," he murmured, almost to himself. "I'd say I'll have an answer on their content and provenance in a couple of months, but I'm pretty sure you're right: they're Byzantine, perhaps even from the early fourth century. It's an astounding find!"

"Excellent!" exclaimed Washbrook. "And I presume I don't need to remind you that your fee is entirely contingent on your discretion in this matter?"

"Of course, of course," replied the conservator, in truth barely listening. "Mum's the word."

"Good," said Washbrook, pushing himself up from the table and making for the door. Over his shoulder he said, "Give me a ring when you're ready. In the meantime, I'll be lining up some buyers."

"Yes, yes, I'll call you," but Washbrook's parting remark barely registered with Parminter, who was far too excited by the task ahead to pay much attention.

Over the next few weeks, Parminter worked day and night on the manuscripts. He barely slept and hardly ate. Had his wife not come down periodically to his workroom from their small flat above, he might have forgotten to eat altogether.

All twelve of the tightly rolled manuscripts were made of parchment, the stretched and dried animal skin – in this case, goatskin – that had been in use as writing material since the third millennium BC. His first task was to cut the fragile material into horizontal strips about a centimetre wide – the only way to access the content without trying to unroll the entire document, which would cause irreversible damage. It took him nearly two weeks to complete this task, following which the strips were laid in turn one above the other on his worktable and photographed from every angle. Each roll, when fully unravelled, formed a manuscript about a metre long. Finally, Parminter divided each document into three parts roughly 30 centimetres in length, and mounted them between two toughened glass sheets.

Now he had thirty-six separate glass panels, together comprising the entire twelve manuscripts, which he photographed once more. Until now he had resisted the urge to begin translating them, preferring to have them all in an easily readable form before he began, but now he was ready. Placing the precious documents in his spacious safe, he left his workroom and trudged upstairs to his flat, exhausted from his labours, but consumed with excitement at what lay ahead the following day.

Over the subsequent weeks, Parminter was preoccupied with ordering and translating the arcane language of the manuscripts and the more he translated, the more excited he became. They were written in the archaic Byzantine Greek that, from the early fourth century, gradually displaced Koine Greek, the lingua franca of the Roman empire. They proved to be religious texts of quite exceptional merit. They appeared to be an account of the life of Jesus penned by a member of his inner circle – but not one of the disciples. Even more astonishingly, as he read on, it became apparent that the author of the manuscript was a woman, which was virtually unheard-of in the ancient world.

Finally, as he reached the end of the last scroll, he had his confirmation, with the closing words, *'Beloved in Christ, sister of Jeshua upon whom the Kingdom is descended.'* My God, he said to himself, falling back into his chair, his heart racing. I've just read the gospel according to Jesus' sister.

CHAPTER 5

"OF COURSE, it's not the original text," Parminter explained to Washbrook, as the two of them pored over the glass sheets. "It was almost certainly copied by a scribe from an earlier document, which had probably originally been written in Aramaic, but it's still one of the most significant Biblical finds since the Gospel of Judas in the 1970s. It's enormously valuable and important."

"That's great news," replied Washbrook with a broad smile. "Given how much I've already had to lay out to get it here, we're going to need a decent return. How soon can you have the scrolls ready to be shipped to a buyer?"

Parminter was experiencing a growing reluctance to let the manuscripts go. They were the most precious artefacts he had ever worked on and he was developing a proprietorial urge to hang on to them. However, to Washbrook he said, "I just want to run one or two more tests – shouldn't be more than a day or so."

"Okay. Have them ready by the end of the week. Looks as if we'll both be booking ourselves a nice trip to the Caribbean for Christmas!" And with that, Washbrook left Parminter to his tests.

Parminter had cut off a very small fragment of one of the scrolls, which he intended to submit to Carbon-14 dating, to establish more precisely when the manuscript had been written. He also expected this to provide clues as to where it had come from, something about which Washbrook remained coy. He had already conducted some tests on the ink, which he successfully identified as a carbon-based material containing metallic elements, probably iron, that would also, in time, help to narrow down its age and source.

But first, there was another test he was keen to conduct. While translating the texts he had noticed some faint shadowing on one of the scrolls which at first he had thought was due to the ink spreading as it was absorbed into the parchment. But as he had looked more closely, an excited suspicion began to form in his mind. He carefully packed the three glass panels containing the scroll in a padded case and left his workroom, hailing a cab on the street which took him to a long, low nondescript building in Bloomsbury. Here he gave his name at the reception desk and was immediately escorted to a laboratory on the first floor.

University College London's Institute of Archaeology is an academic department of UCL's Social & Historical Sciences Faculty and has some of the best-equipped laboratories in the world, to which Parminter, as a member of the faculty, had privileged access. The lab he had just entered was currently empty and he made straight for a large olive-green machine set back in a corner of the room.

X-ray fluorescence imaging is a relatively new technique in archaeology. It uses a combination of X-ray fluorescence and sophisticated image processing to recover text characters written in iron gall on parchment. Having already identified the iron content in the ink, he knew that this would enable him to see the shadowing on the scroll more clearly. Inserting the first sheet carefully into the machine, he made some adjustments to the settings and began to scan the manuscript.

Three hours later, Parminter left the building in a state of high excitement. Hailing another cab, he returned to his workroom and removed the three glass sheets from their protective packing, returning them to the safe. He then withdrew the three printouts he had retrieved from the imaging machine and lay them side-by-side on his worktable. There, displayed as a simple linear show-through model, was a clear reproduction of a second text, hidden below the first. He picked up his phone and dialled a number.

"Tom, you're not going to believe this," he said breathlessly into the phone. "We've got ourselves a palimpsest."

An hour after his call, the two men were once again bent over Parminter's worktable.

Parchment was an expensive commodity in the ancient world and it was not uncommon for it to be reused. The original text would be washed or scraped off so that the material could be written on a second time, hence the term 'palimpsest' from the Greek 'scrape again.'

"I'd like more time to work on it, but I've done a rough translation and it appears to be a letter detailing some sort of important discovery," explained Parminter. I think it was written by someone in a religious order of some sort, probably to their superior – and from the context it seems to have been part of a legacy or a deathbed confession. Here, I've written it down – it's a pretty free translation." He picked up a piece of paper covered with longhand writing and handed it to Washbrook, who read it carefully.

Holy Father,

My heart is in earnest of the Lord's blessing as I go to my rest. In his faithful service I have sought honour for our community and enjoyed the breath of God upon my face each day. The wearing trials of the evil one I have striven to meet and over-come with the strength of his Holy Spirit.

In this blessed wilderness where our Lord sought refuge, I too have found sanctuary. The fellowship of my brothers in Christ has brought me reward beyond measure and the solace of peace in our saviour.

I leave this world as I entered it, as a babe in Christ, naked and unadorned, in awe of his merciful judgment and the joy to come.

I leave to my brothers my writings in the Spirit. May they bring comfort and light in dark times.

And to your care, Master, I entrust the resting place of the burnished scroll. Its unearthing has brought me a deep disquiet that I cannot comprehend and I know it is best left to the secret places and to the will of God. Its treasures will bring no peace to the world. I have returned it to the earth whence it came, to the place of worship of the cursed ones upon whose heads be the blood of our Lord.

May his blessings and peace be upon you always.

In Christ, A

Washbrook looked up quizzically. "What does it mean? Burnished scroll? Treasures?"

"I've no idea. It might help if I knew where it came from," replied Parminter hopefully.Washbrook shrugged. "As I said before, you're better off not knowing. But don't worry, you'll still be well paid when we confirm the buyer."

Parminter pouted. "How can I be expected to do a proper job if I don't have all the details?"

"You've done your job. Now it's time for me to do mine. I'll be in touch."

CHAPTER 6

AARIZ ABDUL-AZIZ AL-SHAMMARI, Ari to his closer acquaintances, put down the phone and sat back in his chair, gazing out of the floor-to-ceiling windows of the elegant Bayswater drawing room as he took another sip of his Camomile tea. The call had come out of the blue, but it was welcome. New funding was urgently needed for the cause and Ari's clients were becoming increasingly restless. This latest transaction sounded fascinating.

He rose from his chair and walked over to the door. He was taller than the average for his countrymen, a little over six feet, with dark skin and a muscled ranginess to his body that spoke of his his Bedouin heritage. His hair was a little long to be fashionable, falling in crisp black curls to his collar, in contrast to a well-trimmed beard speckled with grey. His eyes were liquid brown and appeared, on first impression, to be kindly. He was elegantly dressed in a dark-blue Herbie Frogg suit, iridescent white shirt and light-blue tie set in an immaculate Windsor knot. He wore handmade Crockett & Jones shoes and a Bremont Supermarine watch. This quintessential English uniform stood in stark contrast to his accent, which carried the throaty inflections and musical lilt of his homeland.

He opened the door and called through to the next room. "Mahmoud?" Moments later a well-built bearded man with desert-dark skin dressed in an ill-fitting off-the-peg brown suit slipped into the room. Unlike his master, he had a compact frame, solid with brawn, which seemed to radiate controlled aggression. His eyes were impenetrable black marbles in a darkly tanned face with deep creases around his mouth and a livid white scar running from his right ear to his chin. He stood expressionless with his arms by his sides.

"A valuable opportunity has presented itself, Mahmoud. Please bring the car."

"Sir," responded the man, bowing slightly. He began to turn, then hesitated. "Sir?"

"Yes, Mahmoud?" An edge of irritation crept into Al-Shammari's voice.

"The matter of the young man who was looking into our affairs?"

"The young man who I instructed you to deal with?"

Mahmoud's eyes slid to the floor, his hands clasped before him. "I regret to report that we encountered a difficulty..."

"What kind of difficulty, Mahmoud?" queried Al-Shammari quietly. The irritation had turned to ice.

Again, a hesitation. "The young man appeared to have some protection. My men failed in their mission to apprehend him. They have been – reprimanded." Mahmoud's face had darkened, perhaps a clue to the severe nature of the reprimand that had been metered out.

"You disappoint me, Mahmoud." Al-Shammari paused and walked over to the window, looking down at the street below. He spoke without turning. "I trust you have plans to rectify the situation?"

"Yes, sir." Mahmoud looked up. "I have already issued instructions."

Al-Shammari turned and his eyes bored into those of his

retainer. "Do not disappoint me again, Mahmoud. Have this taken care of. And can I suggest you take more decisive action this time. We have urgent matters to deal with and we cannot allow such a minor inconvenience to distract us."

"Yes, sir." Mahmoud turned and walked quickly out of the room, closing the door quietly behind him.

Al-Shammari's eyes clouded. It had been a good many years, but he well remembered the naïve couple and their innocent involvement in that distant transaction – the first significant trade he had completed, the one that had established his reputation. In the intervening years he had acquired a wide expertise in the international antiquities market. He was familiar with most of the world's leading collections, from the British Museum in London to the Metropolitan Museum of Art in New York, Istanbul's Archaeology Museum, Jordan's Archaeological Museum and even the Eretz Israel Museum in Tel Aviv. He had spent many hours in all of them, learning about their treasures with a fanatical dedication. He also trawled the world's auction houses for rare items. But his real talent lay in the murkier environs of the black market, where the real prizes of his trade were to be found, and he was now recognised in the more discreet circles of the international antiquities market as a discerning – if obsessively secretive – buyer.

Although the demise of the middle-aged British couple had been a regrettable necessity, it had nonetheless saddened him. He took no particular pleasure in the taking of lives, but the cause was great and his paymasters were unforgiving.

When he had learned all these years later that someone was looking into the affair, and when his investigations revealed who the inquisitive young man was, he had directed his acolyte to take swift action to deal with him. He was angered that the operation had been bungled. Given the exacting demands of his clientele, he could not afford any indiscretions, especially not now.

He sighed and readied himself to leave.

CHAPTER 7

AN HOUR later Al-Shammari was in Geoffrey Parminter's workroom looking at the manuscripts laid out on his table. Washbrook was beside him. Mahmoud was leaning against a bookcase at the back of the room, regarding the proceedings with baleful eyes.

"Remarkable," said the Arab. "Truly remarkable. You're sure it's authentic?"

"Well, there are a few more tests I'd like to do, but I'm ninety-nine per cent certain that what we're looking at is a genuine early gospel. It will be earth-shaking when this is made public."

"Yes," responded Al-Shammari evasively. "I'm sure it will. Now, tell me about the palimpsest."

"I'm not sure there's much to tell," replied Parminter. "Without knowing where it was found," he continued in a noticeably petulant tone, "it's impossible to judge its significance."

Al-Shammari exchanged looks with Washbrook, who nodded as if confirming what the Iraqi was thinking.

"Well, I'm sure that will all be made clear in due course," he said. " I would still appreciate viewing the item."

"Of course." Parminter went over to his safe and retrieved the scans, handing them to Al-Shammari.

"Fascinating," glancing over the three panels. "You have translated this?"

"Yes," replied the conservator proudly. "It wasn't easy, but I have a transcript here," and he handed Al-Shammari a single printed sheet of A4.

"I don't suppose you can shed any light on this, sir?" wheedled Parminter. Washbrook threw him a sharp glance.

"Perhaps..." mused Al-Shammari, apparently lost in his own thoughts. "It calls to mind something...something. I am not sure..."

Parminter was struck by the hungry look in the Arab's eyes. He had evidently seen something in the manuscript which had eluded the two men.

Al-Shammari appeared to shake himself out of his reverie. "It's not really my field, he said brusquely. "But I doubt very much it will amount to anything. The antiquities market is awash with such documents and they have no real value. But it does hold a certain interest for me."

Washbrook visibly relaxed. He had a buyer on the hook and that was all that mattered from this meeting.

"What is your price for the entire manuscript?"

Washbrook named an absurd figure and Parminter gulped with excitement.

"I will give it some thought," responded Al-Shammari after a beat. "I would need to be assured of your discretion."

"Naturally," simpered Washbrook. "That goes without saying."

"Is this the only copy you have of the palimpsest and the translation?" Al-Shammari asked Parminter.

"Yes, apart from my handwritten original."

"I would very much like to ensure that all copies are included in the transaction."

After a moment's hesitation, Parminter replied, "Of course. It's here in my safe."

Al-Shammari looked at him expectantly. Parminter eventually wilted under his gaze and went over to the safe, unlocking it and taking out the handwritten draft he had originally shown to Washbrook. He handed it to Al-Shammari, leaving the safe unlocked.

"And there are no others?" Al-Shammari caught the reflex glance that Parminter threw in the direction of a side table, where a mobile phone lay on top of a pile of papers. "No, that's the lot," said Parminter.

"Good. Then I think our business here is concluded. Mahmoud?"

Al-Shammari's retainer stepped away from the bookcase and in one smooth movement, withdrew a Sig Sauer 9mm pistol fitted with a MOD-X titanium suppressor and shot Parminter twice in the head. Al-Shammari was struck by how surprised he looked as he slumped to his knees and slipped sideways to the floor. What did he really think was going to happen?

He turned back to Washbrook, who was frozen to the spot, a look of sheer disbelief and terror on his face as he looked directly down the barrel of the gun that Mahmoud was now pointing at him.

"I apologise that you had to witness that, Mr Washbrook, but I rather think that your colleague was attempting to pull the wool over our eyes." His face hardened. "I do not take kindly to being disrespected in this way – you understand?"

Washbrook nodded dumbly.

"Now, before we take our leave of you, I should very much appreciate you telling me where you came by this fascinating artefact."

Washbrook shook his head energetically. "I don't know!" he spluttered. "It came to me via a third party!"

"And where is this third party located, precisely?"

Washbrook was still eyeing the fat black tube of the pistol suppressor, which was unwavering in Mahmoud's grip. "In – in – in Gaza."

"Ah, once such a beautiful place. Now..." his voice tailed off. "But I fear that that is not where this particular item of merchandise originated. Am I correct?"

There was a long pause as Washbrook calculated options and probabilities. Eventually he reached a resigned conclusion.

"It came from a monastery in the West Bank," said Washbrook quietly, his body beginning to shake with delayed shock. "It was passed to my contact in Gaza by a dealer in Jericho." His shoulders slumped and he leaned over the worktable. "That's all I know."

"Names?" Washbrook gave them.

"Now, please step away from the table."

Washbrook obliged. "I have a wife – and children –" pleaded the wretched dealer.

"I know, I know," replied Al-Shammari in a kindly voice. "So did I."

And Mahmoud shot him twice through the heart.

Al-Shammari walked over to the side table and picked up Parminter's phone and pocketing it before searching through Washbrook's clothes and finding and pocketing his phone too.

Mahmoud had returned his weapon to the shoulder-holster concealed beneath his leather jacket. "Is this thing of so much value, sir?" he asked.

Al-Shammari smiled. "My friend, it may just be the greatest find of our lifetimes." He looked around the room, went over to the safe and checked inside, before gathering up the glass sheets, placing them in Parminter's protective pack and slipping the two translations in beside them. "Please arrange for these items to be shipped home to Beirut."

As Al-Shammari left Mahmoud finished gathering together piles of papers from around the room. He had cleared the front door and was stepping briskly round the corner to the car when Mrs Parminter's screams began to tear through the studio.

CHAPTER 8

WHEN THE BODY of a certain Mr Mustafa Rafa was discovered in his office in downtown Jericho, the blood from his severed carotid artery soaking the expensive Persian carpet beneath his expensive mahogany desk, the Palestinian police quickly concluded that he had been the victim of a robbery. They were encouraged in their thinking by the fact that a number of artefacts were missing from his safe. Given his reputation, he would not be much missed, although the officer in charge of the investigation did wonder why the thief had taken so much trouble to remove most of the man's fingernails before cutting his throat. Well, you live by the sword, you die by the sword, thought the officer.

Father Angelos Bartholomaios never did get to honour his brother with a hospital wing, or any other kind of memorial for that matter. He was found at the bottom of the Wadi Qelt one cold January night with his skull crushed, apparently inflicted by the lengthy fall from his beloved monastery garden. He was quietly laid to rest alongside the few dozen monks who had lived and died in that place over seventeen centuries and earnest prayers were offered for his soul. The elder monk who presided over his interment remarked, in passing, on how peaceful his former colleague looked. Perhaps in the end he had overcome his crisis of faith.

Back in London, Mahmoud packed the glass panels containing the scrolls into a large, vacuum-sealed, lead-lined steel container which would be impervious to the most inquisitive of X-rays. He made a call to a reliable haulage company with which Al-Shammari had had dealings in the past and arranged for the container to be collected and shipped to his master's villa in Lebanon. Accordingly, the following day the chest was transferred to a warehouse in Colindale, from where it would be transported the next day as part of a larger consignment to the cargo terminal at East Midlands Airport.

Shortly after Mahomoud's call, in a sagging portakabin on an industrial estate off the Mile End Road, a middle-aged, overweight man with a bad case of acne and a pretty young wife with a taste for expensive jewellery took another phone call regarding the very same consignment.

He thought it might be the answer to his prayers.

CHAPTER 9

THEY HAD RULED out setting a fire. The presence of residues in the soot left by petroleum-based accelerants would be an immediate giveaway to the most indolent fire investigation officer. Instead, they settled upon the simple expedient of a gas leak, accessorised by a homemade incendiary device – in this case an 'electric match' created by running a fine copper wire through a match head and attaching it to two 9-volt batteries hooked up to a conventional cooking timer, all of which were conveniently lying around in a half-open drawer beneath the cooker hob.

The rear door of the cottage presented no obstacle to the men. The property was a good two hundred metres from its nearest neighbour, so there were no prying eyes. They picked the simple ward lock in seconds, slipping inside and assembling the makeshift firebomb in less than two minutes, before setting the timer to half an hour. Allowing for one or two other precautionary arrangements, they were in and out of the house in less than fifteen minutes.

When the device ignited just after three o'clock in the morning, two things happened in quick succession. First, the butane in the kitchen, which by now had permeated every nook and cranny of the room, detonated with spectacular force, blowing out all the windows and blasting both the interior and exterior doors off their hinges. Second, the flames instantly chased the fuel lines back to the 1,650 litre LPG tank which supplied the cottage, located about three metres from the outside wall. The resulting explosion blew a hole the size of a small car in the side of the house and brought down the ceiling of the hallway and the stairs to the first floor. Debris and shards of metal from the tank rained down on the small cottage garden.

Since Michael's bedroom was directly above the kitchen and just off the landing, it was caught in a flaming pincer movement as the fire instantly took hold, feeding greedily on the carpets and soft furnishings, fanned by the air sucked in through the now open doorways and the breach in the downstairs wall. Lying alone in bed, with virtually no warning, he wouldn't have stood a chance. In less than 90 seconds the entire house was engulfed in a maelstrom of flames which licked at every surface. Within 10 minutes, the whole thatched roof was ablaze. By the time the fire brigade arrived half an hour later, the building was already a hollowed-out shell with every timber alight, showering sparks over the road and surrounding countryside.

The two men watched from their hiding place in a copse on the other side of a field facing the front of the house. When it was clear that the building had been completely consumed, along with its sole occupant, they quietly made their way cross-country back to their car and returned to London.

CHAPTER 10

THE MOST NOTABLE features of the diminutive rural church in the heart of the Hampshire countryside were its eleventh century Doom painting and the weird Green Man carved into one of the wooden roof trusses. The churchwardens had been arguing with the vicar for years that this pagan anachronism should be removed, perhaps worried that it might incite some devilish work at the altar on moonless nights when the villagers' doors were locked and their children safely in bed.

But the grinning fertility symbol still peered through its sculpted foliage, unperturbed by the controversy, and on this cold, dank early spring morning as it looked down on this latest of the many hundreds of funerals which had passed beneath its gaze, it might have wondered why such a young man attracted so few grievers. For apart from the vicar, who had only been retained the day before to conduct the service, there was barely a handful of mourners. The service was perfunctory, as might be expected given that the celebrant knew nothing of the deceased, and the hymn-singing was desultory, nursed along by a wheezing pedal organ played by a local man who appeared only marginally less ancient than the church itself.

There seemed to be a collective sigh of relief as the proceedings drew to a weary close and the vicar took his place at the rear of the church. The coffin was hefted onto the shoulders of four bearers hired by the local funeral director, who made their professionally sombre way through the tombstones to a ready-dug grave near the tall yew hedge at the back of the churchyard. Only two figures, a man and a woman, remained at the grave-side to see the coffin lowered into its final resting place, the other mourners having already melted away.

But they were not the only people watching.

A young dark-haired woman stood just outside the lychgate, unseen by the couple at the graveside, who had their backs to her. As she watched the coffin disappear from view, she sighed deeply, ground the remains of a half-smoked cigarette under her shoe, and turned to walk quickly down the lane to her car, parked just out of view around a bend in the road.

In a small stand of trees on the hill above the church, a dark-skinned man huddled in an oversized puffer jacket, blowing into his hands and rubbing them together for warmth as he surveyed the events below. He watched the woman carefully. He recog-nised her. As she left the church and began walking away down the lane he pulled out his phone and made a call to his colleague, who was parked in a lay-by a mile or so down the road. A minute or so after her car passed him, he slowly pulled out of the lay-by and took up position a few hundred yards behind her. His companion was left with a long, cold walk to the nearest town.

CHAPTER 11

ON A DAMP MONDAY NIGHT, the sickly yellow faux Victorian lanterns outside the Caledonian Club reflected nauseously in the greasy pavement. Steam billowed from the central heating vents in the side alley like a bilious burp. I used to think it looked inviting, sort of reassuringly gentlemen's clubby – all warm red brick and sandstone lintels, with the semi-opaque glass in the door hinting at sybaritic cosiness within. And cosy it is, but beneath the cosiness is a palace of iniquities, the home of dark spirits, the lair of the white worm.

As I pushed open the door just before midnight on that dreary February evening, the warm air pulsed out at me in a fetid wave, a heady miasma shot through with the tang of expensive whiskies, musky perfumes and cigar smoke (proprietor Terry was never much for the niceties of the law). The doorman materialised from his cubbyhole like a crab from a rock pool and my coat miraculously appeared in the crook of his elbow.

"Good evening Mr Carter," he growled, with that smile that always made me feel like a punter in a brothel. "You're becoming quite the regular, sir."

"Where else would I choose to be on a miserable Monday

night, Archie?" I replied. He turned away with a peremptory, "Well, good luck, sir," and disappeared back into his burrow.

The place was packed as usual at this time of the evening: the familiar crowd of sharp-suited sharks, narks, nuts, chancers and no-hopers, most with expensively outfitted consorts fastened to their arms, all clinging to the tables like brightly-coloured sea anemones, waving to and fro with the ceaseless rhythm of the spinning wheels.

I sauntered across to my usual table. Blackjack, under the formidable sway of the club's most fearsome croupier, Modesty Prestwick. I once made the mistake of asking her how she came by such a curiously juxtaposed moniker and in a rare moment of candour she explained her mother was a part-time model, quite a looker and a big fan of Monica Vitti in the 1966 spy spoof.

Modesty had clearly decided from an early age that she wasn't going to live up to her name. I'd never seen her in a dress that was anything larger than two sizes too small for her, usually bright red or green, and always with a cut so low that her chest was on permanent offensive manoeuvres. All this in a petite frame which was only a dyed-blonde hair over five feet one.

I took one of the empty four seats at the table and Modesty fixed me with a pair of lambent green eyes, fingers on autopilot as she broke open a couple of new decks and fed them into the shoe. "All alone, Charlie? Where are your playmates tonight?"

"None of the other boys wanted to come out to play."

"You know what they say about solitary gamblers, Charlie."

"The quickest way for the house to get rich?"

Modesty's mouth turned up a fraction at the corners, the closest it ever came to a smile. "Nothing he likes more," she said with a nod of the head towards the office at the back of the room, "than a guy on his own with a black dog on his shoulder." She paused, as if considering her next words. "I was sorry to hear about your brother, Charlie. Really bad deal."

I nodded, unwilling to engage on this subject. I took my seat and exchanged £100 for chips, then watched as Modesty deftly swept the next deal out of the shoe, two for me, two for her. As the only player at the table, I had her undivided attention, which was now focused on my upturned cards as I decided what to do with my nine of hearts and seven of clubs. A hard sixteen, statistically the worst of all Blackjack hands. Her upcard was the three of spades and so, following the convention that you always assumed a ten in the hole, I dropped a £20 chip on my cards and stuck.

Fortune favoured the brave. Her next card was the King of Hearts, followed by a bust with the nine of diamonds. £40 back to me. Same on the next hand – I rolled with my eighteen and she busted on a fifteen draw. This was fun. But I should have quit while I was ahead. Instead, I played on until it was 2am and I was three hundred down.

"On the tab, Charlie, or will you settle now?"

I gave her my best attempt at an offended scowl, stood up and stretched. "I think I need a drink." That abbreviated smile followed me to the bar and I braced myself for the inevitable wit and wisdom of Barry the barman. He didn't disappoint. "Did you know that eighty per cent of people who come to a casino are up at some point. They just don't have the sense to quit while they're ahead."

"Just get me a Scotch, Barry, a large one, no ice and hold the sarcasm." He laughed as he jabbed the optic and scratched his arse in a single perfectly coordinated movement.

"Tell me again why Terry hired you, Barry. I've forgotten. Was it your matinee-idol good looks or your sparkling wit and repartee?"

It was like water off a duck's back. "No, he just got lucky, I guess." He was six feet four inches of lumpen aggression, with eyes the colour of baked mud, a matted mane of lank hair and a voice you could saw logs with.

Barry moved off down the bar to serve another customer, his

45

interest in me exhausted, and I leaned back against the bar to observe the room. I'd been coming to the Caledonian on and off for a few months, ever since I was dragged here by an old army mate who said it was the best place to get a drink after midnight. I'd fallen in love at once with its dishevelled sophistication. You might say I was now a regular.

A one-time banking hall which had narrowly escaped the clutches of Wetherspoons, it boasted pilastered walls and high ceilings, with low-slung chandeliers and marble balconies. So far so good. But you didn't have to look very hard to see the wear in the carpet, the plaster flaking from the walls and the missing bulbs from the chandeliers. If it were a suit, the Caledonian would have shiny elbows, darned trousers and a hint of mildew behind the lapels.

The copious floor space was occupied by a cramped array of tables boasting everything from roulette, Blackjack and Baccarat to poker, craps and even Bingo. I sipped my drink and watched as the motley gathering of eternal optimists moved listlessly between the tables, testing their luck against the lords of chance.

In all the time I'd been coming here, which recently had been pretty much every evening, I'd only ever played the card tables. Blackjack mostly, poker occasionally, Baccarat on the rare occasions I felt equal to it. I'd never once tried my luck at roulette. I'd always eschewed games of chance, because they removed all control from the wager. True, Blackjack tends to favour the house, but there's still the illusion of skill, the conceit that you can influence the outcome with a smart decision to stick, twist or buy, to outwit the dealer and leave with your shirt firmly attached to your back. But roulette, that was another matter. Pure random luck. And the unerring temptation to bet just a little too much a little too often.

I watched as each croupier spun their wheel with a practised flourish, face professionally deadpan as the ball clickety-clacked across the tracks of the bowl. The punters' demeanours each told a story, if you could read it. There was the nonchalant regular, lounging back in his chair for all the world as if a few hundred pounds here or there were so much pocket-change. The eager optimist, tight-featured and shining-eyed, hands clasped before them on the table as if in prayer. The dilettante, standing behind his girlfriend, proprietorial hands on her shoulders as she alternately sipped Champagne and pushed her (his) chips around the table in a succession of ever more reckless bets. And, roles reversed, the cold-eyed maven in immaculate black tie, girlfriend standing with a brittle smile and perfectly manicured hand on his arm.

I watched and brooded, withdrawing into the memories which so often plagued me in these early morning hours, but which I'd decided I'd rather suffer here with the other desperate denizens of the night than home alone in my tragic bedsit. I reflected, as I did a hundred times a day, that mine had been a life lived and lost barely before it got started. My childhood and adulthood both stolen from me and, barely two weeks before, the remnants of my family gone too, with the death of my brother.

I hadn't even managed to hold my marriage together. Angie and I had barely spoken in months and even when we'd been forcibly reunited by grief at Michael's funeral, we might just as well have been strangers.

I felt brutalised, traumatised, hollowed-out – and spectacularly sorry for myself.

I lifted the glass to my lips and realised to my surprise that it was already empty. Signalling to Barry to bring me another, I wondered – not for the first time – how many more it would take to numb the dull ache that was now a constant companion, constricting my chest, fogging my head, sapping my will.

"Fancy a spin?"

The words hit me a nanosecond before her perfume, a heady miasma that I half-recognised but couldn't put a name to.

47

I turned to meet the crystalline blue eyes, crinkled in a half-smile, of a statuesque girl with jet-black hair. She was holding a cigarillo between manicured fingers tipped with blood-red nails, her elbow propped on her cradled left arm and her weight held on her right leg, accentuating the curve of her hip beneath a close-fitting black sheath dress.

"I'm afraid it's not my thing," I replied lamely, a little dizzy from her perfume and wilting slightly under the directness of her gaze. "You know what they say. It's one of those games where you have the same chance of winning whether you play or not."

"Do they?" Her head tilted slightly, that half-smile still teasing her lips. Coquettish, amused by my dazzling wit, or just by the vacant grin on my face?

"Do you work for the house?" I asked, moving onto what I thought was firmer conversational ground.

"Not exactly." She paused and her eyes narrowed slightly, as if she were pondering a decision. "Tell you what, why don't you come and watch *me* play?" Before I had a chance to demur, she had brushed past me and was sashaying (and that was the only word for what she was doing with her hips) towards the nearest of the two roulette tables, leaving me trailing awkwardly in her wake. She sat down to the left of the croupier and patted the chair beside her, stubbing out her cigarillo in a heavy glass ashtray thrust in her direction by a bright-eyed waiter whose mouth hung open I did as commanded and sat down.

"I'm Rebecca", she said, as she took two £50 notes from her handbag and pushed them towards the croupier, who shoved back a stack of chips in return. She had a faint accent that I couldn't place, possibly somewhere Mediterranean, but with the polish you typically acquire from an expensive English education.

"Charlie Carter", I replied, fighting the urge to hold out my hand. "Do we know one another?"

"Well, we've not met, but..." She hesitated, looked as if she was trying to work out what to say next. "But I do know quite a lot about you."

She watched as the croupier spun the wheel and set the ball rolling, before casually placing all her chips on red.

"I'm sorry," I replied, more sharply than I'd intended. "But exactly who are you?"

The ball stopped rattling and settled into a pocket. Thirty-two red. She appeared not to notice. Her eyes were fixed on mine.

"We'll get to that," she said, in the brusque tone of a nurse removing a catheter. "For now, I'd prefer to talk about you. Or, more particularly, about your brother."

Now she had my full attention. All thoughts of casual flirtation snuffed out. The croupier deposited a matching stack of chips next to hers, but again she paid no attention as the croupier spun the wheel once more and called time on bets. I felt the familiar rage building like a winter storm.

"Who the hell *are* you – and what do you know about Michael?"

She held my gaze without a hint of embarrassment or disquiet. Her eyes were colder now, the pupils anthracite-black in a pool of blue ice.

"You might say I'm a friend of his. And I work for the people who killed him."

CHAPTER 12

THE THREE-AXLE 6X2 Mercedes tractor unit pulling a 20ft dry freight container, registration number RMDU 9752314-3, loaded to its maximum gross weight of 20,000 kg, pulled into a lay-by off the A45 just south of Northampton. The driver was due at the airport early the following morning and planned to get a few hours rest before resuming his journey.

By 1 a.m. he was tucked up in his sleeper cab, dreaming of the rechroming job he was going to get done on his Kawasaki 750cc Mach IV motorcycle, with the cash in hand he'd be paid for this trip. He didn't hear the Nissan pickup pull in behind his truck, or the sound of the seal on the rear doors of his container being carefully cut, and he was unaware of the two men who crept into the container and offloaded several items of merchandise into the bed of the Nissan. But when he woke at dawn and blearily embarked on his routine walk-around check of the vehicle, he noticed the half-open doors of the container and his face paled, nausea immediately clenching his gut.

Wrenching the doors fully open, his jaw dropped when he saw the spaces on the floor of the container where part of his consignment had once sat.

"Oh fuck," he whispered to himself.

His hands trembling, he pulled out his mobile phone, stared at the screen for a moment, then dialled a London number with a shaking finger.

CHAPTER 13

IT WAS 4 a.m. and the club was quieter, its patrons reduced to the hard core who would soon wander out onto the darkened streets, either pondering for the hundredth morning how their winning streak had come to such an abrupt end, or revelling in the unexpected windfall that for now added a satisfying weight to their wallet but would tomorrow night or the next be returned with unerring inevitability to Terry's pocket.

My new acquaintance had cashed £400 of chips, less the croupier's £20 tip, slipped from her chair and left the table before I'd had a chance to catch my breath. I'd followed her, dumbly, to the bar and taken the stool beside her. The drinks, she'd said, were on her. Barry the barman gave us a baleful glare and deposited a brace of neat vodkas before us. My need for alcohol was all the greater after what I'd just heard and I threw back the drink in a single gulp, my hand shaking as I returned the glass to the bar. Rebecca sipped at hers.

She lit another cigarillo and regarded me through the drifting smoke, for the first time exhibiting a hint of uncertainty. "I'm sorry for the cloak and dagger. I have a weakness for the dramatic sometimes." Nothing about this woman suggested weakness of any kind. "But you and I do have something in common."

I looked around the room as I gathered my thoughts. I could see Terry up on one of the balconies, smoking his customary cigar and watching us. He caught my eye and nodded slightly before turning away and heading back towards his office.

"What the hell's this all about? My brother wasn't killed; he died in a gas explosion. An accident."

"Well, that's not strictly true. Michael was a close associate of some friends of mine. He embarked on an investigation which unfortunately led to some dangerous people wishing your brother harm." Her laboured formality was beginning to get on my nerves.

My mind drifted back to that freezing night two weeks before, my breath venting clouds into the bone-dry air, the stream beside Michael's cottage rigid with ice. I remembered the wash of the police car's blue light on the white front gate, the smell of burnt wood, melted metal and plastic – and something else that my subconscious chose not to identify. I remembered the sound of the helicopter overhead, the feel of rough fabric of the blanket covering Michael as they wheeled him out to the ambulance. The over-whelming rage combined somehow with utter numbness at the loss.

"What unforeseen events? And what associates? Michael was just a civil servant, for Christ's sake."

Rebecca sat back on her stool, crossed her legs and gave me a hard look. "I'm afraid there's a great deal about your brother you don't know, Charlie. Including what he did for a living. Michael was very far from being just a civil servant."

"Look, I don't know what you think you know, but I was my kid brother's brother for twenty-five years before he died. We were close. I remember when he got his job in the Foreign Office. Every time we met up he told me how bored he was and how he wished he did something more exciting. He envied me my life in the army – said he'd have swapped places with me any day."

She sighed and stood up. "It's time to go. I really need to show you something."

I was reluctant to go anywhere with this woman I'd only just met. But there was something about her deliberation and quiet assurance that swayed me, against my better judgment, and I found myself following her out of the club.

Melody flipped me a tired salute as we crossed the floor and Archie appeared once more from his cubbyhole when we neared the exit. I slipped a five-pound note into his hand and he handed me my coat, all the while observing my companion in much the same way that a hungry crab observes a shrimp. "Goodnight, Mr Carter," delivered with an unsubtle wink. "See you again soon, I hope, sir."

Terry was loitering on the pavement outside, enveloped in a camelhair coat that looked three sizes too large even for his 100-kilo frame. He placed a hand on my chest, ignoring Rebecca. "I very much hope we're not going to have a problem with your outstanding obligations, Charlie. It would be a shame for it to interfere with our friendship."

I looked down at his hand and clenched my fists, willing him to push, but he didn't. He withdrew his hand and regarded me with hooded eyes. "Friday week okay?" he asked brightly.

"I'm afraid Mr Carter is going to be away for a few days," interjected Rebecca. "But I'm sure he'll take care of any outstanding matters in due course." At which point a silver Mercedes 4x4 purred up to the kerbside and in one fluid motion she opened the door, slid across the back seat and beckoned me to join her. Terry could see that I was as bemused by her interjection as he was, but it didn't stop me from slipping in beside her, pulling the door closed behind me. I saw Terry pull up the collar of his coat against the early morning chill and watch us as we pulled away.

"How much do you owe?"

I looked at her, indignation rising. "None of your fucking business. Now will you please tell me what the hell this is all about. Where are we going and what do you know about Michael's death?"

Rebecca looked away and I saw her catch the driver's eye in the rear-view mirror. Something passed between them, but I couldn't tell what.

"I know this is all a bit sudden –"

"You think!" I yelled.

"– but believe me when I tell you I have no interest in making your life any worse than it already is," at which I visibly bridled, "and you'll be grateful when you've seen what I have to show you. Now please, I know it's hard, but try and relax. We'll be there soon."

We headed west out of London on a largely empty motorway. It was a little too early for the main commuter rush, but there were still plenty of vehicles on the inbound carriageway. A mix of well-heeled City types in Audis and Beemers heading east to London's forest of glass and metal ziggurats, while the less well-heeled in battered Fords and Toyotas headed for the menial minimum-wage service jobs that kept the capital running. Maybe it was the deadening effect of the alcohol, or several nights in succession with very little sleep, but I yawned and decided to go with it. I had nowhere else to be, my curiosity was aroused and I was frankly too tired to mount much resistance. I stared out of the window at the slowly emerging dawn and, while Rebecca tapped away on her smartphone, let my mind drift.

Michael and I were as close as it was possible for two brothers to be. Orphaned when I was 18 and he was 13, victims of a car accident which took our parents at an absurdly young age, Michael had clung to me throughout his adolescence as I had clung to him in early adulthood, a symbiosis of common grief and a shield against the world.

When I joined the army at 20, having eschewed university to look after him for those first couple of years, I made sure that our parents' modest life insurance payout covered his fees at a small private boarding school. While I served out my time on a series of tours in Afghanistan and other parts of the world, my little brother excelled at his studies, and went on to gain a place at Oxford to study Middle Eastern languages.

It wasn't surprising that he should have attracted the attentions of the diplomatic service, given the subject of his degree. They came knocking during his third year, he told me, when he was flying high. He'd already gained a First in his prelims and was a shoe-in for a double-First when he'd completed his finals. I was unspeakably proud of him. When he called me one day in Basra to tell me he was joining the Foreign Office, I felt my job was complete. My little brother was on his way.

There followed three years of what he always dismissed as desk-based drudgery. Analysis of this and that, he said. Writing endless briefs for witless politicians. I was overseas so much that I always accepted what he told me at face value. Why wouldn't I? But the truth was that I didn't really have much idea of what went on in his life. He was still single, although he did mention the odd girlfriend during our phone and Skype calls and in his regular emails, and he seemed to live well. He'd rented a small cottage in Hampshire, close to his beloved River Test where he apparently spent many hours honing his angling skills.

His life seemed set and settled and perfect. Until that fateful day two weeks ago. I got the call at my flat in Lewisham a couple of hours after the fire had been extinguished. Ostensibly they were calling to check on my brother's whereabouts, but it wasn't long before I learned that they had already found a body in the burnt-out wreckage of the house. And the house had only one inhabitant.

It wasn't clear at the time how the gas leak had happened and how it had ignited. Whatever it was, it had torn through the half-timbered thatched cottage in short order. My brother's body was apparently found on the floor of his bedroom, and I imagined his mouth open in an eternal scream, his limbs twisted to unnatural angles by the fierce heat. The firemen said he had most likely died instantly in the explosion, but for the last two weeks I'd been haunted by the thought that he might have been burnt alive, alone, with no one to hear his cries.

Following an investigation by specialist fire safety officers, the consensus was that the ancient rubber piping that fed the cooker with LPG must have perished and begun leaking butane. Something, possibly a switch in some part of the decades-old wiring, had sparked and that was that. One of the most careful people I ever knew had apparently died through a simple accident.

I must have dozed for a while, because the next thing I knew the car's tyres were crunching on gravel and in the gathering daylight I saw a sizeable house drawing closer at the end of a sweeping drive. "We're here," said Rebecca, unnecessarily. The car drew to a halt at the entrance and the driver got out and opened the door for me. Rebecca met me in front of the vehicle as I stretched my tired muscles and gazed up at the imposing portico framing an enormous double front door.

The driver went to the boot and retrieved two suitcases, then walked towards the giant doors, one of which opened soundlessly just as he reached it. He disappeared inside without a word and a middle-aged woman emerged, taking up position in the portico with her hands held demurely in front of her and a small smile on her lips.

"Welcome to Ramsden Hall," she said with a pronounced north-east accent. "I'm Mrs Padbourne. They're ready for you in the library."

We followed her down a seemingly endless panelled

hallway festooned with enough medieval weaponry to arm a small invasion force. Here and there hung gloomy paintings of disappointed looking men in ancient garb, interspersed with the stuffed heads of a variety of small animals, all of which not surprisingly looked similarly disappointed. I was beginning to feel like a character in an Agatha Christie novel. What next? Professor Plum in the library with the lead piping?

As I was gawping at a particularly unpleasant-looking military flail with a massive spiked ball, Mrs Padbourne opened a door off the hallway and ushered us into an enormous room filled with the light of a flaming sunrise. The library was fully two storeys high, with floor-to-ceiling bookcases lining three walls and a gallery halfway up accessed by a ladder on a sliding horizontal rail. The entire fourth wall was occupied by a multi-paned east-facing window, also extending from floor to ceiling, through which the morning sunlight was streaming. A fire was burning cheerily in a giant fireplace in the north wall and the room was furnished with a variety of overstuffed sofas and chairs, surrounding a large map table covered with books and papers. Mrs Padbourne withdrew and closed the door.

I took a few moments to take it all in, then turned to Rebecca with raised eyebrows. "So what is it you want to show me?" But she was looking past me, at the door which I'd just heard open and which I now turned towards.

"Hello big brother," said Michael.

CHAPTER 14

THE MAN in the black Nissan watched and smoked. He had been entrusted with this important job because of who his uncle was and what he did for the movement. He had been told not to let the woman out of his sight and he had stuck to her like glue, all the way to the sleazy club and then out to the unfamiliar green spaces of the English countryside. She thought she had been clever when she left her flat the day before. She thought she had shaken him off. But he had done this many times before and he did not lose her. He continued to follow her until she checked into the hotel. And from the hotel to the club.

And then to this house.

His Zeiss Conquest HD 15 x 56 binoculars were more than a match for the two hundred or so metres between him and the house.

He felt uncomfortable and out of place on this freezing morning in this rural backwater. It was a far cry from the bustle of his home turf on London's Edgware Road and even further from the heat and humidity of his family's well-appointed villa on the shores of the Persian Gulf. But he was being well paid, so he turned up the heating, settled back in the comfortable leather seat and brought the binoculars to his eyes again. He was curious about the man the woman had brought with her. He looked fit and capable. Walked like a soldier. Having been a soldier himself, he recognised the man's bearing.

He wondered if he was going to be a problem.

CHAPTER 15

I STOOD THERE FOR A MOMENT, speechless. The enormous room seemed to compress around me, like those clever movie shots where the camera pulls back and zooms in at the same time. Everything telescoped into the few metres that separated us.

The young man who stood before me with his hands in his pockets and his head cocked was relaxed, tanned and healthy. I took it all in in an instant and everything about him was the same, except for the well-trimmed beard and a small scar above his left eye. He was dressed in chinos and a white button-down shirt, with what looked like expensive loafers on his feet.

He regarded me with a look of abject apology.

"What the fuck?" I finally found my voice. "Michael? What the *fuck*?!"

"I'm sorry, Charlie," his hands spread. "I would have preferred to do this differently, but my colleagues insisted this was the best way." His voice was the same: measured, calm, with that beautiful inflection he'd inherited from our mother. This was indeed my brother. My dead brother. He stepped towards me, his hands outstretched, but I instinctively recoiled.

"Why don't we sit down. We've a lot to tell you," said Rebecca. "What Michael is saying is true - he did want to contact you a while ago, but we persuaded him that wasn't wise. Things have recently – changed. And we need your help."

I could feel the old anger beginning to take hold again, the anger that had so often led to bloody noses, broken limbs and broken promises. I just about held it in check as Rebecca led us all to a sofa and chairs beside the fire. Magically, seemingly without having entered the room, Mrs Padbourne appeared beside us with a tray of coffees and pastries.

"Have you got any idea what you've put me through?" I said, through clenched jaw. "I was at your funeral, for Christ's sake! I threw dirt on your coffin. I said goodbye! I've only just started to come to terms with it. And now here you are, back from the dead, looking like a fucking matinee idol and saying you're sorry!"

I felt the old familiar panic threatening to seize control. My head was pounding and a blackness began to seep into my peripheral vision. I was hyperventilating and knew that I was on the brink of another collapse, not helped by the alcohol I'd consumer earlier. I closed my eyes tightly and was trying to focus on pulling myself together when I felt a hand on my shoulder.

"Easy, Charlie, easy. It's okay," said Michael quietly. His voice was like a balm. I had heard it in my head a thousand times since the news of his death and now that I was hearing it for real, it instantly drew me back from the darkness .

"I know, it's a lot to take in," said Michael, infuriatingly calm and measured. "But you'll soon understand why. In the end it was to protect you as much as me."

"Protect me! Protect me!! You damned well –" I was breathless, half consumed by relief, half enraged by the deception. I fell into a nearby armchair, my arms rigid at my side.

"Please Charlie, just give us the opportunity to explain,"

said Rebecca.

I slowly brought myself under control and sat back in the chair, glowering. There was a brief silence, before Rebecca began. She was perched on the edge of the sofa, her back straight and her eyes locked on mine. I understood that she was beautiful, but that there was something predatory about her. This was a woman you dealt with only on her terms.

"I guess the first thing you need to know is that Michael doesn't work for the Foreign Office."

I looked at him and he shrugged.

"In fact, he doesn't work for the Government at all – at least, not officially. He did spend a short time with your security services," I noted the use of the word 'your,' "but for the last three years he's been part of an independent organisation – I suppose you might call it a consulting group – that was created to meet a specialist need."

"What kind of need?"

Michael and Rebecca exchanged glances.

"We're kind of like a tactical resource," said Michael. "We help solve problems it's difficult to solve through normal channels. Problems that might compromise a country's ability to do business in another country. Or where national security is threatened and a government can't address the threat through normal diplomatic channels, or militarily."

"You're saying you're spooks!" I exclaimed.

"Not exactly," said Rebecca. "Although we do have a fairly sophisticated intelligence and surveillance capability. In fact, that's where Michael's expertise lies. But we lean more towards active measures."

"Look, can you stop talking in riddles and just tell me what the hell's going on? What is this 'organisation' and what exactly do you do?"

"Okay Charlie," said Michael with a sigh, leaning forward with his elbows on his knees, his chin resting on his clasped hands. "You know better than most that the world is a dangerous and complicated place. Rogue states, religious fundamentalists, predatory corporations, ideological terrorists. Conventional warfare's fast becoming a thing of the past. Everything's going asymmetric. Today is about surgical strikes, drones, robotics, nanoweapons, cyberwarfare – all made more complicated by the fact that states and bad actors increasingly fight their battles by proxy rather than risking their own personnel. Our organisation was created to directly address these trends. To find ways of turning them to the advantage of our clients – "

"Who are?"

"Governments, mainly. Occasionally corporations, but only when their interests coincide with the national interests of friendly states. We're the good guys, Charlie. We're trying to make the world a better place."

"And where have I heard that before?" I scoffed.

"Believe me, when I tell you about some of the assignments we've worked on, you'll understand."

"All sounds a bit *Mission Impossible* to me," I said, taking a gulp of coffee.

My brother laughed. "Funny you should say that. One of our team *is* the spitting image of Tom Cruise. Anyway," turning serious again, "some of the people we've had to deal with have been very bad people indeed." He hesitated, pondering for a moment. "And if you'll forgive the euphemism, some of them are pieces we've had to take off the board."

I choked on my slug of coffee. "Hang on a minute. Are you saying you *kill* people?"

Another exchange of looks, this time accompanied by a slight nod from Rebecca.

"People are being killed all the time," continued Michael calmly. "The problem is that too often they're just bystanders in the wrong place at the wrong time, collateral damage. As a soldier, you know this. So-called surgical strikes, smart bombs, drone attacks – no matter how careful you are, in almost every case innocent people get killed. And sometimes it's just not possible to use these long-range methods anyway. The bad guys are too well protected, too well shielded. And occasionally it just pays to remove them without a big bang, quietly and discreetly."

"You've served in some of the world's worst places, Charlie," added Rebecca. "You know how hard it is sometimes to get to the ringleaders, the commanders, the warlords, the ones ultimately responsible for the atrocities you faced every day of your life in the army."

"And that's just the conventional villains," said Michael. "Then you have all the bad guys who hide behind legitimate corporations: the cybercriminals, the billion-dollar fraudsters, the gangsters, the drug barons – people who destroy lives by the thousand and threaten our societies every day of the year. They're the true untouchables, the men and women who even governments can't reach, because half the time they *are* the government."

My head was spinning. My baby brother part of some kind of *assassination squad*? Murderers for hire?

"How long's this been going on," I spluttered.

"The group was founded ten years ago. As Rebecca said, I've been involved for the last three."

This was too much to take in. I was finding it hard to keep up.

My belligerent tone returned. "You still haven't explained why you faked your own death."

Michael sat back in the sofa and Rebecca seamlessly picked up the story. "It was because Michael was in extreme danger. And when I say 'extreme', I mean danger of the worst kind from people of the worst kind. The only way we could protect him was to persuade those people that he was no longer a threat."

"So who were these mysterious people. And why exactly was he a threat to them?"

"Ah, now that's the crux of it," said Michael, looking down at his hands. "They're the same people who murdered mum and dad."

CHAPTER 16

I WAS speechless for the second time that morning. Literally so, because I could not immediately frame any response that would do justice to what Michael had just said. I just looked at him in dumb amazement.

"Perhaps you need a few minutes together," said Rebecca quietly. She rose from the sofa and left the room.

"I know it's a lot to take in," said Michael, leaning forward once more. "Let's take a walk."

I stood in a daze and he led me towards the giant windows. For the first time I noticed that there was a pair of well-concealed French doors in the centre frame. Michael opened one of them and stepped out. The sun was now well above the horizon and the lawn which lay before us was bathed in a golden light, setting off the crisp whiteness of the early morning frost that carpeted the grass and gave a newborn freshness to the day. We walked together in silence towards a ha-ha at the end of the lawn, beyond which sheep grazed on an extensive stretch of parkland dotted with mature trees.

"I know it's no consolation," said my brother, "but I've only just learned this myself." We were walking along the ha-ha towards what looked like a walled garden on the northern flank of the house.

"I think you'd better start at the beginning," I said, with a weariness born of shock and sleeplessness.

What Michael told me next was to change the course of my life.

CHAPTER 17

THE MAN in the Nissan removed the binoculars from his eyes and thought for a moment. He lit another cigarette and removed a photograph from the inside pocket of his quilted jacket, scrutinising it carefully.

Taking out his mobile phone, he quickly dialled a long-distance number and waited for the answering machine to kick in. "It's Anwar," he said to the silence that followed the soft beep. "I've just seen a ghost. I need to know what you want me to do." He rang off and put the phone back in his pocket.

Opening the glove compartment, he removed a Glock 19 semi-automatic pistol. It was an expensive weapon, but worth the investment. Its predecessor, the Glock 17, had been popular with law enforcement agencies for many years due to its light polymer frame, friendly ergonomics and low recoil, but when the 19 was introduced in the late 1980s it quickly became a bestseller. Smaller and two ounces lighter, it was the handgun of choice for both legitimate and illegitimate users who wanted an easily-concealed weapon which would not weigh too heavily on the hip if carried all day. Anwar was holding the Gen5 version of the weapon, launched in 2017, with an nDLC coating, flared mag-well and Marksman Barrel. He checked the 15-round magazine and ensured there was a cartridge in the chamber. He replaced it in the glove compartment, then sat back to wait.

His phone rang 10 minutes later. He explained what he had seen and listened while the voice gave him precise instructions.

CHAPTER 18

MORE THAN A THOUSAND years before the birth of Christ, the Phoenicians were the ancient world's greatest trading nation. Restless seafarers, explorers and adventurers, they traversed the Mediterranean in their fleets of gauloi, or 'round ships,' their holds filled with iron, copper, ivory, glassware and fabrics dyed with the Tyrian purple a must-have fashion accessory among the wealthy nations of the Near East.

But perhaps their greatest legacy were the wines they cultivated in their homeland of the coastal Levant. They domesticated the common grape which had been brought by merchants from the South Caucasus via the Mesopotamian and Black Sea trade routes. They created a thriving viticulture which played a major role in their economy and religion. Phoenician wines were exported all over the known world, from Egypt to Italy and Greece.

The Phoenicians are long gone, but their descendants in Lebanon remain vintners of distinction, especially throughout the country's wine-growing heartland in the south of the Beqa'a Valley, a hundred kilometres east of Beirut.

Deep in the Beqa'a, just outside the small town of Marj, the small independent Karami vineyard has been producing wine since the early 20th century. Watered by the Litani River, the earth is rich and fertile, and while Karami may not be able to claim the heritage of its more famous neighbours like Musar and Ksara, it has yielded some fine vintages over the years and its label can, from time to time, be found amongst the stock of wine merchants and liquor stores in London and New York.

Al-Shammari had purchased the vineyard in 2016 from the family which had founded and nurtured it for the previous 100 years. They were not willing sellers. Al-Shammari was neither a vintner nor a native Lebanese. A Sunni Iraqi, he had been visiting Beirut for many years and when it became convenient for him to take up residence in Lebanon, he deliberately sought out a quiet backwater which was far enough from prying eyes for him to be able to conduct his business in peace. The fact that there was already a flourishing enterprise operating from the property only made it more attractive, a convenient cover for his real interests.

The Karami family – parents, grandparents, uncles, aunts and children – were paid handsomely to vacate their property, but only after it had become necessary for Al-Shammari to persuade them of how misguided they would be to decline his offer. Chaining one of the Karami nephews to the back of a powerful BMW motorcycle and dragging him for three kilometres before dumping him in the courtyard in front of the main house did the trick. The family vacated in two days, leaving Ari to bring in his team to secure the property and settle into his new home. He retained the head vintner and his staff to maintain the operation of the winery and continued to enjoy the proceeds of the business, although as a devout Muslim, he never sampled the merchandise himself.

Since returning home from his London residence the previous evening, Ari had been uncomfortably preoccupied with two unwelcome problems, both of which threatened seriously to interfere with his plans. Firstly, the young man who had been delving into his affairs and who had, he thought, finally been dealt with, appeared to have been raised from the dead.

Secondly – and even more troublingly – the valuable arte-fact that he had only recently acquired appeared to have gone missing. He had spent the last few hours probing the copious research material he had amassed over the last twenty years, focusing on the archaeology of the ancient Levant. What he had discovered only served to confirm his earlier suspicions and reinforce his belief that he had stumbled across something of fabulous value – not only monetarily, but also politically. He was beginning to believe he was on the brink of transforming the fortunes of the cause he served.

It was late morning and he was sitting in the sunshine on the terrace with its fine view of his adopted vineyards, reading the *Financial Times* and enjoying a late breakfast of thick, creamy labneh and olive oil, olives, zaatar, cucumbers and toma-toes, accompanied by Lebanese bread and fresh mint tea. Deep in thought, he did not hear his lieutenant approaching until he heard a discreet cough behind him.

In the lilting Arabic of his native country, Ari asked, "What in the name of Allah is going on, Mahmoud? The annoyance of the young man who has been delving into our affairs? One day I am told that he is dead; a few weeks later I learn that he has enjoyed a miraculous resurrection. Which is it?"

Mahmoud bowed slightly and replied in the harsher tones of his Kurdish homeland, "It appears we were deceived. Before we had an opportunity to deal with him, we were informed that young Carter was killed in an explosion in his home. We believed Allah had taken matters into His divine hands, but it appears that the event was carefully staged. And he obviously did not achieve this alone. We assume he had help from the same people who interfered in our original attempt to appre-hend him.

"But we have had some good fortune." Al-Shammari merely

73

glared at him and waited in silence for him to continue. "I took the precaution of having our people observe the young man's funeral, which of course we now know was a sham. I thought it might be useful to see who attended and perhaps get some clues as to who his helpers were."

"And?" asked Al-Shammari impatiently.

"And there was a woman there, watching but trying not to be seen by the mourners. Our men believe she was one of the three people who interfered with the abduction. One of our people followed her and yesterday she met with another man, with whom she travelled to a house outside London. It was there that our observers saw Carter again."

"This is the second time that you have disappointed me in this matter, Mahmoud. There will not be a third. Have you taken steps to remove him once and for all?"

"Yes sir. Our operative is moving the matter to a conclusion as we speak."

"Good." Ari paused and rose from his chair, his hands clasped behind his back, gazing out across the vines. "Now, to the more pressing issue. What has happened to our merchandise?"

For the second time in the last forty-eight hours, Mahmoud looked abashed. He murmured, "It appears that the consignment was broken into. A number of items were stolen, including your merchandise, sir."

Al-Shammari regarded him with barely suppressed fury. "I need you to return immediately to London and recover that crate," he hissed. "Before I left London I telephoned our clients and told them that we have happened upon something of unprecedented value which could change the course of their campaign. Our clients are very excited. And you know what will happen if we disappoint them.

"It is imperative that no one else views that manuscript before I have had an opportunity to follow up on its contents. I suggest you start with the haulage company. I have been making efforts to contact them since they informed me of the theft, but they now appear unwilling to return my calls." He sighed. "Why is it that it is always your supposed partners who disappoint you. These days you cannot even trust a gangster," he said mirthlessly.

"Sir," with another slight bow. Mahmoud turned to go.

"And Mahmoud? I want no mistakes this time. If you meet with obstacles, remove them, permanently if necessary. Do you understand?"

"Sir." And with a final bow, he slipped through the French windows and was gone.

Ari leaned back in his chair and lit a strong Turkish cigarette. His expression set hard and his unoccupied hand closed into a fist. He was glad to be back in Lebanon. He disliked London and he disliked the British. All those fat and happy people, he thought. What did they know of privation and suffering? He reached into the pocket of his jacket, drew out his wallet and extracted a well-worn photograph. The woman and two small children were playing on a beach, the girls' heads thrown back in laughter, their eyes bright, while the woman's eyes were on the man behind the camera, that familiar smile on her lips, an expression of love which still had the power to squeeze his heart.

He gazed at the photo that captured the last time he had seen his wife and daughters, then he returned it to his wallet and the wallet to his pocket. He sipped his tea and brooded.

CHAPTER 19

WE APPROACHED a small door and stepped through it into a large walled garden laced with footpaths between raised beds that were largely bare at that time of the year. A sizeable greenhouse stood in one corner. We walked and talked.

"As you know, mum and dad were moderately successful art dealers," Michael began. "I was a bit too young to remember their business, but I do know that in the early days they specialised in medieval works and established a decent reputation, especially for tapestries and hanging wall coverings, things like that." I nodded in agreement. "Dad had close relationships with the auction houses and mum had a good business brain. They were a great team."

"I remember," I said.

"It seems that that in later years they began to take an interest in antiquities, particularly from the Middle East. They apparently acted as intermediaries for the sale of a number of pieces to private collectors and made good money. The problem was that some of those pieces had a bit of a dubious provenance."

"What do you mean?"

"It really all goes back to the second Gulf War. When the

US and Britain invaded Iraq in 2003, the campaign was effectively over in three weeks, but that was just the start of the mayhem. Apart from the various insurgencies and the chaos they created, the country became a magnet for thieves and looters who grabbed every artefact they could lay their hands on and dumped them on the black market."

He paused. "Let me give you an example. Have you ever heard of the Mask of Warka?"

I shook my head.

"It's one of the earliest representations of the human face. It's around five thousand years old, from ancient Sumeria, and was one of the most valuable artefacts in the National Museum in Baghdad, worth millions to the right buyer. It was looted from the museum days after the invasion and it was only down to a lucky tip-off that it was ever recovered. American and Jordanian investigators eventually found it buried in a farmer's field. But that was the exception rather than the rule. There were around 15,000 antiquities stolen from that museum alone and most of them have never been recovered, although we know they regularly circulate among illegal collectors."

"Are you saying mum and dad were smuggling these things?" I asked, astonished.

"I don't think they were necessarily doing it consciously, but we're pretty sure they got in over their heads on something at some point."

"We?" I stopped walking and looked at my brother hard.

He stopped too and took a deep breath. "I only know any of this because of the team. When they were recruiting me, they did a thorough background check – a really thorough background check. They looked into me, you and our family."

I didn't like this. "You mean they *investigated* me?" I asked indignantly.

"I obviously didn't know it at the time, but yes. They pulled your army records and, well..."

"Dragged out all my dirty linen and waved it in your face!"

"No, nothing like that, Charlie. They just needed to be sure there was no potential for me to be compromised. They accepted the fact that you were honourably discharged and understood about the PTSD. They were very sympathetic."

"Well, how fucking magnanimous of them!"

"Listen, there were good reasons for them to pay attention to you. And in fact there are even better reasons now, but I'll get to that. It's more important that you listen to what I have to say about mum and dad."

I grunted and resumed walking.

"The team got access to the police reports on the car accident and gave them a good going-over. One of the team is a former DCI with the Met and he was certain something wasn't right."

"Go on."

My mind drifted back to that day in late April fifteen years before. A lifetime ago, it felt like, but the memory was crystal-clear. Michael and I were home alone, waiting for our parents to return from a late lunch in London. We knew they had been celebrating some successful deal they'd just concluded. When it reached eight o'clock and we hadn't heard from them, we called their mobile, but there was no answer. We kept ringing and ringing for the next two hours but got nothing. It went straight through to voicemail every time. And then, just after ten o'clock that evening, the police were at the door.

They were sympathetic and solicitous. They spared us the details at the time, but the essentials were that our parents were only a couple of miles from home when dad somehow lost control of the car, which hit a bridge, came off the road and ended up on the river bank. The only explanation seemed to be that the road was wet from recent rain, dad was blinded by the reflection of the setting sun and misjudged a bend.

We later learned that neither of them died immediately

after the crash. The coroner's report said there were clear signs of them struggling to get out of the car, but both doors were jammed shut by the impact. The car caught fire and they were both burned alive.

"It's actually pretty rare for a car to catch fire after a crash, despite what you see in the movies," my brother said, very quietly. "Even if the fuel lines rupture, there has to be some kind of ignition. That's why you see plenty of nasty accidents on motorways, including multiple pile-ups, but you don't often see fires." He paused, seeing it all in his mind's eye. "But in this case, given there seemed no doubt about the cause of the crash, the fire was just dismissed as a freak event."

"But your – organisation – thought otherwise."

"The policeman who was first on the scene, a smart copper called Ryan Cooper, used to be a traffic cop. He'd seen dozens of traffic accidents in his time and said in his report that this just didn't smell right, but he couldn't put his finger on why. Of course the car was badly damaged and completely burnt out, so he had no way of resolving his misgivings. He did mention that he found fresh tyre tracks on the verge above the ditch. Said it looked as if a heavy vehicle had recently pulled off the road, then reversed back down the lane, but that wasn't exactly evidence of foul play.

"He said the really odd thing was that there was no sign anywhere of our parents' mobile phone. He knew they had one and knew it was working, because one of us had called from home and said it was ringing."

"Did you talk to this copper?"

"Couldn't. He died five years ago. Cancer. He'd only just retired."

"Anyway, none of this was conclusive. It was a quiet road – you remember it only really led to our house and a couple of others – there were no witnesses and obviously no cameras. The inquest eventually concluded it was death by misadventure, down to our dad being tired and possibly blinded by the sun. You know the rest. The car was carted off to a breaker's yard and crushed a few days later."

"So you're telling me you think they were murdered? Why? And what's the connection with their art-dealing business?"

"This is where it gets murky. Let's go back to the house and I'll show you." He turned towards the gate, but I caught his arm.

"Mikey, wait." He looked at me quizzically. It was such a familiar expression, one I recognised from our earliest childhood days: the furrowing of the brow, his head tilted a little to one side, his mouth turned down slightly at the corners. I felt a sudden sharp pang of affection for this man whose life had been so blighted by tragedy and loss at such a young age. "It's good to see you, little brother. It's good to see you alive." And then we were hugging, tightly, a little desperately, and the years fell away and we were back in school, my arms wrapped around him protectively after a spat with the playground bullies that left him bruised and tearful.

We drew apart and I held him by the shoulders at arms-length. We just looked at one another for several moments. "It's good to see you too, Charlie. I'm sorry about the way this has all turned out. But I promise you'll understand when I've explained everything."

We returned to the house and Charlie led me to a small study further down the hall from the library. It was sparsely furnished, just a large partners' desk with two straight-backed chairs on either side. The desk was strewn with papers.

He rummaged around among the various files and binders until he found a small portfolio of photographs, which he passed to me. "Take a look at those."

I flipped through the photos, which showed various items of statuary, with rulers placed beside them to show their dimensions. They were all between 30 and 60 centimetres in height, beautifully carved in a variety of materials – some looked like marble, others obsidian or polished quartz – inset with a variety of expensive-looking gemstones. There were twelve in all.

"They're genuine antiquities," said Michael. "From Iraq, we're pretty sure. Mesopotamian – probably from the second millennium BC according to the experts we've asked. They're very rare and very valuable. They would almost certainly have sold for tens of millions to the right buyer."

"Where did you find these?" I asked.

"That's the thing. The photos were in the safe in our parents' office, along with a catalogue number, but there was no sign of the statues themselves. There's no record of a sale – and for that matter no record of who or where they came from. When the insurance assessors inventoried the items Mum and Dad were holding for sale in their strongroom at the bank, the statues were not among them."

"So what makes you think they ever had them?"

"Dad wouldn't have catalogued them unless they'd actually taken possession of them. But that's not everything." He did some more rummaging and drew out a large desk diary from the year of our parents' death. "Look at the entry for April 27th."

I opened the diary and turned to the page. There was a single notation for 4 p.m. that day: 'JB, Paddington Hilton. Sale SR943'. I looked at Michael questioningly.

"SR943 was the catalogue number of the statue collection. It seems pretty clear from the entry that either Dad or Mum or both were due to meet a buyer. But so far we've no idea who 'JB' is or whether the meeting ever happened. All we know is that two days later mum and dad were dead."

I began to feel a stirring of anger, like a low-frequency thrumming that you only gradually become aware of as it seeps slowly into your consciousness. But it was not unpleasant. It was like the return of an old friend.

"How did everyone miss this at the time?"

"Well, the insurance company didn't have any reason to

suspect foul play. All they had were a few photos, with no documentary evidence that our parents had ever physically had the items themselves. And we only discovered the diary by accident – it was buried in a pile of old archive files which had been stored by Mum and Dad's solicitors and which they'd never got around to destroying. I asked them, on the off chance, whether they still had anything from our parents and they let me have the lot. That's what you're looking at on this desk."

"But what's all this got to do with you faking your own death and hiding yourself away out here in the sticks?"

Michael suddenly looked very tired. "It seems that when I went poking around into our parents' deaths it drew the attention of some unpleasant people," he said.

"Very unpleasant indeed," said a voice behind us. Rebecca walked into the room.

She sat down in one of the chairs and Michael sat beside her. I took one of the seats opposite.

"You have to understand that the illegal trade in antiquities is a very lucrative business," said Rebecca. After the Gulf War all sorts of rogue elements went after a slice of the pie, including a lot of organised crime – and worse. It's always been a cash business and an ideal source of funding for insurgencies all over the world. We believe your parents stumbled into a transaction between some very bad players and it cost them their lives."

"What bad players?" I asked.

"We're not sure, but we suspect, because of their exceptional value, the statues caught the attention of someone representing one of the Middle Eastern terrorist groups. Our working theory is that they were stolen to order and passed on for a fee to an intermediary with ISIS or Al Qaeda. Or some other group with the same credentials. They were then sold on. The proceeds would have bought an awful lot of weaponry for the cause."

"I didn't know any of this at the time," said Michael. "But I just couldn't leave it alone. It gnawed away at me for three years and I repeatedly asked the team to help me get to the bottom of it, but they kept telling me that it wasn't within the organisation's remit. Finally, I took matters into my own hands and stupidly started an amateur investigation of my own. I obviously turned over the wrong rock and something very nasty crawled out – and came after me."

"Michael was lucky," said Rebecca. "We decided to keep an eye on him once we realised he wasn't going to be put off. Which was just as well."

"I was walking back to my house from the station one night. It was late and I should really have taken a taxi, but I always enjoyed the walk – it's only about twenty minutes and it gives me time to think. I was literally just about to open my gate when someone came up behind me and shoved some kind of bag over my head. Someone else kicked my legs out from under me and the next thing I knew I was being carried off like the proverbial sack of potatoes. It happened so damned fast."

"Apparently they were just about to shove me into the boot of a car, but our team were watching my back and intervened." He looked at Rebecca and smiled. "Rebecca here was one of them. I gather bag man's going to be in plaster for a while and leg man's probably still recovering from his headache. Anyway, the team carted me off to their car and brought me here. I've been here ever since."

"Why the hell didn't you tell me all this months – no years – ago?!"

"Like I said, the team argued strongly that I should let it rest. There was no absolute proof that Mum and Dad had been murdered – and it was all too close to home. The guys have a clear rule about steering clear of anything personal. That's not what the team is for."

"When it gets personal, we lose our objectivity, which means we lose our professionalism," interjected Rebecca. "We have always abided by that rule. Until Michael broke it." She looked at him with a mixture of sadness, affection and annoyance. The kind of look an exasperated parent gives a recalcitrant child. And perhaps something else.

"When I decided to investigate this thing, I wanted to solve it myself and present it to you as a *fait accompli*," continued Michael, unperturbed by Rebecca's interruption. "I thought I was being so smart." He paused again. "So smart that I nearly got myself killed – and probably worse."

"You're such a fucking idiot," I said, but the heat had gone out of my temper and all I felt was relief. "So who was the poor sod who ended up as a crispy critter at your place?" I asked.

"He was one of dozens of homeless men who turn up at mortuaries all over the country every month of the year," explained Rebecca. "If they can't be identified, their bodies are eventually cremated. We have contacts in the Coroner's office and used them to find this particular body, which was roughly Michael's height and build, and give it an early cremation – for all we know, the poor guy made a greater contribution by dying than he ever did by living. We had a memorial plaque made and placed in his memory on a cemetery lawn not far from here."

"And did it work? Is Michael safe?"

"We thought so. Until the day before yesterday. That's why you're here, Charlie."

CHAPTER 20

"SO WHAT HAPPENED the day before yesterday?"

"I'm afraid that was my fault," said Rebecca. "I did something foolish."

"I somehow can't imagine that," I replied.

She smiled ruefully. "I went to Michael's funeral. It was a mistake. I wanted to see who else was there, whether anyone was still watching. I just wanted to be sure we were in the clear."

"I was there," I said. "I didn't see you."

"I came in after the service began, sat at the back and slipped out before it ended. I watched the burial from the road. I saw you and a woman –"

"Angie. My ex-wife – well nearly ex," I interjected.

"I watched until the coffin had been lowered and then left. I thought I was being careful, but obviously not careful enough. As I was driving away, I noticed a car parked in a lay-by not far from the church, but stupidly thought nothing of it. Looking back, I'm pretty sure it must have followed me back to London."

"So what happened then?"

"Nothing – yet. But I noticed the same car parked outside my home that night. Clearly watching my flat. I slipped out the back and took a cab to a hotel. Stayed there until I came to find you at the club."

"How do you know you weren't still being followed?"

"I don't. I was reasonably careful, but I can't be sure they weren't still on my tail. I still can't. In any case, if they're taking an interest in me, it's only a matter of time before they find out that Michael's death was a feint."

"But why get me involved? You didn't before – why now?"

"That was my decision," said Michael. "I wanted you here. I worried that if I was still at risk, there was a chance you would be too, if not now, then at some point in the future. I figured that whatever happens, it would be better if we faced it together. Added to which, I think we're going to need your help."

I regarded my brother balefully. "Just like when we were kids. Bailing out my baby brother again."

"Let's get something to eat," said Rebecca. "Then we can talk about next steps. There's also someone else I'd like you to meet, Charlie."

She led us out of the study and back into the hallway, which we followed until we reached a sizeable kitchen with views over the garden where we had recently been walking. Mrs Padbourne was bustling around an AGA at one end of the room. We took our seats at a large scrubbed-pine table beside the window and she laid out a generous breakfast of eggs, bacon, sausages and toast before quietly leaving the room. All three of us tucked in hungrily.

Just as we'd finished, the door opened and a tall, elegantly dressed man entered the room. I guessed he was in his 60s, fit and slim, with a measured step and a confident patrician air. He reminded me a little of Christopher Lee, and when he spoke, his voice was not unlike that of the late actor. He was vaguely familiar.

"Good morning Mr Carter. I'm so glad you could join us.

My name is Simon Spurrier and you are very welcome to my home. I see Mrs Padbourne has been looking after you."

I stood up and shook his hand. Now I realised why he was so familiar. I had seen him on television from time to time. A former trade minister and more recently Britain's ambassador to somewhere. I couldn't remember where.

"Sir Simon is an adviser to our organisation and kindly agreed to put Michael up until we were able to ensure his safe return to London," explained Rebecca. "But it seems we may all now be overstaying our welcome."

Our host dismissed this with a wave of his hand. "You are welcome to stay for as long as you deem necessary."

"Thank you, Simon, but I think it's time we got back to London," said my brother. "I think things are likely to start hotting up and none of us want you to be caught up in it. I think we'll probably be safer back in the office anyway, and it looks as if we're going to have a lot of work to do."

"As you wish."

CHAPTER 21

THE DRIVER WAS WAITING as we walked out. Rebecca introduced him as Tom, taking the front seat beside him while Michael and I climbed into the back. "Where exactly are we going?" I asked. "Somewhere safe," replied Rebecca, turning around to face us. "You're going to meet some of the team and we're going to tell you a little more about what we do – and how you can help."

We passed between a pair of monolithic stone pillars crested with two snarling lions. It had been too dark to see them when we arrived. The car turned left onto a narrow lane and we settled back in our seats.

"How's Angie?" asked Michael suddenly. The question took me by surprise.

"I haven't seen a lot of her," I answered non-committally. "We met up at your funeral," I looked at him sardonically, "but we didn't talk much before she left and went back up north."

"I wish you'd try, Charlie. It's been a long time – you need to put all that stuff behind you."

I grunted in reply and turned away to look out of the window, signalling that the subject was closed. I had put my estranged wife through hell when I was invalided out of the army and I had no wish to be reminded of those days, least of all in the present circumstances. I could sense Rebecca's embarrassment at the brief exchange and I wondered whether she knew all about my imploding marriage, too. I guess she must, if her investigators had done their job.

We retreated into silence, each lost in our own thoughts.

"I think we've picked up a tail," said the driver suddenly. "Shit," hissed Rebecca. "I was afraid of this. Can you lose him, Tom?"

In answer, the driver pushed down on the accelerator and the powerful car surged forward. I turned around in my seat to see a black saloon dropping back behind us. Within a few seconds there were several hundred yards between us. We swept around a left-hand bend and there, barely a hundred feet away, a white panel van was slewed across the tarmac, entirely blocking the narrow road. Tom slammed on the brakes and in a haze of blue smoke and burnt rubber we came to a stop just a few feet from the van.

Immediately the doors of the vehicle flew open and two men jumped out, both dressed in what looked like black jumpsuits and wearing wraparound dark glasses. Both were holding what I instantly recognised as Heckler & Koch MP7 submachine pistols. The sight of the weapons was bad enough, but I also knew from the exercises I had conducted from time to time with the German security services that the MP7 was often chambered for armour-piercing rounds. They were designed to penetrate 20 layers of titanium-reinforced Kevlar at 200 metres and the Mercedes would offer them little resistance.

The two men slowly approached us and signalled with their gun barrels for us to get out of the car. Michael and I looked at each other and an unspoken acknowledgment passed between us. At the same time Rebecca, in a remarkably calm voice, whispered, "Tom..." and a split-second later the driver slammed our vehicle into reverse and we were careering backwards down the lane. The Nissan, as I now recognised our tail car to be, had just cleared the bend and was slowing down.

The driver was clearly surprised to see us hurtling backwards towards him and made the critical error of not pulling across the road as his associates had done. This gave Tom the opportunity to mount the narrow verge, the Mercedes' heavy-duty tyres throwing grass and mud in all directions as it careered between the tall hedgerow and the Nissan. There was a screech of metal and a shower of glass from the driver's window and we briefly glimpsed the shocked expression of the man inside as we rammed our way through the narrow gap. At the same time I also became aware of the too-familiar sound, like ripping fabric, of an automatic weapon loosing its payload.

The MP7 has a cyclic rate of fire of 950 rounds per minute, but even with a 40-round magazine on full automatic this empties the weapon in less than three seconds. Which is where our assailants made their second mistake. The driver of the van paused for just a couple of seconds too long before letting loose an unrestrained volley in our direction, giving us just enough time to get behind the Nissan, which absorbed the multiple rounds of copper-plated solid steel bullets meant for us. As Tom continued skilfully to reverse at maximum speed away from the melee, we saw the Nissan's bonnet blow clean off the front of the car and rise several feet into the air before spinning onto the road between us.

The Nissan's passenger was less profligate with his weapon. As we increased the distance between us, we saw him run around the side of the stricken car, kneel quickly and fire several short, controlled bursts towards us. We all ducked as the windscreen blew in and we felt the dull thumps of several rounds as they thudded into the front of the Mercedes. And then at last we were reversing around the bend and lost sight of our attackers.

As we sped past a five-barred gate on our right, Tom hit the brakes hard and threw the car into four-wheel drive. Steering straight for the gate, he smashed through the timber and powered across an open field, scattering sheep in all directions, heading slightly uphill towards a small copse. As we gained speed, I looked out of the rear window to see the panel van slide to a halt beside the gate and the two men leap out for a second time. They leaned on the bonnet of the van and loosed off another volley in our direction, but by now we were beyond the range of their weapons and in a few seconds we were rounding the copse and the trees obscured their view.

I realised that Rebecca had her phone in her hand and was shouting at someone on the other end of the line while scanning Google maps. Some kind of rendezvous was agreed and she quickly gave the destination to Tom, who nodded and accelerated downhill across a recently-ploughed field to a distant hedgerow. A minute or so later we had burst through another gate, skidded onto a wide lane and were back up to 70mph with the wind blasting into our faces through the shattered windscreen.

It was only after we had covered another five miles or so that Tom brought the car slowly to a halt in the car park of a DIY superstore off a busy dual carriageway and we all finally stopped looking nervously every few seconds out of the back window.

As the three of us were heaving a collective sigh of relief, Tom slumped forward over the steering wheel and slid sideways, his head coming to rest against the driver's door. It was only then that we noticed the blood running freely from his head. It had already soaked his shirt and coat.

"Oh, no, Tom, no –" exclaimed Rebecca as she unfastened her seat belt and reached for his neck, feeling desperately for a pulse. After a few seconds she slumped back in her seat.

"Shit!" she spat. "Shit, shit, SHIT!"

CHAPTER 22

IT WAS a tense half-hour in which little was said, before a black Volkswagen people carrier pulled into the car park, came to a stop beside us, and two men got out. Shielded by the three of us, the two new arrivals carefully transferred Tom's body to the rear of the VW. We stood in silence as the grim task was completed, remembering the brave man – virtually unknown to me – who had risked, and ultimately given, his life to get us safely away from the gunmen.

We climbed aboard and the VW made its way back onto the dual carriageway and from there onto the London-bound motor-way. We made the journey in silence. There was really nothing to say. Rebecca was particularly sombre. I realised that she blamed herself; she understood that the only way the gunmen could have found us was by following her

An hour later we turned into the entrance of an under-ground car park below a nondescript office building near Oxford Street. Michael, Rebecca and I disembarked and waited for the two men to open the tailgate, but one of them said quietly that they would take care of Tom from here and that we should head on up to the office. We made for an elevator in one corner of the car park and stepped in. A few minutes later we were several floors up and standing in front of a frosted glass door. Rebecca placed her hand on a large panel to the right of the door. There was a soft purring sound as it opened.

Inside was a reception area, unmanned, with several doors leading off to the right and left. Directly ahead at the end of the lobby was a floor-to-ceiling glass wall providing a view over the rooftops of central London. Rebecca led us to the far door on the right and we stepped through it into a large room which looked a little like a mini version of the trading floor in an investment bank. Half-a-dozen men and women sat at desks equipped with multiple computer screens showing images ranging from open documents, maps and charts to what looked to my trained eye like satellite imagery. They turned in unison as we entered the room, all regarding us sombrely without a word.

Rebecca nodded to each of them in turn as she continued on to a door in the right-hand wall which she opened by placing her hand on another panel. We stepped into a sizeable board-room comfortably furnished with high-backed leather swivel chairs around a large rosewood table. Coffee and sandwiches were laid out on a side-table.

We sat in uneasy silence, Rebecca on one side of the table, Michael and me on the other. We were all exhausted, but I sensed that a long day still lay ahead of us.

Before we had a chance to speak, the door opened and a man walked in. I put him in his mid-thirties, bearded and dressed casually in jeans and a grey hoodie. He wore the same solemn expression as the rest of us as he took a seat beside Rebecca.

"Charlie, this is Rolf Müller, our head of operations," she said, her voice dull and flat. She looked relieved to be able to pass the baton to someone else for a while. Having made the introduction, she sank back in her chair, her hands in her lap, her eyes downcast.

"I am sorry we meet under such circumstances," said the

new arrival, the German accent faint but detectable. Rolf looked calm and controlled, sitting quite still and regarding me with piercing green eyes that I suspected missed little. In front of him he held a slim red file.

"There will be time later for mourning – and recriminations, if necessary," he began. "But for now we need to focus on the immediate problem. As we feared, Michael's faked death didn't hold them off for long. Obviously, whoever was trying to get to him, now knows he's still alive – and they've given up any pretence of subtlety. They are no longer targeting just Michael. They're happy to take out anyone who's with him. The game has changed."

"Who was the man who died?" I asked. "Did he have a family?"

"He was one of our drivers," said Michael, very quietly. "Ex-Metropolitan Police. He retired several years ago and joined us shortly afterwards. He was a good man. With a wife and two children." A heavy silence fell on the room. "Trust me when I tell you that he will be afforded an honourable funeral, his family will be well looked after, and he will be remembered for his sacrifice. By me especially," he added, his voice catching.

"Sadly he was not the first and I doubt very much that he will be the last of our team to suffer the consequences of the work we do here," said Rolf, matter-of-factly.

Rebecca leaned forward, her hands clasped, and looked at me questioningly. I closed my eyes and shook my head. "It's even more important now that we get on top of this thing, Charlie," she said, her voice still leaden. "Let's recap on what we know. Rolf?" The German opened his folder, took a moment to review its contents, then began.

"As you know, Charlie, we have reason to believe your parents' death fifteen years ago was not an accident. For the moment, let us make that our working assumption. From there it is not unreasonable to deduce that their deaths were connected

94

to the sale of some valuable Middle Eastern artefacts, which were missing and never recovered. A fair deduction, I think, but very difficult to establish as fact."

"With respect, Mr Müller, we've been through all this already."

"Please, call me Rolf."

"But I still don't understand the connection between the two."

He continued, unfazed by my interruption. His tone was formal and to the point. "I honestly believe that if that were the only information we had, then it would have remained just that: a deduction, an inference, nothing more. But all these years later Michael decided to look into the matter. And he obviously awakened an unhealthy interest in himself – and, by extension, potentially our organisation."

Michael shuffled uncomfortably in his chair.

"Michael's cottage was broken into and ransacked. He kept the photographs and diary that he showed you earlier with him, but the police report into your parents' accident was still in the property, and was taken. From that moment we felt it necessary to take steps to ensure Michael's safety, and so managed to prevent his abduction a few days later, as you know."

I listened intently.

"So, we were able to reach a number of conclusions. Firstly, it was now much more likely that our suspicions were correct: your parents' deaths were not an accident and were linked to the theft of the artefacts by persons unknown. Secondly, it was those same persons – or people connected to them – who were apparently now keen to put an end to Michael's investigations. Thirdly, the passage of fifteen years had not reduced the importance to those persons of preventing Michael's enquiries. And this puzzled us." He paused, straightened the papers in the folder before him, and looked up at me.

"We think there is something else going on here."

I looked at him quizzically. "Like what?"

"Well, I don't mean to sound insensitive, but we can't believe that these people, whoever they are, would go to such lengths just to cover up something that happened so long ago. After all, the whole matter was settled to the satisfaction of the authorities and it would be impossible to prove foul play after all these years. No, there is something else. Today's events have only served to confirm that.

In addition our intelligence guys may just have stumbled on something." He paused again. I waited, impatiently.

"Have you ever read any Sherlock Holmes, Charlie?" he asked, locking eyes with me.

"What? What in God's name has Sherlock Holmes got to do with anything?!"

"Bear with me, Charlie, please. You may remember that Holmes's nemesis is Moriarty, who he likens to a spider at the centre of a web with a thousand threads. Moriarty knows and learns from every twitch of every one of those threads. I admit it's ironic for me to be comparing us to the Napoleon of crime, but the analogy is sound. Our organisation has a thousand threads. A network of relationships with governments, security agencies, companies, NGOs and many others. Plus a healthy crop of informants and assets on the ground in countries all over the world. When the web twitches, we watch, listen and learn. And recently our web has been twitching with some very disquieting rumours."

"About what?" I was having trouble keeping up with all this, tiredness once again asserting itself.

"If you'll forgive me for reversing the analogy, it seems that we have uncovered a Moriarty of our own. We don't yet know who he is, but we do know that he is at the centre of an illicit international trade in antiquities going back more than fifteen years, that he is ruthless and that he almost certainly has close links to one of the Middle Eastern terrorist organisations, quite possibly IS or something similar. We think he is a money man, an insurgency banker, a fund-raiser for fanatics, if you will. The man who provides the cash for the weapons these lunatics use to advance their so-called causes.

In the last few hours the web has begun twitching very sharply. There are rumours among our Middle Eastern contacts of an artefact of immeasurable value coming to light. We believe our Moriarty is deep into it. If the rumours are true, and our unknown friend is at the heart of this, someone somewhere is going to have a very big problem on their hands. Because if the sums being bandied about prove to be even half true, they'll buy a hell of a lot of guns and bombs – and a lot else besides." He left the implications of that final statement hanging in the air.

"And that, Charlie, is why we are now becoming more directly involved," said Rebecca. "It's true that we felt a responsibility to Michael and used extreme measures to protect him, even if the ruse appears to have been unsuccessful," she added, with some regret. "We absolutely look after our own. But to be frank, our main concern now is the threat of more serious unrest in the Middle East."

"Yes," Rolf picked up the story. "Ideology is a powerful motivator, but it doesn't lead to power without money – a lot of it. Ever since IS's ejection from Syria, they've been looking for a new home and new sources of funds. Their traditional backers have been getting increasingly queasy about the prospect of these maniacs eventually parking their tanks on their own lawns and have been quietly withdrawing their support. The fewer state supporters they have, the more they'll have to rely on the private sector. And that's where our mysterious new player comes in."

"We think his interest in Michael was purely pragmatic," said Rebecca. "He didn't want any roads leading to his door – even old roads that haven't been travelled for a while. Hence the original clumsy attempt to kidnap your brother, presumably to find out what he knew about his activities. Now the stakes are somehow very much higher and he is determined to deal with Michael once and for all."

"Which, at the risk of sounding clinical, means that all our interests now coincide," concluded Rolf, leaning back in his chair with his hands clasped behind his head.

There was a long silence, eventually broken by Michael, who had been silent throughout the entire exchange. "Let's get something to eat," he said quietly, getting up and heading for the buffet on the sideboard. We joined him, then brought our coffee and sandwiches back to the table.

"So now we have some decisions to make," said Rebecca.

I turned to Michael. "Mike, before we go any further, what exactly did you discover about mum and dad?"

Michael took a deep breath and I watched him as he ordered his thoughts. He was clearly still deeply shocked by the afternoon's events. Finally he spoke: "Okay. Well, I started by trying to find out who JB was. I researched all the main dealers in antiquities and came up with nothing. I went to the big auction houses and asked around to see if anyone knew someone with those initials who specialised in antiquities. Again, nothing. I even called a friend of mine at the Foreign Office and asked him to run the initials through his databases. We came up with names but nothing that could have any relevance."

"So I went back to the artefacts. I took the photos around some of the dealers and asked them what they made of them. They all said they looked rare and potentially very valuable, but they'd never seen them come onto the market in London, although there were rumours of some high-priced Babylonian statuary turning up in various places around Europe and Asia over the years. But essentially I drew a blank there too."

"Sounds like you were making quite a noise. I'm not surprised you tripped a wire somewhere." I said.

He frowned and carried on. "I just came up against dead-end after dead-end. Then I thought about the hotel. The Hilton in Paddington, where mum and dad were due to have that meeting. I went over there and looked around. The lobby's just one big meeting room, businesspeople at tables with laptops, meeting and negotiating or reading newspapers. Not much use to me.

"So I went to the front desk on the off chance and asked to see the general manager – and got lucky. He'd been at the hotel for nearly twenty years and knew all their regulars. Obviously when I asked him if he remembered anyone with the initials JB from fifteen years ago, he laughed in my face. But we got chatting and I told him I'd been reading my father's old diaries and come across these initials several times – it was obviously someone my dad knew and was close to, because they seemed to meet regularly and he spoke very fondly of him, almost like a best friend. My father had recently died, I told him, and I thought it would be nice to try and look up JB and let him know.

"I knew they'd met on 27th April that year and wondered whether the hotel might have a record of a reservation in anyone's name with those initials. It was a pretty thin story, but it seemed to catch the guy's imagination and he told me to hang on a moment and went into his office. He came back 15 minutes later waving a piece of paper with a printed list of all the reservations for that day. Apparently it got so busy in the lobby that it was sometimes advisable to have a table set aside if you wanted to be sure of a meeting place.

"There weren't many names on the list – most people just seemed to turn up and hope for the best. I half-expected to find our name on the register, but I did one better. I found him. Jack Braddock, table booked at four o'clock."

"Jack Braddock," I mused. "Okay, so who was he?"

"Well, that's as far as I'd got. I was going to start checking into him, but the following day my flat got turned over and I was preoccupied with sorting everything out. I needed a clear day to do some research and try and identify him, but never got to it. The following night was when I got bushwhacked."

"So we picked it up," said Rolf, "and made our own discreet enquiries."

"It seems Mr Braddock has quite the reputation," put in Rebecca. "East End gangster of the old school. Protection, prostitution, dodgy property deals, drugs – and theft of the occasional illegal antiquity."

You could have cut the atmosphere with a knife.

I said, "So, this Braddock character meets our parents to discuss the sale of some dodgy statues, which then disappear and Mum and Dad wind up dead a couple of days later. Have you told the police? Surely that's enough to get them to reopen the investigation?"

"Slow down, Charlie," said Rebecca. "It's not that simple."

"Yes, it is. You just go to the nearest cop shop and tell the story. There's definitely enough there for them to reopen the investigation."

"You're forgetting something, Charlie," Rebecca said patiently. "Your brother's supposed to be dead, right? If the police start trampling all over this, how long do you think it will be before they stumble over his faked death? Then our organisation gets dragged into it, and almost certainly you too, and the whole thing just gets out of hand."

"But there's –"

"She's right, Charlie," interrupted Michael quietly. "We need to think this through. Not go off half-cocked." He stood up, walked around the table and stood behind me, put his hands on my shoulders. "Look, why don't we all take a break. You've been awake all night and it's been a stressful morning, to say the least. I suggest we get a few hours' sleep, then reconvene this evening and figure out where we go from here."

"Good idea," said Rebecca, "we need clear heads." She

thought for a moment. "There's a hotel across town – we have a few rooms permanently booked there. Let's meet back here at six. I'll order dinner and we can plan our next steps."

I reluctantly agreed and we all got up to leave. "Just one more thing. I need to know a lot more about who you are and what this organisation of yours is all about," I said, leaning with my hands on the table.

"All in good time, Charlie," responded Rebecca. "Don't worry, you'll get the full rundown as soon as we have the opportunity. As I said, we believe you have a role to play." We stared at one another for a few seconds before I finally broke eye-contact and Michael and I headed for the door, where Rolf stopped us. "Please, take these." He held out two small plastic lozenges, about the size of thumb drives. A tiny green light was flashing at the end of each one."

"What are these?" I asked.

"They're trackers," explained Rolf. "Keep them on you at all times. They will ensure we know where you are – and can keep you safe. If you get into any trouble..." I raised my eyebrows. "...you just press the button on the end of the device and it will send us an alert. We'll be with you in minutes."

"Reassuring," I said, more sardonically than I'd intended.

"From now on, if you'll forgive the cliché, we're all in this together," said Rebecca. "See you at six." And she left abruptly, without looking back. I could see that Tom's death was weighing heavily on her. And I knew that my brother shared the same sense of responsibility.

Michael and I left the room and headed for the lift. As we descended, Michael turned to me. "I'm sorry I got you caught up in all this, Charlie. I bet you thought the days when you had to look out for your little brother were long gone."

I smiled and squeezed his shoulder. "I'm just glad you're OK."

We hailed a cab and took the 20-minute ride to a discreet

mews just off St James's Street. After we'd checked into the boutique hotel, I told Michael to go to his room and get some sleep while I made a quick run to my flat to pick up some fresh clothes and a few necessities. "I'll see you back here in the lobby at quarter to six," I said and headed for the door.

CHAPTER 23

THE TAXI RIDE to Lewisham gave me time to think. Although I was dog-tired, my brain was working overtime, processing everything that had happened. That morning's attack had shocked me, but I was surprised by how calm I'd remained throughout. Even the sight of another death hit me less hard than I would have expected. It had been many years since I'd come under fire, but perhaps the training kicked in when you most needed it. I was even more surprised by how unfazed my brother had been.

The streets and houses of south London passed in a blur as I relived the memories of my final tour. Afghanistan was a disaster. A succession of invasions had brought nothing but misery to the people of that tragic land and Britain had shared in that misery for a generation. My time in the country had been a salutary lesson in why it's a bad idea to interfere in someone else's war.

After serving out the first couple of years of my army career in congenial places like the Philippines, South Africa and the Baltics, it was a shock to arrive in the furnace-heat of a desert outpost where it seemed just about everyone hated us and most of them wanted to kill us.

When I arrived in Helmand for my first tour, the British

Army was in the final throes of its occupation, a prelude to its formal withdrawal in 2014. As I saw it, we had been comprehensively defeated by then and the Taliban were once more in the ascendancy. Time would prove me right. Barely seven years later both the Americans and the last British service personnel would be making a humiliating exit from the country and the Taliban would be back in government.

At the time of the final debacle, only 1,000 or so British troops were still in-country, almost all providing training and logistics support to the Afghan army, but during my first posting we still had a reasonable strength. The incidence of roadside bombs and IEDs had decreased, but we were still suffering casualties and there was a general feeling among both officers and men that it was only a matter of time before we were on a plane home.

My talent with a rifle had been identified very early on in my military career and within six months of my enlistment – an unheard-of speed – I'd been assigned to the Direct Fire Support Division of the Specialist Weapons School at Waterloo Lines in Warminster, to be trained as a sniper. I proved adept, not only at advanced marksmanship and all the technical and mathematical abilities that go with it, but also at the mastery of map reading, camouflage and reconnaissance. Within a relatively short time I proved myself to be an exceptional shot with the L115A3 Long Range Rifle, standard issue for all snipers in the British Army. I entered and won numerous shooting competitions and quickly found myself being posted to infantry units all over the world to train soldiers in this arcane art of warfare, which still retains an almost mystical status in the military world.

My first tour in Afghanistan was uneventful, relatively speaking, by which I mean I was still alive at the end of it, with my limbs and nuts intact and a zero-kill rate. I had spent most of the time providing fire cover for the unlucky bastards who ran patrols from our base at Camp Bastion in Lashkar Gah. For six months I saw virtually no action and returned home to Angie feeling blasé about the whole experience. Then followed a succession of postings to Iraq and the Balkans before my second – and final – tour in Afghanistan, which was very different.

By then the vast majority of our troops had left the country. I had spent the time since my first tour training and working with British special forces and when I returned to Afghanistan I was gung ho and over-confident, proud to be serving with the elite of the British Army and, if I'm honest, a little disdainful of our mission, which was primarily to work with the Americans on training the Afghan Defence Forces.

I was specifically tasked with advanced training of a small group of Afghan snipers who had arguably the most dangerous job of any soldier in that benighted country. They were the guys who had to go deep into Taliban territory, often high in the mountains, to provide reconnaissance on any large forces which looked from satellite surveillance as if they were amassing for some form of engagement. Once they had made their report, their secondary job was to try to identify the commanders – difficult because they all dressed alike, so the only real way to spot them was by the fact that they tended to shout the most – and shoot them. That was the easy part. The hard part was getting out safely after the kill.

Many didn't make it and there was no shortage of lurid stories of what happened to them when they were caught. Most involved employment of the fearsome 10-inch Khyber knife, or pesh-kabz, which had been used for centuries by Afghan tribesmen and was sharp enough to penetrate chain mail. The pesh-kabz struck fear into the hearts of the British during the First Afghan War in the mid-nineteenth century and later the Russians during the occupation of Afghanistan during the 1980s. It was said that it was better to fall into the hands of a Taliban fighter than one of his wives, who felt no compunction about keeping their victim alive for hours or even days as they worked on them with their blades. One veteran Afghan soldier revelled in recounting the tale of the Russian helicopter pilot who had been shot down and captured. The story went that the women managed to keep him alive for three days while they removed all his skin, before leaving him out in the desert sun to die. I don't believe the story was apocryphal.

My nightmare began during a routine training exercise with two young Afghan soldiers, barely out of their teens. We had hiked into the mountains above Baghran, north of Bastion, to practice reconnaissance and ranging in the tricky terrain of the lower slopes of the notorious Hindu Kush. We had travelled most of the way in an armoured Mastiff, with four soldiers as escort, and had just climbed up a narrow defile to a staging post a couple of hundred metres above the valley. There was a hot, strong wind blowing from the south and I was taking the two Afghans through a complex ranging exercise which was made particularly tricky by the heat and the squirrelly passage of the wind through the rocks and crevices around us.

The group of Taliban were as surprised to come across us, heavily camouflaged as we were in our hide, as we were to encounter them. But they overcame their surprise a lot more quickly than we did. Within seconds we were surrounded by six insurgents toting captured US M4 and M16 rifles and even a couple of M249 light machine guns, all pointing their weapons at us and screaming at the tops of their voices. I managed to quickly toggle my radio and send an urgent Mayday to our escort before it and our rifles were torn out of our hands.

Our captors wasted no time dispatching the two unfortunate Afghans. They were forced to kneel with their necks pressed against a rock and their heads were swiftly separated from their bodies with the aforementioned Khyber knives. My hands were quickly bound with cable ties and I was pushed at gunpoint up the mountain. Our escort really had no chance. The moment they tried to follow us up the defile, they were met with two RPGs and a hail of bullets. They retreated to their vehicle and that was the last I saw of them.

Those stories of the brutality of the Taliban coursed through my head as I was led further into the high passes of the Kush. We had been walking for about an hour when we reached a cave system which appeared to serve as this contingent's head-quarters, where there were at least twenty Taliban fighters milling around. I was bundled into one of the smaller caves, my bonds were cut and exchanged for handcuffs, which were immediately attached to a chain hanging from a hook driven into the wall. There I was left to contemplate my fate.

At least I hadn't seen any women.

I spent 15 days chained to that wall. I had time to ponder every potential eventuality, from execution to torture to a star-ring appearance in one of the Taliban's propaganda videos. But as one day became two days, became five, became ten, I concluded that they must have something different planned for me. I was fed regularly, given plenty of water and a bucket was provided for my sanitary needs, which was removed and emptied promptly every morning. I was not abused or maltreated. Each day, a tall bearded Talib dressed in a kamiz shalwar, the typical knee-length dress and baggy trousers worn by many Afghans, would come and squat before me and talk for a while in a hushed voice, his piercing blue eyes boring into mine. He appeared to speak no English and I spoke no Pashto, so they were fruitless encounters from my point of view.

Until one day he did not appear, nor the next. On the third day after his last visit, I saw his familiar figure stoop through the entrance to the cave and he knelt before me as usual, but this time his tone seemed laced with a mixture of sadness and resolve. He placed his hand gently on my cheek, now covered in a two-week growth of stubble, and said slowly in heavily-accented English, "Your people not want you back." Then he paused for a few seconds, rose, and left. I never saw him again.

My next visitor was a thickset, heavily-bearded man who, at around 6ft 2ins, was the first I'd seen who matched my height and was therefore able to look me directly in the eye after he'd dragged me to my feet. He had an ancient-looking Russian AK-47 assault rifle slung over his shoulder and a Khyber knife in his belt, but they were far less intimidating than what I saw in his eyes. Which was nothing. Not a trace of emotion, not even hatred. Just the dead eyes of a man who had been stripped of all empathy.

He put a hand under my chin and spoke slowly, in Pashto. Although I couldn't understand what he was saying, I felt I understood the gist. And I was pretty sure it wasn't good news for me. He barked an order over his shoulder and two other men, their heads shrouded in keffiyeh, came into the cave and set about unlocking my handcuffs. My wrists were raw from the constant chafing of the cuffs and I was unsteady on my legs, which had spent most of the previous two weeks bent beneath me. The two men took an arm each and led me outside.

I could see from the sun that it was near the middle of the day and the heat was intense. Nevertheless, the entire contingent of Taliban appeared to be standing in full sunlight in the small clearing, a very unwelcome welcoming committee. One of them was proudly holding my sniper rifle at high port, wearing a small smile beneath his bushy beard.

My new tall friend barked another order and my two-man escort led me out of the clearing and across a jumble of rocks towards a piece of relatively flat ground about 300 metres from the cave. It was bounded on the far side by a sheer wall of sandstone. One of my captors retreated a few feet, unwound his keffiyeh from his head and pointed his AK-47 at me while the other bound my hands behind me with cable ties after looping them around a desiccated tree root that was baked rigid and ebony-hard.

As he stepped back from his task he also removed his head

covering and I saw with astonishment that he was little more than a child, perhaps twelve or thirteen years old. He regarded me with what seemed to me to be a mixture of fear, awe and – was that sadness? Perhaps I was imagining it. What I wasn't imagining was the slight tremor in the hands holding his rifle. His older companion issued a curt instruction and gestured with his weapon towards the caves.

As the man and boy walked back towards their comrades, I could see a commotion in the tightly-knit group. They seemed to be arguing about something. And then suddenly, I understood. The man I had seen holding my rifle stepped forward and rested the weapon on a waist-high rock, settling the stock into his shoulder.

The L115A3 sniper rifle was at the heart of the UK's £11 million Sniper System Improvement Programme, developed to enhance the reliability and effectiveness of this element of the army's long-range weaponry. Manufactured by Portsmouth-based Accuracy International, my personal weapon was fitted with a x3-x12 x 50 sight and spotting scope and was designed to achieve a first-round hit at 600 metres. In 2014 a Coldstream Guards sniper using the same rifle to hit the trigger-switch on a suicide vest at 850 metres, blowing up six Taliban with a single shot. Its heavy-calibre 8.59mm bullet is substantially weightier than the 7.62mm standard NATO round and inflicts appreciably more damage. At 300 metres, it would blow a hole in me the size of a grapefruit.

The irony of killing me with my own weapon wasn't lost on me. In fact, I understood the symmetry of it, which is perhaps why I was so calm in the face of my impending death. It seemed somehow fitting that a man who had been trained to kill people half a mile away should now face the same fate as my victims, even though to date my roll call in Afghanistan totalled precisely two.

As this thought was passing through my brain, I felt a

colossal sub-sonic shock wave to the left of my head and the rock shattered about six inches from my cheek, showering my face with sharp fragments of stone, followed a split second later by the familiar crack of my rifle's discharge. The shot had apparently caused much excitement among my captors, because they were all cheering and waving their weapons in the air. During this celebration my rifle was passed to another aspiring marksman who took his place on the rock and dispatched another round in my direction, this one landing a few inches to the right of my head, with much the same result.

At 300 metres, with the sighting technology on my rifle, it is practically impossible to miss the centre-mass of a man – which is where, contrary to popular belief, all snipers aim – so it became immediately apparent that I was likely to be the subject of an extended bout of target practice. In all, eight rounds were fired at me, all placed at various points around my body, one tweaking the material of my MultiCam combat trousers as it passed between my legs. By then my entire body was trembling from the build-up of adrenalin and I was soaked in sweat. But I knew that that was where the fun and games would end, because I had only had eight rounds with me when I was captured, and the Taliban would have had no opportunity to secure replacement ammunition for such a specialised weapon.

Sure enough, I saw my two escorts heading back towards me across the rock field and once again they took up their positions, the older man covering me with his rifle, while the boy moved to untie my hands. Which was when I saw my opportunity. The child soldier had propped his rifle against the rock wall a few metres from me, but tucked into his waistband was a tired-looking Russian-made Makarov pistol. As my hands were released from the cable ties I grabbed for the pistol. The boy gasped as my hand seized the pistol grip and yanked the gun free of his belt, keeping him between me and his companion while I gathered myself for the one chance I knew I had.

Wrapping my left arm tightly around the boy, who was only just beginning to recover from his surprise, I reached around him and shot his comrade twice, high in the chest, watching him crumple slowly to the ground with a look of complete astonishment on his face. The boy was squirming in my embrace. He was strong, but I tapped him hard on the side of the head with the butt of the pistol and watched him collapse in a daze.

In the distance I could see the band of Taliban starting to run across the rock field. I grabbed the boy's AK and loosed a volley of shots towards the approaching men, most of whom ducked behind rocks before returning fire. Dropping the rifle and stuffing the pistol in my pocket, I ran at a crouch along the length of the sandstone face; I reached the end of the natural wall and ducked behind it, relieved to see a broad rock-strewn slope below me studded with stunted trees. By now there was a steady crackle of fire behind me as the Taliban quickly covered the 300 metres which separated us. With the rock wall giving me the few seconds of temporary cover I needed, I careered down the slope and threaded my way between the trees, moving faster as the ground became smoother and less cluttered with rocks.

The shouts and shots of my pursuers became clearer as they rounded the rock wall and started down the slope, but I now had a measure of cover and continued to pick up speed as I ran, entering a gully that appeared to lead straight down the mountain. And it was at this point that I got lucky. As I raced between the steep walls of the gully, the ground behind me exploded in a mass of rock and shale. The force of the shockwave blew me off my feet, but a slight bend in the narrow channel protected me from the worst of the blast and as I struggled to my feet I looked behind me to see that the entrance to the gully had been completely blocked by a fall of heavy boulders dislodged by the explosion. It was the one and only occasion in my life when I was glad to have been on the receiving end of an RPG.

The blood running down my left arm and the wetness below my shoulder told me that, despite being largely shielded from the explosion, I had taken a hit, either from shrapnel or rock fragments. So I was less steady on my feet as I resumed my run down the gully and after about 500 metres emerged at the head of a wide valley running north to south. I could still hear the voices of my pursuers in the distance and knew I needed to put more distance between us. I picked up the pace as I ran down into the valley and stumbled along a dry streambed. The voices appeared to fall further behind me as I ran and after half an hour or so I could no longer hear them, so took a chance and stopped, leaning against a rock with my hands on my knees, gasping for breath. I stayed that way for perhaps two or three minutes, grateful for the brief respite, before standing and contemplating the next stage of my escape.

The boy had approached silently while I was recovering my breath. He stood a few feet from me with his rifle pointed at my head. In those few seconds of recognition, I saw a mix of emotions in his eyes. Shame, yes. Fear was there too. But most of all there was an almost childlike petulance. I realised that sheer boyish rage had driven him to outpace his companions, find a path around the gully and reach me before they did. He wanted this. He needed it to restore his honour. But that didn't stop his hand shaking or his cheeks perspiring.

Except, I suddenly realised, it wasn't perspiration. It was tears.

I felt the gun in my pocket resting against my thigh as I stood, my hands hanging loosely by my sides, and regarded him calmly. "You don't have to do this," I said quietly, realising as the words left my mouth what a cliché they were. I regrouped. "This is a stupid war, waged by stupid people for stupid reasons." I knew he couldn't understand me, but I attempted to make myself understood through sheer force of will. "Kill me and you'll just find it easier to kill the next man. And the next.

Until you meet the man who kills you. And for what? We'll be gone soon, and then you'll be on your own. And as far as I can see, it's all been for nothing." I paused. "As for me, I'm done." And I slumped back down against the rock.

The rifle didn't move, although it trembled a little more, and I could see now that the man-child with the big gun and the shame of having lost a captive was already a broken adult. It was too late. The tears coursed down his face and I understood in that moment that they weren't tears of rage or fear, but somehow tears of sorrow for his own lost childhood. This boy soldier intuited that by taking a life, he would be taking a step he could never retrace.

Nevertheless, he squeezed the trigger.

And nothing happened. In the fraction of a second it took me to realise that the large shaped-sheet-metal lever on the right of the AK's frame was pushed up instead of down, I had torn the Makarov from my pocket and fired. The boy looked down at the blooming red flower on his chest and dropped the rifle, its safety still on, then looked up at me with an expression of deep puzzlement, his eyes still streaming. We looked at one another, an instant of mutual recognition passing between us, then he fell to his knees and slid sideways. It seemed to me that his eyes stayed on mine the whole time, and our gazes remained locked together even as he died.

The distant voices were back, as I returned the pistol to my pocket and prepared to resume my journey down the mountain. But first I placed my hand over the dead boy's face and gently closed his eyes.

I ran as fast as I could for another three or four kilometres before the voices had faded behind me again. At which point I needed desperately to rest. The blood had stopped flowing from my arm, but I couldn't lift it. I tore a strip from my shirt to fashion a makeshift sling before continuing on. The poor diet I had been subjected to over the previous weeks was taking its toll and I felt weaker with every metre I ran. It wasn't long before I was reduced to a shambling walk and as night fell I huddled in a shallow depression, covered in brushwood, and slept fitfully.

I was awoken by the return of the voices. They were close by and in the fevered fog that had beset my brain I was convinced that I could hear behind their gruff voices the ululation of their women and the sound of blades being sharpened on stones. My shoulder was on fire and I was covered in sweat, shivering and twitching beneath the shallow carpet of branches. I don't know what instinct or urge took over, but before I knew it, I was rearing out of the ditch and charging towards the sound of the voices, screaming at the top of my voice.

The four Americans in the long-range patrol got the fright of their lives as this filthy apparition in ragged combat clothing dashed out of the undergrowth. I squinted at them in confusion, managed to whisper, "You didn't bring the women," and fell unconscious at the feet of the commanding officer. Two hours later I was back in the well-equipped hospital at Camp Bastion having shrapnel and shards of rock removed from my arm and back.

I never learned who my Taliban captors had approached to trade for my release. My regiment simply said that my escort believed I'd been killed along with the two Afghans I'd been training and nothing had been heard of me since. But I remember to this day that blue-eyed Talib who treated me with respect and dignity and I knew that he hadn't lied. The British Army was not in the business of releasing Afghan prisoners (for which read criminals) in exchange for serving soldiers. Troops were too thin on the ground for commanders to even countenance any kind of rescue mission.

I saw out my tour, returned to the UK and left my army career behind. I had the convenient excuse of the torn ligaments in my left arm, courtesy of the RPG, but the real reason was that I had lost faith in my profession. And realistically I could no longer serve while suffering the nightly nightmares in which a young boy cried as I took his life.

———

I kept the cab waiting outside my bedsit while I gathered a few belongings together and stuffed them into a holdall, along with my passport and some personal items. I dozed, my head against the window, as we drove back through the streets of south London, now busy with late afternoon commuters.

After a long, hot shower and a change of clothes, I napped for an hour or so until my phone alarm woke me just before six. I rose groggily to my feet, splashed some cold water on my face, grabbed my coat and headed downstairs.

Michael was a few minutes late, but in surprisingly good spirits as we rendezvoused in the lobby. "It's so good to have you here, Charlie. I know everything's going to be okay now that you're with me. The Carter boys against the world, eh?"

I smiled. I couldn't help but be infected by his good-natured optimism. Michael's glass had always been half-full, ever since childhood, and he tended to make everyone around him feel better about themselves. We walked out onto the quiet mews and headed off in the direction of St James's Street, where we were most likely to find a cab.

I don't know what it was that alerted me. A too-quick movement in my peripheral vision, perhaps, or the hurried scrape of a shoe on the pavement. Whatever it was, I reacted slowly, still sluggish from lack of sleep, and before my brain had time to register potential danger I saw two quick muzzle flashes followed almost instantaneously by the roar of a large-calibre pistol.

I instinctively dived for the ground, pulling Michael with me, as I looked in the direction of the muzzle flashes. I recognised the face immediately. The man who had been driving the

Nissan we'd rammed a few hours earlier. He had a large gash across his left cheek, his left eye was swollen half-closed and he was limping badly as he walked towards us through the wash of a street light, the gun hanging down by his side. His one visible eye blazed.

I heard a groan and realised it was Michael. I stole a glance at him and saw his face creased in pain, at the same time as I became conscious of a wetness spreading beneath us. I had no more time to think about the implications of this before the man was standing over us, his face calm, his eyes dead. He said something unintelligible in Arabic, raised the gun and shot Michael twice in the head.

CHAPTER 24

AFTER THE GUNMAN'S second shot my training kicked in and I flung myself at him in the fraction of a second that it took him to turn the gun towards me. I used the only weapon I had – my head – crashing it into his nose with the full force of my momentum and pent-up rage. I felt the delicate bones crack beneath my skull and he let out a howl of pain, his hands flying to his face, as we both fell to the ground. The gun flew from his hand and skittered across the road into the gutter. As I withdrew from our tangle of limbs and again sprang to my feet, he leaped up and launched a kick at my crotch. He was off-balance and there was limited power behind the kick, but it was enough to leave me doubled over in pain. I watched, gasping for breath, as he looked frantically around for the gun before running off into a narrow alleyway at the end of the mews. After I'd caught my breath, I limped after him, but he was gone.

The police were on the scene within minutes, but not soon enough to apprehend the gunman, who had run into nearby St James's Park and promptly disappeared. The cops had quickly cordoned off the mews and immediately issued a nationwide APB.

I was in a state of shock. I hadn't had more than a couple of hours' sleep in the last forty-eight hours and my whole body ached. My mind was in turmoil. Only that morning I had rejoiced in the discovery that my dead brother was alive. Now he was dead again – and this time for good. I had seen my share of dead bodies during my time in the army, but nothing could prepare me for the experience of holding my wounded brother in my arms while someone I'd never met and didn't know calmly blew him away. And the look on the killer's face: completely expressionless, emotionless – no more troubled by the act than if my brother had been a wounded dog.

The police drove me to Paddington Green station, siren howling and blue lights flashing. On the way I remembered the tracking device Rolf had given me and took it out, eyeing the flashing green light. Without really thinking, I pressed the button. The light turned red and the device vibrated slightly, but that was all.

Arriving at Paddington Green, I was placed in a bare room furnished only with a table, two chairs and a digital recorder. I saw a camera high up in one corner. After a few minutes a uniformed constable entered with a mug of tea and a plate of biscuits. She left them on the table, mumbled that she was sorry for my loss, then departed. I was left to my thoughts until, about an hour later, a tall ascetic-looking man in his mid-forties came into the room and sat down opposite me, placing a folder in front of him.

"I'm very sorry for your loss, Mr Carter. I'm Detective Inspector Ross." I was too far gone to manage a reply. I just nodded.

"I'm afraid we were unable to apprehend the assailant, but we have a nationwide alert out for him and have every confidence that he will be apprehended."

'Assailant', 'apprehended'. The words seemed strange and foreign, of no relevance to me. Even less so the words 'every confidence'. Something told me that that confidence was seriously misplaced. I was drifting in a fog of grief, unable to think straight, my hands trembling, with a crushing headache. It took me a few seconds after the policeman had spoken to realise that there were tears streaming down my face. And then my whole body was shaking, succumbing at last to shock. I grabbed at the mug of tea and threw the contents down my throat, the hot sugary liquid burning as it went down. Ross regarded me sympathetically and waited patiently for me to regain my composure.

"I know this is very difficult for you, Mr Carter, but you'll understand that I need to ask you some questions. I'll try to take up as little of your time as possible." I nodded tiredly. He had a kind face, with deep-set, brown eyes downturned at the outer corners, which gave the impression of a man who was permanently disappointed by life. He was softly spoken and I thought I detected the slight burr of a West Country accent.

"Did you know the man who attacked you, or did you recognise him?"

In that moment my mind cleared and I understood the trap that lay before me. My brother's death was going to lead to way more questions than I wanted to answer. I had to tread very carefully.

"I have no idea who he was."

"And have you any reason to think anyone intended your brother harm?"

There it was, the killer question. However I responded, truth or lie, what followed would determine the course of my future. I sighed, thought for a moment, and resorted to bluster.

"Well someone clearly did!" I shouted. "They shot him in the head! I think that's a pretty good indication of harmful intent, don't you?!"

Ross was unruffled. "I understand how you feel, Mr Carter. It's been a terrible experience. But we just need to establish the facts as quickly as we can so that we have a fighting chance of catching this man. I'm sure you understand."

I slumped in my chair. I was just too tired to think this through. There were too many implications, too many questions I couldn't answer. And at the back of my mind, throughout this exchange, was the thought that if I weren't careful here, if I didn't give myself some wiggle room, I would lose the chance ever to discover who had killed Michael – and who had murdered our parents. But I just couldn't see any way to avoid telling this policeman the truth.

I opened my mouth to speak, and at that moment the door opened and two people walked in. One was a man I didn't recognise, in his thirties, well-dressed in a dark-grey pinstriped three-piece suit and burgundy tie, with round spectacles and neatly-cut brown hair. The other was Sir Simon Spurrier.

CHAPTER 25

MAHMOUD WAS A CONTENTED MAN. He had just received a phone call, in which it was confirmed that the 'annoyance', as his boss had referred to Michael Carter, was no longer a problem. It had been an embarrassment to be outmanoeuvred for a second time by the young man and the people who were apparently assisting him. The mock explosion and his staged death had been clever, but Mahmoud had been cleverer. He prided himself on his attention to detail and his decision to have one of his men attend Carter's funeral had proven to be an exceptional piece of smart judgment.

The shooting had regrettably been messy, given that it had taken place in the open on a public street, but his operative had successfully evaded detection and had been on a Eurostar train to Brussels within the hour, from where he would this morning catch a flight to Dubai and thence return to his native Kuwait. His boss had been happy to hear the news and Mahmoud was relieved to be back in his favour. Al-Shammari was not a man whose favour one wished to lose.

The killer had neglected to mention to Mahmoud the fact that Michael had not been alone when he had shot him. Had he done so his mood would not have been so benign.

Mahmoud was now walking briskly through the International Arrivals doors of Terminal 5 at London's Heathrow Airport heading directly for the taxi rank outside. Slipping into the seat of the first black cab in the queue, he directed the driver to an address in Canning Town, deep in London's East End. As it happened, the cabbie's family lived in the district and as they shunted their way slowly along the M4 into London, with the late commuter traffic, he cheerfully quizzed his passenger on his reasons for visiting that part of the city.

Mahmoud quietly replied that it was a private matter, and such was the tone of his voice and the expression on his face that the driver decided not to pursue his question with the dark-faced stranger. The rest of the journey was conducted in silence.

Two hours later, the cab drew up outside the gates of a haulage yard near the River Lea. Mahmoud paid the cabbie and made for the shabby Portakabin in one corner of the yard, above which a tatty sign read 'BRS Transport.' There were several cab over semi-trailers waiting no doubt for directions to pick up their next container loads. He surveyed them as he passed and noted that all of them had extended cabs, allowing for sleeping quarters behind the driver's and passenger's seats.

Entering the dilapidated office, he was greeted by an over-weight, middle-aged man with a shaved head and heavily tattooed neck, seated in a swivel chair behind a chipped and stained desk. To one side of the desk was a set of filing cabinets and to the other a small Formica table above which a large-scale map of the country was pinned to the wall. There were various pins in the map and lines drawn between towns and cities, most of which Mahmoud didn't recognise. Behind the man was a window looking out onto the back of the yard and beyond that, the river.

"Can I help you," asked Shaved Head in a gruff voice that suggested he wanted nothing less than to be helpful.

"I wish to speak to Mr Braddock," said Mahmoud.

"You're out of luck, mate. He's not here."

"Could you tell me where I might find him?"

Shaved Head made no attempt to disguise his dislike for his foreign visitor. The swastika below his left ear gave some indication of where his animosity stemmed from.

"Well, he don't like to be disturbed," he sneered, looking Mahmoud up and down as if measuring him for a gibbet.

Mahmoud remained courteous, but there was now an edge to his voice. "I have some important business to discuss with him and would very much appreciate directions as to his whereabouts."

"Well, you could try Piss Off Alley, down at the end of Fuck You Street," replied Shaved Head, obviously mightily pleased with the sharpness of his wit.

Mahmoud lunged with unexpected speed. In one swift move he reached across the desk, placed his hand behind Shaved Head's neck and slammed his face onto the surface, smashing a mug of cold tea. Shaved Head howled as he lifted his head, clutching his shattered nose.

He threw himself up from the desk with a roar, blood flying from his face. "You fucking –"

Mahmoud didn't wait for whatever witticism would be next. Instead, he put his foot against the edge of the desk and rammed it hard into Shaved Head's hips, pinning him against the back wall with his head bouncing off the window. He then took out a slim spring-assisted stiletto, flicked it open and drove it downwards into Shaved Head's left hand. Rather appropriately, noted Mahmoud, the blade entered the flesh dead-centre through a triskele tattoo. Before his victim

had a chance to react or even cry out, Mahmoud slammed his fist, conveniently weighted with a heavy gold ring on his middle finger, into the man's already ruined nose and Shaved Head screamed.

Mahmoud stepped back from the desk and regarded him calmly.

"Now, can we talk again about the whereabouts of your superior?"

Shaved Head stopped squealing and looked balefully at his pinned left hand, evidently considering whether he could pull out the blade before his assailant could renew his attack. He decided against it and slumped forward.

"Spain, he's in Spain," he whimpered.

"Ah. That is unfortunate," said Mahmoud. "Then we shall have to find some way of encouraging him to return. In the meantime, you can perhaps help me with an enquiry about a shipment you recently handled."

Shaved head stared at him, blinking rapidly. "Shipment. What shipment?"

Mahmoud relayed the information that BRS had been engaged to transport Al-Shammari's consignment to Beirut. Shaved Head looked baffled, which admittedly didn't represent that much of a change to his normal demeanour. "Beirut? I don't even know where that is. Suppose it's in Sandland, right?" Seeing Mahmoud's expression darken, he quickly added, "No offence mate. But like I said, I've never heard of it."

Mahmoud mentioned his boss's name and waited patiently. There was a long pause. "Wait a minute!" said Shaved Head, finally, with all the excitement of a toddler who'd just discovered that he could count to ten. "I remember. A big crate that went into one of our regular loads up to the East Midlands."

"Load?" asked Mahmoud.

"Yeah, a container. It was due to be flown out to San– , I mean, to some Arab customers somewhere, you know, out there." He waved vaguely in the direction of the window.

"And you have a record of this consignment?"

Shaved Head, sensing there was potentially a way to get rid of his unwelcome visitor without being subjected to any more pain, lapsed into full-on obsequiousness. "Yeah, yeah – of course. In the filing cabinet, over there."

Mahmoud turned and pointed questioningly at a battered three-drawer cabinet. "Second drawer, under 'S'," enthused Shaved Head, looking pleased with himself. Mahmoud opened the drawer, withdrew a thick stack of files and tossed them on the desk. "Show me," he said.

Shaved Head, operating one-handed with difficulty, shuffled through the files until he found the one he wanted, which by now was covered in blood. "Here it is." He read through the document slowly. "The shipment was packed with a load of other stuff into a rented container. It left our warehouse in Colindale on a wagon at six in the evening on January 14th. All the stuff was uncrated and loaded onto a cargo plane the next morning. According to this," he peered myopically at the document, his nose practically touching the paper, "the plane was on its way to Dubai and then on to Abu Dhabi. It landed at Beirut on the way to drop off some of its load."

"The problem," said Mahmoud, "is that somewhere along the way, before it reached the airport, our shipment was removed from the container."

Shaved Head sensed more pain coming his way. "I don't know nothing about that!" he spluttered. I just handled the papers and booked the job. They don't tell me nothing about stuff like that. You'll have to ask the boss about that."

Mahmoud, realising the man had nothing to tell him, regarded him with barely disguised disdain. "I fully intend to," he said. "Now, I would be most appreciative if you could return my knife."

CHAPTER 26

WITHIN A FEW MINUTES of Sir Simon's arrival, I was whisked with bewildering speed into a waiting car and shortly afterwards we were once again heading west out of London, the younger man in the front seat beside the driver, Sir Simon and I seated in the back.

I still wasn't entirely sure what had happened. As he had entered the interview room Sir Simon had asked the younger man, whom he did not introduce but addressed as 'James', to escort me outside while he had a word with DI Ross. The Detective Inspector protested, but without much conviction. He seemed to understand something about the arrival of our visitors that I did not. He remained seated as I was led from the room.

We waited in silence in the corridor and about five minutes later Sir Simon re-emerged and took my arm, leading me gently back to the front desk of the station, where he murmured something to the desk sergeant before directing me to the waiting car. "I'm so sorry about what has happened, Mr Carter," he said as we walked. "I'm sure you'd like an opportunity to rest and recover after your terrible shock. You will be my guest."

"What happened in there?" I asked, as we sped along the motorway.

"It's a simple matter of jurisdiction," said James, turning around in his seat to face me. "Since 2001 Britain has introduced seven separate pieces of counter-terrorism legislation, each designed to protect our citizens from extremist threats. Under normal circumstances, those counter-terrorism laws are enforced by the police, except in cases where national security is involved. More specifically, cases which are covered by the Official Secrets Act. This is one such case."

"The agency that Michael worked for – and with which, as you know, I am associated – has some productive relationships with the security services, Charlie. May I call you Charlie?" asked Sir Simon. I grunted an affirmative. "It has been useful on this occasion to make use of those relationships." As he said this he indicated, with a shift of his eyes, to James in the back seat. "As you know, attacks by extremist groups and individuals are being foiled every day by our security people, but unfortunately we cannot prevent every lone attacker from getting through. As the IRA so memorably said, we have to be lucky all the time – they only have to be lucky once. This was one of those occasions when a lone attacker got lucky."

"But he wasn't a terrorist, was he?" I objected. "He specifically targeted Michael because of his investigation into our parents' death. God knows what dirty secrets lie underneath all this, but he wasn't some lone maniac and we both know it!"

"You're right, Charlie," soothed Sir Simon. "But that is something to which only you and I and a select group of people are party. As far as the rest of the world is concerned, there was a terrorist incident in London this evening in which a member of the public – not yet named for family reasons, but whom we believe will turn out to have been a foreign national – was killed in a random attack by a man who unfortunately escaped, but whom the police fully expect to apprehend in due course. The matter will be forgotten as soon as the newspapers tire of the story, which they will, because they will be given only just enough information to satisfy them for a few days and no more."

I was too tired and distressed to argue. I turned and looked out of the window while Sir Simon continued in that infuriatingly soothing voice.

"Tomorrow, when you have rested, we will meet with Rebecca and her team and decide how best to proceed. I can promise you one thing, Charlie. With or without the police, the person or persons responsible for your brother's death *will* be brought to justice. The full resources of our organisation will be brought to bear to ensure that happens. We look after our own. And you are now one of our own."

I dozed for the rest of the journey, my disconnected dreams haunted by the sight of Michael's face and the wetness of his blood beneath my hands. For some reason his face occasionally became the face of the boy I had killed in Afghanistan and it was *his* head I was cradling as the wetness spread, his eyes staring accusingly into mine.

At the house we were once again greeted by Mrs Padbourne, who led me to a wide staircase to the left of the passage we had walked down earlier that day. Sir Simon and his mysterious companion, James, wished me goodnight and carried on down the passage. At the top of the staircase she opened a door off the main landing and showed me into a large room with a four-poster bed. I walked over to the window and saw that it looked out onto the same lawn, now floodlit, that I had walked across hours earlier with Michael. I thought I saw two dark figures moving slowly at the extremity of the lights, but it may have been my tired imagination.

I went into the bathroom and looked at my unshaven face in the mirror. Was it only 24 hours since I had walked into the Caledonian, blissfully unaware of any of this? A dead brother suddenly alive and dead again just a few hours later. Murdered parents. Shady quasi-governmental agencies. Middle Eastern gunmen. As I stared at my face, I suddenly realised just how similar in looks Michael and I were. I could have been looking at his face in the mirror, aged by a few years.

But Michael would never age. I had been granted a brief respite from grief but now it had returned a hundred-fold. I rarely wept – the tears just wouldn't seem to come, no matter how tragic the circumstances – but now I gave myself up fully to the anguish of loss. Not just of Michael, but of my parents, my marriage, my career, my self-respect. The tears streamed down my face as I sobbed at myself in the mirror.

After a few minutes the crying stopped and I began to feel something else besides the grief. A coldness and a calm determination. I recognised it as a growing rage. The rage of an orphaned son. The rage of a brother whose only sibling has been ripped out of his life, twice. The rage of a brother left alone. The face I now saw in the mirror, though still tear-streaked and anguished, was the face of a man who would bring all his experience and resources to bear on a single mission: to find the people who had killed my family – and end them.

With that thought, calm once more, I returned to the bedroom, pulled off my clothes, fell into the bed and was immediately asleep.

CHAPTER 27

I AWOKE to a gentle knock at my door. "Come in," I ventured groggily.

Rebecca walked into the room and stood at the end of the bed. She was dressed in a dark blue silk shirt and jeans and her hair was tied in a ponytail. She looked good, despite the lack of any detectable makeup.

"What, no breakfast in bed?" I quipped.

She smiled indulgently. "Breakfast is ready. We're just waiting for you." She turned and walked to the window, drawing back the curtains. In spite of myself, I couldn't help sneaking a look at her long legs rising to a firm backside encased in tight-fitting Levis.

I reluctantly broke my gaze and looked at my watch. Nine o'clock. I'd slept for nearly nine hours. "Give me time to get a shower and I'll be right there."

Rebecca returned to the foot of the bed. "We have some news, Charlie."

"About what?"

"About who killed your parents – and quite possibly a lead on who killed Michael." I sat up straight and leaned against the headboard. The sheets slipped down to my waist and I was conscious, despite the unprepossessing circumstances, of Rebecca appraising me.

"OK," I said. "Tell me."

"It's complicated. We have a conference downstairs in an hour. We'll explain everything then."

"But –"

"An hour, Charlie." She crossed the room and was gone.

Somehow my holdall containing all my clothes and other belongings had appeared during the night and was sitting on the upholstered bench at the end of the bed. It took me fifteen minutes to shower and change. As I was about to leave the room, I glanced out of the window and saw two men walking in opposite directions on the far side of the lawn. They were dressed in black and had what looked like automatic weapons slung over their shoulders. I guessed Sir Simon had decided to step up his security after yesterday's events.

The dining room was full when I entered. Sir Simon was sitting at the head of the table, with Rebecca to his right and a man I didn't recognise to his left. He was in his forties, clean-shaven with dark hair cropped short, wearing a lightweight windcheater over a casual blue shirt. He held himself erect and I immediately thought: military. Next to him was Rolf and opposite, next to Rebecca, was another woman, blonde, attractive, I guessed in her early fifties. There was no sign of James the spook.

"Good morning, Charlie. I hope you managed to get some sleep. And once again, on behalf of us all, let me say how sorry we are for your dreadful loss.

"Now let me make some introductions. Rolf you know." I nodded at the German, wearing his familiar jeans and hoodie. "This is Bruce Havelock, our head of security." The dark-haired man nodded, eyeing me appraisingly. "And this is Aleysha Fox, our head of intelligence. Michael worked closely with her."

"A pleasure to meet you, Charlie," said the woman, her

voice low and throaty. "I had a very high regard for your brother. And he talked about you often." I nodded in acknowledgment.

"Please, help yourself to breakfast and then we'll get started," said Sir Simon briskly. There was food laid out buffet-style on a side-table and I helped myself to coffee, orange juice and a plate of bacon and eggs. I was surprised at how hungry I was, despite the events of the previous evening. There followed a few minutes of small talk, a lot of it about the internal politics of the organisation, before Sir Simon slapped his hands down on the table and suggested that we begin.

Mrs Padbourne immediately came into the room, loaded up the breakfast things on trays and removed them, leaving the six of us alone at the table.

"Well, the team have been very busy over the past few hours and we've learnt a lot," he began decisively. In deference to you, Charlie, I propose that we start with what we have established about the death of your parents and go from there to the rather more urgent matter which is now preoccupying our organisation. Aleysha, why don't you take us through what you have discovered."

Aleysha cleared her throat, took a sip of water, and began to speak. "You will recall from our last conversation that Michael discovered your parents had a meeting with a certain Jack Braddock at a hotel in Paddington. It seems that Mr Braddock was, and probably still is, a dealer in many commodities. Drugs, prostitutes, illegal immigrants. He has quite the little empire in his part of London. He also began many years ago to take an interest in antiquities, when he realised that there were literally thousands to be traded and a great deal of money to be made from acting as a middleman."

"How did you find all this out?" I asked.

"We have spoken to a number of individuals in the trade," replied Aleysha cryptically. "Many of them were not best pleased to be woken in the middle of the night," she smiled, "but we can be very persuasive in our efforts when we need to be. Let us just say we have greased the right palms and believe what we have learnt to be accurate." She paused, then continued. "It seems that after a while Mr Braddock tired of being an intermediary and was keen to become a principal. More money to be made that way, of course. So he began intercepting consignments here and there, stealing the contents and using his contacts in the London underworld and elsewhere to find buyers.

"It seems that shortly after your parents' deaths, a number of valuable Babylonian statues began to be placed very discreetly on the international market by a private seller."

"Who?" I asked.

"I'm afraid we haven't been able to establish that yet. All we know is that whoever eventually took delivery from Braddock and placed them in the market lives somewhere in the Middle East and, as I think we've already indicated, we believe the proceeds of the sale went to one or more terrorist groups. We believe this individual is still very active in the trade, but as I think Rolf told you yesterday, they are now in pursuit of an item which may have serious consequences if it falls into the wrong hands. We aren't talking about a few antiquaries – this is of a completely different order of magnitude."

"Go on," I prompted.

"Well, it seems that Mr Braddock felt it necessary to remove any potential connection between himself and the statues. In fact, there's a suggestion that the Middle Eastern party had insisted on this as part of the negotiation for the artefacts." She dropped her voice. "I'm afraid your parents were no more to him than an inconvenient obstacle."

I felt the rage rising again. Evidently everyone in the room could see it, because all heads turned to me and Sir Simon leaned forward and addressed me in an earnest tone. "Charlie, we understand what you must be feeling – and believe me, we will completely support you in whatever steps you feel you need to take in this matter. But we must be judicious in our choice of action. Please, just hear us out."

Rolf picked up the story. "We have one more relevant item of information," he said, almost reluctantly. "It seems that Mr Braddock dislikes getting personally involved in any," Rolf paused, searching for the right word, "unpleasantness. He tends to delegate such work to others. In the case of your parents..." He tailed off.

"Yes?" I prompted.

"We had a talk with one of the men who used to work in Mr Braddock's organisation, someone who's known him for a long time. He used to drive for him and he remembers the events of that night because he was usually charged with cleaning the company's trucks when they came back off the road. According to him, it wasn't Braddock who killed your parents." Rolf paused, seemingly unsure of how to put his next point into words. "Apparently, Mr Braddock considered the completion of this particular task as a useful rite of passage."

"A rite of passage for who?!" I demanded impatiently.

Rolf hesitated again, then: "For his son. He had just turned twenty-one when his father commissioned him to murder your parents. And it seems he did it without a single qualm. His name is Jimmy."

CHAPTER 28

JOHN ALBERT BRADDOCK was a man of substance in London's East End, respected and feared in equal measure. He had come up the hard way, carving out his turf with a combination of shrewd judgment and extreme violence. It was said that Jack Braddock was your best friend and your worst enemy. And it is certainly true that his most trusted partners had made a lot of money, while those who crossed him fared badly, often in profoundly unpleasant ways.

Jack had never known his parents. His father had by all accounts impregnated his mother in an alley behind the Roxy Cinema in Catford during the break in a double bill of *East of Eden* and *Rebel Without a Cause*. He took her out a few more times in the weeks that followed, but soon made himself scarce when he found out she had a bun in the oven. She was duly dispatched to stay with a distant relative until she was due, returning to London and a council house in Plaistow ten months later, endowed with the well-worn backstory of a single mother whose merchant sailor husband had been lost at sea.

She lasted eighteen months before the drink took her. Jack was supposedly a handful even as a baby, and his twenty-two-year-old mother simply couldn't cope with the strain of a young child, no work and no money. She died propped against a wall in the local park with her veins opened and a cutthroat razor on the ground beside an empty gin bottle and a still-smouldering Player's Navy Cut.

Jack went to live with his grandparents back in Catford for a while, until his tantrums became too much for them, and at the age of five he found himself in an orphanage on Haverstock Hill, where he remained, making a nuisance of himself, until he inveigled his way into a job on the docks at the ripe old age of fourteen.

London's dockland was a cornucopia of opportunity for an enterprising young man in the late 1960s and early '70s. There was serious money to be made from the interception of cargoes, smuggling of booze and cigarettes, and the general larceny that comes with the movement of high-value commodities through a trading pinch-point. Jack first made his name at barely twenty years of age, running a nifty protection racket in Tilbury. The masters of ships docking at the port, and the haulage companies which collected their cargoes, either paid Jack and his colleagues for their security services, or found themselves the victims of burnt-out trucks, smashed merchandise, or shipments which just inexplicably fell into the river during transfer from vessel to shore.

Legend has it that the captain of one livestock carrier decided he had no need of Jack's services and, taking exception to Jack's threats, had him carried bodily from his ship and dumped on the quay. The following night, the captain was awoken in his stateroom by shouts and screams and rushed on deck to discover that his entire cargo of more than three thousand sheep were burning alive in their pens. When he went looking for Jack the following day, he found him tucking into a roast leg of mutton with all the trimmings and was invited to join him for lunch. Enraged by Jack's audacity, he threatened him with the police, at which point Jack had his men hold down the captain while he force-fed him the remainder of the mutton-leg until he was on the brink of suffocation and patiently explained that the next time the captain threatened him he would roast him instead.

As the years went by, Jack grew craftier and bolder. He opened brothels on the wharves around the Port of London and took a healthy cut of the tarts' income. He slowly built a distribution network for smuggled cannabis and over time graduated to heroin and cocaine. In the ten years he worked on the docks, Jack created an illicit business empire turning over the best part of a million pounds, equivalent to nearly £15 million today. He had diversified into taxi firms, coffee bars, laundrettes and later property. The only thing he didn't touch was fruit machines, which remained the preserve of his competitors south of the river. Police and local officials were only too happy to turn a blind eye to Jack's criminal activities, as long as he continued to quietly subsidise their mortgages, cars and mistresses.

As he became stronger and wealthier, Jack grew more vicious. By the time he reached his mid-thirties, he had been personally responsible for the deaths of more than a dozen men and women. The fortunate ones turned up dead with a hole in their head. The less fortunate were victims of Jack's party piece, reserved for those who had offended him in especially egregious ways. Jack would have them dragged from their homes in the middle of the night, tossed in the boot of a car and driven to a remote section of the Thames mud flats, where they would be buried up to their necks at low water. It was said that one of Jack's greatest pleasures was enjoying a cigarette whilst watching the sun come up over the estuary, accompanied by the dwindling screams of his victims as they were gradually smothered by the incoming tide.

These days many of Jack's businesses were legitimate and, like a lot of hoodlums, he had developed an innate desire to be accepted into the more elegant echelons of society. He had accordingly married a famous socialite in the late '80s and they had moved to a mansion on the outskirts of Epping Forest where they threw extravagant parties for friends, business contacts, senior police officers and the odd Member of Parliament. As time went by, the parties became less exaggerated and more discreet and Jack decided the time had come to settle down and start a family. In due course Sandra gave birth to James Frederick Braddock. It was not an easy birth and Sandra's body never recovered from the trauma, leaving her unable to have more children.

So fortune dictated that Jimmy was Jack's only son. And the apple of his eye.

One of Jack's numerous business interests was the wholesale importation from the Far East of sex toys. It had grown out of his early forays into the porn movie business, which itself had evolved from his highly successful escort operation. Why not widen the margin he made on the girls by making better use of their downtime between clients? The girls doubled their income, so they were happy, and Jack had the added benefit of being able to watch the filming – and perhaps have a taste or two of the talent himself if the fancy took him when the crew wrapped for the day.

When he realised how much the various film props were costing him, he decided to scale up his purchase of toys, lubes and underwear and sell them on to the plentiful network of sex shops around the country who were only too happy to deal with Jack at prices more competitive than those of their more reputable suppliers.

The warehouse in question was located just off the East India Dock Road. Jack had built it himself. Inside was a large storage area for his sex toys and other erotic accoutrements, together with a sealed-off room where the coke could be safely extracted, cut and repackaged for onward distribution.

Mahmoud briefly surveyed Jack's warehouse with his eyes then took a pair of wire clippers out of the pocket of his dark-coloured overalls. He quickly snipped a hole in the fence before crawling through and running on light feet to the corner of the building. He could see two cameras high up on the wall by the entrance, and noted the sensor between them which would fire up the floodlights the moment someone tripped it. But that didn't bother him. He was happy to be seen. He spotted the two men tasked with guarding the warehouse leaning against the large up-and-over door, smoking. He watched until one of them walked off around the far corner, obviously about to do his rounds, while the other walked towards him.

He took a large wrench from another inside pocket of his overalls and waited until the man turned the corner, then hit him a roundhouse blow. He dropped like a sack of cement and Mahmoud moved off towards the next corner, round which he expected the second man to emerge shortly. When he did, Mahmoud meted out the same treatment and the man collapsed in a heap on the gravel.

It took Mahmoud less than five minutes to prise the two locks off the warehouse bay doors and pull them up. An alarm immediately began screaming, but again Mahmoud was not worried. He wouldn't be here long.

He glanced about and saw evidence of the sex toys and cheap lingerie that he knew constituted a part of Jack's business. The items were completely ridiculous to him. It wasn't a moral judgment, just that he couldn't see the point of any of it. Women were there to be used, yes, but there seemed little point in making the act more complicated than it needed to be with all these absurd plastic devices and ludicrous bits of clothing. Mahmoud was a simple man and liked to keep sex simple, like everything else in his life.

There were three delivery vans parked just inside the doors and when he investigated one of them he found the key conveniently in the ignition. Powering up the vehicle, he drove it straight through the cinder-block wall of the packing room and came to rest against a line of lockers ranged along the far wall, which he assumed contained Jack's current inventory of narcotics. Finding a dust sheet folded neatly on one of the benches, he shook it out, removed the fuel cap of the van and shoved one corner of the sheet into the mouth of the tank, pushing it in as far as it would go. The other end of the dust sheet he draped over the wooden bench. Pulling out just enough of the now petrol-soaked dust sheet, he flipped open his cigarette lighter and ignited the cloth, withdrawing swiftly from the room.

As he crawled back through the hole in the fence, there was an explosive whoosh from inside the building and he watched briefly as an orange glow grew gradually brighter in the open doorway. By the time he had made it back to his car three blocks away, two further explosions had torn through the warehouse, liberally sprinkling a colourful variety of spankers, ticklers, rabbits and penis rings across the gardens of adjoining houses.

As the first of the sirens sounded through the night, Mahmoud lit a cigarette, started up the car and drove away.

CHAPTER 29

OUR SMALL GATHERING in Buckinghamshire had been making plans throughout the day.

Learning the identity of the man who had murdered my parents, and was probably indirectly responsible for the death of my brother, refined my rage into a cold fury. I stood and walked away from the table to the window, while silence fell in the room. Still with my back to the table, looking out over the garden, I asked, "Are you absolutely sure of all this?"

"Yes," replied Aleysha. "Our sources are very reliable."

"Then I want them. I want them all. The son, the father – and the bastard Arab who was behind it."

The silence lengthened.

"We understand that, Charlie," said Rebecca, speaking for the first time. And we're with you. But as Rolf explained yesterday, there's something else going on here. Whoever it was who sold those statues is still active, still in the market, and chasing the biggest score of his life. We have to find him, find out what he's got, and prevent him cashing in. This is why we exist – to prevent the kind of mayhem this character is capable of causing if he gets his hands on the vast sums of money we think are at stake here."

"I don't care about that," I retorted, turning around to face them all. "My entire family has been wiped out by these people," I shouted. "Before we do anything else, I want this taken care of. You told me yesterday that you solve problems like this, that you have resources. Then use them. Give them to me."

There was a long pause and then Bruce Havelock spoke for the first time. "I think Charlie's right," he said. He spoke with a gruff American accent and I pegged him as US military. "And it may be useful to us to flush out some of the other players in this game. But we need to move quickly, because it's clear that whoever is pulling the strings hasn't finished with you, Charlie. And attack is the best form of defence, for sure."

"Do we know where the son is?" I asked.

"We have him under surveillance," replied Havelock. "He's been building a nice little operation of his own over the last few years, trying to loosen his father's apron strings, but the apple hasn't fallen far from the tree. In fact, it looks like his business is fast outgrowing daddy's. He's bringing in heroin by the truckload, most of it now spreading out from London through the county lines racket, employing kids as young as eleven to do his dealing for him." Havelock couldn't keep the contempt from his voice. "According to our sources, he has a signature punishment. If one of his county lines kids makes the mistake of dipping into the merchandise, Jimmy takes one of his hands. With a machete. The last one to be taught that particular lesson was a thirteen-year-old girl."

There was a shocked silence in the room.

"Anyway," resumed Havelock, "Jimmy's been doing the rounds of his businesses today. We had a word with one of his employees who was in the middle of a transaction on his behalf in Hackney early this morning. He was very helpful."

Why did I think that was a euphemism?

"I'm afraid we rather screwed up whatever deal he was

doing," he smiled wryly, "but after a bit of encouragement he told us where Jimmy's going to be tonight."

I felt a tightening in my chest and said quietly, "Then tell me. I want to be there."

"Slow down, Charlie," said Havelock gently. "We have a better idea." And he outlined it to me.

Two hours later we had a plan mapped out. By the time Mrs Padbourne arrived with lunch for the team, arrangements had been made and events had been set in motion. Bruce Havelock left to carry out a related errand and Aleysha returned to London to continue her investigations into the 'Middle Eastern connection.' Sir Simon had retired to his study to attend to some business and I was left in the dining room with Rebecca and Rolf. The three of us moved to the library and took our seats in front of the fire. Through the floor-to-ceiling windows we could see the two black-suited men walking slowly back and forth. Rebecca assured me that they were not the only ones patrolling the ground.

"We will deal with Braddock, Charlie. But we need you to understand that this is not what we do," said Rebecca. "We were created to help make life better for people, for ordinary citizens. We are not vigilantes."

"So why are you doing this?" I queried.

"Because Michael was special. And he was one of us. And —" She hesitated.

"And?"

"And because Jimmy Braddock and his father are filth!" I was taken aback by her vehemence. "They poison and corrupt everything they touch. They destroy people's lives."

"But most importantly," added Rolf, more calmly, "as Rebecca said, they made the mistake of tangling with one of our own – even if it was a long time ago and before he became involved with us. The simple fact is that no one the Braddocks victimise or terrorise can stand against them." He leaned forward, his gaze intense. "But we can."

He leaned back again in his chair. "Also, as Rebecca said, there is something much bigger going on here – and the Braddocks are up to their necks in it."

"When this is over, Charlie, we'll take you to our network centre, introduce you to the work we do and talk about the role we think you can play. We think you'd enjoy working with us."

"But isn't your HQ blown?" I asked. "Whoever's behind all this must know all about it by now. Surely they'll come after you there?"

Rebecca laughed. "Oh, that wasn't our headquarters, Charlie. That was just an outpost. Call it a branch office – and it's already been emptied of people and equipment. No, I think you'll find our network centre a whole lot more impressive."

I passed the rest of the day impatiently. I walked the grounds, nodding passing acknowledgments to the men who had been tasked to protect us. I explored the house, a beautiful Queen Anne building which had been extended over many years and boasted more rooms than I was able to get around. I looked through the books in the library. I even tried to engage Mrs Padbourne in conversation in the kitchen, but she turned out to be taciturn and reserved. Rebecca left for London later that afternoon and Rolf and I had dinner alone together before Havelock finally returned and joined us back in the library. He was pulling a large black container on wheels, which I immediately recognised as a portable rolling tactical rifle case. He set it down in front of the sofa and flipped the catches.

It's all set, Charlie. The car's outside – and this is for you." He lifted the lid of the case and nestling inside, protected by shaped foam, were the matt black components of a powerful rifle. To me, it was a thing of beauty. "A Barrett M82," I breathed, impressed.

Havelock smiled grimly. "It'll do the job, Charlie."

The M82 was a lot different to the L115A3 that I had used for most of my army career. Better known by its US Army designation, the M107, it was a fearsome weapon. It was originally designed in the early '80s by Barrett Firearms Manufacturing of Christiana, Tennessee as an anti-materiel weapon, intended for long-range use against sensitive radar equipment, trucks and aircraft, due to its ability to penetrate brick, concrete and even tank armour at a close enough range. But over the years it had become popular with snipers in more than fifty of the world's armed forces.

A little heavier than most sniper rifles, at around 14kg, it is equipped with a ten-round detachable magazine loaded with .50 BMG centrefire cartridges and, with a muzzle velocity of over 850 metres per second, has a firing range of nearly two kilometres. However, I had no intention of testing it to its limits – or of coming back with anything less than nine rounds in the magazine.

Snapping the lid shut, I grabbed the handle, slung my overnight bag over my shoulder and followed Havelock outside, pulling the bulky case behind me. Ten minutes later, we were on the M40 in Havelock's Range Rover, heading back into London.

CHAPTER 30

ON THIS, the last morning of his life, Jimmy Braddock was where he shouldn't have been, with a suitcase full of someone else's money, having sex before breakfast.

The woman in question was a pliant thirty-one-year-old blonde flying high on a potent mix of vodka and MDMA, which even for a girl with her exotic career was a little hectic for 8am on a chilly February morning. Jimmy didn't mind. It was all the same to him whether she was drunk or sober, awake or asleep.

The spacious penthouse apartment on the top floor of the Thameside high rise had been Jimmy's secret gift to himself when he'd cut his latest big deal, two months ago in the back of a Discovery on Hackney Marshes. Everything in it was top-of-the-range, including the Italian marble kitchen work surface over which the woman was currently bent, naked except for the black Yasmine Eslami knickers around her knees, while Jimmy indulged his simple tastes with loudly-expressed enthusiasm.

The woman, too, was top of the range. Which was why he'd made an exception to his usual rule that, where whores were concerned, a couple of hours were more than enough. This one had stayed the night – costing him an extra two large – and kept him interested enough that she was still here, splayed out on his marbleware at breakfast-time. Who would have credited it?

Drawing his labours to a conclusion with a satisfied grunt, Jimmy pulled up his jeans and gave her an appreciative slap on her upturned arse before taking a drag on his cigarette and a gulp of his coffee. Foreplay didn't feature heavily in Jimmy's sexual repertoire, so the coffee was still hot and the cigarette only half-smoked. Waste not, want not, he thought as he watched the girl straighten up and restore her knickers to their rightful place, before heading wordlessly back to the ensuite bathroom.

Draining the coffee cup, Jimmy stubbed out his cigarette, drifted into the living room and reached for his mobile phone. He switched it on and as the screen came to life six messages revealed themselves, all from the same number, each one more impatient than the last, culminating in a pithy "WTF enough of this shit where tf r u!!" He wasn't exactly expecting Shake-speare, but even Jimmy appreciated a bit of punctuation here and there. It was only polite. He sighed and tossed the phone on the sofa.

Gazing out across the bristling London skyline, slumped under a sodden blanket of rain-soaked cloud, he smiled as he pondered the many and varied ways in which this great city's denizens could be fleeced, conned, duped and swindled. Life is sweet, he thought. When you're the one doing the squeezing, that is. When you're the one being squeezed, not so much.

He heard a toilet flush and the girl reappeared, dressed once again in the tight black mini skirt and white Tommy Hilfiger T-shirt which he'd so enjoyed removing the night before. Now, his mood forfeited to post-coital indifference, he just wanted her gone. He reached into his pocket and pulled out the two grand. In one seamless movement, she stepped quickly past him, swept the fat bundle of cash from his hand into her oversize handbag and was out through the front door before he even had a chance to tell her to fuck off.

He did have time to notice, though, that her freshly-applied mascara was smudged. As if she'd been crying. Women, eh?

———

I took my place on the rooftop, kneeling in front of a low parapet, partially hidden by an array of satellite dishes. Unfastening the case, I withdrew the contents and assembled the weapon with practised hands. It had been years since I'd handled a rifle, but muscle memory kicked in and it took me only a couple of minutes to complete the task, before screwing on the wrapped suppressor and snapping the box magazine into place.

I calculated the range at less than 250 metres – a breeze for me. But nevertheless, I approached the operation with the same discipline I would have if I were taking on a target at five times that distance. Delving back into the case, I took out a small anemometer that came with the weapon, switched it on and held it above my head, allowing the gentle breeze to register on its electronic display. Making a note of the wind speed – a gentle 3 knots – I consulted a set of wind tables, again supplied with the gun, and began the complex job of calibrating the 20x scope which I had already mounted on the top of the rifle.

My preparations complete, I leaned back against the parapet, took out my phone and waited.

———

Jimmy was suffering a severe sense-of-humour failure. He'd spent the best part of an hour on the phone with one of his partners, listening to him explaining how, thanks to a spectacular fuck-up by one of Jimmy's bag-carriers during a routine exchange of merchandise in Hackney, he, Jimmy, was now going to be seriously out of pocket. A subsequent five minutes on the phone ripping said bag-carrier a new arsehole hadn't improved his mood.

With a sigh, Jimmy dialled the number of the man who'd been texting him since the night before. Excuses made, he listened with growing disbelief while his father brought him up to speed on the night's events.

If he felt he was already having a bad day, it was about to get a whole lot worse.

———

I looked at my watch for the umpteenth time and tried to keep a lid on the tension which was slowly building and releasing a heady mix of adrenalin and endorphins into my body. I could not allow the anticipation to get the better of me and affect the steadiness of my hands or eyes. I gazed across the building to the horizon, beyond the forest of rooftops, where a sickly sun was struggling to make headway against the sullen cloud cover. I felt droplets of mist coalescing on my face and hair, reflecting the heavy humidity that threatened rain – and which I'd already factored into the calibration of the rifle sight.

Gradually, I brought my breathing under control and began to retreat into what I always thought of as my pre-fire zone, a place in which there was no yesterday, today or tomorrow – just now. Just me, the rifle and the target, in perfect symbiosis. I adjusted my position, making myself a little more comfortable, and continued to wait.

———

Jimmy by now was incandescent. The news from his pa had enraged him. Someone, somewhere, was seriously taking the piss. Sometime in the middle of the night that someone had broken into one of the family's warehouses, which Jimmy had been tasked with overseeing, put two of his guys to sleep with a monkey wrench and torched the place, along with three of his trucks. At least two million euros of merchandise, gone.

His father was still at the villa in Spain, but had reacted predictably and brutally, giving clear instructions to his most trusted lieutenants in London. Both the sleeping beauties were now wishing they'd never woken up, given that neither would walk again without sticks and one was going to need a lifetime's dental treatment. It wasn't that the swiftness and viciousness of his response particularly bothered Jimmy, it was the fact that it was his dad, not he, who had meted out the punishment. When was he going to grasp the fact that Jimmy was a grown man with his own firm and his own way of doing things? If it had been left to Jimmy, both men would now be hugging paving slabs at the bottom of the Thames.

But all that would have to wait. Right now he had a more pressing priority: his Albanian partners. He'd taken delivery of their shipment a couple of days ago and it was already being cut and repackaged in one of his lockups. He just needed to drop off their cash at the chicken shop on Green Lanes, then he could get back and sort out the clusterfuck in Hackney. He knew the Albanians didn't like to hang about. They had a reputation. They were among the very few people in London who frightened Jimmy. You didn't keep Albanians waiting.

Grabbing his overcoat from the kitchen chair where he'd tossed it the night before and shrugging it on as he moved, Jimmy strode into the master bedroom and yanked open the fitted closet. The small carry-on Samsonite suitcase was tucked behind a set of golf clubs, which he dragged out and tossed on the floor before reaching for the suitcase. The moment his fingers curled around the handle and lifted it free he knew something was very wrong.

Tossing the case on the bed, he wrenched it open, suddenly finding it hard to breathe. Instead of £600k in twenties and tens, which was what it used to contain, he was looking at a pair of lacy black panties and nothing else.

He finally caught his breath and, clenching his fists, he let out an animal roar.

"Bitch!" he screamed. "You fucking little bitch!"

Turning on his heel, Jimmy staggered drunkenly to the front door, across the hallway and into the lift, stabbing hard at the rooftop button, still cursing, but with his anger now beginning to give way to something else. Something Jimmy hadn't felt for a long time. Doubt. And not only that – something even more unfamiliar, more toxic. Fear.

Reaching the roof, he ran to his car, a black BMW with smoked glass windows and J1 MMY number plate. Under normal circumstances Jimmy would have taken a moment to admire his latest acquisition, with its 600-horses under the bonnet, its £3,000 sound system and its hand-stitched cream leather. Today he simply threw himself into the driver's seat and slammed the door shut before hitting the ignition Start button. But instead of the usual throaty growl of the car's 4.4-litre V8 twin turbo-charged engine, there was nothing. Not even the gentle ping of his seat belt warning.

Jimmy poked at the Start button again, repeatedly pressing it, to no avail. He cursed and frantically surveyed the dashboard for any sign of warning lights, but there was nothing. The car simply refused to come to life. All 600 of its stallions hobbled and silent.

He threw open the door and leaped from the car, only just resisting the temptation to kick the fucker. Instead, he just stood there, seething, thinking how an eighty grand motor is just so much junk metal if it's going nowhere. Just as he was having second thoughts about giving the useless piece of shit a hefty booting, his phone rang. The old man again, no doubt, whining on about his warehouse. But instead, when he looked at the display, he saw 'Withheld number.' Very few people had access to his private number, so he knew it must be one of his coterie, and so didn't hesitate to answer it.

"Hello, Jimmy," said a voice he didn't recognise. Posh, it sounded. Like some cunt from up West.

"Can I suggest you take a look on the rear right tyre of your car, Jimmy. There's something there I think will interest you."

"Who the fuck's this?" he spat. "And how did you get this number?"

"Just take a look, Jimmy, there's a good boy." Jimmy suddenly had a flash of understanding. It was the girl, the slag who'd done him over. She was up here with some chancer and they were about to put the squeeze on him – something they wanted from him in return for returning his money. Well, they had another thing coming. Still feeling that unexplained uneasiness, Jimmy looked around, could see no one, and walked as nonchalantly as he could to the rear of the car, which was backed up against the low wall of the car park.

Stooping down and reaching into the right-hand wheel well, he withdrew an A3 manila envelope, blank on both sides, but with the flap open. Holding the phone between his ear and shoulder, he shoved his hand inside and pulled out half a dozen high resolution photos. "What the fuck's this?" he breathed, leafing through them. They all seemed to be pictures of some antique shit – foreign-looking statues. He couldn't for the life of him think what they had to do with him.

"Do you recognise them, Jimmy?" asked the voice, now a low growl. "Do you remember?"

Jimmy hadn't got a clue. Why the fuck would he be interested in pictures of fucking little Buddhas, or whatever the fuck they were? "Look, I don't know who the fuck you think you are, but do you know who *I* am, sunshine? Do you know who my family –" His voice trailed off as a distant memory suddenly emerged from the primordial soup that passed for his brain. Statues. Foreign things, from somewhere out in Sandland. What was it...?"

"Ah, I see it's beginning to register," said the infuriatingly calm voice. Jimmy shot up and looked around him, realising from what the voice had said that he was being watched. From somewhere. But where?

"Listen, you cunt. Whoever you are, I'm gonna fry your balls and feed them to you." But the bravado was leaching from his voice, and he knew it. That unaccustomed fear was beginning to grow.

"My parents," said the voice, softly. "Fifteen years ago. There was a car, and a fire." Jimmy span on his heels, still holding the phone to his ear, desperately trying to see where the fucker was hiding. For once in his life, he could think of nothing to say. He remembered it all. His first job for his dad. Some posh cunts from the home counties. How the hell had they tracked him down? And who were they?

In the next instant, all those memories were wiped from his mind by a powerful blow to his left arm. He looked down and was astounded to see a bloody mess where everything below his elbow used to be. It took a few seconds for the pain to kick in and then he began to howl in agony.

"I wasn't sure whether you're left- or right-handed Jimmy. Which one was it you used to light the fire with?"

With that, Jimmy's bravado evaporated. He sank to his knees, the phone still clamped to his ear.

"That's a nice car you've got there, Jimmy," said the voice after a pause. "A lot nicer than my mum and dad's. But I'll bet it burns just as well." A split-second later he felt rather than heard a loud thump beside him which he barely had time to register before flaming fuel erupted from a six-inch hole in the side of the BMW and the whole vehicle seemed to lurch into the air. Jimmy was instantly engulfed in flaming petrol from the waist down. It took a second or two for the pain to begin, but when it did, it was intense, searing, agonising – beyond anything he would have thought possible.

He stared down in disbelief. His remaining hand was now ablaze, as well as his legs, and he leapt to his feet and began running in frantic desperate circles, too panicked even to think of falling to the ground and trying to roll out the flames. He could smell his own flesh scorching, as the burning gasoline ate through his skin, instantly cauterising the nerve-endings. He could no longer breathe because his throat was seared closed, his hair was alight and his face was melting like candle-wax.

He never felt the second shot, which tore through his face at around 2,000 mph, vaporising most of his head and leaving his blazing body standing for just a second before it sank to the ground.

———

I dismantled the rifle and packed it away carefully. I expected to feel exhilaration at the death of the man who had destroyed my life and the life of my brother, but I'm not sure what I felt. Satisfaction? Closure? Relief? I think it was a mixture of all of those, laced with a deep weariness and profound sadness. I took no pleasure in the man's death. It just felt like a balancing of the scales, a kind of restoration of equilibrium. I thought of Michael and wondered what he would have thought. I suspected he would have disapproved. But he would also have comprehended. When I was eventually free to bury him properly, I would explain it to him. And he would understand.

I picked up the handle of the case and walked to the head of the staircase on the roof of the office tower which stood a couple of hundred metres from, and thirty or so metres higher than, Jimmy Braddock's apartment block. In the end, the shot had been easier than I'd imagined. And I had no regrets about my decision to leave seven, rather than nine, rounds in the magazine.

———

When I got back to the Range Rover, where Bruce Havelock had been waiting for me, he had news. "It appears that events have taken an unpredictable turn," he said carefully. I raised my eyebrows and cocked my head expectantly.

"Late last night someone set fire to one of Jack Braddock's warehouses and apparently destroyed several million pounds' worth of drugs and merchandise," said Havelock.

"Who?" I asked.

"We have absolutely no idea," he answered, his hands spread wide. "But it wasn't us."

CHAPTER 31

JACK BRADDOCK'S phone beeped just as his plane was landing at Gatwick Airport. It was lunchtime and Jack was hungry. He'd had no breakfast and was at his worst when his blood sugar was low. Sandra was always nagging him about getting regular meals. The first message was from a voice he recognised and it sent him into a cold rage as he battered his way through the disembarking passengers. That foreign cunt had not only torched his property, but had had the front to ring him up and admit to it.

Jack was dreaming of all the ways he was going to fuck the cunt up when the second voicemail kicked in. This one was from Gazza, a mate from his docklands days and now his most trusted lieutenant. What Gazza said stopped Jack dead in his tracks, leaving hurrying passengers flowing round him like a river round a rock while he stood stock still taking in what he'd heard. After a few seconds his head dropped, along with the overnight bag he'd been carrying in his right hand, and then he threw up his arms, dropped to his knees, raised his face to the ceiling and bellowed at the top of his voice: "Noooooooooo!"

A few minutes later, after all his disconcerted fellow passengers had passed by and Jack was alone, he slowly stood up, lifted the phone that he'd been holding in a death grip in his left hand, and punched in a number from memory.

"Gazza, get the guys together. At the house. Council of war. Now." He rang off without waiting for a response, rolled his shoulders and neck, picked up his bag, paused for a few seconds, then began to walk briskly towards passport control.

CHAPTER 32

JACK BRADDOCK SAT at the head of the table in the dining room of his spacious home in Wanstead, East London, Sandra standing by his side, her eyes red from crying, her hand resting lightly on his shoulder. The table was large enough to comfortably seat twenty guests and was made from a solid piece of redwood which Jack had had cut and shipped over from the States two years before. Dining tables didn't excite him that much, but Sandra had insisted that if they were going to hold important meetings in his home, the table needed to make a statement, and at $90,000, not including the chairs, Jack reckoned the statement was clear enough.

On this occasion only nine chairs were occupied, including Jack's. Gazza sat to his right and Pete Berriman, his head of security, on his left. The other six seats were occupied by the heads of his various enterprises. The mood was solemn and the looks being exchanged around the table were nervous. Everyone in the room knew what had happened and each of the men had first-hand experience of what befell people who crossed Jack. But this – this was of a different order of magnitude and the tension in the air was taut as piano wire.

Jack rested his elbows on the table and looked at each of his subordinates in turn. None, apart from Gazza and Pete, could meet his gaze. "My boy," said Jack quietly. "My boy. The fuckers took my boy." The silence was as thick as the menace in Jack's voice. "They fucking roasted him next to his own car, then blew his brains out." He paused for a moment, looked down at his hands. "Jimmy could be a fucking idiot sometimes and we all know it." There was a murmur of half-hearted disagreement around the table. "But he was my boy. My only boy." He felt Sandra's grip on his shoulder tighten and her hand shook.

"The warehouse, fair enough. Someone wants to hit me hard, that's business. Plenty more where that came from. And we'll deal with those cunts, trust me. But my boy – that was out of order. That needs answering. That requires a fucking head on my table!" And his fist crashed down on the polished wood in emphasis. All six men jumped – only Gazza and Pete remained unperturbed.

"It's time to show these ragheads who runs this town," said Jack, drawing in a decisive breath. "They don't come shitting on my manor and walk away." There were compliant nods around the table. "Pete, tell 'em what we know."

Berriman had been a boxer back in the day and his face showed it. His nose had been broken countless times, his jaw was out of kilter from being repeatedly dislocated, one ear was mashed to a mess of cartilage and one cheekbone was crushed from a lucky punch early in his career. He rarely smiled, but when he did, the copious number of missing teeth made it an unpleasant experience for the recipient. His voice sounded like the rustling of crows' wings.

"The guv'nor got a call. From our Arab friend. Said he'd torched the warehouse to get our attention. Said we'd helped ourselves to something that didn't belong to us." The men shifted uncomfortably on their well-padded chairs. "And they want it back."

"Any idea what they're talking about?" asked Jack, looking again at each man in turn. "Anyone?" There was a nervous shaking of heads.

"What makes it worse is that this – this Arab fucker's a good customer. We've traded a good few bits of merchandise with him over the years, going all the way back to those statues we blagged. That's what got us started in that little sideline – and it's been fucking good business!" this last with his voice rising. He paused again and the silence lengthened. "But no one knows nothing, right?" Still no response from the assembled group.

"Well pardon me for calling bullshit on that!" shouted Jack, who shot up from his chair and began to walk around the table. "Pete?"

Berriman continued, "Apparently one of our Arab friend's associates came to us to take a piece of merchandise up to East Midlands Airport. It was valuable, but they trusted us because we've done good business together in the past and they needed it transported discreetly. We put it in one of our regular containers doing a backload out to Sandland. Somewhere along the way, that piece of merchandise seems to have grown legs and done a runner."

Jack continued walking around the table, whose occupants were now looking at one another with growing unease. He reached the end of the room and poured himself a coffee from a pot on the sideboard, waving the pot at the assembly. "Anyone else fancy a cup?" Murmured demurrals all round. "Sure?" He resumed his walk around the table, still holding the pot.

"You see, what I can't understand is why someone would be so fucking stupid as to steal a customer's gear without telling me. I mean, do they think I'm a fucking wanker? Perhaps they'll be round here next bending me over my dining table and giving me one in the arse! I mean, where will the liberties end?"

Jack had stopped behind one of the chairs and seemed to be closely examining the coffee pot. He unscrewed the top and nosed the aroma. "Best Brazilian beans. I have them flown in special." He suddenly let loose a laugh. "Do you remember that old 10cc song? How'd it go? They make a lot of coffee in Brazil, but the price is gonna make you ill. Yeah, well this is definitely gonna make you ill!" With which he upended the pot and poured the scalding contents over the head of the man in front of him.

The man screamed, his hands flying to his burning face. "Did you really think you could do me over like that and I wouldn't find out, Paulie?" Jack nonchalantly picked up a heavy paperweight from an occasional table behind him, weighed it in his hands for a moment, then slammed it down onto the back of the man's head.

"Did. You. Really. Think. I. Was. That. Stupid?!" Hammering blow after blow into the back of the man's head with each carefully annunciated word. The man was now slumped on the table, blood, brain matter and splinters of bone from his broken head spattering the men on either side, who were too shocked and terrified to move. Panting heavily, Jack dropped the paperweight onto the expensive Persian carpet and wiped his red-soaked hands on the shirt of the dead man.

"Now look at the state of my fucking table."

He thought for a moment, looking down at the spreading stain on the redwood, then stood up straight and said brightly, "Now, does anyone want to tell me what Paulie did with the fucking merchandise?"

CHAPTER 33

HAVELOCK and I were back in the car, heading once more into London, both lost in our own thoughts. I had a strong sense of foreboding. Rolf had told me that we were going to the nerve centre of the organisation he worked for. That I would get to see the full extent of its resources and influence.

Havelock was adroitly negotiating a network of streets in west London, eventually turning onto Wandsworth Bridge Road and crossing the Thames. On the south side of the river we bore left along York Road and after a few minutes turned back towards the Thames and drew up at London Heliport. I immediately recognised the Bell 505 Jetranger parked on the pad, its rotors beginning to spool up as we got out of the car.

Rebecca and Rolf were already aboard the five-seater aircraft and she was leaning out of the door beckoning us to hurry. Havelock and I ducked under the spinning blades and stepped up into the cabin, Rebecca handing us each a set of headphones. No sooner had we fastened our seatbelts than the helicopter was in the air, rising fast through the dark sky. The chopper swooped low over the City of London and headed north-east, accelerating fast.

"I thought we were going to your headquarters," I said to

Rebecca, puzzled by the direction we were heading in. "And so we are," she replied. We'll be there in about an hour. Just relax."

As soon as we were clear of what I assumed was Heathrow Approach, the machine nosed up and climbed quickly. I looked ahead of me into the cockpit and saw that we were already at 3,000 feet and still ascending at just over 100 knots. After a few minutes we crossed the coast and headed out into the darkness of the North Sea. I looked questioningly at Rebecca and Rolf, who were both sitting opposite me. They just smiled and looked out of the windows.

After forty minutes or so, I saw a cluster of lights in the darkness below, which gradually resolved into a brightly illuminated vessel of some kind. We tracked towards it, now slowing and descending quickly. The pilot expertly hovered over a helipad on the upper rear deck of the vessel, which must have been a good 300 feet in length, and settled gently onto the surface.

"Welcome to *Triton*," said Rebecca.

CHAPTER 34

ARI AL-SHAMMARI WAS WAITING for Mahmoud's call. When it came, he became angry at his employee's lack of progress. "I thought I had made it clear, Mahmoud, that time is of the essence. Where is our merchandise?"

"Please be assured that I have the matter in hand, sir. Braddock has returned to England and I will be making the arrangements shortly. I have no doubt that the items will be back in our hands very soon."

Al-Shammari put down his mobile phone and walked with his glass of orange juice out onto the balcony of his villa. He could smell the scent of the mimosas drifting up from the gardens below. He reflected on the last two thousand years of conflict and strife in this troubled land and how little had been resolved. Brothers were still killing brothers, his people still lived in poverty and the preening nations of the West still treated them with contempt.

But that was all about to change, he thought. Provided his recent find didn't fall into the wrong hands and was soon back in his possession. He took another sip of his drink and began to formulate his plans.

CHAPTER 35

TO MY UNTRAINED eye *Triton* looked like a pretty substantial vessel. As Rebecca led me down the steps from the helipad and along a companionway towards the bow of the ship, she explained that NV *Triton* was a former Canadian oceanographic research vessel which had been decommissioned ten years earlier. Her organisation had purchased and completely refitted her as a floating headquarters.

She went on to give me some stats. She was 85 metres long, with a 17-metre beam, displacing over 3,200 tons. She had a crew of twenty and capacity for 40 passengers, all of them full-time employees of the organisation. It was large enough to accommodate all the personnel they needed, together with all the equipment necessary to conduct their business wherever in the world they happened to be. Operating in international waters made life much easier for them, she explained, and over the years the ship had travelled around the globe several times and visited any number of countries.

"But who pays for all this?" I asked, dumbfounded, as we climbed several flights of stairs and emerged high above the main deck of the brightly-lit ship. "Our clients have deep pockets, Charlie. The deepest, you might say. A few hundred million dollars can easily get lost in the rounding, which is helpful since most of our funding is off the books and, as far as I know, has never found its way into the minutes of any appropriations committee."

We walked along another short companionway and Rebecca led us through a door into a room bustling with people and activity. Front and centre in the room were too high-mounted swivel armchairs in front of a long, curved console with a dazzling array of screens and controls. The windows were angled outward from the base and I could see the floodlit foredeck several levels below, where crewmen were busying themselves at tasks which eluded me.

Seated in one of the comfortable chairs was a dashing black man in a short-sleeved shirt with four stripes on his shoulder-boards. "Charlie, I'd like you to meet Taylor Jackson, our captain." The man swivelled around in his chair and rose to greet me, holding out his hand. He was tall by any standards, at least six six, I guessed, and built like a rugby front-row forward. He had lively eyes – and a crushing grip. "Welcome to *Triton*, Mr Carter," he said in a rich growl. "Charlie, please," I responded. "Charlie, then," he replied, and his face broke into a broad grin. "We're glad to have you. Have you ever been on the bridge of a ship before?" "No," I answered, "and never expected to. I get seasick looking at seaside postcards."

Jackson laughed, a good-natured rumbling deep inside that huge frame. "Well, I doubt you'll even notice you're on a ship, Charlie. She's steady as a rock, even in a decent swell."

I became aware of someone's eyes on me and turned to find a short, dapper man dressed in a pink button-down shirt and stone-coloured chinos regarding me closely from the back of the bridge. He had thinning sandy hair and a head that seemed a little too large for his body, with a prominent forehead, small nose and wide mouth. He continued to look at me for a few more seconds, then stepped forward and offered his hand.

166

"Nathaniel Lowell," he said, in a clipped American accent. "I head up Vanguard." I looked sideways at Rebecca, questioningly. "The name of our organisation, Charlie," she said, then turned away to say something to the captain, who had returned to his chair.

"I've heard a lot about you, Charlie," said Nathaniel. He was cool and humourless, but I had the immediate impression of a man of exactitude and discipline. "I'm sorry for your loss."

"Thank you," I replied, meeting his gaze evenly. "Quite the operation you have here."

"Oh, you've no idea," said Lowell with a slight smile. "Please, come with me."

He led me out of the bridge, past what looked like a radio room and another control room, and down a set of steps to the level below. Rebecca followed. A little way along the deck he turned and pressed a button and two doors opened silently, revealing an elevator. "Please," he said, extending his hand towards the interior. I stepped in, followed by Rebecca and Lowell. He pressed a button on the wall and the doors closed. After thirty seconds or so the doors reopened and we exited into a companionway which was obviously deep in the bowels of the ship. There were no windows and the corridor was softly lit. I was surprised to find carpet underfoot.

Lowell walked along the corridor for a few metres and turned to face a door. For a few seconds he placed his face in front of a facial recognition scanner and the door opened. We all stepped through into an enormous room which seemed to occupy the full width of the ship and was perhaps 50 metres long. For a moment I thought I'd fallen asleep and woken up at Cape Canaveral. The room was on two levels, with a central well populated by two rows of back-to-back workstations at which perhaps twenty people were pecking away at keyboards, tapping screens or talking on headsets. The upper level, around four metres wide, ran around three sides of the room and accommodated various meeting tables, a coffee area and what looked like four small sleep pods. The far wall ran from the base of the well straight up to the ceiling and was mainly taken up with three giant screens which were all currently displaying a global map with various flashing dots and lines.

At the far end of the room on our right was an elevated glass window, through which I could see more people at work in another room. Maybe a dozen more were deep in conversation at the various tables around the upper area of the room or at the coffee station. Even though it was now close to midnight, the whole place was buzzing with activity.

"This is Vanguard's nerve-centre, Charlie," said Lowell from behind me, as I regarded my surroundings open-mouthed. "From here we can manage our entire global network. We have state-of-the-art comms, one of the most powerful supercomputers in the world and the best talent money can buy. What you're looking at is the heart of the best non-state-owned intelligence agency on the planet." He said this with the pride normally reserved for a father introducing his newborn son.

"We're making excellent progress with our investigations into the circumstances surrounding your brother's death," he continued. We'll convene in the conference room first thing in the morning. But for now, I've no doubt you'll appreciate some rest and something to eat. We've assigned you a stateroom and arranged for a late dinner to be provided. Now, if you'll excuse me, I need to talk to some of my colleagues." Abruptly he turned away and walked down a short set of steps into the well of the control centre.

"Come on, Charlie," said Rebecca, taking my arm. "Plenty of time for action tomorrow. Now we both need some sleep." Did I detect the merest hint of innuendo in this? She led me back into the elevator and we rose once more through the ship, this time exiting on the main deck, where we walked past what looked like a series of large cabins. Rebecca stopped in front of one and opened the door. "This is you, Charlie." She moved ahead of me and spread her arms. "I hope you'll be comfortable here."

The stateroom was spacious and well appointed, with a large double bed, a desk and leather chair, an occasional table on which a covered plate and bottle of wine had been placed, and a door which I assumed led to a bathroom. The sizeable windows gave onto the deck and the sea beyond, with wooden blinds for privacy. Rebecca sat down on the bed and crossed her legs, regarding me with head cocked on one side. Despite my tiredness and the shock of the last few days, I couldn't help but be distracted by the sight of long legs clad in dark stockings beneath her tight-fitting black skirt.

She smiled as if she could see my thoughts being played out on my face. "We're going to do some good things together, Charlie," she said, perhaps a little more throatily than before. She seemed to pause and think for a moment, as if trying to make a decision, then pushed herself up off the bed and made for the door. As she passed me, she reached up and kissed me on the cheek, her lips lingering for what felt like a fraction of a second longer than was necessary. Operating on pure instinct, I cupped her chin in my hand and turned her face to mine. Her blue eyes seemed to have darkened into cobalt pools with infinite depths. As I moved to kiss her and slid my arms around her waist, she let out a small gasp and I felt her warm breath on my face a moment before our mouths met.

I felt her rise onto her toes as her arms encircled my neck and we kissed gently, our lips just brushing one another's, an unhurried prelude to what we both knew was now unstoppable. And then her mouth opened, her tongue a sinuous darting explorer, and I was hungrily crushing her body against mine.

There was a desperation to her passion which took me by surprise. She had always seemed to me to be so perfectly in control, so cool and detached. I intuited a profound need in her, born of some great loss. It was as if she had buried some inestimable pain deep inside and it was at last finding an outlet.

I began to unbutton her blouse, the white cotton stretched tight across her breasts as she arched her back, her neck muscles taut and her throat milky white in the dim light of the cabin; but she placed her hands lightly over mine, gently compelling me to stop. Then she took control. She didn't even bother to unbutton my shirt, just pushed it up and over my head, before running her hands over my shoulders, her fingertips briefly brushing the scar tissue, then down my arms and over my chest to my belt. She quickly unbuckled and unzipped my jeans and pulled them down in one smooth movement, followed by my underwear. Then she was pushing me back on the bed, tugging off the last of my clothing.

She stood there, her head on one side, and regarded me frankly, a smile playing around her mouth. She took her time unbuttoning her blouse, her eyes locked on mine, before unzipping her skirt and letting it fall to the ground. Her white strapless bra came next, revealing tanned breasts, her nipples already erect. Hooking her thumbs into her panties, she slid them over her hips and let them fall around her ankles and it was my turn to regard her candidly. Her breasts were small, but in perfect proportion to her slim, toned body and her legs were long and well-muscled, meeting in a trim triangle, at the base of which I could see the cleft of her sex.

She knelt on the bed and sat astride my ankles, then began inching her body slowly up my legs, her stockings rasping against my legs, until the intimacy was complete. It felt intoxicatingly new and yet profoundly familiar as she guided me gently inside her and began to move in a smooth circular rhythm which pulled me deeper into her, her back arched once more, her head thrown back, my hands on her waist, encouraging the slowly accelerating rotation of her hips. We moved like that for what seemed like an eternity, faster and faster, my body rising to meet hers, pushing against her as she moved ever more urgently against me. In reality, the eternity lasted no more than a brief few minutes, before we climaxed simultaneously, a surging, juddering release that left us both gasping for breath and clinging to one another like two souls lost at sea.

We lay, both bathed in a light sheen of sweat, Rebecca's head on my chest, my arm around her shoulders, lightly stroking her arm.

"I need to tell you something," she said quietly. And in that instant I realised that I already knew. I'd known from the first moment I saw them together. A subtle intimacy that perhaps only the subconscious can detect.

"My brother," I replied. There was a long silence, during which neither of us moved.

"I can't believe he's gone," she said after a while. "He was a real force of nature, you know. Well, of course you know." She paused. "It was just once, shortly before his funeral. It was almost as if he needed the reassurance of life after faking his own death, and I..."

"You?"

She didn't respond for a moment. "I needed him for different reasons. But that's a conversation for another time." She sat up, turned and looked down at me. "It's difficult to explain, Charlie. I loved him. Not in the old romantic sense, but as – well, as a sort of – fellow traveller." My puzzlement must have shown. "Let's just say that we had shared experiences which drew us close. The important thing is that I loved him, fraternally I think is the best way to describe it, and I will do anything to avenge his death." I saw again that familiar steel that she had displayed in the previous days.

It surprised me that I wasn't hurt or upset by what she'd told me. There was a certain symmetry to it that softened the blow. Now I understood something that had been puzzling me all along – why she had felt such a pressing need to be at Michael's funeral. And I felt somehow that Rebecca's and my futures were now inextricably bound together, for good or ill. I felt a tenderness towards her that I hadn't felt towards a woman in a long time, tinged with a little a certain wariness.

"I think I understand. We'll pick this up later," I said gently, the cue for us to part. As Rebecca quickly dressed and headed to the door for the second time, she turned and looked at me. "You're more damaged than your brother, Charlie. But stronger. I can feel your strength and it gives me hope for what lies ahead."

"And I can see why Michael loved you too," I said.

The door closed and she was gone.

CHAPTER 36

IN THE EVENT, the scheduled morning meeting was postponed until the afternoon, due to a delay in some incoming intelligence. Rebecca explained this as she gave me a full tour of the ship. I was surprised, given what had taken place between us the evening before, at how easy we had become with one another. There was no hint of embarrassment or awkwardness. We were both comfortable with what had happened and, I suspected, both fully expected it to happen again. But today, now, it was all business and Rebecca's demeanour was nothing but professional as she showed me around Vanguard's HQ.

It felt to me like nothing less than a small floating town. On the first level there was a full-size conference room complete with a comprehensive communications setup, a fully-stocked library, a dining room and cafeteria and a ship's lounge where the crew and Vanguard team would meet and play chess and backgammon. Above that, on the second level, was a working deck with two MCT-1565 cranes, hydrographic winches and a fully-equipped hospital. On the third level, below the bridge, were the captain's and senior officers' staterooms.

On the main deck, beneath the helipad, *Triton* boasted an electronics lab, a computer lab and, at the stern, a sizeable A-frame which I was told could tow anything up to 18,000 lbs in weight, and another crane – a Morgan Marine 18000 tele-scoping boom version. All this together with 3,500 feet of open deck space.

Below decks, and below the operations room I had visited the night before, were the engineering spaces, machinery control room and machine shop, propulsion motor room, and the majority of the staterooms occupied by Vanguard's employ-ees, who operated on an eight-hour three-shift system. Finally there was a room that you would be hard-pressed to find on any other merchant vessel. Behind a six inch reinforced steel door was a seriously impressive armoury, stocked with everything from pistols and automatic rifles to rocket-propelled grenade-launchers, C-4 explosive and a whole shelf full of limpet mines.

Rebecca explained the workings of the Vanguard opera-tion, whose activities ranged from intelligence-gathering at one end of the spectrum to paramilitary intervention at the other. Throughout the morning I repeatedly asked her how the team's investigations into my brother's death and the people behind it were progressing. My enquiries always met different versions of "We're making very good progress, Charlie. Mr Lowell will give you a full briefing when we have all the facts." In the end I gave up asking and abandoned myself to the wonders of the ship which, for the first time in my life when aboard any kind of waterborne craft, did not produce regular bouts of nausea.

As we were finishing a brief sandwich lunch, Lowell himself came to collect us from the dining room. He led the way to the conference room, which looked out on the operations centre through the elevated glass window I'd noticed the previous evening. Already seated were Rolf, Aleysha Fox and Bruce Havelock, all of them peering at a large screen on the wall at the head of the conference table. I sat down and Lowell took a seat beside me. Two young women, who were not introduced, sat quietly at one end of the table taking notes throughout the session.

"Well, Charlie, we've got a lot of ground to cover, so let's get started," Lowell said briskly. "Aleysha?"

The intelligence head turned a page in her file and began. "Over the last twenty-four hours our operatives have been pursuing a number of leads on the ground and we've had the opportunity to analyse some extensive electronic intelligence, too."

"What kind of intelligence?" I asked.

"Well, we've had a root around in a number of encrypted email accounts, intercepted some useful text messages and listened in to some fascinating telephone conversations," replied Aleysha candidly. "We've learnt a lot. And what we've learnt is frankly terrifying."

I was shocked at Aleysha's bluntness, but no one else in the room seemed fazed by it. It certainly made me sit up and pay attention.

"It seems that when he started delving into the past, your brother stumbled into a situation with very high stakes indeed."

She picked up a small remote control and a photograph flashed onto the screen of a well-dressed middle-aged man of Middle Eastern appearance, snapped while getting out of a car on a busy city street. Well groomed, with a neatly-trimmed beard, the man looked every inch the international banker.

"This is Aariz Abdul-Aziz Al-Shammari, or Ari as he's known to his friends, an Iraqi currently living in Lebanon with an unhealthy interest in Middle Eastern antiquities, among other things. His interest is not personal or cultural, but purely transactional. He finds stolen artefacts a remarkably easy way to raise substantial sums of money without a paper trail, money that can be used to finance certain groups with which he has sympathies. This is the man who acquired the statues your parents were dealing with fifteen years ago."

I felt the breath catch in my throat and I leaned forward, listening intently. "Go on."

"If we've pieced together events accurately, it seems that your parents were employed as legitimate intermediaries in the purchase and sale of the statues. We still don't know at this stage who the seller was and in a sense that's not important. What is more pertinent is that Mr Braddock somehow caught wind of the transaction and decided to intervene on his own account. It appears that he stole the statues and somehow, probably through a third party, made contact with Al-Shammari.

"Al-Shammari paid Braddock a handsome sum for the statues – but nowhere near what they were truly worth. We understand that Mr Al-Shammari netted himself something in excess of thirty million dollars when he eventually placed the items on the market. And we have a shrewd suspicion where that money eventually ended up – and what it was used for. Let's just say that thirty million dollars will pay for a lot of lethal hardware."

Aleysha paused and let this sink in, before I asked the question she had obviously been anticipating. "But why kill my parents?" I asked quietly. "And Michael?"

"To be honest, I'm not sure Braddock himself would have found that necessary," she replied, "but evidently Al-Shammari doesn't like loose ends, and likes even less the possibility that any transactions of this sort will lead back to him. Or, more precisely, to the company he keeps. As I said when we last met, for him the death of your parents was purely a matter of expediency. And it was simpler to get Braddock to do it than to go to the trouble himself. No doubt Braddock received an additional fee for their murder which, as we all now know, he delegated to his son as some twisted rite of passage.

"As for Michael, Al-Shammari is obviously paranoid about anyone poking around in his affairs. Which, given the nature of his clients, is perhaps not surprising. Now that he's involved in a sensitive potential transaction which we think will net him immeasurably greater gains than a few Babylonian statues, he cannot afford even the remotest chance that we or anyone else should get wind of it."

"Unfortunately for Mr Al-Shammari, Michael wasn't just a lone member of the public trying to find out how his parents died. He was a member of Vanguard and, as Simon told you, we look after our own. But more importantly – and this is in no way to downplay your personal tragedy – there are far more serious issues at stake here. Issues which have made it imperative that Vanguard takes action, and quickly. Because the fact that we are aware of Al-Shammari means that he may also now be aware of us. And he has considerable resources at his disposal."

I absorbed all this while looking at the image on the screen. If this was the man ultimately responsible for the death of my entire family, he would pay. I swore it silently to myself. Out loud, I said, "How do we get to him?"

"We don't," interjected Havelock. "At least, not yet. We believe there's one more scene to be played out in this little drama before we have a complete picture. It appears that the night before Braddock's son –" he paused, evidently searching for the right words, "– before his son met his end, Mr Braddock senior suffered a serious business setback. Someone burned down one of his warehouses and a couple of million pounds worth of drugs went up in smoke. We have good reason to believe that Al-Shammari was behind it.

"But why?" I asked.

"Because we believe the merchandise that Al-Shammari is so keen to acquire was mislaid while in Braddock's possession. Which is causing some serious grief on both sides of the transaction. At the moment we're letting it play out and keeping an eye on Braddock's little firm. If our suspicions are correct, we don't think it will be long before Braddock and Al-Shammari get together and that will present us with an opportunity."

Silence fell on the room once more. "Okay," I said, "So what about this transaction that Al-Shammari's involved in? What's he trying to get his hands on – and why's it important enough to kill people over?"

At this point, Lowell took over. "For that, Charlie, we need to go back a couple of thousand years. What do you know about first century Palestine?"

PALESTINE, AD66
THE BURNISHED SCROLL

CHAPTER 37

THE BIBLE RECOUNTS THAT, shortly before Jesus of Nazareth was captured and crucified, he rampaged through the Temple in Jerusalem, outraged by the money-changers and merchants who were plying their trade and getting rich in the courtyards of Israel's holiest place of worship.

The irony is that it was that very Temple which, legend has it, housed some of the most fabulous treasures then known to man, amassed over centuries by the Jewish priests and their acolytes who protected, maintained and controlled access to the shrine. Quite apart from the priceless historical artefacts the Temple was said to contain – the great majority of them made from gold, silver and precious stones – the religious authorities earned enormous revenues from the half-shekel of Temple tribute which was required each year from every male Israelite of age, including their slaves and proselytes.

By the time Jesus was born, more than five centuries of treasure had been accumulated, stored, preserved and inventoried in the inner sanctum of the Temple.

And when the Jews decided to rebel against their Roman occupiers in AD66, there was one thing uppermost in the minds of the Jewish aristocracy: should the rebellion fail, how were they to keep that immense wealth out of the hands of the Romans?

CHAPTER 38

BENJAMIN BEN ABRAHAM was eighteen years old and a hothead. He had spent his entire childhood and adolescence under Roman rule and his resentment had grown with each passing year. He could not remember a time when his country had not been on the brink of rebellion and war. His very birth had been tainted by the depravities of the Occupiers. He had been born in the year 48, on the day when one of Rome's loathed Greek auxiliary soldiers had provoked a riot by pulling down his breeches on Jerusalem's Temple Mount and farting at the packed crowd of pilgrims who were gathered there for the Feast of Passover. While his mother was bringing him into the world, his grandfather was leaving it, clubbed to death by one of the soldiers from Procurator Ventidius Cumanus's garrison, which had been sent to quell the unrest.

And that was a mere eight years after an even greater outrage, when the Emperor Caligula had had the temerity to try and erect a statue of himself – fashioned in the guise of Jupiter – in the heart of the Temple, so that he could be worshipped alongside Yahweh. That had brought Palestine as close to war as anyone could remember, as the citizens of Jerusalem rose up as one against the defilement of their holy place. Would the Romans never learn?

And yet the persecution had continued, year in, year out. And as the oppression worsened, the populace grew more and more restless, especially in Galilee and the rural heartlands outside the capital. A ragtag army of militias sprang up in the countryside, among them peasants with legitimate grievances over punitive taxes and growing anti-Semitism, bolstered by bandits and rioters who saw an opportunity to profit from the chaos.

Not long after the Temple Mount incident, another soldier provoked outrage in the coastal town of Caesarea by tearing up a copy of the Torah and burning it, prompting thousands of people to descend on the city and force Cumanus to have the soldier executed. And it wasn't just the Romans and their hired mercenaries who appeared to have it in for the Jews. Samaria, which sat inconveniently between Galilee in the north and Judaea in the south, had been at odds with their Jewish neighbours for as long as anyone could remember. When a Galilean pilgrim was murdered in Samaria on his way to Jerusalem and Cumanus refused to take action, the veteran Jewish bandit Eleazar ben Dinai took matters into his own hands and wrought havoc throughout the southern Samaritan villages, sparking a wave of communal violence that continued to simmer for a generation.

As the unrest grew, Rome was forced into action, partitioning Palestine between a new client-kingdom under Herod Agrippa II in Transjordan and a reduced Judean province under a new Procurator, Marcus Antonius Felix. Felix was competent enough, but a little too close for comfort to the Herodian aristocracy, since his second wife was Agrippa's sister. This didn't help at a time when the monarchy and priestly aristocracy were seen as hopelessly out of touch with the citizenry and had come to be hated almost as much as the Roman occupiers. The high priesthood itself had degenerated into naked greed, despatching bands of thugs to seize tithes from the peasantry and prevent them from being given to their village priests. Bribes were exchanged for top positions in the priesthood and the story goes that on one occasion rival factions actually fought it out on the streets. It was no surprise that by the early 50s the Jews were literally throwing themselves into revolutionary activity.

Felix did his best to stamp out the banditry. He captured Eleazar and sent him to Rome for trial, executing many of his associates and coming down hard on the rural militias in an effort to restore order across the three territories. But the Jews' blood was up and by now the revolutionary Zealot movement was in full swing, harassing the Roman military and effectively mounting a paramilitary insurgency throughout the province.

Benjamin had been a breathless admirer of these brave guerillas since early childhood and revelled in their stories of derring-do. He had been particularly admiring of the Sicarii, the arch-Zealots led by the legendary Menahem ben Yehuda, who had carved out a formidable reputation as silent assassins. They made a speciality of mixing with the Jerusalem pilgrim crowds, with short, curved knives concealed in their clothing, quietly stabbing to death prominent political figures before melting away into the throng. Their first victim was the high priest himself, Jonathan, a blue-blooded Sadducean aristocrat, and many others followed, despite Felix's ruthless acts of retribution.

When Felix was recalled to Rome and succeeded as procurator by Clodius Albinus, the Sicarii became even bolder. Albinus had redoubled Roman efforts to quell the insurgency, carrying out mass arrests of the revolutionaries, and the Sicarii responded by kidnapping a clutch of aristocrats and using them as hostages for the release of the detainees, including the secretary of the Governor of the Temple Precincts. Albinus was forced to capitulate and ten of the revolutionaries were released. The legend of Menahem was secured.

As if violent revolution were not enough, the Jews also had their share of supposedly divinely-inspired millenarians who believed it was their God-given mission to overthrow the state. Benjamin had no time for these self-styled messiahs, but he did admire their pluck. His father used to regale him with the story of the Egyptian 'false prophet' who everyone in his family thought was a soft-headed loon, but who still managed to mobilise 4,000 men, bring them out of the desert and camp on the Mount of Olives before storming the Roman garrison in Jerusalem. He failed, like all the messianic upstarts, but he and his ilk were just one more reason why the Romans were forced repeatedly to intervene in Jewish civil affairs, further stoking civil unrest.

By the time Benjamin celebrated his eighteenth birthday, the whole of Palestine was in a state of foment. The ruling class had effectively broken down, large areas of the countryside and hill country were controlled by bandits and Jerusalem was plagued by urban guerrilla warfare and street protests. Albinus had been succeeded as Procurator two years before by Gessius Florus and it was his arrival in Jerusalem which finally lit the touch paper that would set off an incendiary chain of events over the ensuing four years – and change the course of Benjamin's life.

Florus was a thick-necked, uncompromising bully who had no time for the conciliatory overtures of some of his predecessors. He saw that his province was out of control and set about restoring order in the only way he knew how: with an iron fist. He sent his cavalry into Caesarea, where a series of violent demonstrations had recently erupted, butchering hundreds of demonstrators. He enraged the Temple authorities in Jerusalem by ordering them to hand over Temple funds for the Procurator's use, provoking more violent protests which he met with massed troops and indiscriminate killing.

When Florus called up reinforcements to intensify his bloody suppression, the Jews' anger finally boiled over into full-scale insurrection. The citizenry of Jerusalem came out to confront his troops in unprecedented numbers.

In Benjamin's nineteenth year, all-out war with Rome became inevitable.

CHAPTER 39

BENJAMIN LOUNGED on his sleeping mat as he watched the sun rise over Mount Zion, across the Tyropaean Valley from his home in the lower city. He had gone to bed late, after playing too long at draughts with his younger sister Miriam, and felt groggy and out of sorts. His father had left the city before dawn for his olive grove on the slopes of Mount Olivet, but Benjamin was not expected at the stonemason's yard until later that morning: his boss was across the city repairing the wall of one of the dozens of synagogues that interspersed the cramped housing of south-east Jerusalem, and Benjamin had been tasked with purchasing some new tools from the market before setting off for work. So he was able to relax a little.

He could hear his mother clattering about in the courtyard below, punctuated by the occasional squeals of his sister as she attempted to milk one of the tethered goats, which was obviously being uncooperative. His family were not wealthy, but his father made a good living in the fields and his mother took in washing from some of the rich merchants in the upper city. His own stonemasonry apprenticeship would soon be completed after the obligatory five years, enabling him to legitimately claim status as a craftsman and join one of the guilds, with a commensurate rise in income.

Their home was modest, but comfortable, occupying half of a fieldstone apartment on one side of a communal courtyard in the north of the lower city, just below the upper city walls. He shared a small room with his sister, across a narrow passageway from his parents' sleeping quarters, above a spacious living area on the ground floor. But Benjamin's favourite part of the house was the small roof terrace, where during the spring and summer he would often sit and watch the city come to life in the mornings and return to slumber in the evenings, looking south across the cluttered rooftops of the lower city towards the Hinnom Valley, or north to the towering walls of Temple Mount, Jerusalem's most holy site.

He loved the sounds and smells of the city. The perpetual cries of the hawkers as they plied their trade through the narrow streets and alleyways. The friendly greetings exchanged between neighbours. The periodic muted sounds of prayer from his local synagogue. The scent of jasmine, citron, sage and pomegranate. The heady mix of spices and rich cooking smells. The occasional whiff of incense. And, best of all, the intoxicating eucalyptus-mint smell of persimmon, which well-off women dabbed on their heels, teasing the young men they encountered in the streets by stamping their feet and diffusing the pungent scent into the air around them.

But at present his city was in turmoil. Florus's demand that the Temple Treasury be raided for funds for his own use had scandalised the citizenry and Jerusalemites' simmering hatred of the Romans had reached fever pitch. As the sky brightened in the east, Benjamin could hear the harsh cries of angry men in the streets, as bands of protestors coalesced and streamed up the sloping main thoroughfare that connected the upper and lower cities. Benjamin felt the tension in the air and craved the excitement of the demonstrations that he knew would soon be gathering on the steps before the Temple, just as they had for the previous few days. But his father and mother were adamant that he should not get involved. It was too dangerous and there were already more than enough young hotheads squaring up to the Romans and putting their lives at risk.

Benjamin was a dutiful son, so he obeyed his parents, although he longed to be among those of his friends who had already joined one of the many groups of agitators itching to cross swords with Florus's men. Instead, he got up from his bed with a sigh, dressed and headed downstairs into the courtyard, where his mother was already hard at work in the courtyard, beating a fine piece of wet purple cloth with a flat stone on the step outside the wooden front door of their apartment. He kissed her and cuffed his little sister affectionately before grabbing a handful of fruit and heading for the arch that led out of the courtyard.

"Wait, we'll come with you," called his mother as he was about to step out into the street. "I need some bread and herbs for the Sabbath." Benjamin smiled indulgently. He knew the real reason his mother Ruth wanted to join him was because she was proud of her son and loved to show him off to the other women in the market. His late departure for work gave her just such an opportunity. Miriam was no less adoring of her big brother. He truly loved them both.

They set off through the dusty maze of streets and alleyways towards the upper market, nodding greetings to friends and neighbours as they walked, his mother forever on the lookout for a suitable match for her handsome son. He boasted a tall, slim frame, with muscular arms strengthened from wielding the stonemason's hammer and lugging the heavy stones of his trade. His eyes were the colour of matured honey above a strong, aquiline nose and full mouth, his head a tangle of dark curls. He attracted more than his fair share of attention from the opposite sex and Ruth knew she could afford to be choosy when it came to selecting him a wife.

They walked through a gaggle of open-air shops where the city's weavers, dyers, potters, bakers, tailors and carpenters all sat at work. Benjamin went straight to the metalworker's shop to buy the hammers and new chisels he needed, while Ruth and Miriam continued on up the broad steps which led from the lower to the upper city and into the enormous space which lay in front of the south-facing wall of the temple and which, on market days like today, was filled with stalls bursting with bustle and colour, displaying everything from fruit, vegetables and dried fish to clothes, perfumes and jewellery. The noise of shouting tradesmen, overlaid by the squawking of sacrificial animals used in the many rituals of the Jewish faith, was deafening. The two women made straight for the bazaar, where they would find the foodstuffs they sought.

Benjamin was haggling with the metalworker and looking forward to a cup of wine or beer and perhaps some fried locusts at one of the many local taverns, when he became conscious of a din from beyond the market. This growing noise was different from the ambient hum of activity: it was laced with the sound of iron-shod hooves and clanging metal, accompanied by the roar of a crowd in full throat. Benjamin turned towards the sound and quickly understood that it signalled danger. He swiftly thanked the metalworker and set off at a run for the bazaar.

As he entered the tightly-packed area of shops and stalls, he looked to his left and saw the vanguard of a sizeable crowd rushing into the market from the direction of the viaduct which led from the upper city to Temple Mount, pursued by armoured men on horseback. He looked frantically around for his mother and sister, but couldn't immediately see them among the mass of people. He called out their names and ran from stall to stall, desperately searching for a glimpse of them. Just as he was losing hope of ever finding them in the melee, he spotted Ruth at one of the bakers' stalls, a loaf of unleavened bread in each hand, frozen in terror as the crowd swamped the market, followed by a troop of Roman auxiliary cavalry at the gallop.

The crowd was streaming down the steps into the narrow streets and alleys of the lower city, while the horsemen slashed their way through the throng with their spathas, the fearsome metre-long double-edged swords that sliced through everything but chain mail. They were casting around them indiscriminately, leaning from their mounts to cut at heads, limbs and legs, while their horses reared and neighed, their nostrils flaring with the smell of the blood of injured and dying men and women. It made no difference whether the victims were fleeing demonstrators or citizens quietly going about their daily business – the Romans made no distinction.

Benjamin saw a soldier thrust his sword through the back of an old man trying to hobble to safety behind a carpenter's shop, its sharp point emerging from his chest in a haze of gore. A young man put up a pitiable defence with his staff before his head was hewn from his body in a single stroke. An elderly blind woman, her eyes bandaged, stood in the middle of the street, her arms outstretched in supplication, until a soldier slammed the pommel of his sword into the crown of her head and she sank to the ground, blood flying from her long grey hair.

It had been barely a minute since the thirty or so horsemen had arrived, but already there was carnage. Everywhere he looked, Benjamin saw his fellow citizens being slaughtered like animals. The market was littered with bodies, some writhing in agony, punctured or limbless, most unmoving.

And then he saw his mother, still rooted to the spot, still holding the bread she had purchased for the family's forthcoming Sabbath supper. His sister was standing beside her, her eyes wide with terror. As Ruth stood helpless and motionless with fear, a cavalryman tugged on the reins of his warhorse and its front legs lifted clear of the ground, the rider holding his sword aloft as he leaned back in his saddle and let out a blood-curdling cry. Ruth turned and saw her son. Their eyes met and in that instant Benjamin saw in them the certainty of her own death as the horse's hooves descended, crushing her skull like an egg before trampling her into the ground as it continued on its way.

Letting out a howl of anguish, Benjamin ran full pelt towards his fallen mother. Miriam had collapsed onto her body and was screaming at the top of her lungs. Benjamin reached them and threw himself over their bodies as another three horsemen galloped past, letting out the same battle-lust roar as their compatriot. He grabbed his sister by the arm and tried to pull her from her mother's prone form, but she clung on with a grim strength. He finally managed to drag her away and was starting to pull her to her feet when everything seemed suddenly to go silent. He turned and saw a soldier in the uniform of a decurion, the troop's commander, seated on a great jet-black horse which was wheeling hard in the confined space.

The rational part of Benjamin's brain knew that the shouts and screams in the market hadn't diminished, but his ears seemed suddenly to filter out all background noise so that he was conscious only of a heavy silence broken solely by the jangling of the horse's bridle, the panting of the beast and the ringing of its hooves on the cobbles. The soldier looked down at him with complete indifference as he wheeled above him, before his eyes slid to Miriam and a leer crept onto his face. She was barely thirteen years old and still painfully shy, but had matured early and her beauty had already caught the attention of many a local boy, entranced by her pale skin, soft brown eyes and lustrous mane of chestnut hair.

Benjamin regarded him with growing horror as he realised the danger his sister was in. He moved in front of her and held her against his back, his eyes blazing with hatred and unspoken challenge as he locked gazes with the officer. For a moment, neither spoke nor moved. Then, with a swiftness honed on countless battlefields across Europe and North Africa, the decurion raised his sword and swiped the flat of the blade against the side of Benjamin's head. His ears ringing and eyes tearing, Benjamin fell to his knees, dazed. Momentarily incapacitated, he watched helplessly as the decurion reached down and with a single movement swept Miriam from the ground and up onto the horse's neck in front of him.

Before Benjamin could raise himself, the soldier had wheeled once more and galloped off in the direction taken by his troop, holding Miriam tightly across his chest with his left arm.

Benjamin finally managed to regain his feet and stumbled clumsily after the cavalryman, following the shouts and screams which were receding southwards through the lower city. His mother was dead – there would be time to purify her body and grieve for her later. For now, there was only one thought in Benjamin's head: the rescue of his sister.

For an hour or more Benjamin roamed the streets, drawn hither and thither by the voices of fleeing citizens or the gruff shouts of soldiers. As the sun reached its zenith, he turned into a street famed for its taverns and heard the sound of raucous laughter coming from one of the hostelries. A number of horses were tied up outside. Cautiously approaching the door, he listened. He heard voices shouting excitedly in Greek, the lingua franca of the Roman empire, together with the screams and whimpers of a woman crying out incoherently in her native Aramaic.

Benjamin slowly pushed open the door and looked in silent revulsion at the scene before him. About a dozen cavalrymen, all of them Macedonian auxiliaries, were standing in a semi-circle on the other side of a rough-hewn table, on which a young girl was splayed out, most of her clothes torn from her body. As the soldier pleasured himself, his comrades cheered him on, settling into a rhythmic chant in time to the abuser's quickening thrusts. Even as he climaxed with a grunt and a shudder, the next soldier was lowering his leather breeches. As the soldier withdrew to make room for his comrade, the girl pulled her knees up to her chest and fell sideways, curled up in a defensive ball, and Benjamin saw her face. It was Miriam.

He lunged forward with a scream of rage and despair, but no sooner had he launched himself towards the men than a strong hand seized him by the collar of his tunic and yanked him backwards off his feet. "Not so fast, young master," growled the owner of the hand in a commanding voice, using heavily-accented Aramaic; he had evidently been standing behind the door when Benjamin entered. There was a sudden silence in the room – the soldiers surrounding Benjamin's sister instantly stopped laughing and cheering and the man who had pulled down his breeches held them at half-mast. The pitiful curled-up figure on the table did not move.

Benjamin squirmed around, screaming at his captor, a mixture of rage, impotence and shame wracking his body, and saw that it was the decurion from the market. He was still holding Benjamin easily by the collar with his right hand. With his left he now withdrew a dagger from his belt, wrenched Benjamin around, pinned him against the wall and held the razor-sharp point of the blade at his throat.

"Well, well. We have a real little polecat here," he sneered, his voice low and contemptuous. Benjamin became completely still. The decurion switched to Greek, which Benjamin had learnt in his lessons at the synagogue. "I suggest you draw in your claws, young master, or you may find a paw missing." Benjamin could smell the foetid breath of the Roman as he leaned closer. He had a saturnine face, deeply lined, with a livid scar running from his left ear to the side of his mouth. His dark, oiled hair lay flat on his scalp, indicating that he had not long removed his helmet. His eyes were blue and penetrating.

"You fucking animal," hissed Benjamin. "You fucking bastard animal!" He lifted his chin as the soldier pressed the point of his dagger a little further. Benjamin felt the skin break and a rivulet of blood ran down his neck.

"Animal, is it?" smiled the decurion. There was a murmur of laughter from the men across the room. "Well, if that's so, then I must be the lion sent to devour you, my little polecat.

"What do you think, boys?" he called over his shoulder. "Shall we eat him?" There was another ripple of laughter. The soldier cocked his head on one side and looked thoughtfully at Benjamin. "No, I don't think so. I like you, little polecat. I like your spirit. Unlike your pathetic, whining, simpering Jew friends out there. You'd really like to kill me, wouldn't you? Eh?"

Without warning, Benjamin drove his knee hard into the soldier's crotch. He was never going to do much damage due to the studded leather groin-protector the decurion wore over his skirt, but it did have the element of surprise and the soldier stepped back momentarily and the dagger was withdrawn an inch or two. Benjamin took the brief opportunity to duck and dart under the decurion's arm, racing towards the table on which his sister lay. His way was immediately blocked by two of the soldiers who grabbed him and held him fast, one on each arm, while he cursed and kicked.

The decurion walked toward him, no longer smiling. "Enough of this shit," he growled. "The only reason I'm not going to cut your throat right here is because I want you to learn a valuable lesson, little polecat. We are in charge here, do you understand? I could be sunning myself in my olive grove in Umbria now, but instead I'm here in your shitty little country propping up your shitty little king while your shitty little rebellion gets dealt with. And believe me, it is being dealt with. I don't know how many ways we have to show you that you don't fuck with Rome!" This last shouted in Benjamin's face.

"Now, we're going to leave my boys to their fun. They've

earned it. It's been a hard morning. And if you feel the need to show me that you haven't understood a word I've said, come and find me and I'll give you another lesson. Felix Maximus Drusus will be waiting for you.

"Now you're going to have a little sleep." And he punched Benjamin hard in the face, breaking his nose, followed by a hammer blow to the side of his head, which sent him sprawling across the tavern floor. As he fought unconsciousness, Benjamin heard the screams of his sister rising in pitch above him. And then everything went dark.

CHAPTER 40

THE DECORATED clay lamps on their shallow wall shelves threw shadows across the room. They had been a gift from Abraham to Ruth on their wedding day, in accordance with Jewish tradition. Now their flickering light illuminated a very different scene: a dead wife, a broken husband, a traumatised daughter and an angry son.

Abraham had personally taken on the task of washing his wife's body, which he had done gently and lovingly over the course of two or more hours. This flew in the face of religious practice, which required a rabbi to perform the ritual, but Abraham had insisted. A devout Pharisee, he believed that God would forgive him this small act of selfishness. She now lay in her shroud, her face covered by a sudarium, her hands and feet bound with linen and her body perfumed with nard, myrrh and aloes. Soon the family's relatives and friends would be admitted to pay their respects and early the next morning she would be carried to the family tomb outside the city, the procession led by the women, who would keen loudly and throw dust in their hair, as tradition demanded.

Benjamin had seen a few funerals over the years, but this was the first in his family. He knew that the following day theirs would be far from the only procession snaking out of the city. Rumour had it that nearly a hundred people had died in the Roman onslaught that morning.

While Abraham wept over his wife's broken body, his stout farmer's frame wracked with sobs, Miriam sat silently in the corner, her body motionless and her eyes unseeing. When Benjamin had recovered consciousness earlier that day he had found his sister lying in a foetal position on the floor of the tavern, now empty of her attackers, her clothes drawn tightly around her small form, her legs streaked with blood. He had cradled her head in his arms, crying quietly and repeating over and over his sorrow and shame that he had been unable to protect her. He received no response. Eventually, he lifted her gently and carried her back to their home, where their father was waiting to receive news of the double tragedy.

Benjamin knew that it might have been better had his sister died in that tavern. She would now be untouchable, unclean. She would never marry, never have children. Her life was effectively over. As he sat beside his father and grieved for his mother, he no longer shed tears. Instead, he seethed with a cold fury that now vibrated through every sinew of his body. And beneath the rage was a shame and humiliation so profound that he could never have imagined it. He knew that it would define him for the rest of his life.

As he sat with his ruined family, his face bruised and throbbing from his broken nose, all his dreams of becoming a master stonemason evaporated. He had only one career now, a single mission. To meet Felix Maximus Drusus, decurion of the third troop of the Tenth Legion Fretensis, once again. And to kill him.

CHAPTER 41

GENERAL CESTIUS GALLUS, Roman senator and Legate of Rome's Syrian province, arrived in Judaea with his Twelfth Legion Fulminata in September 66, under orders from Emperor Nero to put a stop to the upstart rebellion once and for all. But it would be no easy task. Despite having 30,000 men at his disposal, bolstered by 14,000 Transjordanian troops provided by Herod Agrippa, Gallus's force was faced with putting down a growing revolt that by now had spread throughout Galilee, along the Judaean coast and into Jerusalem itself.

Following the atrocity in the upper market four months earlier, the people of Jerusalem had come out in unprecedented numbers to challenge the Romans, turning violent protests into a full-scale insurrection. The rebels were emboldened by a number of spectacular successes, defeating Florus's auxiliaries shortly after the massacre and driving them from the city after days of bloody hand-to-hand street fighting. Then in August the rebels defeated a major counter-revolutionary incursion backed by units of Herod Agrippa's army and slaughtered the Roman garrison. As Gallus drew up his troops to the gates of Jerusalem, he was effectively confronting a city that had seceded from the Empire.

The leader of the Jerusalem rebellion was Eleazar ben Simon, who had assembled a formidable rebel army of nearly 2,500 men, now known throughout Judaea as the Zealots, who were thirsting for more action against their Roman oppressors. Among them was Benjamin ben Abraham.

A week after his mother's funeral, Benjamin had bidden an emotional farewell to his father and sister. Abraham tried hard to persuade him not to go, even offering to make him a partner in his olive oil business, but Benjamin was a different man now and his father reluctantly accepted it. Eventually he gave up trying to persuade his son to stay and one morning shortly after dawn Benjamin stood at the threshold of his childhood home, a small pack of clothing on his back, and prepared to leave. He kissed his father and then turned to his sister. Miriam had not uttered a single word since her ordeal and showed no signs that she heard anything either. Her face was a permanent blank mask. But as Benjamin hugged her tightly and kissed her, he saw a single tear roll down her face and, for just a moment, saw recognition in her eyes. "I will avenge you, dear sister," he whispered into Miriam's ear, before squeezing her tightly one more time. And then he walked out into the courtyard, and was gone.

Benjamin immediately made his way to Eleazar's headquarters in the upper city and asked to enlist. Eleazar's quarters were surprisingly cramped for someone whose renown as Judaea's greatest revolutionary leader had been cemented by his recent victory against the Romans and who now had effective military control of his country's ancient capital. They were housed in a storeroom off the lower courtyard of a well-to-do house near the old Hasmonaean Palace, not far from the council chamber of the Sanhedrin, the Jewish religious authority. It appeared that the wealthy owners of the house still occupied the upper two floors, but had given over the lower levels to Eleazar and his retinue.

The place was full of armed men, bustling about the room

shouting at one another, with a constant stream of messengers darting in and out with communications from Jerusalem's various defensive positions and lookout posts. The air was thick with the smell of unwashed bodies and a plethora of sacks and stone jars were stacked against the walls. In the middle of the clamour a man was bent over a small desk, flanked by two earnest-looking men, poring over a map. Eleazar was not at all as Benjamin had imagined him. He had envisioned a roughneck brawler, seasoned by years of guerrilla warfare, but instead he found himself looking at an ascetic-looking man with thinning fair hair, sharp features and a calm, almost tranquil, demeanour. Benjamin put him in his early forties.

He looked up as Benjamin approached and regarded him with a pair of intense blue eyes. Benjamin noticed that they were flecked with brown, like flotsam adrift on a deep sea.

"Can I help you, young man?" His voice was low and musical, again a contrast to Benjamin's expectations.

"I am here to enlist, sir."

Eleazar pulled himself upright and Benjamin realised he was unusually tall. There was a pause while Eleazar and his two companions looked him up and down, then he came around the table and leaned against it, folding his arms. "We are always glad of recruits, lad, but what can you do that we might need?"

For the first time, Benjamin felt a little foolish. He had no military skills and no experience of fighting. "My back is strong, sir, and I am willing to learn. I can read and write, both Aramaic and Greek, and a little Latin. And if you ever have need of it, I can hew stone."

Eleazar smiled and turned to his comrades. "We have an intellectual among us." The men laughed, but not unkindly. He turned back to Benjamin. "What is your name, boy?"

"Benjamin, sir."

"Well, you are welcome, Benjamin. We will certainly find work for you."

"I want to fight, sir. I want to fight the Romans."

"And so you shall, young man. But first we discover your mettle, then we decide how to use it. Now, go, report to Ezra across the courtyard. He will show you the ropes." And he returned to the other side of the table and bent over his map once more, Benjamin forgotten.

Once again Benjamin was surprised when he met Ezra, who was giving instructions to some young men on the other side of the house's lower courtyard. He was barely older than Benjamin himself. But he was shorter, stockier and swarthier, with twinkling brown eyes and a mouth with deeply-etched laughter lines at its edges. His hair was long, down to his shoulders, and Benjamin instantly recognised him as a Galilean.

"And who have we here?" asked Ezra with a grin, dismissing the young men.

"My name's Benjamin. The general sent me to you. I've just enlisted."

"Have you, by God! Well, it's good to have you on board, Benjamin. You're just in time for a late breakfast. I hope you like dried fish and dandelion greens, because that's about all you'll get to eat for the next few weeks. Come on, I'm just about to go and inspect the slingers. You can tag along and then we'll eat."

Ezra led the way out of the house and through a warren of streets to a large lithostroton, an open space with an ornately decorated stone floor just below the walls of Herod's Palace. Herod himself had fled Jerusalem weeks earlier when the Roman garrison in the Antonia Fortress had been overrun, but had left a full contingent of servants and slaves to ensure that the enormous complex was kept immaculate until the king's return. The rebels seemed happy for the moment to leave them to their labours.

According to Jerusalem lore, it was here on this expanse of decorated flooring more than 30 years before that the then

Procurator, Pontius Pilate, had presided over the trial of Jesus of Nazareth, the itinerant preacher who had subsequently been crucified at Golgotha, just outside the city walls.

Set up on the other side of the space against the walls of the palace was a line of straw targets, shaped like men, some arrayed in various bits of Roman uniform, including one or two battered helmets. On this side of the pavement was a line of young men with slingshots, small piles of rocks beside them on the intricately decorated mosaics of the lithostroton. They were furiously slinging their projectiles at the straw targets, with varying degrees of success. Among them were a handful of archers wielding captured Roman bows, the professional composite versions made of laminated horn, wood and sinew that were such deadly long-range weapons in battle.

Just as they stepped into the open space, a rock whistled past Benjamin's left ear and Ezra cried out to the unfortunate young man, a boy, really, whose technique was so poor that the stone had flown out of his sling in precisely the opposite direction to that intended. Calling him over, Ezra boxed his ear and said sternly, "How many more times, Nathaniel! A vertical swing and then step forward as you release!"

The boy looked crestfallen as Ezra took his sling and picked up three smooth stones from the pile on the ground. Dropping the first stone into the leather pocket, he gripped the knotted ends of the woven hemp cords and let the pocket fall to just above the ground. Then with a practised flex of his arm he sent the sling into a wide vertical arc, speeding up until the pocket and stone were just a blur. At the peak of the third revolution he released one of the cords and the stone flew through the air, striking one of the dummy helmets dead-centre and sending it bouncing across the ground. No sooner had the distant clang faded than another projectile was arrowing through the air, followed by third seconds later. In the time that it took Benjamin to take four or five breaths, Ezra had loosed three rounds at the makeshift targets, every one of them finding its mark.

"Now remember, Nathaniel. Step forward!" He tossed the sling back to his unfortunate pupil and then walked on down the line of slingers and archers, giving a word of encouragement here, a gentle admonishment there. It was clear that all the men – none of whom could have been more than twenty-five years old – worshipped him and were desperate to please him, redoubling their efforts as he passed by.

"Can you teach me how to do that?" he asked, somewhat abashed, as they walked on.

"Of course," replied Ezra cheerfully. "You'll be dinging Roman helmets in no time!"

Ezra led the way into a tavern just beyond the south wall of the palace and they settled into a quiet corner with a loaf of fresh bread and plates of the promised dried fish and dandelion greens, washed down with a fine beer, which the innkeeper assured them had been brewed to an ancient Egyptian recipe. As they sat back with full bellies, Ezra told Benjamin how in the last few weeks Eleazar and his Zealots had successfully repulsed two major offensives on Jerusalem by the Romans and their auxiliaries and were now well entrenched in the city, with the widespread support of the peasantry who were doing such a good job of harrying the occupiers beyond the walls of the capital.

"But it's about to get a lot tougher," he explained. "General Gallus is marching on Jerusalem with over 40,000 men and we'll be hard-pressed to resist them. Now that we've taken the Antonia Fortress, we've not only given them a bloody nose, but we've really damaged their pride. They won't let us forget it."

He was right. Over the next three months rumours flew around the city of bandits being rounded up by the Romans in the surrounding countryside. In late October, the inhabitants of the city saw for themselves what was likely to happen if the city were ever overrun. Early one morning, a forest of crosses appeared on the Mount of Olives across the Kidron Valley opposite the Sheep Gate. Benjamin counted over a hundred men silhouetted against the rising sun, hanging from rough-hewn crosses, some breathing their last, some destined to hang there in the hot sun for hours or even days before they finally expired.

Far from invoking the terror in him that the Romans intended, the sight fortified Benjamin. He recognised a building bloodlust that would only be satisfied by a full-on engagement with the hated oppressors. He longed for the day that would happen.

Over the last few weeks he had practised relentlessly with his sling, under Ezra's expert tutelage. They had become fast friends, recognising in one another the same fearlessness born of tragedy. Ezra's father had died fighting the Romans at Akeldama and he was bent on revenge, just as Benjamin was. Benjamin found he had an affinity with the weapon and a natural expertise, learning to load and loose the smooth stones with increasing speed and accuracy. He was even more efficient with the bow, whenever he could persuade one of the archers to lend him one of the sought-after weapons. He thrilled to the sensation of sending the fearsome iron-tipped arrows, now being produced by the thousand in the city's forges, across unheard-of distances to their target. The bows were capable in the right hands of a range of more than two hundred metres, and Benjamin was fast proving to have just the right hands.

By mid-November, when Gallus's troops were camped outside the western walls of the city and preparing for their final assault, Benjamin and Ezra were ready, comrades, bound in common cause, determined to bring death to their enemies wherever they met them.

CHAPTER 42

THAT DAY CAME in early November. It dawned brightly, a cold crisp morning with clear skies and a light wind. Gallus's troops were massed to the west of Jerusalem, facing the Gennath Gate, and as Benjamin and his comrades stood on the city walls and looked across the plain, the army seemed to them to stretch to the horizon and beyond, the morning sun glinting off thousands of shields and helmets. They could hear the low rumble of an army awaking and preparing for battle.

Gallus had chosen to attack from the west for a number of reasons: the northern wall was much easier to defend, with the Antonia Fortress in a commanding position at the north-west corner of the city, while the Dung Gate and Essene Gate to the south were flanked by the Hinnom Valley, which would have made his forces highly vulnerable to attack on their approach. The eastern wall of the city was built along a steep escarpment, with a sheer drop into the Kidron Valley, which ruled that out, too.

Eleazar was walking along the top of the western wall, encouraging his men and checking their deployment. Every metre of the wide walkway seemed to be occupied by men under arms. The Jewish defenders had been strengthened by deserters from the various auxiliary units which had been conscripted by the Roman army and there were also many hundreds of men from the countryside who had sought refuge in the city from the predations of Gallus's forces. But at the heart of this formidable defensive force were Eleazar's battle-hardened Zealots, who had already repulsed the Romans twice from their holy city and prepared to do so for a third time.

Slingers, javelin-throwers and archers lined the ramparts, while those without weapons hefted huge rocks onto the walk-way, ready to be dropped on the Romans when they attempted to put their ladders against the wall. Large cauldrons of pitch were boiling over braziers, which would inflict terrible injuries on the first of the Roman infantry to attempt scaling the ramparts. Benjamin and Ezra stood shoulder to shoulder, their slingshots at the ready. Eleazar finished his rounds and a silence settled over the packed line of defenders. They waited.

They did not have to wait long. As the sun rose higher over the mountains to the east, they heard the cacophony of trumpets from the massed Roman infantry and the front ranks coalesced into a series of testudos, the highly effective close-defensive formation which had served the infantry so well in dozens of campaigns across the empire. With their shields aligned at the front and on top, the men in the testudo were effectively protected from arrows and slingshots, and they moved fast despite the constraints of the formation. It took less than half an hour for the vanguard to reach the walls, advancing as was their custom in complete silence. The defenders had rained down hundreds of arrows, stones and javelins on their heads, most of which bounced harmlessly off the locked shields.

As the ranks of testudos grew in depth, now extending several hundred metres from the wall and reaching along most of its length from the Joppa road to the crest of the Hinnom

Valley, the Romans passed their siege ladders through the massed ranks, beneath their shields, until they reached the men at the base of the wall. At a shouted command, the front rank lifted its shields and with practised speed ran the ladders up the wall. The first of the soldiers immediately began to climb, but all were struck down by a hail of projectiles from above, some with their skulls crushed by rocks, others left screaming from the boiling pitch which had flayed their exposed skin where it was unprotected by armour. The ladders were toppled by the defenders and fell back onto the shields of the second and third ranks of the attackers.

But they regrouped, like the highly trained soldiers they were, and once again approached the wall in tight formation. Once again their ladders were toppled and once again they withdrew. By now the pile of bodies at the bottom of the wall was obstructing their progress, as they had to climb over their fallen comrades and find spaces to lodge the ladders. The assault went on for hours, and the defenders were amazed at the dogged perseverance of their enemies in the face of such terrible losses. There were howls of triumph from the ramparts as the Romans continued to throw themselves against the impenetrable barrier.

The defenders did not have it all their own way. Highly skilled archers standing back from the front line were loosing their arrows at the ramparts in controlled waves and dozens of Jews were taken in the head, throat and chest as they briefly raised themselves above the parapets to launch their own missiles at the attackers below. Still further back from the massed ranks of infantry were the Roman artillery, comprising the giant ballistas which were hurling iron bolts and rocks at the top of the wall. The finely cut masonry with its enormous blocks of interlocking stones had withstood centuries of assaults like this and were more than a match for the missiles, which did little damage, but from time to time they would find their mark on the ramparts and two or three men at a time would be blasted from their positions by the incoming fire.

Benjamin and Ezra were stationed on the section of wall just below the Gennath Gate and it was here that something odd was happening. As the defenders were occupied repelling the ranks of attacking infantry, the approach to the gate was empty and there appeared to be no soldiers on the distant stretches of the road that led from Jerusalem to Joppa. The gate-keepers peered through their arrow slits, but saw nothing. For several hundred metres on both sides of the road, they saw only open ground. It was as if the way were being kept clear for some kind of procession.

The conundrum was answered soon enough. Just after the sun reached its zenith, a few hundred metres from the city wall two cohorts of cavalry, each comprising several hundred horse-men, detached themselves from the body of the army and took up station on either side of the road. Then behind them there appeared what looked like a large house on wheels, which began to trundle down the road toward the gate. As it drew closer, Benjamin realised what it was.

"It's a ram!" he exclaimed to Ezra. "Inside that contraption, see?"

Ezra and the tightly-knit band of fighters all looked on as the machine moved slowly down the road towards them. They could now see a wooden frame inside the wheeled housing, from which was slung a colossal tree trunk with a giant iron wolf's head at its tip. The arrows and slingshots began once again to rain down on the attackers, but they had no effect on the well-protected ram and the horsemen held back just out of range. Behind the ram came several more testudos. Slowly the ram drew closer to the gate.

Eleazar appeared beside them. "Don't worry boys," he said quietly, clapping them both on the shoulders. "While their infantry keeps our men on the wall busy, they will try to take down the gate." He paused. "And they will probably succeed."

Benjamin was astonished and drew a sharp breath. "But the city will be taken!" he exclaimed.

"There are more ways to rid oneself of an infestation of ants than to stamp on them," said Eleazar cryptically. "Be of good cheer. The day is long." And he was gone.

The fearsome contraption had now turned towards the gate, which was set in the side of a massive corner buttress projecting from the wall, and the fire from above intensified. The defenders on the wall to the south were so far unaware of what was happening at the gate. The efforts of the attacking Roman infantry were keeping them busy and there was no abatement of the shouts and screams coming from that direction.

The machine was now pressed against the timber of the gate, which comprised overlapping planks of hard acacia wood from the north of the country, formed into a formidable barrier more than twenty feet tall. There was a commotion in the front rank of the testudo behind the machine and the defenders watched as the men pulled hard on something which appeared to give a strong resistance before letting go. A thunderous crash sounded from below and all the nearby defenders felt the vibration as the enormous ram made its first assault on the gate.

Benjamin could see Eleazar standing some way off, looking down impassively as blow after blow was delivered against the gate. He had no idea how long it could withstand such an onslaught. Minutes went by, the gate shuddering with every strike. Then Benjamin saw Eleazar turn to one of his lieutenants and give him a quiet order, before striding off in the direction of the steps down into the city. A few minutes later there was a howl of triumph from below as the gate appeared to give way and the ram pushed forward, driving the two giant doors apart on their hinges.

The cry of triumph was taken up by the cavalrymen waiting

on either side of the road and with a peal of horns they now converged, as five hundred or more mounted soldiers all bore down at a canter on the now wide open door to the city, followed by a stream of infantrymen with shields raised and swords drawn.

CHAPTER 43

BENJAMIN AND EZRA ran full pelt down the steps into the chaos below. They descended into a narrow street running parallel with the main thoroughfare that led from the gate past the Hasmonaean Palace and on to the viaduct which gave access across the Tyropoean Valley to Temple Mount. They could hear the deafening sound of hundreds of hoofbeats on the ancient stones to their left and caught glimpses of the riders between the houses. They were followed by dozens of their compatriots, who were similarly anxious to find some way of engaging with the invaders.

By now the horsemen had ridden onto the gently sloping approach to the viaduct that led from the upper city to the western entrance of the Temple complex and were pressing on towards the Temple itself. Benjamin and Ezra burst out into a small square just below the double-arched viaduct, looked around desperately for a vantage point and spotted a grand-looking house which boasted three storeys and what looked like a tower projecting from the roof. They dashed through the doorway and ran past the startled occupants, breathlessly demanding access to the roof, which they were immediately granted. They ran up three flights of stairs and emerged onto the roof, from which the tower reached up another two storeys. Crashing though the low door they ran up another four flights and found themselves in a small open area with low walls on each side and a commanding view of the viaduct, which was now almost at the same level.

They were confronted with an extraordinary sight. Along the full length of the viaduct, men were hanging from the side of the structure, a couple of feet apart, slung from leather straps attached to what looked like iron spikes driven into the stone of the parapet. They were all leaning out from the wall of the viaduct, their legs braced against the stonework, with bows and javelins at the ready. As the horsemen mounted the flat stretch of the viaduct, they let loose their weapons and perhaps a hundred arrows and lances found their mark in the flanks of the speeding horses. Benjamin could see that exactly the same hell was being unleashed from the other side of the viaduct.

The sound was horrifying, as two hundred horses fell to their knees, tossing their riders onto the stone surface of the viaduct, crushing them beneath them, or throwing them over the parapet to fall fifty feet to their deaths. Moments later a second volley of projectiles were loosed and a hundred or more horses and men fell. Without their mounts, the cavalrymen milled around in confusion, to be picked off by the archers and javelinmen. They were now joined by slingers at the head of the viaduct and on the high western wall of the Temple, who loosed volley after volley with deadly accuracy into the melee below. Benjamin and Ezra joined in, picking off soldier after soldier with their slings across the fifty or so feet that separated their eyrie from the viaduct.

And then Benjamin saw him. He screamed to Ezra, pointing, "There he is, the bastard who killed my mother!" Drusus was still on his horse towards the rear of the column, wheeling around in tight circles and screaming orders at the confused men. Behind him, several hundred infantrymen were converging on the lower slope of the viaduct, but they too were met with a relentless rain of stones and arrows, this time from behind them as another cohort of defenders appeared on the inside rampart of the wall. As Benjamin and Ezra watched, Drusus's horse was struck in the head by a well-aimed arrow and crumpled to the ground, instant deadweight.

Drusus slipped to the side and sprang to his feet, his sword unsheathed, and began to run along the parapet, hacking at the leather straps from which the Jews were suspended. Several of them were cut loose and fell, thankfully only a few feet at this lower level of the viaduct, but Benjamin could see that many more at higher levels were in greater danger from the decurion, who was wielding his sword like a madman.

Benjamin felt a great calm descend on him. The sounds of battle around him faded and he was conscious of the presence only of himself and this man who had robbed him of his mother and his sister. He took a stone from his pocket, aware of its beautiful smoothness in his hand. Sliding it into the leather pocket of his sling, he started to swing the weapon in a wide arc beside him – once, twice, and on the third revolution he loosed the missile. It flew from his sling in a perfect trajectory, crossing the sixty or seventy feet in less than a second, and struck Drusus square on the side of his helmeted head. He immediately fell from sight.

Benjamin felt a strange ambivalence about what he had done. While he was glad to have taken revenge on the murderer, he was disappointed that he had not had the opportunity to dispatch him at close quarters, face to face and eye to eye. Ezra had only been vaguely aware of the silent duel that had played itself out beside him; he was too busy with his own sling.

The surviving horsemen were now racing back down the causeway, only a handful of them still mounted. The soldiers on foot had also turned tail and were streaming back towards the gate, harried all the way by the slingers and archers on the wall above them and by javelins thrown by other men hiding between the houses that flanked the retreating men. Benjamin estimated that as many as four hundred men had perished in that short hour.

He shouted to Ezra that he would meet him back at their muster point below the wall and headed downstairs at a run. Threading his way between the houses, he made his way to the entrance to the viaduct, which was now empty of the enemy but littered with Roman dead and injured, and ran up the slope. He jogged to the place where he had brought Drusus down and looked for his body. But there was no body. He spotted a helmet lying nearby and picked it up. It was emblazoned on two sides with the crest of a decurion and in the very centre of the left-hand crest was a deep depression. His missile had found its target, but failed in its objective. Drusus had escaped.

———

As the sun began its slow descent to the west, Benjamin and Ezra were reunited at their muster point. Ezra eventually asked what had happened to Drusus and a subdued Benjamin told him. His deep disappointment at being thwarted in his revenge had plunged him into a depression, which Ezra did his best to drag him out of. "I have a feeling we'll meet him again, Benjamin. Be patient." But Benjamin was not to be soothed. He soon slunk off by himself to stew in his own misery.

Eleazar was clapping everyone on the back and congratulating his Zealots on another small victory in the war against the reviled occupiers. It transpired that the Gennath Gate had not yielded after all, but at a judicious juncture the bolts holding the great locking bar had been withdrawn and the gates simply fell open, just as Eleazar had planned.

Furthermore, just as Gallus's cavalry and infantry were pouring into the city, a thousand or more rebels emerged from the countryside and attacked the Roman flanks, surprising them before they had a chance to deploy their skirmishers. After picking off several hundred more of Gallus's army, they melted back into the hills and valleys, pursued half-heartedly by a handful of auxiliaries, who were quickly dispatched by the departing Jews.

General Cestius Gallus had just suffered his first defeat of the war.

CHAPTER 44

THE GREAT SANHEDRIN, the rabbinical body that administered the law in Jerusalem, met as usual the following day in the Hall of Hewn Stones, built into the north wall of the Temple. But this was no ordinary day and no routine gathering. The president and chief of the court sat on elegantly decorated chairs on a raised dais in the chamber, which resembled a modern-day basilica, light and airy with entrances both to the Sanctuary and to the outside courts. The sixty-nine general members sat before them ranked in a half-circle, whispering to one another as they waited for the president to open the proceedings.

The president stood and silence fell on the room. He looked down for a moment, as if collecting his thoughts, and the chief of the court laid a reassuring hand on his arm, as if to give him courage to speak the words he was about to utter.

"My brothers," began the president. Then, more quietly, "My friends." Those nearest to him could see that his eyes were shining, on the brink of tears. They had never seen him like this before. "We were fortunate yesterday. Our fine young men fought bravely and Yahweh delivered a great victory to us." There was a general murmur of agreement and nods around the chamber. "But we cannot deceive ourselves into thinking that the Romans will simply give up and go home." The silence seemed to thicken, every member of the Sanhedrin listening intently, beginning to understand that something momentous was about to happen.

"It is true that they have withdrawn for the time being. But they will return. We will resist and our young men will once again repulse them. Yahweh may well give us more victories." Heads nodded once more. "But make no mistake, my brothers. Eventually, Jerusalem will fall."

A simultaneous sharp intake of sixty-nine breaths was followed by a rising babble of shocked voices. The president raised his hand and the noise gradually abated. The sense of shock in the room remained palpable.

"It is time to consider how best to protect the Temple possessions. We cannot allow the treasures of Yahweh to fall into the hands of the Romans." Every eye was now locked on the president's face. "I have consulted the high priest and his officials and they agree. We must take steps to remove the treasures from Jerusalem."

The Sanhedrin rose as one to their feet, completely taken aback. What the president was suggesting was unconscionable. The Temple treasures had always resided in the Sanctuary, ever since Nehemiah had rebuilt the Temple half a millennium ago. The thought of removing them and denuding the holy of holies of the ornaments which were so intrinsic to the nation's worship of Yahweh was beyond any of their wildest imaginings.

Once again the president raised his hands and slowly, one by one, the members took their seats again. He turned to the chief of the court and whispered something to him, at which the chief turned and beckoned to an elderly man who had been standing in the shadows behind his chair, unnoticed until now. The man stepped forward and bowed to the president before turning to face the congregation.

"This is Eli," said the president. "He is the most experienced – and expert – of all the scribes in Jerusalem." The old man stood with head bowed, clearly awed by his surroundings. "We have tasked him with producing an inventory of every treasure in the Temple. Every chalice, every vestment, every jewel, every vessel of gold and silver, talent by talent. Every item will be accounted for, itemised and noted by Eli. Then, when the time comes," he paused, his breath catching in his throat, "they will be taken from the city and secreted until such time as they can be returned to the Sanctuary.

"His work begins today."

CHAPTER 45

NO ONE COULD RELIABLY EXPLAIN why Gallus chose to withdraw his army from Jerusalem. The more optimistic residents suggested that he had been so comprehensively beaten that Rome would give up its claim on their holy land, embark once more on their cursed ships and sail home. The millenialists argued that Yahweh had intervened, as they always knew he would, and that the defeat signalled the coming of the End, as the Hebrew scriptures had prophesied. The more pragmatic among them, including the Zealots, recognised a tactical withdrawal when they saw one.

The fact was that Jerusalem was a ferociously difficult city to take. Its strategic position bounded on three sides by valleys and by a massive fortress to the north, made encirclement impossible. The walls were many feet thick and superbly built by ancient masons, designed to withstand any siege engine so far known to man. The gates were relatively small, ensuring that attackers, even if they gained entry, would find themselves bottlenecked and vulnerable. And, as the previous day had demonstrated, once inside the city, a conventional army was in a weak position, unable to deploy effectively in the narrow streets.

Above all, there was the Temple Mount, the perfect

redoubt, where the rebels and citizens could withdraw and hold out for weeks if necessary, with relative impunity – a formidable, easily defended fortress at the heart of the walled city.

Whatever his reasons, Gallus's army was preparing to leave. Benjamin and Ezra had seen from their lookout on the wall that camps were being struck, the baggage train was being packed up and the cavalry were being brought to order, riding up and down the slowly forming column that everyone now thought would turn and head west towards the Mediterranean.

"Gallus will wait for reinforcements," proffered Eleazar the morning after the victory. "He needs to keep the countryside under control."

He stood before his most trusted lieutenants as they break-fasted, the greater mass of men around them listening carefully, and spoke in his quiet, considered voice, explaining from experience what he understood to be happening. "We know that the Romans believe the only way to deal with resistance is to strike hard and strike fast, with no mercy. That is what Gallus hoped to do yesterday. He failed." A small cheer went up. "But mainly because his flanks were vulnerable to our brothers in the hills. He needs a bigger force to contain them and prevent them from harrying his men while they plan a more effective assault on the city.

"Which is why we need to follow them."

This was met by dozens of gasps. "But why can't we leave it to our countrymen to give them a bloody nose on their way to the sea?" asked one of Eleazar's men, puzzled. Benjamin and Ezra, who were far back on the edge of the group, strained to hear his worlds

"Because we are going to apply the lesson we have learnt from the Romans," replied Eleazar in a louder voice. "We are going to give them no relief. We are going to hit them and hit them again. Our comrades in the country are brave and well-intentioned, but they are farmers with scythes and pitchforks, not trained men. It is we, the Zealots, who can mobilise and lead them most effectively." There was a murmur of general agreement.

"I will shortly send scouts to the militia leaders in the hills, to ensure they are well prepared for an engagement with the enemy. We will then leave a small contingent in the city and tonight, under cover of darkness, our main force will leave by the Damascus Gate and travel north and west, to get ahead of the Roman column, which will be moving more slowly than Gallus would like with so many men and so much heavy equipment. God will help us find the right place to meet them and when the moment is right we will descend on them like the locusts in the scriptures and devour them." The men cheered again.

"Now go, ready yourselves. Ensure you are well armed, but do so while preparing to travel light. We have a hard few days ahead of us." Eleazar nodded to his adjutant, who began barking orders to the men, and walked slowly back to his quarters.

Benjamin and Ezra had had little rest since the previous day's engagement, so returned to their billet and slept for a few hours before heading to the bazaar to replenish their food supplies. Then, with their packs readied and slings checked, but no swords or arrowheads to sharpen and little else to do, they retired to a tavern and sat quietly in a corner, surrounded by other Zealots who were similarly engaged in muted conversation with their comrades as the sun began to set and Eleazar's men all over the city pondered what the coming days would bring.

The two young men were deep in conversation, so Benjamin didn't at first notice the young woman who brought their wine. As he became conscious of the limestone cups being placed before them, he looked up and straight into the eyes of the most beautiful girl he had ever seen. She did not turn away, but returned his gaze frankly and directly. Her eyes were a deep sea-green, unusual for a Jewish girl in Judaea, set above a small, delicate nose in a heart-shaped face with a honeyed complexion that seemed to glow with an inner luminescence in the lamp-light. Her mouth was full and sensual and a mischievous smile played on her lips.

"Can I get you boys anything else?" she asked, her eyes still on Benjamin, who was entranced. She spoke with the unmistakeable lilt of an Idumaean, the land to the south of Judaea where Herod the Great himself had been born. When her question elicited no response, she nodded familiarly to Ezra and turned to go.

"Bread," spluttered Benjamin. "Um – a loaf of bread if you please." She turned back and regarded him with her head cocked and her smile a little more pronounced. Benjamin noticed now how slim and diminutive she was, fully a head shorter than himself, he guessed. She wore a simple blue woollen dress, embroidered at the neck, with a dark green shawl that set off her eyes, and a white headscarf that only served to accentuate the lustrous mane of dark hair beneath it.

"Bread," she repeated. "Yes, sir." And she turned once again and walked into the back room of the tavern.

Ezra poked Benjamin in the ribs. "Takes your fancy, does she?" he asked with a salacious grin.

Benjamin was still looking at the door she'd passed through. "She's gorgeous," he replied, a touch of awe in his voice.

"Her name's Rachel. Her father owns the tavern," said Ezra. Benjamin turned to him in surprise. "How do you know that?"

"Her father and my father were friends before he died. This was the first tavern he brought me to as a boy. I've known Rachel since she was a girl."

At this point Rachel returned with the loaf and placed it on the table before them. For no reason he could explain, Benjamin immediately stood up and, catching the edge of the table with his leg, sent the cups and bread flying. He watched in horror as a liberal quantity of deep red wine ran down the front of her dress. She looked down at the mess and the smile on her face vanished, replaced with a sharp gaze. "I'll wager you're not that clumsy with your sling," she said hotly. Then turned on her heel and was gone.

At that moment the door flew open and one of Eleazar's lieutenants stalked in. "Time to go, lads," he shouted, and stood by the door as the men in the room gathered their belongings and began to leave. Ezra picked up his pack and made to follow them, but Benjamin put a hand on his arm. "Wait," he said, and hurried to the door of the back room. Rachel was poised to wipe down her dress with water from a stone pitcher. He blundered between the storage jars and chalk vessels which littered the floor and stood before her.

"Benjamin," he said breathlessly. "My name's Benjamin."

"And I'm hardly likely to forget *you*, am I? she replied, the ghost of a smile returning to her lips.

"I'll come back and I'll buy you a new dress," he blustered. "A better one." Did I really just say that, he thought? Her eyebrows arched and her eyes began to sparkle.

"I have other dresses," she said. "But I have very little jewellery." Benjamin's face fell and she laughed. "Just come back sometime and finish your wine. It's on the house."

The raised voice of the man next door called for the last stragglers to leave. Benjamin bowed his head and smiled at her. "Rachel," he said. "What a beautiful name." They looked at one another for a few seconds longer and something passed between them. An instant intimacy.

Then Benjamin turned and walked quickly back into the tavern, rejoined his friend and they left without another word. Rachel looked after him, her brow furrowed. It's as if I've known him all my life, she thought. And set about cleaning her dress.

Benjamin and Ezra were assigned to a band of sixty or so Zealots who were ordered by Eleazar to travel fast through the night and link up with a militia commander in the hills above Gibeon, about 30 kilometres from Jerusalem. They were to combine forces and harry the right flank of the retreating Roman army while moving north-west towards Joppa. Eleazar would send word of the place he would muster his full complement of 2,500 men, where they were instructed to rejoin him.

Benjamin remembered little of that night. They travelled fast on roads, tracks and sheep trails, threading their way north through the foothills of the Judaean mountains, their way lit by a bright moon, their breath clouding the cold November night air as they alternately walked and jogged through the countryside. They occasionally encountered other men, emerging from villages or camped beside the road, calling out encouragement to one another as they passed by. As dawn was breaking, they rendezvoused with a large group of rebels who were milling around a cluster of stone houses in a hollow below a low line of hills.

They were led by a giant of a man with a great bushy beard, who introduced himself as Joshua. "I was named after the conqueror who won this land for us," he told the leader of the band. "We have lost it again and again. But this time I will be the man who wins it back!" He laughed, a great rumbling belly laugh, with his hands on his hips and his shoulders shaking. "Now come, rest. Tonight we will show the bastard Romans how we Jews fight. And we fight dirty!" He laughed again and then led them to one of the larger houses, where they found food and water prepared for them. They crammed into the small space, ate and rested.

As the sun was setting, they heard Joshua's booming voice

cry out, "It is time, my friends! Come, let us go and skewer some Romans!"

Benjamin and Ezra found themselves among a group of perhaps two hundred men, variously armed with slings, swords, javelins and stolen bows, moving quickly over the flat ground towards the Joppa road, spurred on by Joshua who, despite his bulk, set a relentless pace. After about an hour, they became aware of a low murmur in the distance and shortly afterwards saw a glow low on the horizon, at which point Joshua called back for the group to remain silent for the rest of their approach. Another half an hour or so later, they crested a shallow rise and saw below them the Roman column, lumbering north-west along the paved road. Unusually, they encountered no skirmishers.

"They're like a big fat calf just waiting to be slaughtered," observed Ezra in an excited whisper as they surveyed the column. Gallus had clearly decided to abandon the Romans' standard marching formation, which would have left his column strung out over many miles and highly vulnerable to attack. Benjamin later learned that the previous night Gallus had camped on Mount Scopus, a mile or so from Jerusalem, only to be assaulted in a rearguard action by hordes of Jewish rebels and deserters from Herod's army, so he had evidently decided that for the rest of the retreat it would be safer to adopt a shorter, wider squared-column formation which would enable each unit to quickly wheel into a battle line when attacked. This had the added benefit that the baggage train, with its slow-moving ox-carts and pack animals carrying the army's heavy equipment, would be better protected within its own squares.

The problem for Gallus was that this formation made progress very slow. Instead of his troops being confined to the well-surfaced Roman highway, they were now spread out on either side of the road, meaning that the men marching along it, burdened by more than fifty kilos of equipment, were continually having to halt and wait for those of their comrades who were travelling more slowly on the rough ground on either side. The lack of Roman skirmishers was partly explained by this: Gallus was opting for security over speed, which meant keeping all his men as far as possible within the safer confines of his column.

Joshua had clearly spotted the opportunity this presented. They watched as Gallus's tribunes and centurions moved ceaselessly up and down the column, chivvying their men to keep up the pace. Joshua passed the word that his force should descend slowly down the slope and on his command let fly with slings, arrows and javelins at the exposed outliers of the column, giving the Romans as little time as possible to close ranks and wheel towards them. They were aided by a cloudless night and the many swinging lamps and lanterns that the Romans were using to light their way.

Benjamin felt the excitement build in his chest as they crept down the shallow incline towards the road, any sound from their advance muffled by the noise of the marching column. When they were a hundred or so metres from the nearest soldiers, Joshua sounded his horn, a clear bright sound in the crisp night air. Instantly the band let loose a blizzard of stones, rocks, javelins and arrows. Benjamin's sling looped and whirled, spinning as many as five stones a minute at the vulnerable men below. In response the Romans moved quickly into battle formation, but they were hampered by the rough ground and Benjamin saw many of them stumble as they tried to keep their footing.

Joshua knew that he would not be able to maintain the momentum of the attack for long. His men would be no match in close combat for the highly trained and disciplined Romans. So after a few minutes his horn sounded again and they withdrew, scampering back up the slope and melting into the folds of the land, before regrouping and moving quickly along the road to harry another section of the column. The Romans could not pursue them far for fear of being cut off from the main column, which gave the advantage to the attackers, who attacked again and again, until they saw a large cohort of horsemen galloping up the flank of the column towards them, which signalled the moment to call off the attack and retire.

Benjamin had seen many Romans fall, most of them injured but not dead. Broken limbs and hands, copiously bleeding head-wounds, blinded eyes and deep cuts to exposed flesh were even more debilitating to a retreating army than those who were killed. Bodies could be discarded by the roadside for the vultures and wild beasts to prey on, but a wounded man slowed his comrades down and threatened their own safety. In most cases the injured were simply left behind to fend for themselves and the rebels made short work of them with their knives and swords.

Benjamin felt elated at the success of their first encounter with the hated occupiers. He had tried to spot Drusus among the approaching cavalrymen, who had pursued them a little way into the countryside before withdrawing under a hail of stones, but had not seen him in the confusion and the darkness. But he knew that they would meet again.

They arrived back at their camp as the sun was rising and a messenger from Eleazar was already waiting. The following morning they were to travel to Beth-Horon, fifteen kilometres to the west, and join his main force there, where their first direct engagement with the Romans was planned. The messenger told them that Gallus's army had been dealt a series of heavy blows by the Jews over the previous day; their scouts reported that a tribune, a cavalry leader and even the commander of the Sixth Legion himself had been killed during a series of skirmishes and the demoralised Romans were presently seeking refuge at their fortified camp in Gibeon, where Eleazar expected them to remain for a day or two while they regrouped before the next stage of their retreat towards the coast.

Benjamin and Ezra, tired from the night's exertions, were glad of the chance to rest and they dropped to the earthen floor of their stone house, their packs beneath their heads and their cloaks wrapped tight around them, and immediately fell asleep.

The camp was bustling with life when they re-emerged. Fires were lit and cooking pots were steaming in the cold air. The mood was cheerful, with a palpable sense of anticipation and excitement. Men wandered from group to group, bantering with one another, telling ribald jokes and trying to outdo one another with their bravado in the face of the coming engagement with their adversaries. Benjamin and Ezra sat with a Galilean javelin unit who were ribbing two Herodian deserters busy polishing their bows.

"Bet you never expected to be roughing it with the likes of us!" laughed one of the Galileans. "Must be a bit different from those feather beds you were used to in the palace." The two soldiers growled a muted response. "Come on, boys, tell us what it was like. Must have been roast mutton and beer every night, with a couple of those minxy Palace servants thrown in for good measure. Eh? Eh?" And he poked his javelin across the cooking fire at one of the deserters. Faster than any of them could have imagined, the soldier had drawn his bow, nocked an arrow and planted it between the Galilean's legs. After a second or two of shocked silence, the group erupted in laughter. "That was close, Ishmael! If your balls weren't the size of sheep's pellets, you'd be singing higher than an Egyptian eunuch!"

As night fell, Joshua's force, which had now swollen to around 250 men, embarked on a raucous chorus of traditional tavern songs, their throats lubricated with beer captured from the Roman baggage train. Much later when the camp quietened, as the ale took its toll and each man contemplated what faced them in the coming days, a lone voice struck up in the darkness beyond the fires – a young Judaean, barely out of childhood, embarked in a high, clear voice on one of King David's best-known psalms, a traditional battle hymn sung before joining with the enemy. The full company of men now took up a full-throated refrain.

The psalm ended with the resounding stamping of feet around the camp. And so every man was left to his own thoughts as the fires burned lower and the moon re-emerged to bathe the company in its haunted light.

CHAPTER 46

THE FOLLOWING morning dawned cold and wet. During the night the heavens had opened and deluged the land, creating runoff from the hills which left the camp laced with small streams and dotted with puddles. It was a rather less enthusiastic band of men who emerged from their sleeping quarters to find their camp fires extinguished and facing the prospect of a desultory breakfast of bread, olives and figs. They huddled together in their cloaks, their breath steaming. There was little conversation.

The rain intensified as Joshua mustered them for departure. It was a sorry and bedraggled group that emerged from the hollow and made its way slowly across the undulating countryside towards Beth-Horon. "I can't feel my feet and there's more water inside my cloak than outside it," grumbled Ezra. "At least the Romans are suffering the same as we are," answered Benjamin with an effort at a smile. "And they have to worry about a lance in the belly as well as their breakfast."

Ezra grunted.

The rain persisted as they quickened their pace, leaping across newly-seeded streams which rushed through the natural gulleys and defiles, their sandals slipping on the wet grass as they struggled up the steeper slopes. At around noon the rain abruptly stopped and the clouds parted, revealing a watery sun and before them a landscape of high hills and deep valleys. For the first time that day they could hear birdsong, punctuated by the distinctive hoot of a hoopoe somewhere in the undergrowth. Joshua called a halt and they rested, glad of the respite from the rain. After a while their cloaks began to steam and their spirits to lift. As they gathered themselves to leave once more, they even managed a marching song or two.

They arrived at their destination early in the afternoon. And what a sight met them. Beth-Horon was a steep-sided pass through which the main road from Jerusalem to Joppa snaked, reaching a height of more than 2,000 feet before dropping down into the open land that stretched from the Judaean mountains to the coast. It was the final challenging piece of terrain that the Romans had to negotiate before they could accelerate their march to Joppa across the flat agricultural plain of Aijalon. Benjamin could see immediately why Eleazar had chosen this place for his coordinated assault on the retreating enemy. His comrades told him that King Saul himself had won a great victory against the Philistines here, as had Joshua against the Amorites many years later.

Eleazar had deployed his 2,500 men along both sides of the pass between the twin villages of Upper and Lower Beth-Horon. The archers were ranged along the top of the ridge, with his slingers and javelinmen below them. He had also assigned skirmishers, who Benjamin watched as they picked their way down the steep slopes of the pass, scouting the best and easiest routes for their ascent and descent.

There was a boisterous atmosphere as Joshua led his men to the upper village where the headman's house had been requisitioned as Eleazar's quarters. Benjamin watched as slingers and javelinmen practised their aim against makeshift targets and he heard the unmistakeable clang of swords from the distance, almost certainly more Herodian army deserters. Everywhere he looked men were sharpening blades and spear tips, foraging for stones for their slings, or restretching leather over the woven frames of their shields.

Eleazar and Joshua conferred for a time and then Joshua re-emerged to pass on the commander's orders. A hundred of the company were to deploy to the other side of the pass to join the slingers and javelinmen there, another hundred to the same roles on this side of the ridge. Finally, Joshua asked for volunteers to descend below the main force, to the head of the pass, to block the road ahead of the advancing Romans. Only the most determined and courageous of the Jews chose to raise their hands for this most dangerous of missions. Benjamin and Ezra were among them.

As the two young men and their group of fifty or so rebels picked their way along the ridge and then down into the throat of the pass, one of them murmured that it was like descending into hell. And it was true that, as the sunlight was blocked by the steep walls of the pass and they moved into deepening shadow, it felt as if they were being swallowed by the bowels of the earth itself. Arriving at the head of the pass where it began to slope more gently down to the plain, they encountered another similar-sized company of men who had already made camp for the night. It was a very different atmosphere from the previous evening: tempers were short and conversation muted. Everyone sensed that there would be no hit-and-run harrying of the Roman flanks tomorrow. They would be in the thick of the fight, at close quarters, challenging head-on the most powerful army the world had ever seen.

Benjamin and Ezra bedded down beside their campfire and tried to sleep, but sleep wouldn't come. Eventually they rose and offered to relieve the two sentries who had taken the first of the night watches and who were only too glad of the opportunity for an extra few hours' rest. "I hope he's here tomorrow," whispered Benjamin. Ezra didn't have to ask who 'he' was. "I pray that God will bring him to me and that I can watch his face when I kill him."

"The time will come," replied Ezra cautiously. He knew he could not offer his friend the encouragement he wanted. Not only were the odds against the two men ever coming up against one another again, but even if they did they would be ill-matched and Benjamin would almost certainly be the loser, for all his courage and determination. They fell into an uneasy silence, which was broken only by the snoring of their companions and the occasional cry of an oryx in the distant hills. The wind was soughing gently through the pass and they wrapped their cloaks more tightly around them as the night deepened and it grew colder. When the next watch came to relieve them, they demurred and remained at their post until the sky began to brighten above the ridge, once again sharpening the shadows in the pass and reinforcing the sense of foreboding among the men, who breakfasted quietly before checking their weapons and shields for the hundredth time.

The morning dragged on with no sign of the Roman army. Benjamin wondered if they had decided to remain in the safe haven of their camp at Gibeon, but then dismissed the thought. Gallus would not want to be trapped there with 30,000 men, limited supplies and no prospect of immediate relief. He would continue with his retreat to the coast, where reinforcements would land and bolster his forces in preparation for a more concerted attack on Jerusalem.

Finally, as morning was giving way to afternoon, a runner arrived from Eleazar with news that the Romans were approaching Upper Beth-Horon and would be in the pass within the hour. Benjamin clapped his friend on the back and said, "Care to make a bet on our tally today?" Ezra laughed. "After your dismal performance at the viaduct? It would be

cruel to take your money!" Benjamin punched him affectionately on the shoulder. "We'll see!"

The two men hoisted their packs, checked their slings and
made their way to the main body of the company, which was
deploying across the pass, slingers and archers behind the
swordsmen and a small group of intense-looking Sicarii walking
back and forth ahead of the line. A hundred or so metres in
front of them was a line of wickedly sharp stakes which had
been driven into the ground facing the direction of the enemy,
just before a bend in the pass.

They heard it before they saw it. The cacophony of battle,
amplified and echoing down the pass. The clash of metal, the
cries of men, the stamping of thousands of feet and hooves.
Benjamin understood that the Romans would no longer have
been able to hold their squared columns, but would now be
bunched together more closely in Beth-Horon's narrow confines
and would undoubtedly be trying to rush forward to escape into
open country as quickly as possible. The hail of missiles from
above must have been terrifying. Even his hatred of the occupying enemy could not prevent Benjamin from feeling a pang of
sympathy for the brave infantrymen who were simply following
the orders of their officers in a strange faraway land where none
of them wanted to be, fighting people they didn't understand,
and no doubt by now dying in droves from the momentous
onslaught being visited upon them.

Benjamin and his fellow fighters did not have long to wait
before the battle came to them. A growing tumult sounded from
around the bend in the pass and the ground seemed to shake
with its approach. Moments later two full cavalry troops of sixty
men and horses thundered into view, careering around the bend
at the gallop. They did not see the stakes until it was too late and
the front rank ran full onto the sharp points, the horses speared
in the chest and their riders flung over their necks. Aspirated
blood flew in clouds from the doomed animals, which had

pitched forward and onto their sides with the vicious stakes still embedded in their chests. The second rank did not fare much better, the horses rearing in terror as their fellow animals lay screaming in pain. Within seconds there was carnage and chaos as the surviving horses wheeled in panic, some racing back the way they had come

Which was when Benjamin and his fellow slingers let fly. Although the soldiers were protected by the armour hinged and laced around their chests and over their shoulders, their necks were unprotected, but for a woollen cloth to stop the armour chafing, as were their faces in their open iron helmets and their legs, which were bare but for the leather straps running from their sandals the length of their lower legs.

This left plenty for Benjamin and his companions to aim for. As the dismounted cavalrymen tried to recover, they were hit by a volley of stones. Some were taken between chest and chin, the sharp missiles opening their throats and leaving them writhing in agony as their arterial blood sprayed from their necks. Others took rocks full to the face, smashing cheeks, noses and eye sockets. Some were struck in the shin, with enough force to break the bone and leave them defenceless on the ground.

Their job done for the moment, the slingers withdrew and the javelinmen ran forward, launching their two-metre lances thirty metres or more at the remaining horses, bringing them down by the dozen. With their foes weakened by the suddenness and lethality of this initial assault, the rebels ran forward with a howl of triumph and set about finishing off the surviving soldiers, most of them auxiliaries once again from the eastern realms of the empire. Their bloodlust left no room for mercy. Men were stabbed and hacked at, javelins were retrieved and thrust into unprotected groins and faces. Bellies were torn open and loops of entrails freed to flop out on the ground.

Everywhere Benjamin looked there were dead and dying,

the groans and screams of men mixed with the bellowing of terrified animals. The smell too was horrific, sweat and urine laced with blood and faeces from the opened bowels of men and horses. None of which halted the rebels, who hacked their way through the downed men in a frenzy. As they dispatched the last of the cavalrymen, they raised their arms in victory, waving their javelins, knives and slings above their heads.

They should not have celebrated so soon.

As they were collecting the weapons of the dead soldiers, they heard the cries of an enraged body of men and turned to face the massed infantry of the front ranks of the Roman column, bearing down on them with swords raised. It was the rebels' turn to collapse into disarray. They tried frantically to retreat down the valley in order to regroup, but the swiftly advancing Romans gave them no chance. They were further hampered by the mass of bodies of men and animals, over which they had to stumble as they ran.

The Romans came on at a relentless pace, ordered, disciplined and determined. The stragglers in Benjamin's band were quickly struck down by the fearsome gladii of the soldiers, their heads separated from their bodies in many instances. Their enemy then formed into a square, their shields raised protectively before and above them, ready to drive forward through the Jewish company and cut it to ribbons. Benjamin and the other slingers were hurling missiles at the square, but they were bouncing harmlessly off the metal carapace. And Benjamin watched in horror as rank after rank of Roman infantrymen rounded the bend in the pass behind them.

They were pushed back further and further down the pass and now the Romans could smell victory. They could see the plains below them and only this ragtag army of Jewish vagabonds stood between them and a swift march to the sea over open ground. A few brave Sicarii broke from the retreating band and darted forward with their razor-sharp knives to hack at the tendons of the Romans beneath their shields, which in places succeeded in fragmenting a square – but not for long. This was what the imperial army was trained for and they came on remorselessly.

As the square overtook the first members of the main rebel body, they took their revenge with grim determination, battering through the throng, hammering their shields into their adversaries' bodies and thrusting beneath them to disembowel and castrate. Benjamin had become separated from Ezra and saw him frantically warding off blows from a giant of a centurion with his plundered shield. Falling backwards, he tried to scramble away from the advancing Roman, who raised his sword for the killing blow. Benjamin's missile struck him cleanly between the eyes with the same shot that David had used a millennium before to take down Goliath and the centurion dropped like a stone to the ground. Ezra jumped to his feet, turned, saw Benjamin and waved a thank-you before plunging back into the melee.

It was obvious, despite their bravery, that the Jews would be overrun. The Romans were just too well trained and disciplined. More rebels were falling under their swords and lances. Perhaps thirty of their number had already been killed or maimed and Benjamin knew that this was now a fight to the death. He ran forward to join Ezra in his doomed onslaught, but was pushed back. The last he saw of his friend, he was overrun by another square and disappeared beneath their sandaled feet.

Further and further back they were pushed, with the Romans now unquestionably in the ascendant and more and more infantry pouring into the shoulder of the pass behind the front ranks. It was over.

And then Benjamin heard a cry of surprise behind him, then another and another. He turned around and saw an extraordinary sight. Rebel after rebel was backing down the pass and then disappearing. One moment they were there, the next they were gone. One by one they vanished from view. Benjamin ran towards the retreating band and became aware of a pungent smell emanating from where his companions had disappeared. He slowed to a cautious trot and was confronted by a broad ditch, perhaps three metres wide and with a depth twice the height of a man. At the bottom he saw a tangle of bushes, brush and wood, stained dark with pitch, which he recognised from the smell, a derivative of tree resin. The six men who had fallen into the ditch were clambering over the branches and up the shallower sides to the steep walls of the pass.

From further down the canyon came shouts in Benjamin's native Aramaic and as he watched in astonishment he saw a horde of rebels emerge from the rocks and gullies on either side of the road and come running up the hill. At the same time, he heard voices above him and saw outlined against the sky more rebels, standing on either side of the pass with arms raised in salute.

Eleazar evidently had one more trick up his sleeve.

Benjamin and his companions scrambled up the sides of the pass and around the ditch. As soon as they were clear a group of the new arrivals ran forward with flaming torches and tossed them into the ditch, which immediately burst into flame with a roar.

The fire leapt several feet into the air above the ditch and the men had to pull back sharply to avoid being burnt. Seeing what was happening, the Roman advance had slowed and there was evident confusion in their ranks about what to do next. But as they paused, the rebels on the high ground above the pass let loose a lethal volley of rocks, stones, javelins and arrows. Despite their armour and shields, the Romans were in such disarray that dozens of them immediately succumbed to the onslaught.

Some tried to climb around the edges of the flaming ditch, but were immediately cut down by slingshots, arrows, or – in some cases – by Sicarii who rushed forward to dispatch them as they scrambled in ones or twos over the rocks. Meanwhile in the throat of the pass it was mayhem. Unable to move forward, the Romans in the vanguard were bunching up, pressed from behind by their fellow soldiers who continued to march around the bend in the pass. As they were pushed relentlessly forward, some fell screaming into the fiery ditch. And it was at this point that Eleazar launched his most deadly attack. Along the heights of the pass, on both sides stretching for as far as Benjamin could see, appeared men armed with bows plundered from the Romans and their auxiliaries, ready-strung with flame-tipped arrows. An awestruck silence fell over the pass as the rebels looked down upon their helpless foes and the Romans, who immediately understood what was about to happen, stopped milling about and were still. It was as if time had stopped. Acrid smoke from the arrows drifted down into the pass and as one the archers lifted their bows high into the air, their arrows pointing at the sky, before lowering them to point directly at the floor of the pass. Then, with a single blow of Eleazar's horn, they let their arrows fly.

There must have been a thousand flaming darts loosed in a series of waves along a length of many hundreds of metres in the first minute of the attack. From the high sides of the pass Benjamin and his companions watched in horrified wonder as the arrows found their marks along the Roman column. They thudded into shields, immediately setting them ablaze. They struck heads and necks, arms and legs, and as they landed the flaming resin ran freely across faces and limbs. The very ground seemed to catch fire. The Romans were screaming in pain, some writhing in agony on the ground, some running around in circles trying to pat out the flames on their bodies. Others, unable to go back against the press of bodies, tried to leap over the ditch and disappeared into the flames.

The slaughter continued unabated for several minutes, with

volley after volley of arrows fired, until finally the officers in the rear somehow managed to pull their troops back up the pass. Gradually, the deadly stretch of the narrow defile emptied as the Romans withdrew, leaving hundreds dead and dying on the killing ground. Even the rebel archers seemed overcome with the sheer horror of what they had accomplished. As the Romans retreated, they lowered their bows and stood silently watching their enemy withdraw. Some even saluted with their weapons, in recognition of the bravery of their foes. Then Eleazar's horn sounded once again and the entire rebel force withdrew from the high ground and melted back into the countryside.

CHAPTER 47

IT TOOK the Romans some time to regroup and pull back to the village of Upper Beth-Horon, but as darkness fell they posted sentries, sent skirmishers out into the hills and the body of the army rested, badly bruised from their encounter with the rebels, coming as it did on the back of several days of retreat under heavy daily attack. Fires were lit, food was cooked and army surgeons began the grim work of tending to the hundreds of wounded. In the numerous valetudinariums, the Romans' tented field hospitals, men howled as bodies were roughly bandaged and limbs were amputated with crude saws and no anaesthetic other than copious draughts of wine.

For their part, the rebels had withdrawn to a camp some miles from Beth-Horon and were celebrating their victory. Benjamin was still in a state of shock from what he had witnessed, and he was not alone. Many of his companions were similarly afflicted by the scale of the slaughter they had witnessed. As a result, the victory celebrations were more muted than they might otherwise have been. Furthermore, Benjamin was deeply saddened by the loss of his friend, along-side whom he had trained and fought for many months.

Both sides of the conflict were exhausted and Benjamin

sensed a need for his companions to pause their campaign. Eleazar seemed prepared to permit this, believing as he did that after the punishment they had been dealt, the Romans would remain camped at Beth-Horon for a day or two before attempting once again to move through the pass to the coastal plain.

This was one of the rare occasions on which Eleazar was wrong.

That night, under the cover of a moonless darkness, Gallus ordered 400 of his men to take up position on the roofs of the village and periodically call out the watchwords of the camp sentries, to give the impression to any watchers that the whole army was there. Meanwhile, in the early hours of the morning his entire army marched in complete silence out of the village and back along the road through the pass. Timbers were laid across the ditch and the Romans picked up speed as they cleared the canyon and entered the open ground beyond. They covered three and a half miles without a sound and by dawn were marching in battle order at great speed across the Sharon Plain towards the coast.

When the Jews discovered the Romans' escape, they fell upon the unfortunate defenders of Beth-Horon in an angry frenzy, killing all four hundred men before setting off in pursuit of the main body of the army. However, Gallus had learnt from his mistakes and his forces were now well ordered, properly defended by skirmishers on more congenial open ground and were simply moving too quickly to be caught. In reality, they were now fleeing headlong from their pursuers, abandoning in the interests of speed the remnants of their baggage train with all its supplies, artillery and heavy equipment, which were to be captured by the victorious Jews and brought back to Jerusalem in triumph.

The Romans might have escaped, but the Jews had secured an extraordinary victory. Over the course of their retreat from

Jerusalem, most notably at the battle of Beth-Horon, the Romans had lost more than five thousand of their infantry and nearly five hundred cavalry, along with a number of senior officers, a mountain of heavy weaponry and, most humiliating of all, the prized Eagle Standard of one of Gallus's legions. Beth-Horon marked the moment at which the break with Rome became irreversible.

Benjamin trudged wearily along the road out of Upper Beth-Horon. He had been among the force despatched by Eleazar to kill the Roman rearguard in the village and was bone-tired from his exertions of the past few days as they began their slow march back to the capital. The death of so many men had also had a profound effect on him. He understood the imperative behind the revolt of his people, and he more than most had powerful personal reasons for wanting the Romans out of his country, but he also understood that many of his enemies were simply young men like him, sent to fight in a distant land, under orders with no recourse.

That night they camped not far from Gibeon, its garrison now empty of Roman soldiers. He was sitting quietly by the fire, half-listening to a group of his companions regaling one another with stories of how they had personally killed at least a dozen Romans each, but deep in reflection on the fate of his family. He missed his mother and sister more than he could put into words, and was coming to terms with the fact that his youth, his career, his hopes for the future, had all been sacrificed in the cause of a war whose scale and seriousness was only now becoming apparent. He and his rebel companions had chosen to face down the power of Rome, the most successful and efficient imperial power in history, with an army of unprecedented strength. He asked himself where it would all end, but in his heart of hearts he knew the answer.

As he was pondering these things, he heard a commotion behind him and turned to see a small group of men run panting into the camp. The sentries were jumpy and held them at lance-point until Eleazar himself could be summoned. He walked into the clearing and ordered the men to come closer to the firelight so that he could see them. As they came closer and the flames lit their faces, Benjamin was overjoyed to see that one of the men was his old friend, Ezra, dirty, bedraggled and apparently covered in blood, but with that same familiar smile on his lips.

Benjamin ran to his friend and threw his arms around him. "You bastard, you left me!" he cried. "What did you think you were doing, trying to take on the whole Roman army by yourself, you idiot?!" Ezra hugged him tightly, then gently pushed him away, holding him by the shoulders at arm's length. "You don't think I'd let you forget our wager do you? I got twenty-three of them with my sling and two more with my dagger. I bet you didn't even come close!"

Benjamin couldn't help but laugh. He caught him in a tight embrace once again and then stepped back as Eleazar demanded a report from Ezra and his companions. It transpired that when Ezra had been overrun by the vanguard of the Roman infantry, his small size had worked to his advantage. He had simply lain flat and still on the ground beneath the advancing square and the Romans had evidently mistaken him for the body of one of their own, so had stepped around him as they advanced. As soon as he'd been cleared, he rolled sideways unnoticed and hid in the cleft of a rock in the side of the canyon. He had seen the carnage wrought by Eleazar's men and had narrowly escaped a flaming arrow himself, but in the noise and confusion that followed the rebel leader's attack he had managed to escape unscathed. And he had news.

"I saw him, Benjamin. The Roman from the viaduct. The

bastard who killed your mother." Benjamin became very still and his blood seemed to freeze in his veins. "Tell me."

"He was leading the second rank of cavalry, behind the first wave of infantry. He only just missed the attack and escaped when the army was told to turn around and head back to the village. He had a new mount, a great black beast in full horse armour. He was thrashing the men with the flat of his sword, calling them all sorts, trying to get them to fight back. He even got off his horse at one point and punched a man in the face who answered him back. Then he was back in the saddle and was gone."

Another opportunity missed, thought Benjamin. But his time will come, he swore to his mother and Miriam – his time will come.

CHAPTER 48

BENJAMIN AND EZRA returned to Jerusalem with a triumphant Eleazar and a mountain of captured Roman armour and weapons, including whole batteries of artillery and supplies of their fearsome iron darts, together with Gallus's entire baggage train of supplies. Beth-Horon had been a stunning victory for the insurgency and positioned Eleazar to become one of Judaea's most powerful leaders.

After taking leave of his friend, Benjamin headed back to his home in the lower city, where he found his father and sister's conditions unchanged. Abraham was still a broken man and Miriam a mute shadow. On the first evening, after his father had gone to bed, Benjamin sat up with his sister beside the fire in the courtyard and told her the story of their exploits in the mountains, but they elicited no reaction from her. Miriam's face remained blank and her lips sealed.

The following morning his father rose as usual before dawn and made his desultory way to the olive groves outside the city, while Benjamin pondered his future. He knew that he was no longer a stonemason. That profession had evaporated along with his old life. He was a revolutionary now and the only question was how he could best serve the revolution. He started by meeting up with Ezra in the tavern where they had had their last drink together before leaving for Beth-Horon.

Neither man felt particularly victorious, despite their success on the battlefield, but both were as committed as ever to expelling the Romans from their land. Both were also driven by a visceral need to avenge their lost loved ones, but in Benjamin the hatred burned white-hot, like a fiery bolus in his chest.

"What will you do now, Benjamin?" asked Ezra.

"Fight," replied his friend.

"Where?"

"I think in Galilee. That's where the action will be. Gallus won't bring his troops back to Jerusalem for a while, not until he's reinforced them and is confident of being able to take the city. Assuming that ever happens. But up in Galilee they're still fighting hard."

Ezra was silent for a moment. "I think I'm going to stay here," he eventually said, quietly. "I was born and raised in Jerusalem and this is where I belong, defending David's city. Won't you stay?"

Benjamin cast his eyes down. "I just can't bear the sight of my father and sister, Ezra. It breaks my heart every time I look at them. I can't just sit here splitting stones and going home every night to a house of the dead. I need to take the fight to the Romans. I need to be out there where I can make the biggest difference. I have to hope that when I come back things will be better. The more so if I can ever find the man who did this to our family."

Ezra nodded. "I understand." He reached across and put his arm around his friend's shoulder. "We've not known each other long, but we've had some times together, eh?" Benjamin smiled. "Well, if you mean I've saved your skin a few times, yes!" Both men laughed.

"I'm glad someone has something to laugh about," said a

voice. Both men turned to find Rachel standing there with her hands on her hips, regarding them with a playful smile on her lips.

Benjamin immediately lapsed into gibbering incoherence, babbling about their adventures over the previous few weeks and stumbling over each sentence. She continued to look at him with that enigmatic smile while he jabbered on, Ezra leaning back and enjoying his discomfiture. Eventually Benjamin ran out of inconsequential chatter and lapsed into silence, just looking into those deep-green eyes with growing embarrassment at his tongue-tied rambling.

"Well that's all very interesting, I'm sure," said Rachel. "But I presume you boys would like a drink," and she turned on her heel and headed for the back room.

"I'm going to marry that girl," said Benjamin abruptly, his confidence returning now that she was no longer in his eye line. "You see if I don't."

"Well, you'd better come back from Galilee in one piece, then!" exclaimed Ezra. Now, let's get drunk!"

Rachel was as good as her word. She had promised them wine on the house during their last visit, and wine on the house they received. Rather too much of it. The following morning it was a very sore-headed Benjamin who made his way gingerly to the jewellery quarter of the market and surveyed the cornucopia of brooches, pendants, rings and necklaces on display. It took him more than an hour to make his choice, but when he had, he knew it was the right one.

Returning to the tavern, he found the place empty of patrons at this early hour. Rachel was mopping the stone floor and didn't hear him approach her from behind.

"I'm going to Galilee," spluttered Benjamin. "I think I might be away for a bit." Rachel spun round, taken by surprise. "Well thanks for letting me know. I'll be sure to keep a candle burning in my window."

Benjamin's face flushed with embarrassment. "I – I – you said you liked jewellery." He rooted around in his pocket, pulled out a small leather pouch and handed it to her. For the first time, Benjamin thought she registered genuine surprise. "Why, I didn't really mean..."

"I hope you like it," he said. Rachel pulled on the drawstring and pulled out a silver chain with a beautiful smooth oval gemstone suspended from it.

"It's a moonstone," said Benjamin. "It symbolises new beginnings."

"Really?" replied Rachel. "And what kind of a new beginning did you have in mind?"

"One for both of us," said Benjamin. And for the first time Rachel noticed the underlying sadness in this young man whom until now she had seen only as a shy suitor. She lay the stone in the palm of her hand. "It's really lovely, Benjamin. Thank you. Will you put it on for me?"

Benjamin's heart was beating so hard he thought it might burst from his chest as he stepped behind her and fastened the chain around her neck. It nestled in the hollow of her throat and seemed to glow against the creamy tawniness of her skin. "It suits you," said Benjamin, more loudly than he'd intended. "Yes," she replied quietly, "I rather think it does." She looked directly into his eyes, which sent Benjamin's heart into new paroxysms.

"I have to go now, but I wondered if – perhaps I might – erm – maybe if you would, erm..." Rachel smiled that unsettlingly brilliant smile that seemed to melt all of Benjamin's vital organs. "Yes, Benjamin. I rather think I would." And now his lungs were competing with his heart in a breathless struggle for control. "Then I'll see you when I get back," he said, then turned quickly on his heel and bolted for the door.

"Benjamin." He turned and somehow she was right there in front of him, so close that he could feel her breath on his face.

She reached up, put a hand on his shoulder and placed a soft kiss on his cheek. "I'll consider that a promise. And Benjamin?" He looked at her questioningly. "Maybe I will keep that candle burning." Then she turned and was gone. And a few seconds later, the tavern was empty once more.

CHAPTER 49

AS BENJAMIN WAS SETTING off in that November of 66 with a small band of Zealots across the New City and out of the Northern Gate onto the Damascus road, tumultuous political events were taking place in Jerusalem. With the Romans repulsed, most of the remaining Herodians had left the city and a provisional Judaean government had been formed under the high priest Ananus ben Ananus, re-establishing the old ruling class with the tacit support of the Sanhedrin. The revolutionaries and militiamen who had seen off the Romans – along with the peasantry and impoverished majority of inhabitants in the capital – were once again sidelined by a corrupt, grasping aristocracy. Even Eleazar, only recently feted as a national hero, was confined to his power base on Temple Mount, his writ extending no further than the outer wall of the temple complex.

And so the city settled into an uneasy calm as the war continued to rage across Galilee, the Golan, Samaria and the Sharon Plain. The Romans had clearly decided that the priority was to quell the rebellion in the countryside and so subdue the wider province before taking on the greater challenge of conquering its capital.

In the spring of 67 an increasingly impatient Emperor Nero

tasked his top general Vespasian with the job of retaking Judaea from the rebels. Vespasian duly landed at Caesarea with his fifth and tenth legions, bolstered by his son Titus's fifteenth legion and thirty auxiliary battalions, and promptly invaded Galilee. Over the course of the next year, town after town fell to the Romans and by July only four major strongholds were left.

Jotapata was the first of these to be overrun after a siege lasting more than six weeks. Towards the end of the siege the Galilean commander Josephus was trapped in an underground bunker with 40 of his men, all of whom committed suicide rather than be captured by the enemy, following which Josephus promptly defected and the city fell. Mount Tabor and Gamal quickly followed and finally Titus took Gischala. However, Titus was deprived of the pleasure of killing the rebel leaders as they escaped in the middle of the night and fled to Jerusalem, led by their legendary leader, John ben Levi.

During this time, Benjamin was attached to a cohort of rebels based in Tiberias on the western shore of the Sea of Galilee, led by his old commander Joshua. They had become expert skirmishers, venturing as far afield as Capernaum in the north and Agrippina in the south, harrying the Romans wherever they found them and seizing copious quantities of weapons. As a result, Benjamin had been able to indulge his growing appreciation of the Roman composite bow, with which he had now reached a high level of proficiency and so was most commonly to be found among Joshua's elite group of archers who were tasked with keeping the Romans' heads down while Joshua's skirmishers and Sicarii did the close-up damage.

Whenever they engaged with any of the legions' cavalry he would scour the enemy for a sign of his sworn enemy, but so far he had remained elusive.

One of the consequences of the steady conquest of Galilee and its neighbouring political regions was that refugees began to pour into Jerusalem from all over the province. By the winter of

67, when Benjamin returned home from his Galilean campaign, there were around 250,000 people in the city, which was struggling to cope with the massively increased numbers of Jews who had to be housed, fed and employed. As he walked back through the Northern Gate, Benjamin was astonished by how much the New City, enclosed between Jerusalem's recently renewed second and third defensive walls, had grown. There was now a sprawling mass of humanity, many living in makeshift tents and shelters.

The chaos was even more apparent as he passed through the second wall and crossed the market quarter, past the gigantic Antonia Fortress, to the original first wall, built by the Hasmonaeans nearly 140 years earlier. The wall, which ran parallel to the viaduct where Eleazar had wrought such havoc on the Romans a year before, had recently been rebuilt and strengthened, and once through the gate Benjamin was confronted with an even denser mass of humanity milling around the upper city and down Herodian Street into the lower city.

He made straight for the tavern, where he found Rachel busy serving a room packed with raucous customers. He stood on the threshold and looked at her. Her smile never left her face, despite the fact that she was rushing from table to table, constantly being accosted by men demanding faster service. She had a calming word or a quip for every patron and her eyes flashed warningly whenever a hand wandered out of place.

Finally he moved into the tavern and sat down on a stone bench in the far corner of the room. She spotted him a few minutes later and his heart sang when he saw her face light up in the broadest, sunniest smile he had ever seen. She walked over to him, hips swinging. "You're back then."

He laughed. "So it would seem."

He saw she was still wearing the moonstone, resting as before in the hollow of her throat, which he suddenly had an overwhelming desire to kiss. Instead, he stood up, took both her hands in his and said, "Marry me."

Rachel cocked her head to one side, the enigmatic smile back on her face. "Not before you've had a bath," she said.

Benjamin sought her father's permission that same evening, a procedure made easier by the support of Ezra, whose father vouched for him, and by the fact that Rachel's father was a widower, which avoided the potential difficulty of a challenge from her mother, who would probably have preferred a negotiated match with a well-known family friend. Immediately after his meeting with Rachel's father, Benjamin went home and told Abraham of his plans. His father seemed more relieved than anything else. Benjamin supposed his father thought that marriage would cool his hot-headedness and keep him away from dangerous revolutionaries. When he sat beside Miriam and told her that he was to be married, he watched as her eyes clouded and tears began to run down her cheeks. He held her tightly in his arms, stroking her fine auburn hair, and they remained like that for a long time, until finally Miriam fell asleep on his chest.

Benjamin and Rachel were married the following spring in a quiet ceremony, with Ezra as best man. Since Rachel had no sisters, Miriam was invited to be her bridesmaid, which seemed for the first time to bring Benjamin's sister out of the shadows of her ordeal, eliciting her first words since Benjamin had carried her home that fateful day. "You are beautiful together, brother. May God bless your union." Before returning to her mute silence.

The newlyweds moved into two small rooms above the tavern and Benjamin gradually took over her father's duties as proprietor, revelling in the social life of the hostelry and falling ever more deeply in love with his wife as the days and weeks passed. It was no surprise to any of their family and friends when Rachel announced in the summer that she was expecting their first child.

The war had quietened somewhat. Vespasian had evidently chosen to delay any attack on Jerusalem and had instead focused his attention on the conquest of Idumaea to the south and Peraea to the east, which wise heads judged to be a means of protecting his back and flank when the assault finally came. Meanwhile, the political situation in Jerusalem had deteriorated badly.

The flood of refugees had created a crisis of leadership in the capital, with various factions competing for influence. John ben Levi, the man who had escaped by night from Gischala the previous year, had drawn a host of hotheaded radicals to him and allied himself with Eleazar, creating a combined armed force of more than 8,000 men. A third armed faction was led by a wily Idumaean called Simon, a romantic idealist who had brought a 20,000-strong army to Jerusalem to support the Zealots.

It was inevitable that these revolutionary forces, thirsting for confrontation with the Romans, should eventually clash with Ananus's government, which saw them as a profound threat to the natural aristocratic order. Matters came to a head when the rebels deposed the high priest, Matthias, and instituted election by lot rather than by royal appointment from among the Sadducean aristocracy. The Zealots followed this up by summarily executing swathes of the nobility, together with several members of the Herodian royal family who had remained in the city.

The final confrontation came when Ananus wrote to Vespasian inviting him to take over the city, in a bid to subdue the growing threat from the revolutionaries and prop up his corrupt regime. Predictably, it had the reverse effect, galvanising and uniting the disparate militias, who finally brought down the interim government and took over the city. Ananus and his retinue were executed and the revolution was given a new lease of life, once again spreading from Jerusalem out into the countryside.

Benjamin remained loyal to Eleazar throughout this tumultuous period, but was too busy with the tavern to become involved in the internecine politics that were ravaging his city. He and Rachel lived quietly and peacefully, his thirst for revenge temporarily assuaged by care for his wife and newborn son, Daniel, who arrived loudly proclaiming his presence in the spring of 69. Of the Romans, there had been no sign for over a year, until in the summer of 69 watchmen on the western walls spotted a contingent of Roman cavalry in the distance. Vespasian had come briefly to view the city he had vowed to take, before withdrawing once again.

By now there were around 25,000 fighters holed up in Jerusalem. Ten thousand Judaeans and Idumaeans were mustered under Simon bar Giora's leadership, allied with 5,000 Idumaean militia in units of 500, who together defended the New City, upper city and most of the lower city. A further 6,000 Galileans were under the command of John of Gischala, allied with Eleazar's 2,400 Zealots, who between them controlled the Antonia Fortress, Temple Mount and Ophel Hill, site of the original City of David.

It was another nine months before the Romans returned to Jerusalem in force. By this time Vespasian had been declared Emperor by the Senate and was headed back to Rome. His 28-year-old son Titus was now commander in chief of the enormous military machine that had successfully brought Palestine to heel. With Judaea, Samaria, the Galilee, Golan and Peraea all now subdued, Titus was finally able to turn his attention to the Jews' last stronghold.

He arrived with his entire army in April 70.

CHAPTER 50

IN A SMALL ANTEROOM off the Hall of Hewn Stone, the president of the Sanhedrin and his faithful chief of the court were meeting together in secret.

"It is time, Jonas," said the president, affectionately addressing his colleague by his given name for the first time in many years. "It will not be long before the Romans encircle the city and it will be too late. It must be now. I am entrusting you with the dispatch of the Temple treasures. You and you alone among the members of the Sanhedrin will know where they are to be hidden.

Jonas nodded sadly. "It is a great honour, master. But I wish it were not to be."

The president threw his hands wide. "I know of no other way, Jonas. The treasures must be protected." His face darkened. "There are very bad times ahead for the people of this city and I know not how they will end. I fear the worst. I fear our beautiful Zion will face the same fate as it did under the Babylonians."

Jonas paled. The president was referring to the conquest of Palestine six hundred years before when Jerusalem had been overrun, its leaders exiled to Babylon and Solomon's great Temple completely destroyed. "But surely –"

"No, Jonas, we cannot take the risk. Without those treasures, worship in the Temple will be impossible. Their value is beyond even the wildest imaginings of our people. I will not countenance them falling into the hands of the Romans and being used to finance the further expansion of their benighted empire."

"I understand, master," replied Jonas reluctantly.

Over the following two weeks, on selected moonless nights, a series of mule trains made their stealthy way out of the city through each of its gates, most bound for distant parts of the country and in the care of trusted men who had sworn a blood oath never to reveal their purpose or destination.

By the time their mission had been completed and they had returned to Jerusalem, around which the Romans' noose had begun to tighten, the Temple's Sanctuary was completely empty.

CHAPTER 51

BENJAMIN WAS AWAKE EARLY on 23 April 70. A large order of wine was due to arrive that morning and he needed to clear space for it in the storeroom at the back of the tavern. Rachel was still in bed, nursing Daniel, who had given them both a sleepless night. He had no sooner dressed and eaten a quick breakfast of fruit and olives than there was a thunderous knocking on the tavern door. Annoyed that someone should be demanding entrance so early in the day, Benjamin scowled and prepared to berate the offender as he unbolted the door.

A hot and excited Ezra stood on the threshold. "They're here!" he exclaimed breathlessly.

"Who's here?"

"The Romans. They've come at last."

Benjamin shrugged on his cloak, ran upstairs to kiss his wife goodbye, promising to be back before the delivery arrived, and rushed back down to join Ezra, who was hopping impatiently from foot to foot. They ran through the still deserted streets of the upper city and across the market quarter and New City to the Northern Gate, where they pounded up the steps to the ramparts atop the outermost wall of the city, known to everyone as the Third Wall. There was already a large gathering of young men on the walkway, all looking north-east over the olive groves towards Mount Scopus. There they saw more than 500 horsemen gathered on the near slope of the mountain, their armour flashing in the early morning sunlight.

Benjamin and his companions surveyed the mounted men throughout the morning, but they made no move to approach the city. They simply watched. Occasionally, a rider or two would break from the main troop and gallop back around the mountain, obviously delivering some intelligence or other on the disposition of the city. Then, as the sun passed its zenith, a large contingent of Jews crept up on the troop and ambushed them with slings, arrows and swords. Benjamin and Ezra watched as the extraordinarily brave men dashed up to the armed horsemen and slashed at the horses' fetlocks, severing their tendons, before hastily retreating as the animals collapsed and their riders were thrown to the ground. The Romans were taken completely by surprise and as their horses reared and wheeled in panic Benjamin and Ezra saw men trampled beneath their hooves before being dispatched by the Jews.

Eventually the riders regained the initiative and mounted an orderly charge at the marauders, but they simply melted away into the rocks and gulleys of the mountain before retreating to the city. Finally, they galloped north, disappearing round the eastern flank of the mountain, leaving dozens dead and dying on the mountainside.

By now unit commanders from Simon, John and Eleazar had joined their men on the wall and word quickly spread about the reconnaissance party that had been scrutinising the approach to Jerusalem. The perceived wisdom was that, despite the formidable defences ranged against them in the north of the city, with the mighty Antonia Fortress dominating Jerusalem's second line of defence, the Second Wall, the Romans would not make the same mistake as Gallus had four years before and would avoid an attack via the Western Gate. Instead, it was felt that they were more likely to mount a frontal assault from the gently sloping terrain to the north or north-west.

It was obvious to the defenders that the cavalry scouting party was part of a much larger force hidden by the mountain. In fact, Titus was in the process of camping the entire Fifth Legion behind Mount Scopus and over the next few days the citizens of Jerusalem watched with growing alarm as the body of soldiery expanded until it seemed as if the whole mountainside was covered with tents. Throughout this period the Romans were constantly harried by Jewish sorties from the city. The day after the reconnaissance party had been driven off, there were also two massed attacks on the Tenth Legion, which was making camp on the Mount of Olives across the Kidron Valley to the east of the city. The Jews were only driven off after several hours of heavy fighting, in which the Romans suffered substantial losses.

A few days later, the Jews used the ruse of a false surrender to draw a sizeable detachment of Romans to the northernmost stretch of the Third Wall, where they were slaughtered by a large attacking force led by Simon. This was Benjamin's first taste of action since the Galilean campaign and he relished being on the ramparts letting loose volley after volley of arrows from his beloved bow.

At this point Titus finally lost patience. Over the next couple of days he deployed his Fifth, Twelfth and Fifteenth legions to camps north-west of the city and set about preparing for a head-on assault. As April became May, the general's army readied itself for the final battle of the four-year war. Over 100,000 men were ranged against the city, including 20,000 legionaries, 20,000 auxiliaries and 20,000 allies, among them soldiers from the exiled Herod Agrippa's army, together with many hundreds of cavalry.

The Romans' first action was to clear and level the ground between Mount Scopus and the First Wall, giving his army a clear run at the defences. The attack finally came between the Western Gate and the Psephinus Tower at the north-west corner of the New City. Titus built three earthen ramps and up each one an iron-plated wooden tower was moved into place below the nine-metre-high wall, providing cover for the soldiers who were now raking the ramparts with arrows, supported by a heavy artillery battalion which was flinging iron bolts at the defenders. Beneath this suppressing fire, three giant rams were brought into position, protected by the towers, and began their work on breaching the wall.

Despite its thickness, after a week the wall eventually succumbed to the relentless battering and a breach opened through which the infantry streamed. The New City, protected by the now breached Third Wall, was now occupied by the Romans, who established a forward base at the Camp of the Assyrians in the north-west corner and prepared to attack the city's next line of defence: the Second Wall.

That evening Benjamin and Ezra stood on the highest turret of the Antonia Fortress. They had both been among the defenders of the Third Wall near the Psephinus Tower and both had been shaken by the sheer disciplined efficiency of the Roman onslaught. This was a formidable fighting force, emboldened by a string of victories across Judaea, and its full force was being brought to bear against their city, which was defended by a ragtag army of brigands, bandits and hastily-assembled militia. Battle-hardened though their comrades were, Benjamin and Ezra both knew in their hearts that they could not hold out against this mighty enemy forever.

They looked down from their perch across the New City to the Roman camp, where hundreds of campfires burned and the unmistakeable distant sound of forges at work carried to them through the still night air. They wondered how long it would be before Titus ordered an assault on the Second Wall, which they would next be called upon to defend.

"It's the skirmishers I feel sorry for," sighed Ezra. "Going up against all that Roman armour. Despite all the kit we've managed to scrounge, we're still not well enough protected. You've got to be pretty brave to leave the gates and confront the bastards head-on."

"Well I dearly love being among the archers, but I sometimes wish I was down there, toe to toe with the bastards. It just doesn't feel like proper warfare chucking arrows at them."

"Be careful what you wish for, Benjamin. I have a feeling it's a wish that will be coming true all too soon." They lapsed into silence, watched the campfires, listened to the forges and brooded on the days to come.

When the Romans' assault on the Second Wall came, it was ruthlessly executed. On 11 May Titus launched a fearsome artillery barrage at the defenders on the wall, raining heavy iron bolts and enormous rocks onto the ramparts, while moving his rams into place against the base of the wall. It took just four days for one of the rams to bring down the middle tower of the wall and open a breach and just after dawn a thousand legionaries poured through. They found themselves in a relatively new suburb of the city, bounded to the north and west by the Second Wall, by the soaring forty-five metre platform of Temple Mount to the east and by the First Wall, Jerusalem's original defensive boundary, to the south. It was a maze of narrow streets, courtyards and rundown buildings surrounding the city's market quarter, which on a normal day would have been bustling with wool-sellers, blacksmiths and rag traders, but as the Romans spread out across the suburb they found it eerily quiet and empty.

The Jews had simply disappeared.

CHAPTER 52

BENJAMIN AND EZRA stood once more on the ramparts of the Antonia Fortress, which anchored the north-west corner of Temple Mount to the Second Wall. It was a formidable defensive position, built on an eleven metre high outcropping of rock with sheer sides and soaring to forty-three metres above the ground at its highest point. Standing on its topmost tower, as they had a few days before, they had a birds-eye view of both the New City and the apparently deserted suburb through which the puzzled Romans were now dispersing. They watched as legionaries and mounted auxiliaries combed the streets for signs of life.

It was mid-morning when the narrow streets of the market quarter suddenly erupted with armed men. They swarmed through the suburb, appearing without warning from alleyways and gates, from tumbledown houses and from the concealed entrances of tunnels. Once again the Romans were taken completely by surprise. All of a sudden the rebels seemed to be everywhere. From the rooftops the Romans were pelted with rocks, slingshots and arrows. As they retreated through the streets they were flanked by more men with swords, daggers and slings, who darted out of the shadows to launch guerrilla attacks on the enemy before disappearing again into the warren of streets.

Gradually they were pushed back to the breach, where they were completely surrounded by the Jews. The problem for them was that the breach was narrow and partially blocked by fallen masonry, so only a few soldiers at a time could clamber back through the gap. The rebels took full advantage of their disarray, pushing them hard against the inside of the wall as more and more men poured forward from the suburb to support them. From their eyrie on the Antonia tower Benjamin and Ezra could see that a massacre was about to take place. The Jews were evidently blinded by bloodlust, frustrated to the point of madness by their inability to prevent the Roman assault on their city. They hacked and stabbed their way through the tightly-packed shield-walls leaving dozens of men dead and dying.

It was only when a massed contingent of Roman archers arrived and began to rain arrows down on the rebels that the trapped soldiers were given the breathing space they needed to escape through the breach. The Jews followed them, surging onto the wall and driving the Romans back into the New City before barricading the breach.

The Romans wasted no time in counter-attacking, but the Jews still managed to hold them off for another three days before they were finally driven back and the wall was breached once more. Having learnt his lesson, this time Titus tore down a length of the wall several hundred metres wide and garrisoned the towers with seasoned soldiers before taking proper control of the suburb.

The Jews were now behind their last line of defence: the First Wall, which encircled the upper and lower cities with the Temple Mount and Antonia Fortress at the eastern end of its northern fortifications. John ben Levi's Galileans and Eleazar's Zealots held the Temple Mount and the fortress, while Simon bar Giora's Judaeans and Idumaeans held the wall between Temple Mount and the palace a kilometre to the west.

For their part, the Romans celebrated their capture of Jerusalem's suburb by staging a military parade of the entire occupying army on Betheza Hill in the New City. The Jews looked on from their fortifications half a mile away as 40,000 men in full armour, accompanied by hundreds of cavalry and a cortege of heavy weaponry, put on a breathtaking display of military might that was intended to strike terror into the hearts of the defenders. During the parade Titus made one last effort to avoid an all-out assault on the Jews' final redoubt, dispatching the defector Josephus to appeal for the city's surrender. As on all previous occasions, the Roman emissary was sent away with taunts and insults ringing in his ears. The final stage of the long war was about to begin.

———

Benjamin had taken a couple of days' leave from the defences to spend time with his wife and son. Rachel was increasingly apprehensive about the days ahead. She knew that if the Romans succeeded in taking the city there would be no mercy. Titus would give his soldiers full rein and they would sack Jerusalem, quite probably killing every last defender. And worse would follow for the women of the city.

"It's our last chance to leave," she said to Benjamin quietly as they lay in bed on the second night, Daniel snuggled between them. "We can go south to my family in Idumaea. It's peaceful there and we can open another tavern or you can return to your stonemason's job. There's no shame. You've done your bit."

Benjamin stared into the darkness. Eventually he replied, "This is my city, Rachel. I was born here. It's given me everything I have. My father and sister are here and everything I know is here. I love Jerusalem." He paused, then turned towards her. "And I have unfinished business with the Romans," he said finally.

Rachel sighed. "I will follow you whatever you decide, Benjamin, you know that. But we have Daniel to think of now." They both listened to the gentle breathing of their son and for a while there was silence.

"I will protect you both," said Benjamin. "Nothing will happen to you, I swear."

Rachel put an arm around his neck and drew him to her. "I believe you, Benjamin." And they lay in one another's arms, sleepless as the night hours passed and the grey light of dawn crept through their window, both wondering how he would ever be able to keep his promise.

Benjamin and Ezra were assigned to the defence of the Antonia Fortress and after an emotional farewell to Rachel, Benjamin met up with Ezra and they made their way up the viaduct to Temple Mount and north along the western colonnade to the Fortress. In order for the Romans to take the city, they first had to take the Antonia. Its massive square bulk, with its four high turrets and deep ditches on three sides, was a serious impediment to an assault on the First Wall. It had to be conquered and Eleazar's Zealots were tasked with ensuring that they did not succeed.

Titus brought all four of his legions to bear in the attack. The Fifth and Twelfth built two enormous ramps up to the wall of the Antonia Fortress, while the Tenth and Fifteenth built two more leading up to the western wall of Temple Mount. Benjamin and his comrades delivered a constant rain of missiles onto the heads of the attackers, while from inside the walls more than three hundred captured bolt catapults and forty stone-throwers loosed a relentless artillery barrage. Yet despite suffering severe casualties, the Romans completed the ramps in just seventeen days and on a warm cloudless day at the end of

May their rams were moved into position on the four platforms in preparation for the final assault.

Benjamin and Ezra were deployed in separate towers at opposite ends of the fortress's battlements. Both men could see that, despite its formidable defences, it was only a matter of time before the Antonia was overwhelmed by a combination of ramming and assaults by ladder as the Romans made full use of the well-protected platforms they had built at the tops of the ramps. Soon enough, they heard and felt the first blows of the gigantic rams on the wall below and the first of the ladders appeared. They prepared themselves for the hand-to-hand fighting they knew would be sure to ensue.

It was just as the last of the machines were being manoeuvred into position at the tops of the two ramps that the most extraordinary thing happened. A deep rumble began to reverberate through the feet of the defenders, growing in intensity. As they gazed down from the top of the wall, looking for the origin of the sound, they watched in astonishment as both the Roman platforms, complete with machinery, ladders and men, simply disappeared into the ground. The two ramps collapsed in an enormous cloud of soil and dust, leaving two enormous craters filled with splintered wood, bent metal and broken bodies. The screams of those buried beneath were terrible to hear.

Eleazar himself was standing beside Benjamin as the catastrophe unfolded. "I should have known John would have a surprise up his sleeve," he said, smiling. "Now we know why so many of our men have been busy burrowing about under the city. Cunning bugger." And he turned and calmly walked off.

Benjamin later learned that John ben Levi had been extending a number of the existing tunnels beneath the city, eventually culminating in a large underground chamber directly beneath the two Roman ramps, which were only ten metres apart. Held up with timber props, against which were piled pitch-soaked faggots of wood, it was a simple matter at the right moment for John's men to set light to the faggots and, when the flames ate away at the props, to bring the roof of the chamber crashing down along with everything built above it. This was a stunning setback for the Romans, but more was to come.

Two days later a small party of rebels sallied forth and set fire to the other two ramps against the western wall. In just two days the Jews had destroyed what it had taken the Romans two weeks to construct. Fired by their success and bolstered by a wave of rebels pouring out of the city, the Jews pressed their advantage and drove the Romans back through the suburbs and onward as far as their camp in the north-west corner of the New City. It was only there, after Titus called up his heavy artillery, that the rebels were finally stopped and forced to retreat.

Benjamin and Ezra were among the fighters who had participated in the rout and they were exhilarated by their spectacular victory. They began to believe that they could actually drive the Romans out of their city once and for all.

But Titus had once again learnt a valuable lesson from his latest encounter with the revolutionaries. He knew that even if he were to construct new ramps and towers – which would be difficult enough given that practically every tree on the hills around Jerusalem had already been cut down for timber – there was no guarantee that they too would not be destroyed. He held a council of war with his commanders and they made a decision.

They would besiege the city and starve the defenders into submission.

CHAPTER 53

SIEGE WARFARE IS the last resort of an attacking army and it is brutal and remorseless. It involves the enforced deprivation of many thousands of innocent civilians, as well as the men under arms who are charged with defending them. It strips the citizenry of their freedom, their health and their dignity. If prolonged, it inevitably results in the total collapse of order and the creation of a moral vacuum in which any atrocity is possible. It is intended to destroy a city's will to resist. It is designed to crush hope.

The 250,000 inhabitants of Jerusalem were about to be subjected to an incomparable horror. And they did so, in the full knowledge of what would befall them, rather than submit to their Roman masters.

At the beginning of June 70 Titus ordered the construction of an eight-kilometre wall that was to encircle the entire city, beginning and ending at Bezetha Hill in the New City and following the line of hills which surrounded the capital skirting the Kidron and Hinnom Valleys. The wall was fortified by thirteen forts, garrisoned by Roman auxiliaries, and created a virtually hermetically-sealed blockade of Jerusalem.

The impact on the inhabitants was immediate. The city had never before had to accommodate so many people, its population inflated many times over by militiamen, bandits, refugees and the pilgrims who had come to Jerusalem for the Feast of Pentecost the month before. Food was already in short supply when the siege began and it wasn't long before hunger began to take a firm hold. A few upper-class Jews and monarchists, whose sympathies had always lain with their Roman colonisers, managed to negotiate their escape by promising to be politically helpful in the future, but the vast majority of Jerusalem's inhabitants remained bottled up within its new, heavily patrolled walls and slowly began to starve.

Benjamin had invited Ezra to stay with him and Rachel for the duration of the siege and two months after it had begun they sat talking early one morning over a desultory glass of wine, heavily watered-down, and a shared crust of mouldy bread.

"It can't go on much longer," said Ezra. "We're beginning to behave like animals. The city stinks of the dead, even though the bodies are being thrown over the walls. The valleys are filling up with them and I've never seen so many rats and flies. People are starting to get sick and very soon we'll have a plague on our hands as well as a famine."

Benjamin agreed. "It's coming to a head. It looks as if Titus is concentrating all his forces now on the Antonia. They're having to travel miles to find timber, but somehow they're managing it." And it was true. The Romans had almost completed construction of four enormous new platforms in front of the fortress. It wouldn't be long now.

"Those bastards with money still seem to be able to get out," said Ezra bitterly. "There's a steady trickle of them sneaking down into the lower city and out of the Dung Gate. I'd cut their throats myself if I could get my hands on them."

"Rumour has it they're swallowing their gold to get it out of the city," countered Benjamin. "I heard the other day that some of our Arab and Syrian allies are catching deserters and cutting them open."

"Serves them right. Being gutted is too good for them. We should lock them up and let them starve to death like everyone else. Do you know there are people eating weeds and stable sweepings? I've even heard of women boiling belt leather and picking bits out of cow dung and sewage."

Benjamin scowled. "Did you hear that awful story about Mary Absalom down by the Pool of Siloam? She was so desperate that she killed her own baby, roasted it and ate half of it. She offered the other half to a passing gang who were attracted by the smell of cooking."

Rachel appeared from the back room, Daniel on her hip. She looked painfully thin, even though Benjamin and Ezra had foregone most of their meagre rations in order to keep her as well fed as possible while she nursed their son. But to Benjamin she was still as beautiful as ever, even though her hair was lank from lack of nourishment and her eyes were dull.

"We're just about to go out and find some bread, my love," proffered Benjamin. "And maybe some goat's milk for little Daniel." Rachel smiled. "There's no need, Benjamin. We have enough for a few more days." Which was a lie, thought Benjamin, but he said nothing.

There was a sudden sharp rap at the door and as Benjamin got to his feet, it burst open and Rachel's father stumbled breathlessly into the room.

"What on earth's the matter, father?" exclaimed Rachel.

"It's your father, Benjamin! The Romans have him. I was with some of Eleazar's boys patrolling the eastern colonnade of the Temple when I saw them dragging a group of men away from just below the Sheep Gate. One of them was your father!"

"What! But I left him at home with Miriam yesterday

evening! He said he felt unwell and was going to try and sleep it off. What on earth was he doing outside the wall?"

"The word is they were night-foraging in the valley and got caught. And you know how the Romans are dealing with foragers, or anyone who tries to creep through their lines."

Benjamin's blood ran cold. He knew exactly what fate awaited his father.

He ran out of the door and dashed headlong down to his father's house, followed by Ezra, only to find it empty. Turning tail, he ran up Herodian Street and took the broad steps leading up to the Temple concourse two at a time, quickly crossing the Outer Court and rushing into the eastern colonnade that looked out over the Kidron Valley. There was a crowd of people halfway along the colonnade and among them Benjamin immediately spotted his sister, who was clinging to another woman, in floods of tears. He ran to her and swept her up into his arms.

"Miriam, Miriam. It's alright. It's all going to be alright." But she was not to be consoled, her body was wracked with spasms and she was keening, repeating over and over, "Papa, papa, papa..."

Benjamin held her tightly to his chest and looked in the direction that everyone else was looking. He felt Ezra's hand tightly gripping his shoulder. Seven bedraggled looking men had been rounded up and were being held at sword point outside the Roman siege wall, just across the Kidron Valley near the Garden of Gethsemane, by a small contingent of Roman infantry, protected by a troop of cavalry. One of the seven men was Benjamin's father.

As they watched in horror, the seven men were stripped naked and each bound face-first to a post which had already been driven into the ground. Benjamin could see his father shaking with fear. He suddenly tore himself loose from Ezra's grip and began to run up the colonnade towards the Shushan

Gate, which led down into the valley. Ezra tore after him and caught him just as he was about to charge at the gatekeepers.

"Benjamin, there's nothing you can do! Please, don't do this!" He held Benjamin tightly as he wriggled like an eel in his arms. Finally, he went limp and slumped to the ground, his head in his hands.

"I couldn't save my mother, I couldn't save my sister and now I can't save my father. Ezra, what use am I?!"

"You have Miriam to take care of, Benjamin. Think of her. If you go down into that valley you'll just suffer the same fate as Abraham. Please, come to your senses."

Tears were streaming down Benjamin's face as Ezra led him back down the colonnade to the huddled group looking across the valley.

"Come on, let's take Miriam and get out of here. You don't have to watch this, my friend."

"No. My place is here. With my father. I want him to know that I'm here with him." He turned to the woman to whom Miriam was still clinging, a neighbour of his father's. "Please," he asked, "would you take Miriam home with you? I will come and collect her later." The woman hesitated, obviously finding it difficult to tear her eyes away from the spectacle across the valley, then sighed, said "Of course," and led Miriam away, his sister appearing to be completely unaware of what was happening to her. Benjamin watched until they turned the corner into the Outer Court and then returned his gaze to the opposite side of the valley. He was no longer weeping and his face was set hard.

A large Roman had stripped to the waist and was now approaching the seven bound men, a scourge hanging loosely by his side. It was a terrible instrument of punishment: three strips of heavy leather attached to a wooden handle, with small fragments of bone and metal embedded in the leather.

The soldier approached the first of the bound men and

swung the scourge through a wide arc. The assembled watchers heard the sound of the flail meeting flesh, followed a split-second later by an agonised scream. Eleven more lashes followed, each accompanied by a wet slapping sound and an even louder scream, as the man's flesh was torn from his body. The soldier moved on down the line of men, and the valley echoed to the sound of mocking jeers from the rest of the Romans.

The watchers could see that the soldier was sweating from his exertions as he delivered twelve lashes to each of the men in turn, until finally he reached Benjamin's father. He was panting now and his body was covered in spots and splashes of blood and torn flesh. The scourge, too, was dripping with gore as he raised it to deliver the first blow to Abraham's back.

Benjamin watched expressionless as his father squirmed beneath the lashes and his back ran red. But Abraham, unlike his companions, did not scream. In fact, he didn't utter a sound, just flinched with each blow until, at last, it was over.

But his father's suffering had only just begun. The watchers on the colonnade looked on with growing revulsion as each of the men was untied from their stake and carried a short distance to where seven ready-assembled rough-hewn crosses lay on the ground. This time, Abraham was the first to be dealt with. His arms were stretched wide on the crossbeam and a pair of small wooden boards were placed on his arms, just below the wrists. One of the Romans then hammered a large nail through each board, the nail passing through Abraham's arms and into the crossbeam beneath. Now his father at last let out a terrible cry of pain.

The soldier was impervious to Abraham's cries. With mechanical precision he drew Abraham's knees up and drove another, larger, nail crosswise through a third board and on through both heels deep into the vertical post. Benjamin remained impassive as his father's cross was lifted up and dropped carelessly into a readymade slot in the ground.

Abraham immediately tried to pull himself up to relieve the unbearable pressure on his lungs, pushing against the nail which held his feet firmly to the post. The nails through his arms had now locked against his wristbones and the scene was set for a slow and increasingly painful death as Abraham repeatedly pulled himself up to relieve his lungs, only to sink again when exhaustion overtook him. Eventually, weakness would take its toll, along with blood loss, thirst and sunstroke, and Benjamin's father would suffocate to death. But that could take hours or even days.

Ezra felt his friend gently remove his hand from his shoulder. As he turned towards him he saw Benjamin seize a bow from one of the archers who happened to be standing in the crowd. The man looked at him angrily and had opened his mouth to shout when he saw the expression in Benjamin's eyes and his mouth closed without uttering a sound. Benjamin now reached for the leather pouch of arrows at the archer's waist and, after a moment's hesitation, the man drew the pouch from his belt and passed it to him.

The second unfortunate victim was now being nailed to a cross, his shrieks of pain once again echoing around the valley. Benjamin walked calmly to the low parapet which ran the length of the colonnade and rested his knees against it. Lifting the bow, he withdrew an arrow from the pouch, nocked it and drew back the bowstring. At that moment, his father lifted his head and looked directly at Benjamin, his face etched with agony as once again he attempted to pull himself upright. For just a moment, the pain seemed to clear from his face and, even at this distance, Benjamin could see the father who had raised him and loved him from boyhood to manhood, his face momentarily serene. And as the arrow flew from Benjamin's bow, he thought he saw his father smile, before the iron tip drove through his forehead and sank deep into the wood of the cross.

Benjamin stood for a moment in silence, and there was silence all around him in that crowd of watchers. Then he calmly turned and handed the bow and arrows back to the archer.

"Now we can go," he said to Ezra.

CHAPTER 54

THE NIGHTMARE of the siege continued. As the weeks went by, order in the city broke down almost entirely as desperation grew and the various factions fought increasingly bitter battles for influence. Matters came to a head when the rump of Sadducean aristocrats, priests and Herodians who remained in Jerusalem banded together and tried to fill the moral vacuum, presenting themselves to the people as the party of peace, with a mandate to surrender to the Romans and bring the suffering to an end.

Simon responded by promptly executing the high priest, his three sons and a host of other aristocrats, tossing their bodies over the wall. When a dozen others tried to defect, they too were executed and their bodies thrown into the valley.

Meanwhile, Roman preparations for an assault on the Antonia Fortress were completed and the city waited in trepidation for the inevitable attack. In early July the rams were hauled up the four ramps and began pounding the wall of the fortress, while soldiers protected by the wooden housings attempted to crowbar out stones from the base of the tower, but with very limited success. They need not have worried. Shortly after the rams had begun their work, part of the fortress's wall collapsed into one of John's tunnels and Titus's men eagerly scrambled though the breach, only to be met by a second wall which the Jews had hastily constructed inside the first.

Several attempts to penetrate the wall failed, until Titus finally ordered a night assault, using John's tunnels to gain entry to the Sanctuary. But here, once again, his forces were pushed back. One frustrated centurion, a Bithynian called Julian, could no longer bear the repeated repulses and launched a suicidal lone attack on the defenders, only to be torn apart by the Jews holding the Mount. The Romans responded by tearing down the remainder of the fortress's wall, leaving only the towers standing, from where Titus now commanded his troops.

At this point the defence of Jerusalem rested on the shoulders of a few thousand battle-hardened revolutionaries on Temple Mount itself. It was a formidable final line of defence, resting on a platform forty-five metres high supported by walls five metres thick, the jewel in Herod the Great's massively ambitious national building programme of a century before.

The entire Temple complex covered one-and-a-half square kilometres. The Outer Court, or Sanctuary, was an open concourse surrounded on three sides by twin marble colonnades eleven metres high and topped by cedar roofs, including Solomon's Portico, the impressive colonnade on the eastern side of the Mount from which Benjamin launched the arrow that killed his father. At the southern end of the concourse, broad steps led down to a wide plaza looking out over Ophel Hill to the Lower City.

At the centre of the Sanctuary was the Inner Court, surrounded by a low balustrade beyond which Gentiles could not pass. Jewish pilgrims and priests would enter through one of nine gates into the Inner Court, passing through the Court of the Women, Court of the Israelites or Court of the Priests depending on their position or rank. The Temple itself was a magnificent 45-metre high marble and gold edifice accessed from the Court of the Priests by two giant golden gates leading into the Holy Place, beyond which was the Holy of Holies, the most sacred place in Judaea, entered only once a year by the high priest himself.

In the middle of July Titus ordered a full-frontal assault on Temple Mount, with over 7,000 soldiers led by Sextus Cerealis, commander of the Fifth Legion. Defended by javelin-throwers placed just behind the front line, and with archers deployed behind them, the front rank of the Roman infantry moved forward from the ruins of the Antonia into the open space of the Outer Court, where the Jews were waiting for them. In addition to the massed ranks of men on the concourse itself, archers and slingers were stationed on the roofs of the northern and western colonnades, among them Benjamin and Ezra. The Romans were quickly engaged in vicious hand-to-hand fighting with the rebels while being pelted with heavy missile-fire from above. Unable to bring his full force to bear because of the narrow 300-metre width of the concourse, Cerealis finally capitulated and withdrew his men after just a few hours' fighting.

Once again Titus took stock and decided to resort to platforms, building four ramps against the north-western corner of the Sanctuary and the flanking colonnades, and proceeding to destroy most of the northern colonnade. What the Romans did not know was that the Jews had filled the roof spaces above the remaining pillars with pitch and bitumen and as soon as the first few hundred Romans swarmed onto the roof of the unbroken section, the rebels fired the flammable material and the attackers were engulfed in flames.

The advantage this gave the Jews did not last long. The relentless pressure of the Roman advance eventually took its toll and the rebels fell back further and further until they were holding a line just to the north of the Inner Court.

After four long years of war, waged on multiple fronts from Golan in the north to Idumaea in the south; after the deaths of thousands of Palestinians who stood up to the Roman war machine; after the brutal siege of the capital which took thousands more lives; after all this, it came down to a few thousand stalwart insurgents who would soon be defending a few thousand square metres of the Holy Land against the full might of four imperial legions. And Rome was in no mood for compromise.

CHAPTER 55

BENJAMIN AND EZRA had been manning the northern colonnade with fifty or so archers, slingers and javelin-throwers when they saw the Romans preparing for their final assault. Their commander immediately ordered them to fall back to the Inner Court and the men raced south along the eastern colonnade and through the Beautiful Gate, the eastern entrance to the Court of the Women, and joined up with Eleazar's fighters just beyond the Corinthian Gate.

While hand-to-hand fighting raged across the front line a few yards north of the Inner Court, it was curiously quiet inside the Temple complex. The thousands of men who were crammed into the Court of the Priests, the final approach to the Temple itself, were silent and reflective. Some knelt and bowed their heads in prayer, some took a final opportunity to sharpen their blades and arrowheads, others hugged companions, while still others just sat quietly by themselves in silent contemplation of the final battle to come.

Standing before the covered porch and giant golden gates which marked the entrance to the Temple, Eleazar prepared to address his men, as the sounds of fighting from the Outer Court gradually became louder. He spoke with a quiet force, his deep voice carrying easily across the crowd.

"My brothers, we stand here on the site of our holiest place, the house where God dwells and our hopes rest. More than six hundred years ago our forbears faced another occupying army on this very same spot, defending the great temple built by King Solomon. We all know the outcome. Our ancestors were carried off to Babylon and the temple was raised to the ground. Not a stone remained.

"But Nehemiah rebuilt our temple and, after our people's return from exile, they worshipped here for over five hundred years in peace and prosperity. When Herod rebuilt and expanded the temple seventy years ago, my father used to say it was an abomination – a monument to man rather than God. An extravagance that served the ambitions of our monarchy and our priesthood, rather than our people. And maybe he was right. I don't know whether all this marble and gold is to the glory of God, or just a giant vanity project. But I do know this: it is the heart of our nation. It is a sanctuary for every Jew who seeks safety and succour, wherever in the world they come from. It is a testament to our endurance and our will to survive.

"Our temple has stood on this mount for more than a thousand years, and it will stand for a thousand years more. I'm not talking about the pillars, the arches, the plazas, the stones. I'm talking about the soul of our people. That which can never be taken from us. That is what we fight for.

"I am proud to have led you. I am proud to have fought beside you. I am proud to be with you, here, at the end. So take up your bows and your slings, unsheath your swords and your daggers. Let us show these barbarians how we Jews can fight! And may God watch over us and give us strength!"

A great shout went up from all the assembled men, as bows and swords and lances were held high in the air and they joined to recite the great battle cry of the Jews from the time of Joshua:

"Sh'ma Yisrael – Hear Oh Israel! You are about to approach battle on your enemies. Let your hearts not whither and do not fear, tremble, or be broken before them. For Hashem will go with you, fight with you, and save you."

As their voices subsided and the men broke up into their various dispositions, Eleazar stepped down from the plinth where he had been standing and walked over to Benjamin and Ezra, who were preparing to climb to the Temple roof to provide covering fire for their companions.

"Boys, your fighting is done." They both looked at him in astonishment. "I have a task for you which is of immeasurably greater importance than anything your arrows and slingshots can accomplish today. Come with me." And he led them through the golden gates into the Temple. They followed awestruck as Eleazar pushed his way through the heavy embroidered curtain that lay just beyond the entrance and into the Holy Place, the last chamber before the Holy of Holies itself.

Eleazar paused and turned to face them, his thin face drawn and tired. "This is where the most sacred and precious of our religious objects were stored. If you had walked through here a few months ago, you would have seen treasures beyond your wildest imaginings. These shelves were heavy with gold and silver and precious gems. There were the richest of priestly vestments, chalices and menorahs, vessels too numerous to count. The wealth of our nation was housed safely within these walls.

"But we could not deceive ourselves about what was coming. Eventually the Romans would take possession of this sanctuary and everything would have been plundered and carted back to Rome, to adorn the villas of rich noblemen and their vacuous wives and mistresses. We could never allow that." He looked wistfully around him at the empty walls and floors. "So the Sandedrin took steps to ensure that those precious things would be safe."

Benjamin was conscious that his mouth was hanging open

and he turned to Ezra, who was obviously similarly overwhelmed by what Eleazar was telling them.

"Before the Romans began building their wall and the siege began, the treasures were packed up and placed in the care of twenty trusted men, who carried them out of the city by night in a caravan of mules. A few of the items have been secreted close to Jerusalem, but most of them were carried to distant locations and hidden in places where they would not be found even by chance. Follow me." Eleazar resumed walking to the far end of the room, where he pulled aside a double curtain and led them into a small, unfurnished space. Benjamin and Ezra were speechless. They were now standing in the Holy of Holies, the very place where God Himself resided. The walls were bare and the room was unfurnished. It was entered only once every year, and only by the high priest himself. Eleazar walked over to the far corner and picked up a bundle of cloth.

"This is one of two copper scrolls listing where the Temple treasures are hidden," he said, unwrapping the bundle. Inside Benjamin and Ezra saw a scroll about 30 centimetres wide, gleaming a burnished red in the candlelight. "When the men returned from secreting the treasures, two of our most experienced coppersmiths spent many days inscribing the scrolls with their locations.

"But the Sanhedrin's court chief was a clever man. Not only did he choose the most cunning hiding places, but he listed them in such a way that both scrolls are needed to identify them. One scroll details the precise placing of the treasures in their hiding places. The second scroll identifies the towns, villages and cities where those hiding places are located.

"He wisely decided that the scrolls should then be separated. The first scroll has already been taken out of the city and delivered to a place of safety. This one must be similarly secreted. That is your task."

Benjamin could contain himself no longer. "But why us, master? Why not one of your commanders? We're just two ordinary boys from the Lower City. What do we know of all these things? We're not even religious!"

Eleazar rested a hand on Benjamin's shoulder. "I know what has happened to you and your family," he said quietly. "I watched you end your father's life on that hill." Benjamin went still. "I know that you more than most have reason to hate the Romans and I believe you are in need of a purpose, something which will give you peace in its accomplishment and which will deprive the Romans of the spoils of their desecration." He smiled. "I am giving you that purpose."

"But – but – it's too much!" cried Benjamin. "We're not equal to this, we –"

"You will serve the revolution by doing this, Benjamin. More so than if you kill a hundred Romans today. And I also know that you two are bound by a friendship which is unlikely to be broken. You will need that friendship in the days ahead. You will need to depend upon and protect one another if your task is to be completed.

"Now, we must hurry. There is not much time."

"But where are we going? And how do we get out of the city?" asked Ezra.

"Samuel will show you the way," answered Eleazar and as they turned back towards the entrance Benjamin and Ezra saw a man standing quietly inside the curtain, a sword at his side. He was a short, burly man with a well-trimmed beard, thin lips and sharp eyes. He regarded them both unsmilingly.

The four of them walked quickly back to the main entrance of the Temple and Eleazar turned to them one last time. "May God protect and guide you both. Now I must go. There is much to do before we entertain our Roman guests." And he was gone, striding across the court to his commanders.

Samuel said gruffly, "This way. And hurry, we have a long way to go."

Benjamin didn't move. "I need to get my wife and child and my sister," he said.

"There is not time," answered Samuel firmly. "Then I am going nowhere," said Benjamin, hefting his bow and turning to follow Eleazar, Ezra in his wake.

"Wait!" said Samuel. "There is no time to argue about this. We must move quickly if we are to get out of the city before all hell breaks loose."

"Then we had better get moving," retorted Benjamin, and the two of them set off at a run across the three courts and out of the Beautiful Gate, with Samuel trailing behind. The Jews were still barely holding the Romans off to the north of the Inner Court, but for now the southern concourse of the Sanctuary was clear of the enemy, although crowded with fighters. The three men rushed across the concourse, down the steps of the royal portico and through the Triple Gate onto the broad plaza which fronted the southern wall of the Temple complex. Turning right, they hurried along the western wall and across the viaduct into the Upper City, making straight for the tavern.

"The city is lost," exclaimed Benjamin breathlessly as he burst through the door. "Pack some things quickly, Rachel. We must go." Rachel had been sitting in the corner nursing Daniel, but when she saw her husband's face, she didn't hesitate and ran straight upstairs. Ten minutes later they were all on the move, with Samuel again trailing behind as they ran across the Upper City and down Herodian Street into the Lower City. As they ran, Rachel said, "Benjamin, what about father?"

"He was in the Temple with Eleazar's men. He will make his stand with them." Rachel didn't respond, but bowed her head as she ran and Benjamin saw the tears on her face. "Your father would never leave the city, you know that, Rachel. He is where he wants to be." She nodded, but the tears still flowed.

Miriam was sitting in the courtyard outside their family home when they arrived. Benjamin rushed up to her and took her in his arms. She fell against him as he swept her up and half-carried her indoors. Setting her down, he put his hands on her shoulders. "We have to go, dearest. Are you ready to come with me?" Miriam looked at him with her dark eyes and he saw behind them the world of suffering that she had endured. He felt his heart swell with love for his small sister who had borne more in her fifteen years than most people did in several life-times. And then he saw something else in her eyes: a bright spark of resolution, which once it had taken hold grew into something akin to the fierce obstinacy that he remembered from her childhood. She broke from his hands and walked purpose-fully to the corner of the room, where her cloak was hanging. She shrugged it on and nodded slowly.

Benjamin smiled. "Now we're ready," he told Samuel. "Take us where we need to go."

Samuel now took the lead and guided them through the streets of the Lower City into the southern district, just above the Tekoa Gate. They finally halted beside the Pool of Siloam, one of the major sources of water in Jerusalem, which today was deserted as most of the city's residents were watching events in the north of the city. To everyone's surprise, Samuel immedi-ately jumped into the pool and began to swim across it towards what appeared to be a sheer rock wall on the other side. When he reached the wall, he turned onto his back and beckoned them to follow, before disappearing below the surface. The four companions looked at one another in amazement, before returning their gazes to the water. Minutes passed and there was no sign of Samuel.

Eventually, Benjamin said, "I'm going to take a look," and jumping into the water he followed Samuel's course and came up against the wall. Treading water, he felt along the stone, but evidently found nothing, so the group watched as he ducked below the water and vanished. Two minutes later, his head popped up again and he cried out excitedly, "There's a tunnel. Come on. Samuel's waiting. You just need to duck under a bit of rock – Daniel will be fine, Rachel."

Rachel and Miriam dropped cautiously into the water, Rachel holding Daniel at high port on her chest. It transpired that Ezra couldn't swim, but as he hesitated on the parapet of the pool, Miriam reached up her hand and drew him gently into the water, holding him beneath his arms as they paddled towards the other side of the pool. When they reached the wall, Rachel immediately ducked below the surface with Daniel and Miriam followed, gently pulling Ezra down with her; he held his breath as she drew him carefully through the water and upward again to the surface.

They emerged to find Samuel, Benjamin and Rachel standing on a stone ledge in front of what appeared to be a rough-hewn doorway through which water was flowing freely. As Ezra and Miriam clambered out and joined them, they saw another man standing just inside the entrance with a flaming torch. "This is Ephraim," said Samuel. "He will lead us through the tunnel."

"What is this place," asked Benjamin, bewildered. "I've lived my whole life in Jerusalem and swum in this pool a hundred times, but never knew it was here."

"We have Hezekiah to thank," replied Samuel, as they followed Ephraim along the gently upward-sloping tunnel. He went on to explain that Jerusalem had been besieged at least once before, eight hundred years before during the reign of Hezekiah, the thirteenth king of Judah. At that time the great colonial power was Assyria, which had already conquered most of the Levant and in the early seventh century BC was stampeding through Judah. Flushed with the success of his campaign, the Assyrian king Sennacherib finally laid siege to Jerusalem, the last stronghold of the Israelites.

"He would have taken the city, too," said Samuel, "had it not been for this tunnel. In those days – just like today – the city's main water source was the Gihon Spring, just across the Kidron Valley. But of course when the city was besieged, access to the spring would have been cut off. But Hezekiah foresaw this and long before the siege was mounted he found a natural fault in the rock and opened it up into a tunnel which brought water from the spring underground directly into the city, ending up in what is now the Siloam Pool.

"It was an amazing feat of engineering. One thousand seven hundred and fifty feet long and up to fifteen feet high, carved out of solid rock. Look," and he called Ephraim back to hold his torch against the wall, where they saw an inscription. "This is where the tunnelers met," he explained. "They started from opposite ends and worked towards each other. It's amazing how they managed to meet up, but they did. The party peered at the inscription in an Old Hebrew script which dated from before the Babylonian Exile:

While the labourers were still working with their picks, each toward the other, and while there were still three cubits to be broken through, the voice of each was heard calling to the other, because there was a crack in the rock to the south and to the north. And at the moment of breakthrough, the labourers struck each toward the other, pick against pick.

They all wondered at the achievement of their forbears who had managed to build this extraordinary life-saving tunnel without the benefit of any of the modern tools available to Benjamin and his stonemason's craft.

"This tunnel saved the city," concluded Samuel, resuming their journey. "It enabled Hezekiah to break the siege and Jerusalem was never conquered – at least, not for another hundred years."

At last, after walking for perhaps twenty minutes through the shallow water, they saw daylight ahead and Ephraim called a halt, putting his finger to his lips. They all stopped and listened, Rachel shushing Daniel as he began to whimper. Slowly, Ephraim led them quietly upward toward the light and the ceiling began to drop sharply until there was only a couple of feet of clearance above the water. They all ducked and followed Ephraim as he crawled through the narrow space and emerged into a deep depression into which a waterfall perhaps five feet high was falling. Stepping to the side of the falling water, Ephraim put his hands on the top of the rock and lifted himself up cautiously, peering around before dropping back down.

"It's all clear at the moment," he said. "Follow me," and he pulled himself up and out of the natural cistern onto the surface, reaching down to help the women who were immediately behind him. After a couple of minutes the company were all gathered together beside a rocky outcrop masked by thorn bushes, out of which the spring itself was bubbling energetically. Once again Ephraim held his finger to his lips and, stepping through the thorn bushes, disappeared. Five minutes later he was back. "I can see Romans," he reported. "We must be very quiet," this said with a nervous glance towards Daniel. "Don't worry," said Rachel. "He'll be quiet."

Ephraim led them through the thorn bushes and out onto the hillside above the Kidron Valley, just outside the new Roman wall. Ducking low, they made their way along a shallow gulley south-east away from the spring. They could hear the shouts of the Romans in the distance, but no alarm seemed to have been raised. They gained in confidence and with it, speed, hurrying along the gulley in the gathering gloom of the early evening.

And it was half an hour or so later, just as they were beginning to think they had escaped without detection, that they heard the soft thud of hoofbeats behind them and, before they had a chance to hide, heard a mocking voice, "Well, what a little mischief of rats we have here." They all turned towards the voice and Benjamin felt his blood run cold. There, mounted on a jet-black charger and accompanied by four other cavalrymen, was Felix Drusus.

CHAPTER 56

"MY, my. Isn't this cosy. Four little Jewboys and their whores, all on a family outing. Are we going for a nice picnic?" He chuckled and dismounted, as did his four companions, and took off his helmet. "It must be my lucky day. Exactly what I needed to liven up a boring scouting job out here in the middle of fucking nowhere." He paused, looked quizzically at Miriam. A slow smile spread across his face.

"Well, well, if it isn't my little girlfriend. I never forget a pretty face." He leered and swaggered towards her, while his companions spread out to encircle the group, swords drawn. Benjamin had tensed to the point where his muscles were screaming for relief. Ezra put a warning hand on his arm.

"What do you say, boys? Fancy a second date with our girl-friend?" The five men laughed in unison. "Then maybe we can have a bit of fun with mum here, eh?" Rachel held Daniel even more tightly to her chest and glared at Drusus. "And do you know what we do with Jew brats when we've finished with their mothers? We stick 'em and toss 'em on the fire. Nice bit of Jew fat keeps it burning nicely."

Benjamin broke free of Ezra's grip and lunged at Drusus, who quick as a flash drew his sword and swept it sideways, cuffing Benjamin on the head just as he had the first time they'd met. This time the stroke was more powerful and Benjamin collapsed to the floor, his head ringing, with Drusus's sword now pricking the back of his neck. "No need to get over-excited young pup. Plenty of time for you and I to play after we've finished with the girls." He pressed the point of his sword harder, breaking the skin on Benjamin's neck and producing a thin rivulet of blood.

As Drusus was cuffing Benjamin, the other four horsemen had grabbed hold of Ezra, Samuel, Ephraim and Rachel and were holding them tightly, daggers pressed against their throats. Daniel, now crying in alarm, was clutched even more tightly to Rachel's chest. She could smell the sweat on the soldier holding her. Miriam, untouched for the moment, stood silently, watching what was happening with apparent disinterest.

"What, don't want to run, little Jew-whore? That's a shame. I like a bit of a chase. Gets my blood pumping. Or perhaps you're looking forward to it? Eh?" He sniggered and licked his lips. "Let's get 'em trussed up, lads, then we can have a bit of fun before we head back. I reckon we'll get extra rations for picking up this lot. And they'll look pretty as a picture all hanging side by side on the hill tomorrow."

At that precise moment a loud crash sounded from the undergrowth behind Drusus and he turned involuntarily as a pair of wild boars plunged out of a small ravine and careered towards them. In the second or two it took for the Romans to recover from their surprise, the four men being held captive moved as one. The swarthy soldier holding Ephraim was knocked off his feet when Ephraim flicked back a foot and swept it sideways, unbalancing the Roman and sending him sprawling in the dirt. Ephraim was on his back in an instant, grabbing his helmet and pulling back his head as he drew his knife across the soldier's throat. The Roman slumped back onto the ground, clutching at his neck, trying to hold back the blood pumping from his throat.

Simultaneously, Samuel grabbed the arm of his captor and wrenched it downward, snapping his wrist with an audible crack and causing the knife to fall to the ground. Samuel followed up with a punch to the man's throat driven by the full force of his formidable shoulder muscles. As he fell to the ground, gasping for breath, Samuel calmly stepped forward and stamped once on the soldier's already broken throat. His eyes went wide, he convulsed twice and was still.

Ezra had a tougher time of it. The soldier holding him had recovered quickly and the knife barely left his throat, so he had no opportunity to wriggle free and tackle his captor. But Miriam did. Within three or four seconds of the wild pigs' explosive arrival, she had picked up a handy rock, turned and smashed it with all her strength into the back of the man's head. She felt his skull give way with a wet crack and he collapsed to his knees before slipping slowly sideways to the ground.

While his companions were being dealt with by their captives, Drusus had recovered fastest of all, turning back a split-second after his instinctive reaction to the frightened animals. He moved to drive the point of his sword downward, but Benjamin was no longer there. He had rolled quickly away from the sword-point and was now scrambling to his feet. Drusus grinned. "Want to make a proper fight of it, eh, like a real man rather than a Jew dung beetle?" He hefted his sword and out of the corner of his mouth grunted to the soldier holding Rachel not to let her go and to slice her throat open if anyone made a move. His own eyes never left Benjamin's.

Ezra, Samuel and Ephraim seemed uncertain what to do next. The soldier holding Rachel pressed the point of his knife harder against her throat, drawing blood, while Daniel started to howl in outrage. Benjamin was backing slowly away from Drusus, looking for an opening, anything that would give him an advantage over his foe, but Drusus was wily and quick-witted and was not going to be thwarted twice. His grin grew wider as he advanced on Benjamin. When suddenly a look of surprise crossed his face and he dropped his sword, putting his hand up to the left side of his head.

Benjamin saw a stone fall from Drusus's hand and blood start to pulse between his fingers. He turned to his left and Benjamin followed his gaze. Miriam stood holding an empty sling. Benjamin instinctively felt for his own on his belt and realised it was gone. Drusus sank slowly to his knees, shaking his head in apparent confusion.

The soldier holding Rachel hesitated a moment, then released her and backed away, holding his hands up palms forward. But to no avail. In one seamless movement, Ezra drew his dagger from his belt and threw it, catching the soldier neatly between his breastplate and his kilt, the knife sinking to the hilt in the soft flesh of the man's belly. He let out an anguished wail and fell backwards clutching his stomach. Samuel withdrew the dagger and finished the job with a flash of the blade across his windpipe.

There was silence now except for the gurgling death-rattle of the last soldier and a kind of murmured whimpering coming from Drusus, who seemed completely baffled by what had happened to him. Benjamin walked up to him and put his sandal in the man's chest, pushing him backwards. He sprawled in the dust, his left eye bulging unnaturally from its socket, as Miriam walked slowly towards him, removing her dagger as she approached.

"Please, please, I have a wife and a child," blubbered the decurian. "Please."

Miriam looked down at the man who had robbed her of her childhood, her womanhood, her life. Then she knelt and, almost tenderly, slipped her hand behind his neck and lifted his head, pulling it up gently until he could see the full length of his body.

Then in one swift movement she lifted his kilt and brought the blade up between his legs. His scream of pain echoed around the hills as blood ran across the dirt.

Miriam laid his head gently back on the ground and stood up without a word, watching the writhing figure beneath her. His lifeblood was flowing freely now and, despite the confusion wrought in his brain by the impact of the rock, she could see from the blaze in his one good eye that he could see the end coming and was consumed by fury and humiliation. Miriam stooped once again, wiped the knife on Drusus's tunic, stood and turned away.

Benjamin ran to his wife and child and caught them up in his arms, then did the same to Miriam. "Where did you learn to use a sling?" he asked her in amazement.

"Why should you boys have all the fun?" she asked coyly, her face breaking into the first smile Benjamin could remember since that fateful day in the tavern. "Now perhaps we should go."

The entire company regarded Miriam with something approaching religious awe. Then they gathered their belongings, including the cloth binding with its precious cargo, and set off towards the east, away from Jerusalem and the setting sun.

CHAPTER 57

AS BENJAMIN'S party left their dead captors behind and headed further into the Judaean hills, Jerusalem was entering its death throes. As resistance finally crumbled in the face of a determined onslaught by the Romans on the Inner Court of the Temple, John, Simon and their supporters fell back through the Upper City to the Royal Palace, where they made their last stand. Eleazar was killed with his men defending the Holy of Holies from the first of the Romans to enter the sacred enclave.

The Temple itself was not completely abandoned. A group of millenarians – civilian mystics who believed that the destruction of Jerusalem was the final act of the Apocalypse before the coming of the Messiah to wreak revenge on their enemies – took refuge on the roofs of the Inner Court colonnades. There they chanted and prayed in a fever of divine anticipation. Which was swiftly dashed when the conquering Romans set fire to the colonnades and burned them all to death.

The sack of the Lower City quickly followed. The soldiers of four Roman legions had been held at bay by the city's defenders for six months, their attacks repeatedly frustrated and their comrades dying in unprecedented numbers. Now that they had finally taken Jerusalem, they were in no mood for compassion. The Jews of the city's poorest areas, already weakened by four years of war, followed by months of hunger and privation, suffered the full force of Rome's retribution. The Lower City was burnt to the ground and its inhabitants slaughtered by the thousands, with no quarter given regardless of age or sex.

Meanwhile, the Romans were once again at work with their siege engines. John, Simon and the last of their fighters were now committed to a final stand, in the certain knowledge that, if defeated, their fate was sealed. They took up positions in the three towers of the Palace – Mariamne, Hippicus and Phasael – from where they rained arrows, rocks and burning pitch onto the heads of the Romans who were once again building ramps, this time across the Hinnom Valley against the western wall of the Palace and against the eastern wall not far from the entrance to the viaduct.

On 7 September 70, the Romans brought their rams up the ramps and began battering the walls, which were quickly brought down. What followed was a rout, in which those fighters who did not manage to escape into the Upper City were massacred where they stood. Those who did reach some kind of safety in the warren of streets below the viaduct were soon rooted out and killed. The conquest of Jerusalem was complete.

Titus himself stood victorious that day in front of the golden doors of the Temple, watching his troops applaud him with the traditional chant reserved for the leaders of great military conquests: *Imperator! Imperator! Imperator!* And when the cheering had subsided, he stepped down from the podium on which he had been standing with arms raised in triumph, and casually ordered his men to raze the Temple to the ground.

———

Six months after the destruction of Jerusalem, a sorry spectacle presented itself in Rome. To the shouts and jeers of thousands of Romans, seven hundred rebels were paraded in chains through the city's streets as part of a grand Triumph led by Emperor Vespasian and his son Titus to celebrate victory in the Jewish War. At the head of the chained procession were John of Gischala and Simon bar Giora. John, as a man of former wealth and rank, was destined for life imprisonment, but Simon – the perceived commander in chief of the rebels – suffered a humiliating end: after being dragged across the Forum, viciously scourged and beaten, he was slowly strangled to death in front of the crowd.

It had taken more than two thousand years for Jerusalem to evolve into the beautiful, golden jewel of the nation that it had become by AD70. It had more or less survived the predations of the Assyrians, Babylonians, Persians and Macedonians, only to fall to the greatest imperial power the world had ever seen. Its people were scattered like chaff after the destruction of their physical and spiritual capital and it was to be another two thousand years before they would return.

CHAPTER 58

AFTER SPENDING a restless night camped just outside the city of Bethany, the exhausted band of refugees made their way through the forests, scrub and grassland of eastern Judaea, before entering the vast desert wastes where Jesus was said to have wrestled with Satan forty years before. As the sun reached its zenith they crested a rise and looked down across the shimmering wilderness to the shores of the Dead Sea, the great salt lake fed by the River Jordan and called Asphaltitis by the Roman occupiers. Their destination was an eccentric settlement on the north-western shore of the lake.

Over the centuries, Judaism had evolved into three distinct traditions: the Sadducees, the upper-class custodians of the Temple and priesthood, closely allied with the Herodian monarchy; the Pharisees, a socio-religious movement that thrived in the towns and villages of Palestine; and the Essenes, an ascetic sect with a fundamentalist view of the Hebrew scriptures who lived in segregated communities. It was to one such community that the companions were now being led by Samuel.

Qumran was a hot, remote outpost of Judaism founded some three hundred years before by the Essenes as a monastic retreat for those who adopted an even more rigid interpretation of Jewish law than their fellow acolytes. There were only a few hundred inhabitants and very few were women – most of the Essenes of Qumran were celibate and those who were not had married only after three years of engagement. All possessions were owned collectively, so they had no slaves, and they practised strict communal living, under the direction of an elected leader, sharing all meetings, meals and religious celebrations. Unlike their fellow Pharisaic and Sadducean Jews, they did not sacrifice animals and were dedicated pacifists, only carrying weapons for defence against robbers.

All new members of the community were required to serve a three-year probation, during which they were expected to take an oath to serve God, maintain a pure lifestyle, adhere to the community's rules and preserve the Essenes' extensive library of religious texts. Again in contrast to their Sadducean and Pharisaic counterparts, they believed in the immortality of the soul. Community rules required a life of repentance and constant purification, beginning with baptism and maintained through regular bathing in the community's ritual rain-fed baths or 'mikveh.' So seriously did they take their personal purity and adherence to Judaic law that they would not even defecate on the Sabbath.

It was into this strange world that the six companions walked, tired and dusty, that afternoon in early September.

They entered Qumran via a shallow stairway at its southeastern corner, which led up to an open space where congregants were busy at a series of potters' wheels, producing tableware and vessels for the community. They passed by a kiln on their right, marvelling at how the potters could work at such a task in the already fierce heat of the desert. The labourers looked at them curiously as they passed, nodding in recognition to Samuel, but did not stop working. The band continued on their way, led by Samuel, into the heart of the community.

They approached on their right a large complex of buildings

303

which, Samuel explained, housed the kitchens, pantry and assembly hall where all the community would gather for their meals, religious ceremonies and important meetings. To their left, across a wide courtyard, they noticed a sizeable cattle pen, from where they could hear the soft lowing of numerous beasts. Directly ahead was a long, low building which Samuel explained was arguably the most important structure in the entire complex. It housed the Essenes' reservoir, located alongside the community's original ancient cistern, which was supplied by a rainwater-fed aqueduct running into the commune from the north.

Samuel led them into the assembly hall, where they were met by a small, dark, wiry man called Aaron, whom Samuel introduced as the Bursar of the Congregation. Aaron embraced him fondly and turned with a smile to his companions.

"You are welcome to our community," he said with the strong accent of the Decapolis, the ten cities east of the Jordan from one of which Aaron undoubtedly hailed. He called out a name and a young man appeared from the pantry on the south side of the hall with a tray of fruit and cups of wine, together with a small cup of milk for Daniel, who seemed awestruck by his surroundings and was uncommonly tranquil. They sat at the long table in the centre of the room and ate and drank hungrily.

Before they had an opportunity to embark on any meaningful conversation, the door opened and a tall man entered and walked briskly to the table. "I am sorry I was not here to greet you," he said with a smile. "My duties are many and the hours are few! My name is Lemuel and I am the Guardian of our community." Aaron had already explained that the Guardian was the leader of the Essenes at Qumran, periodically elected by the congregation, and respected for his religious erudition and leadership skills.

Lemuel cut an impressive figure, dressed in black with long limbs and an austere cast to his face, from which dark eyes seemed to search their souls as he regarded each of them in turn. They noted that, unlike most Jews, his hair was long, probably marking him out as a Nazirite who had taken a vow never to cut his hair, as well as a commitment not to drink wine.

"I regret that we meet under such circumstances. The rumours of war have reached us even here and it was only a matter of time before the heathens in Jerusalem met their just end." It was the first time the company had heard the religious authorities in the capital spoken of in this way and it puzzled them until Samuel later explained that the Essenes had originated nearly three hundred years before as a breakaway from the Zadokite priesthood, which they saw as poisoned by pride and avarice. Today's Sadducees, descended from the Zadokites, were therefore viewed by the Essenes as a rotten corruption of the original Aaronic priesthood.

Lemuel eyed the bundle in front of Benjamin. "One day these treasures will be restored to their rightful place in the Temple under the leadership of the true believers," he said quietly. "Until then, their whereabouts will be safe here in our custody. Now, please, eat, drink and rest." And he stood up, smiled at Daniel and chucked him under the chin, then left as briskly as he had arrived.

Aaron showed them to comfortable, if basic, quarters in a tower in the north of the settlement which had breathtaking views of the lake and the mountains which towered over its farther shore. Samuel left them to return to his own home and the companions settled down to sleep, the deepest and most restful repose that any of them could remember.

At dawn the following day, Samuel came to rouse them with a modest breakfast of fruit and milk. Ephraim then bade them all farewell, explaining that he needed to return to Jerusalem to find out what had happened to his parents. He feared the worst.

The remaining companions were joined shortly afterwards by Aaron, who led them from the tower through the maze of connected buildings to a room fronted by a beautifully carved set of double cedar doors. Pushing them open, he entered and they followed him into an enormous room lined from floor to ceiling with shelves on which rested hundreds of scrolls. In the middle of the room were several large tables at which scribes were hard at work.

"This is our library," explained Aaron proudly. Here we have preserved copies of every book of the scriptures along with a host of other texts, hymns, poems, wisdom literature, scriptural commentaries, liturgies and blessings, together with the laws which guide our community."

Benjamin, Ezra, Rachel and Miriam gazed around them in wonder. They had never seen so many volumes in one place. For Ezra in particular, who was an avid reader, it promised a treasure trove of learning.

"Ah, good morning," said a cheerful voice from the shadows on the far side of the room, and the Guardian emerged into the sunlight which streamed across the tables in the centre of the library from windows high in the walls. "I see you are all well rested. Then we can begin."

He beckoned them to follow and led them to the far side of the room. There in the shadows was a small shallow opening about half a metre square, with a plain hinged door which appeared to be made of bronze. Taking an elaborate key from within the folds of his cloak, he opened the door and withdrew a small metal casket. Another, smaller key, appeared in his hand and he opened the box, revealing a copper scroll which appeared to be identical to the one carried by Benjamin and his friends.

"Samuel brought us this scroll for safekeeping before the siege of the city began," he explained. "Now it can be reunited with its companion."

Benjamin looked at the man, stupefied. "But I thought the whole point was that the scrolls should remain apart, until it was safe to reunite them! Our mission was to bring the second scroll out of the city and ensure that it was safely hidden until then."

A shadow of confusion crossed the Guardian's face. "I know nothing of this," he said, clearly puzzled by Benjamin's outburst. "I know only that our loyal Samuel was entrusted with the scrolls and instructed to take them to a safe place."

Benjamin and Ezra both turned to Samuel, who was standing a little apart from the group. They simultaneously registered the sly look that flitted across his face and almost instantly disappeared. "It is better this way," he said, beginning to move towards Benjamin. "My people are worthy custodians of these precious things and will take great care of them until the time comes for them to be restored to their rightful place in the Temple, under the rule of the true believers."

"No," said Benjamin firmly. "That is not what Eleazar instructed – or what the Sanhedrin intended. The scrolls must remain separate."

Samuel's expression changed: his eyes darkened, his chin lowered and his lip curled. "The Sanhedrin – the damned Sanhedrin. What do they know of the will of Yahweh? They and their Sadducean upstarts are liars and apostates! Jerusalem is being punished because of their sinful pretensions! It will soon be time for the true believers to take their place and these treasures will ensure we create a kingdom that glorifies God for a thousand years!

"Now give me the second scroll?!" and he lunged for Benjamin.

In the chaos that followed, no one quite realised what had happened until it was all over. Samuel, imagining that Benjamin was carrying the scroll somewhere in his clothing, pushed him back against the wall and began rummaging in his cloak. Ezra instinctively ran to his friend's aid and, wrapping a strong arm around Samuel's neck, tried to pull him away. Samuel, his face twisted in fury, turned and punched Ezra hard in the stomach, leaving him reeling. As he staggered backwards, clasping both hands to his gut, Samuel turned back to Benjamin, who realised to his horror that the man now held a short paring knife with a wickedly sharp blade – he barely managed to grab his adversary's wrist in time, preventing him from slashing the blade across his throat.

The two men struggled together for what seemed to their dumbstruck observers like minutes, but was in reality only seconds, the knife held chest high between them, Samuel trying with all his might to bring it to bear on Benjamin's neck. As they strained against each other, neither gaining the advantage, a loud voice rang out: "Samuel – for God's sake, stop!"

Benjamin saw it in his face, inches away from his own, before he felt it: the slight relaxation in Samuel's body. It was as if a shadow passed from his eyes, leaving them clear-sighted once more, and the snarl vanished as swiftly as it had appeared. The tension went out of Samuel's arm and the knife began to move downward, away from Benjamin's throat. It was as Benjamin cautiously began to relax his own grip that Samuel's hand surged upward once more and buried the blade in his own throat.

There were screams and shouts as he fell to his knees, blood pumping from his wound and air whistling through his severed windpipe. Clutching his neck as if to try and stem the flow, the man raised his eyes to the Guardian and, struggling to get the words out through his ruined throat, said hoarsely, "I'm – sorry – master..." and slumped to the ground face down, his lifeblood ebbing away across the flagstone floor.

As the gathering looked on in shocked dismay, the doors to the library flew open and more members of the community rushed in. The Guardian was kneeling beside Samuel, holding his head as the man's struggle to hold onto life gradually gave way to a peaceful resignation. A few moments later, he was gone.

As soon as Benjamin had gathered his wits, he ran to his friend, who was leaning against the wall, still clutching his stomach. It was as he reached for Ezra's hands that he saw they were both covered in blood. Miriam noticed this a moment or two later and ran to his side. "How unutterably stupid of me," gasped Ezra with a lopsided smile pushing through the pain. "After all those Romans who tried to kill me, to be gutted by a homegrown religious maniac..." And then he was sliding down the wall, his eyes closing. "Noooooooo!" cried Miriam, flinging herself on his prone body.

———

Benjamin and the Guardian were alone in his office, seated across the table from one another. The events of the previous few days had taken their toll on the community's leader and he was grey and stooped, no longer the imposing figure they had met on their arrival. He regarded Benjamin balefully.

"I do not understand why Yahweh has seen fit to visit these trials upon us," he said quietly, seeming to squeeze out every syllable through a welter of sorrow. "But I am truly sorry for what has happened – and for your friend."

Benjamin just shrugged. There was nothing to say.

"But I have made a decision," continued the Guardian. I have prayed on it and I know it is the right one." He hesitated for a moment, looking out of the window at the main courtyard, where his people were gathered to pay their formal respects to the dead in one of their arcane ceremonies. "Samuel was not a bad man. Just over-zealous and misguided. I pray that Yahweh has mercy on his soul." He leaned forward and placed both hands on the table in a gesture of decisiveness.

"You will take the second scroll and ensure it is safely hidden far from here. That is Yahweh's will, I am sure of that."

Benjamin nodded. He had no wish to stay in this place that now held such tragic memories.

"So," said the Guardian. "It is done." And he rose from his seat, opened the door and left the room without another word.

Benjamin cut a disconsolate figure as he walked slowly back to their lodgings. After all the horrors he had witnessed in Jerusalem, he would never have believed that he would encounter yet more violence and bloodshed in this peaceful haven.

Rachel was sitting quietly with Daniel on her lap when he entered the room. He regarded them sadly.

"So why are you looking so miserable?"

Benjamin turned towards the voice. Ezra was sitting up in bed, naked from the waist up apart from the broad bandage around his middle. As always, his smile was infectious and Benjamin couldn't help but grin too. "How are you feeling you old malingerer?"

"Never better," replied Ezra. "After all, I've got the best nurse in the land!" He turned towards Miriam, who was sitting beside his bed holding his hand.

Miriam was gradually emerging from the shadows that had shrouded her since her ordeal in Jerusalem, but she was a different girl. The death of Drusus had helped to exorcise her demons, but there was still a deep sadness behind her eyes that her brother knew would take a long time to fade. She had lost her childhood and her innocence overnight and been catapulted into adulthood in the most brutal way; he sensed that her mind was still trying to catch up. But Benjamin could also see her inner strength asserting itself and he sensed that, despite everything, she was finally beginning to find some peace.

For his part, Ezra had spent many hours closeted with the Guardian and had decided, once he was fully well again, that he would stay with the Essenes. He had already been accepted as a potential probationer. He didn't in the least mind the three years it would take to achieve membership of the community, because coincidentally it was exactly the same length of time as his engagement to Miriam, with whom he had fallen head over heels in love from almost the first moment he set eyes on her, and for whom Ezra was the kindest and most attentive of prospective husbands.

The four companions remained together at Qumran for several months, recovering from their recent ordeals. Benjamin grew strong as he resumed his work as a stonemason, helping the community build an additional pottery and kiln to enable them to increase their output. Rachel made new friends among the few women of the congregation and settled happily into domestic life, while spending increasing amounts of time with the scribes, learning their skills.

During this time the first scroll remained in its locked repository, watched over by the Guardian, who had sworn to protect it until such time as Yahweh made clear his intentions for it.

While Benjamin and Rachel tarried at Qumran, the second scroll lay concealed in a cleft of the rocks not far from the community walls, its whereabouts known only to Benjamin. And when it came time for them to leave the community, the second scroll went with them. Benjamin had no idea where it was supposed to be secreted – the intended destination had been known only to Samuel, who had clearly disobeyed the instructions he'd received in Jerusalem by leading them to Qumran rather than to the hiding place envisioned by Eleazar and the Sanhedrin. But Samuel was now dead and the secret of its proposed location had died with him. Benjamin knew only that it now fell to him to ensure that the second scroll was taken somewhere it would be safe and well hidden.

They took their leave on a bright April morning, the air fresh and clear, the sound of hymn-singing and the lowing of contented livestock in their ears as they walked down the steps they had ascended six months before. They were setting out on the first stage of their journey north to a village on the western plain of Jericho, where Rachel had distant relations. Daniel, who had grown into a strapping two-year old, insisted on toddling beside them for the first few steps until he tired of the effort and demanded to be carried.

At the foot of the steps, Ezra embraced his friend and accepted with tearful surprise Benjamin's gift of his treasured bow. "Keep practising, my dear friend. I will be back one day to test your skills against mine."

Then Benjamin hugged his sister tightly. "My dearest sister, may you be as happy with Ezra as I am with Rachel. I hope you bear him many nephews and nieces for me, because one day I will be back to spoil them. I love you."

"I love you, too, my brother. Go peacefully and be happy. You deserve it."

Benjamin and Rachel turned to the north, took the bridle of the donkey they had been given by the community, which was laden with their few belongings, popped Daniel on top, and walked slowly away without looking back. They never returned to Qumran.

As the community gradually forgot about their departed visitors and Ezra and Miriam settled into its fellowship, the life of Qumran went on unchanged and undisturbed by the upheavals in the lands around it.

CHAPTER 59

IN THE WINTER OF 73, doom finally came to Qumran. Since their conquest and destruction of Jerusalem, the Romans had conducted mopping up operations throughout the south of Palestine, where sporadic guerrilla attacks continued to be mounted against them. Finally, they dislodged the remnants of the revolutionaries from their last redoubts in Herodium near Bethlehem, Machaerus east of the Dead Sea and the Forest of Jardes on the southern slopes of Mount Hebron, before finally besieging the mountaintop fortress of Masada, near the southern shore of the Dead Sea, where the last of the Jews were holding out.

When the Romans eventually overran the fortress, they found every building burnt to the ground and nearly a thousand dead, the defenders having all committed suicide rather than fall into their enemy's hands. Only two women and five children were found alive. With the last stronghold of the revolution now in their hands, the Romans headed back along the western shore of the Dead Sea, towards Qumran, fifty kilometres to the north.

The Essenes at Qumran had been well aware of events at Masada. In the early days of the siege, some of the civilians there had escaped and made their way to the commune, and the congregants had followed developments over the subsequent two years as various travellers brought them news from the south. So when the fortress was eventually taken and Lucius Silva's Tenth legion turned north, they knew exactly what to expect.

The Guardian immediately ordered all the scrolls in the library, including the first copper scroll, to be removed, placed in protective jars and transferred to a cave complex to the south-west of the community. Many of the caverns were natural, but the Essenes had added to them with a number of artificial caves, making thirteen in all, in which the sacred books, including the copper scroll, were secreted. It took two full days for all the books to be moved and sealed in their hiding place and only just in time, for the Romans arrived the next day.

The soldiers were as ruthless at Qumran as they had been in their previous conquests. Most of the men were killed and the few women and children enslaved. Within hours the peaceful religious community was transformed into a charnel house. The potters were thrown into their own kilns. Many died in the main assembly hall when the Romans locked the doors and fired the building. The Bursar was decapitated with a single sword stroke when he tried to prevent entry to the albeit now empty library. The Guardian himself was thrown bodily from the tower and left to die from his injuries.

Ezra and Miriam were among the fortunate few to escape the mayhem, slipping out along the aqueduct and into the desert before making their way north to Jericho, where eventually they were reunited with Benjamin and Rachel in their new home.

The Essenes' priceless library remained undiscovered by the Romans.

The first of the two copper scrolls slept safely in its new

hiding place for many long centuries, until it was unearthed two thousand years later.

By contrast, the second scroll, which had travelled north with Benjamin and Rachel, passed into obscurity, its whereabouts unknown.

KHIRBET QUMRAN, JORDAN, 1947

CHAPTER 60

DURING THE FINAL months of the British mandate in Palestine, in early 1947, three young Bedouin shepherds were tending their flock of goats in the hills above the Dead Sea, near Ein Feshkha in what was then Jordan. The story goes that Muhammed Ahmed el Hamed, nicknamed 'edh Dhib', or 'the wolf' and his cousins Jum'a Muhammed and Khalil Musa, from the Ta'amireh tribe, spotted a small opening in the side of a rocky cliff and, curious, one of them idly tossed a stone into the hole. To the boys' surprise, they heard what sounded like pottery shattering in the darkness below.

Night was falling, so the cousins made camp and the following day Muhammed edh Dhib rose early and climbed inside the hole. What he discovered was to electrify the debate about the origins of the Bible, Judaism and Christianity itself. In the corner of the cave were a collection of earthenware jars containing seven papyrus scrolls. Muhammed did not recognise the language, and neither did his cousins, but they took the scrolls to Bethlehem and sold them to an antiquities dealer, from where they changed hands several times, arousing progressively greater interest in scholarly circles until eventually three of them ended up in the possession of a professor at the Hebrew

University and the other four were sold to a Syrian Orthodox priest, both in Jerusalem.

Meanwhile, the original find had prompted repeated searches for the cave where the scrolls had been found, but it took almost two years before it was finally located. On 28 January 1949 a Belgian United Nations observer, Captain Philippe Lippens, and Captain Akkash el-Zebn of the Arab Legion, rediscovered what came to be known as 'Cave 1' at Qumran, prompting an initial excavation of the site by the Jordanian Department of Antiquities, which yielded more scroll fragments.

Two-and-a-half years after the initial find, the American Schools of Oriental Research commenced a full-scale excavation at Qumran. Over the subsequent five years, eleven caves were discovered, yielding some 972 manuscripts, including all but two of the books of the Old Testament, together with a huge range of mystical and prophetical texts and copies of the various Rules which governed life in the long-dead Essene community. It was the greatest archaeological discovery of religious texts in history and it revolutionised academic thought in Jewish, Christian and Muslim theological circles.

It was early on in the excavation, on 14 March 1952, that archaeologists discovered a strange copper scroll at the back of Cave 3, the last of fifteen scrolls to be discovered in that particular cave. It was unique among all the scrolls discovered at Qumran, in that it was not only made of copper rather than papyrus, but it also contained, not a religious text in literary Hebrew, but an inventory.

Since 2013 the so-called Copper Scroll has been on display for all to see at the Jordan Museum in Amman. Two separate sheets of rolled copper, totalling two-and-a-half metres in length, contain a list of sixty-four locations, all but one of which describe jaw-dropping quantities of hidden gold and silver treasure. In one location alone, the copper scroll refers to 900 talents of buried gold, equivalent to 868,000 troy ounces, which today would be worth nearly $1.2 billion.

In all, the scroll lists literally thousands of talents of gold and silver coins, bars and vessels, together with a host of jewel-encrusted priestly vestments.

The problem is that the descriptions of the locations for the treasure are obscure and arcane. For example, the opening lines, which are a fair guide to the style of all the other entries, refer to *'the ruin that is in the valley of Acor, under'*; *'the steps, with the entrance at the East'*; *'a distance of forty cubits, a strongbox of silver and its vessels'*; *'with a weight of seventeen talents'*. Scholars and treasure-hunters from all over the world have pored over the scroll in an effort to identify the locations of the treasure. Expeditions have been mounted and thousands of square metres of land explored, without success. The locations referred to just aren't specific enough.

One of the frustrations of the many academics and explorers who have tried to unravel the mystery of the scroll is that there is a tantalising reference at the end of the inventory to a second scroll:

'In the underground cavity which is in the smooth rock north of Kohlit whose opening is towards the north with tombs at its mouth there is a copy of this writing and its explanation and the measurements and the details of each item.'

Scholars have long pondered that this second scroll may hold the key to the first, that the two were always intended to be read as a pair, and that anyone in possession of both will at last be able to decipher the precise locations of the treasure. Unfortunately, the second scroll has never been found.

Until now.

CHAPTER 61
TODAY

THE MEETING HAD BEEN ARRANGED on neutral ground, in a public place, in the middle of the day. Jack Braddock, always prepared, always cautious, arrived an hour early to check out the location and ensure there was no chance of being caught unawares. The café in Regent's Park, not far from the famous zoo, was a favourite haunt of London's cosmopolitan fashionistas whose eclectic tastes ran to chai lattes and vegan quiche. But Jack wasn't there for the rabbit food.

He and his trusted lieutenant, Gazza, took their seats at one of the round tables outside the café and looked around. They were just off the Inner Circle road that looped around the core of the park, surrounded on three sides by over 160 hectares of gardens, lakes, ponds and grassy expanses. The café was busy with the lunch crowd, emitting a low hubbub as people passed in and out, settling for an hour or so before returning to their offices in Marylebone or in one of the elegant Regency buildings that surrounded the park.

He could see no one watching, although he knew that six of his men were concealed close by, keeping an eye on things. Always best to be prepared for all eventualities.

Five minutes before the allotted time he saw the Arab

approaching from the direction of York Bridge, which linked the Outer and Inner Circles of the park, accompanied by his bodyguard – at least, that's what Jack assumed him to be – but otherwise apparently alone. Jack wasn't, however, stupid enough to believe that Al-Shammari hadn't made similar preparations, which meant that the surrounding parkland was undoubtedly bristling with well-muscled men of various ethnicities.

Al-Shammari and Mahmoud took their seats opposite the two men. "Why don't you go and get us some coffees, Gazza," opened Jack. "Mine's black." He made no offer to Al-Shammari, who nevertheless added, "Yes, Mahmoud. The same for me." And the two subordinates headed inside to stand uncomfortably together in the lengthy lunchtime queue.

"How long have we conducted business together, Mr Braddock?" Jack knew a trap when it opened up before him. "As long as it has suited you, Mr Al-Shammari," he replied after a beat. The Iraqi smiled. "Please call me Ari. It seems to me that we have made a great deal of money together over the years and I am puzzled as to why you have chosen to compromise that arrangement when it has been so profitable for us both."

Jack leaned back on the bench and shrugged expansively. "Sometimes you can't account for the behaviour of your employees, even when they know the consequences can be – harsh."

Al-Shammari raised an eyebrow.

"Look – Ari. We both know what happened shouldn't have happened. One of my team got a bit overenthusiastic and decided to help themselves to some of my shipment. As it happens, they didn't know what they were nicking or who they were nicking it from. There were a few other bits of merchandise in that container that they thought they could turn a quick few quid from and your goods got caught up in the blag. As far as I can tell, they never even opened the crate."

Al-Shammari watched Jack closely. He had a sixth sense for lies, but could detect none here.

Jack sat back in his chair, crossed his arms and regarded the Iraqi coolly. "Anyway, I don't understand why you didn't come to me first to get hold of this package, whatever it is. I thought I'd proved my worth to you over the years. It was a bit disrespectful just treating me like a fucking bag-carrier."

Al-Shammari nodded in capitulation. "You are right, Mr Braddock. But on this occasion the seller came to me via a more direct route. However, we still thought it best to use your company to transport the item."

Braddock harrumphed.

"But," continued Al-Shammari, "I would have expected a more dependable service."

Now Braddock leaned forward. "I get that. But what you did was well out of order and needs answering. The warehouse was one thing – I can almost understand that. It was business. But my son. That was something else." His voice dropped to a threatening growl. "That was personal. And I can't let it pass." His eyes were boring into Al-Shammari's.

The Iraqi was taken by surprise. He had expected this to be a difficult meeting, had anticipated a negotiation, but this mention of Braddock's son meant nothing to him. "I'm afraid I don't understand, Mr Braddock. I have had no dealings with your son. I have never even met the boy, nor, to my knowledge, have any of my associates."

It was Jack's turn to scrutinise his adversary. Although he reckoned your average Arab was a duplicitous son of a bitch, Al-Shammari appeared to be genuinely taken aback by what Jack had said. Nonetheless, he wasn't going to give ground until he knew more. "My son was killed the morning after my ware-house burnt down. It was a professional hit. And as far as I'm concerned there's only one suspect."

"Jack. I am a practical man. I use whatever measures are necessary to achieve my objective. Sometimes that means adopting extreme measures to gain a person's attention. But I have never taken a life unless it were necessary in the pursuit of my objective. In your case, I had already sent you a clear message. There was no advantage to me in adding your son to the equation."

Jack continued to stare hard at the man, who regarded him impassively, his posture relaxed, hands resting together on the table. At this point, Gazza and Mahmoud returned with two coffees. Apparently neither of them was thirsty.

"Mahmoud, when you completed your assignment at Mr Braddock's premises in East London, what did you do?" Mahmoud looked confused. "I returned to your home, sir, as you know."

"Did you or any of our associates take any further action against Mr Braddock?" Again, Mahmoud looked baffled. "No sir. You gave me no other instructions."

Al-Shammari looked back to Jack. "It seems someone has been inserting themselves into our business, Jack." He thought for a long moment, then added, "And I have a suspicion who that might be."

Jack was still not entirely convinced. "Go on."

"There was a young man who had been making enquiries into my affairs. A young man who I believe was indirectly of your acquaintance." It was Jack's turn to raise an eyebrow. "You may remember our first transaction together?"

"Them Persian statues. Yeah, I remember. Neat little deal, that was."

"And you recall that it was necessary to remove two of the parties involved in that transaction, lest they disrupt our arrangement or bring it to the attention of the authorities?"

Jack thought for a moment. It had been a long time ago and, while he remembered the deal, the details eluded him. Then, in a flash of understanding, he connected all the dots in one go.

"The bloke and his missus who Jimmy took care of?" Al-

Shammari nodded. "And the young bloke you talked about. He was some kind of relative, right?"

"The couple's youngest son."

And so everything fell into place. It seemed their fortunes were all interlinked. "So, this boy took out my son, what, for revenge?"

"No, Jack. We felt it necessary to take action as soon as we realised that he was delving into our business. He died some days before your son was killed."

Jack dismissed Michael's death without a thought, moving immediately to the only possible conclusion.

"Someone else then? Another member of the family?"

"The young man's brother."

Jack went very still. "An eye for an eye, eh?" He paused and regarded Al-Shammari carefully. The Iraqi nodded slightly. "Well, it seems he took a bit more than an eye, doesn't it? Which means he needs dealing with." Another pause. "Who is he? Where do I find him?"

Al-Shammari sighed and turned to Mahmoud, who straightened up on his seat and said, "His name is Charles Carter, the older brother of the young man Mr Al-Shammari referred to. He is a former soldier. We have reason to believe that his younger brother was involved in some kind of government agency and that Mr Carter has recently also become involved in that organisation."

"Just stop talking in riddles and tell me where the fuck he is!" exploded Jack, slamming his fist on the table.

"I'm afraid we do not know Mr Carter's whereabouts," responded Al-Shammari calmly. "He seems to have disappeared."

Jack stood up and leaned over the table, his face inches from Al-Shammari's. "I want to know where that cunt is. If you know anything, now's the time to cough up."

As soon as Jack stood up, two figures appeared soundlessly

out of the bushes lining the café garden. Both were dark-featured and both were wearing black leather jackets, which they pulled aside just far enough for Jack to see the guns in their shoulder holsters.

Al-Shammari remained calm. "As I said, we do not know where Mr Carter is. But we do know the whereabouts of his wife."

Jack resumed his seat and the scowl fell from his face, to be replaced by a slyly calculating expression. The two men melted back into the shrubbery.

"Ari, as soon as you give me that address, your merchandise will be on its way to wherever you want it delivered."

"It will be my pleasure, Jack. And as a gesture of goodwill, I am prepared to make a contribution of, let us say, one million pounds, in part recompense for your loss of property."

Jack smiled for the first time. "Pleasure doing business with you, Ari."

CHAPTER 62

"WHAT DO you know about first century Palestine?" repeated Lowell. I still couldn't understand why the Vanguard chief was suddenly talking about something so arcane.

The conference room deep in the bowels of *NV Triton* was becoming stuffy, despite the air conditioning. It had been a long meeting and everyone around the table was tired. Outside the windowless room, night was falling on the ship as it steamed steadily south through the North Sea.

Lowell sighed. "Let's start with something that happened a few weeks ago," said Lowell, "there were two murders in a building in Bloomsbury, near the British Museum. It belonged to a manuscript conservator called Geoffrey Parminter. He was shot, along with another man whose body wasn't immediately identified. You might have seen it in the papers; it made a bit of a splash.

"There were a couple of security cameras outside and the police ran the footage for that day and saw two men enter and leave the building before and after the murders. They both had their heads down, but the cops reckon they saw enough of one of them to say that he was dark-skinned, possibly Middle Eastern. That was as much as they got, though. The two guys just disappeared – no sign of them on any of the neighbouring cameras. They obviously knew what they were doing."

"We picked up on the story while we were looking into your brother's death, as part of our research into the illegal antiquities market," interjected Aleysha. "It's an iffy trade, for sure, but it's not every day that someone gets murdered. So we did a bit of digging with our friends in the Met. Transpires that Parminter had regular dealings with a fellow called Washbrook, a dodgy dealer in stolen manuscripts."

At this point the door opened and a tall, red-headed woman walked confidently into the room and sat down in an empty chair beside Lowell. She was dressed in jeans and a black T-shirt printed with *My career lies in ruins*. I judged her to be in her mid-thirties. She had an open face and smiled broadly as Lowell introduced her.

"Charlie, this is Dr Charlene Ramirez from the University of Houston," said Lowell. "She's a distinguished paleographer – in the same field as Parminter. Rare manuscripts. She was in London speaking at a conference, but agreed to fly out and help us."

"Morning everyone," said the woman crisply in a broad Texas drawl, laying a briefcase on the table in front of her and taking out a sheaf of papers. "I'm here out of respect for Professor Parminter. Whatever happened, he was a tremendously gifted academic and one of my heroes. He didn't deserve what happened to him."

"Thank you, Charlene," Lowell continued. "After we picked up on Parminter's death, we had a look at his movements over the previous few days and discovered that he'd spent most of one afternoon in UCL's archaeology department," continued Lowell. "He used to teach at the university, so had free access to all the facilities there. Some discreet enquiries and a few pounds in the right hands and we managed to establish what he was doing there."

"Which was?" I asked.

"He was in one of the labs operating something called an X-ray fluorescence imaging machine. Among other things, it's used to uncover texts on ancient parchment which have been over-written with other writing or pictures. They're called palimpsests. Parminter spent a few hours with this machine and when he left, our sources say he was in a state of great excitement."

"Have we any idea what he was doing in there?" I asked. "And what's this got to do with us or with this Iraqi you were talking about?"

"Well, that's where we got lucky. The machine logs all the tests carried out on it and in certain circumstances keeps digital copies of whatever material the user prints from it. Charlene?"

The Texan rummaged among the papers before her, withdrew three sheets of A4 and handed them to me across the table. I looked at them in puzzlement. All I could see was line after line of what looked like gobbledegook, but Charlene was quick to explain.

"It's written in a language called Byzantine – or mediaeval – Greek. It was the lingua franca of the Byzantine Empire from the early fifth century until the empire collapsed with the conquest of Constantinople in 1453. I'm pretty sure it dates from very early in that period."

"But what does it say? And why's it relevant?" I asked.

"We're getting to that, Charlie," countered Lowell. Charlene continued: "This palimpsest was obviously an original document which had been overwritten with some sort of religious text. We're not sure what that was – it seems to be some kind of account of Jesus's life, but without the context or the rest of the document, we've no way of knowing. Anyway, clearly what had excited Parminter was the palimpsest itself. So I translated it." She handed me another sheet of paper on which what looked like a short letter had been printed. None of it made any sense to me.

"Look at the last paragraph" and she clicked her remote, bringing up the words on the screen.

And to your care, Master, I entrust the resting place of the burnished scroll. Its unearthing has brought me a deep disquiet that I cannot comprehend and I know it is best left to the secret places and to the will of God. Its treasures will bring no peace to the world. I have returned it to the earth whence it came, to the place of worship of the cursed ones upon whose heads be the blood of our Lord.

"I still don't understand," I said, sounding a little peevish even to myself.

In answer, Charlene flicked another image onto the screen. It showed a series of illuminated glass display panels encased in a heavy black cabinet. Behind each pane of glass I could see what looked like a fragment of flat greenish-grey metal covered with arcane script.

"This," she said, "is the Copper Scroll. It's on display in the Jordan Museum in Amman. It was one of the scrolls discovered back in the '40s and '50s in a remote part of the Judaean desert in Israel. You might have heard of the Dead Sea Scrolls?" I nodded. "There were literally thousands of fragments of papyrus discovered in a network of caves near the Dead Sea, but this was the only scroll made out of copper.

"It caused huge excitement, because it appears to be a detailed inventory of a fabulous treasure, which was supposedly hidden in various places across the Levant. It dates from the mid-first century and most scholars agree that what it lists is all the treasure from the temple in Jerusalem, which was removed and taken to safety shortly before the Romans conquered and looted the city during the Jewish War in AD70. Needless to say, no one has ever found the treasure – although countless expeditions have been mounted over the years. It remains one of the world's most fascinating mysteries.

"But what's really intriguing about the scroll is that the final line refers to a *second* scroll, presumably also made out of copper, which apparently contains the missing information needed to locate the treasures."

I was beginning to see the light. I looked back at the translation Charlene had given me. "And you think the 'burnished scroll' mentioned in the palimpsest could be this second scroll. But why? It could refer to any number of things."

"A lot has to do with where it was found," explained Aleysha patiently.

"And where was that?" I asked.

"In Israel. Or more correctly, on the West Bank, in the Occupied Territories. Our friend Al-Shammari's henchmen have been very busy there of late, most recently in Jericho, where another antiquities dealer was recently tortured and killed. And our sources in Israel think it's no coincidence that his murder happened just hours before another death a few miles away at a remote monastery in the desert. A monk in his 50s who just happened to fall off a balcony and end up with his head pulped in the ravine below.

"Putting two and two together, we believe it's safe to assume that the palimpsest – and the original document that overlaid it – originated at that monastery. Perhaps our monk found it and decided to do a bit of dealing on the side, cutting out his monk-brothers. Who knows? But if our assumption is correct, we have a big problem on our hands."

"Because...?" I asked.

"Because if the palimpsest does give a clue to the whereabouts of the second copper scroll, then our friend Al-Shammari could be about to lay his hands on one of the greatest and most valuable archaeological finds in human history," said Lowell.

I turned to Charlene. "So what do you think this treasure's worth?"

Charlene paused before answering. "Taking the Copper Scroll at face value, academics and historians believe the treasure it documents could be worth up to – three trillion dollars."

There was an awestruck silence in the room and I suddenly realised I was holding my breath. "Good God," I finally said. "Now it all makes sense. Why this guy was so keen to shut down any investigations into his business."

Havelock nodded. "And why you were so lucky to get away." I nodded slowly in acknowledgment of this simple truth.

"So do you think Al-Shammari knows where this thing is hidden?"

"Not yet," replied Aleysha. "But Charlene thinks she does."

"So why not just give what we know to the authorities. To the Israeli Government – or the Palestinian Authority?"

"Because, Charlie, we don't know where these treasures are," answered Lowell. Most of them could be on the West Bank, or in Gaza, or Egypt, Jordan, or in Syria or Lebanon, for all we know. The geography and political boundaries were very different in the first century and all these countries are less than a hundred miles from Jerusalem – an easy distance to travel even two thousand years ago.

"Can you imagine the chaos if billions of dollars of ancient Jewish religious artefacts suddenly started being dug up all over the Middle East? These are treasures from Temple Mount, the most viciously disputed fifteen hectares of land on the planet. The Palestinians would claim it belonged to them. So would neighbouring countries. Israel would go ballistic. With those sums at stake, every nutcase and fruitcake within a thousand miles would have a field day stirring up hatred and resentment.

It would be used to finance a massive terror campaign and the entire region would go up in flames."

Havelock cut in. "We need to find that scroll first. It's now Vanguard's top priority – everything else is on hold. And we have one advantage. As far as we can tell, Al-Shammari doesn't know that anyone else is aware of what he's discovered. If we're lucky, it will take him time to figure out where the scroll is. Whereas we might just have the edge – if Charlene is right."

At that moment my phone rang. Despite being in the middle of the North Sea, the ship offered a powerful satellite cellular network. I glanced at the screen, but there was no caller ID. I punched a button to accept the call. It was short – no longer than five seconds – but I felt myself go cold as adrenalin instantly flooded my body.

"What is it, Charlie," asked Rebecca, speaking for the first time that day.

"It's my wife. Angie. She's been kidnapped."

CHAPTER 63

EIGHTY KILOMETRES SOUTH of Beirut and less than twenty kilometres from the Israeli border, on the Mediterranean coast, lies Tyre, one of the oldest continuously inhabited cities in the world. The historian Ernest Renan once described it as 'a city of ruins, built out of ruins,' and the richness of its archaeological heritage has earned it the status of a UNESCO World Heritage Site. It is also home to three of the twelve Palestinian refugee camps in Lebanon, which helps to explain the particularly strong Hezbollah presence in the city.

On the outskirts of Tyre, in the Jabal Amil mountains, lies the village of Shama'a, whose principal claim to fame is that it is supposedly the burial place of Simon the Zealot, one of Jesus's twelve apostles. In a graphic illustration of the paradoxical symbiosis of the Christian and Muslim traditions, he is better known locally as Prophet Shamoun al-Safa, who is believed to be an ancestor of Imam Mahdi, the messianic figure whose return to rid the world of evil and injustice is eagerly awaited by many Shia Muslims.

A number of mosques and shrines have been constructed in the Mahdi's honour across the Shia world, the most prominent at Samarra and Kufa in Iraq, and the Jamkaran Mosque in the

Iranian holy city of Qom. One of the smallest among them is this modest shrine in southern Lebanon. As an ancestor of, and claimant to the blood lineage of, the Mahdi, Shamoun is revered by Lebanese Shias, who regularly visit his tomb in Shama'a to pay their respects.

On a morning in early March, the small shrine was packed with a party of forty Shia pilgrims who had been touring the country's religious sites for the past two weeks and for whom this visit was the culmination of their trip. They were excited but respectful as they filed past the prophet's tomb, looking forward to a final celebratory lunch in the city before boarding the coach back to their homes in the northern Lebanese city of Tripoli.

When the bomb exploded, all forty pilgrims were packed inside the small space and the concentrated blast from the four pounds of Semtex instantly vapourised most of their bodies, pasting the interior walls of the shrine with blood and shattered limbs as the entire building blew outwards in a maelstrom of stone, glass and twisted metal. Including visitors and staff, fifty-two people were killed in the blast and another ten were left with life-changing injuries. As the dust settled on the rubble and the first sirens began to wail, the keening of the village women was already reaching a crescendo.

CHAPTER 64

AL-SHAMMARI TOOK the call in his villa in the Beqa'a, a hundred kilometres north-east of Tyre.

"Have you seen the news," asked the voice at the end of the phone in heavily accented Arabic, betraying the caller's origins in the Caucasus.

"Yes," replied Al-Shammari quietly. "It is well done."

"That was merely a timely demonstration. We need to remind our enemies that we are still able to strike anywhere, at will, against the apostates and infidels. Our shahid are ready to launch a hundred such operations!"

At one level Al-Shammari detested dealing with these people. As a committed Sunni, he shared the movement's loathing of the Shi'ite renegades who ran Lebanon with the backing of their poisonous sponsors in Tehran. His animus was also deeply personal: his father, an Iraqi tank commander, had been killed on the front line of the Iran-Iraq War in 1980 when he was a small child.

However, he also recognised that his clients were exceptional soldiers. Fanatical and fearless, they had efficiently harnessed the twin weapons of guns and propaganda, even if they had a limited understanding of how to achieve their political ends. There was no finesse or subtlety about them, but they were brutally efficient.

And, he reminded himself, this was about more than what he personally regarded as a perverse internecine war between Muslim factions. For him, dealing with these savages was merely a means to an end. As long as they could be relied upon to wreak the same havoc on the Jews and their western poodles as they did on their Islamic cousins, his objective would be achieved.

"This is just the beginning," said the voice. "Your discovery will enable us to take jihad to our enemies in every corner of creation. There will be no hiding place for the kuffar bastards. We shall light a fire under their world that will burn for a thousand years!" he said, his voice rising.

There was a brief silence, then the voice – calmer now – said quietly, in measured tones, "We have operatives ready to descend on every site as soon as you provide us with the locations. They will strike as one. Every last piece of the Jews' gold will be seized within hours of your confirmation. When can we expect you to complete your mission?"

Al-Shammari sighed. 'His mission'. He wondered at what point his paymasters thought they had assigned him this task, rather than his having brought the opportunity to them. It was ever so. With religious fanaticism came arrogance and hubris. This man, a former leader of IS in Syria and one of the most wanted terrorists on the planet, thought he was invincible and infallible.

"Soon," replied al-Shammari. "Very soon. Just be ready, my brother, because when the time comes you will need to move with the speed of a mamba."

The voice on the end of the phone grunted. Then, "You have a week." And the line went dead.

Al-Shammari sighed again. He would not be goaded by these people. They were, after all, going to make him rich, while exacting the revenge on his enemies for which he had thirsted since the day his family were slaughtered. And he saw with great clarity how it would all play out.

Ever since Islamic State had been ejected from Iraq it had been seeking territory for a new power base. There had been constant skirmishes along the Syrian border between IS fighters and Shi'ite Hezbollah guerrillas, who reluctantly collaborated with the Lebanese army against their common enemy. In recent years the risk that Lebanon would slip into the same sectarian violence that plagued Syria and Iraq had increasingly driven minority groups in the country to take up arms, making the situation even worse.

The fact that refugees from Syria now accounted for fully one-third of Lebanon's 4.5 million population, coupled with the sheer volume of weaponry that had seeped into the country during the course of its neighbour's civil war, had created unprecedented unrest. The situation was exacerbated by the alliance between IS and Syria's al-Qaeda affiliate, the Nusra Front, who had together established footholds in the mountains along Lebanon's north-eastern border and were launching daily incursions, while recruiting jihadists by the hundred in preparation for an all-out assault.

Al-Shammari had gathered from their various conversations that his clients' first strategic objective was a lightning strike to drive through a passage from the Qalamaoun Mountains in Syria to the Sunni Lebanese enclave of Akkar on the coast, splitting the country in two and giving them a powerful foothold from which to extend their reach north and south across the rest of Lebanon.

But that was merely the first skirmish in the war.

Once they had their hands on the treasure from the scrolls,

they would embark on their ultimate aim: a catastrophic conflict across the southern border with Israel.

Al-Shammari well understood the chaos that would ensue once the Jews' treasures were unearthed. Overnight, everything would change. The Israelis would puff up with rage at the prospect of their ancient religious treasures being stolen by their enemies. The Palestinians would be emboldened to lay claim themselves to any treasure found in the Occupied Territories. The surrounding Arab states would be forced to take sides – and the West would be dragged into the inevitable conflict that followed.

It would be the jihadists' wet dream, the ultimate prize for an apocalyptic death cult that yearned for a conflagration in the Middle East with the potential to spread across the globe. The treasure from the scrolls would be a twin weapon in IS's hands: a source of fabulous wealth to fund their cause and a catalyst for the war to end all wars between Islam, the Jews and the Christian infidels. The entire Middle East would be consumed in the inferno, an Armageddon worthy of the most febrile religious prophecy.

Walking to the window that looked out over his vineyard, Al-Shammari withdrew the familiar photograph from his wallet and gazed once more upon the faces of his wife and two daughters. He had taken the photo himself in the garden of their home in Ramadi, the provincial capital of western Iraq. It was 2015 and a few months after Islamic State had crossed the border from Syria, swiftly occupying large swathes of the province. As usual, the Americans had responded with indiscriminate air strikes. Al-Shammari had been in Europe on business on the day that an American bomber loosed its payload on the Ramadi suburb where his wife and children were eating lunch in the family home. Their house and four neighbouring properties had been obliterated.

The ISIS commander whom US intelligence had mistakenly placed in their street that afternoon was in fact a hundred miles away to the west taking delivery of an arms shipment from Syria.

He replaced the photo in his wallet and stood, brooding.

What happened next was now in his hands

CHAPTER 65

THE NEXT FEW hours were spent in furious planning. I still had no idea who had taken Angie, but following the phone call I had been instructed by text to be at a specific location in Thamesmead, east London, at 7am the following morning. It was now 5pm in the afternoon. Havelock led the planning and for the first time in a long time I was relieved to be back in the company of a military man who knew what he was doing. We spent several hours working out how we would approach the rendezvous and what contingency plans we needed to have in place, before splitting up to get a few hours' rest.

The helicopter was in the air at 5 a.m. There were three of us. Bruce Havelock had insisted on personally accompanying me, together with another of his team – a cheerful young Somali called Omar, who seemed to approach the whole thing as a great adventure. Havelock had reassured me that Omar, contrary to appearances, was as serious as it gets when confronted with a tactical situation and was also one of his best shots. Both men were outfitted in what I recognised as special forces gear: light Nomex suits with Komperdell ballistic protector vests and fully-loaded Viper chest rigs complete with V-cams. On their laps sat light, compact Modular Integrated Communications Helmets with Pyramex I-Force anti-fog goggles.

Across their chests, they held LWRC PSD rifles. Derived from the US M6A2 rifle, the PSD is an ultra-short carbine with an eight-inch barrel chambered for 5.56mm NATO rounds and capable of a rate of fire of up to 900 rounds per minute. It is perfect for close engagements. They also wore Sig-Sauer P226 pistols on their thighs. As the chopper turned west across the North Sea, Havelock passed me a spare Sig and concealed-carry holster, which I slipped inside my waistband and clipped to my belt.

"I believe you know how to use this," said Havelock. "It's got a full mag with one in the chamber. And a little something extra," he explained.

I thanked him and settled back with my scrambled thoughts as we sped across the sea towards the east coast. I thought back to that fateful night a few months after I got back from Afghanistan, to the final confrontation with Angie. I was still in pain from the injury to my shoulder, still in therapy and popping too many painkillers washed down with too much whisky. Under the circumstances, the outcome was inevitable.

She and I had met at a regimental dinner two years into my service. She was the daughter of the RSM and the apple of his eye. When we began going out, her father was less than enthusiastic about our relationship. He had always wanted his baby to marry outside the army and so be spared the pain inflicted on her grandmother when two officers arrived on her doorstep one day to inform her that her husband had been killed by a land-mine in some grubby little East African war that his UN peace-keeping force was trying to keep a lid on.

But I had found a kindred spirit in Angie. She understood my need to overcome the nagging pain of my parents' deaths by driving myself to tackle new challenges, even if it meant putting myself regularly in danger. She was a gentle soul, a diminutive blonde with green eyes and delicate features who had an inner strength that belied her fragile exterior. She had found her vocation as a primary school teacher when she was barely out of university and her pupils adored her. We fell head-over-heels in love and were married just six months after we met. As he gave her away at the altar, her father whispered to me, "I have only one request of you, son. Stay alive." It was an exhortation I had done my best to abide by.

But as the years passed, we grew apart. I was away much of the time and Angie refused to leave our home in Winchester and travel with me on my postings. Her school kids were too important to her to leave them behind and I understood that, so never pressured her. But our marriage suffered as a consequence. Neither of us were built for a long-distance relationship. The final straw came when I returned from the Middle East with shrapnel in my arm and shoulder, demons in my head and a giant dose of self-pity. We had an explosive argument within minutes of sitting down for our first dinner together for six months and, like the juvenile I had become, I walked out, slammed the door and headed for the nearest pub.

Angie made all the running in the weeks that followed, doing her best to nurse both my body and my heart back to health, but my head was in a state of permanent revolt and, little by little, I pushed her further away until somehow the bond finally broke and we called it a day. When I boarded the train for London one dismal morning in late November, I couldn't even summon up any tears of farewell.

Months of TV dinners, short-term security jobs and occasional labouring work followed, with too many nights spent alone with a bottle, until I decided that if I were going to drink, I might as well do it in company, so I embarked on a series of heroic night-time tours of London's dingiest bars until I happened on the Caledonian Club, where I doubled down in my pursuit of self-destruction by acquiring a gambling habit to go with my drinking.

Angie and I talked only occasionally on the telephone, exchanging the odd email when the occasion demanded it and, until we met briefly at Michael's funeral, it had been months since we'd last spoken. But for some reason we still hadn't got around to making our separation final. In any case, her father, needless to say, was not my biggest fan and made every effort to ensure that I stayed away from her. It seemed to him that I had done something even worse than getting killed. I had stayed alive and killed my marriage instead.

Despite the damage I'd done, I knew deep down that I still loved my wife. And I believed she still loved me. There was no one else in her life, as far as I knew. She put all her energy into the kids at her school and there seemed little time left over for romance. Although I had created a gulf between us, Angie didn't seem in any great hurry to file for divorce. And neither was I. I just think neither of us knew how to find a way back to one another.

I pushed these thoughts aside and tried to focus on what lay ahead.

We were now flying low over the Thames Estuary, heading west up the river towards the Barrier. A couple of kilometres before we reached the Woolwich Ferry crossing, the pilot veered south and descended fast towards an area of open parkland just off the Eastern Way, setting us down on a stretch of patchy grass. All three of us leapt out of the aircraft and ran north-west across the park as the chopper immediately took off and headed back the way it had come.

Keeping low, we reached and vaulted the line of metal fencing that marked the boundary of Southmere Park and jumped into the black people carrier that was already waiting for us on Bazalgette Way. After a swift recap of the plan, I jumped back out of the vehicle and began walking quickly

344

north along a footpath between two hedgerows towards the river, while Havelock and Omar headed off in the van.

The voice on the phone had been explicit. I was to come alone (naturally) and walk west along the Thames Path from just north of the Crossness Pumping Station and keep walking until I was contacted on my phone. We saw from the map that the area south of the path at this point was given over to several hectares of wasteland, dotted with small hills, gulleys, trees and bushes. There were plenty of places to hide and it was an area that was simple to seal off. The open path could be blocked to the west and east, and the river provided a natural barrier to the north.

I duly arrived at the Pumping Station at 7 a.m. precisely and turned left onto the path, anxiously waiting for my phone to ring or beep with a new message. I knew that Havelock and Omar were close at hand, but at this point I didn't know where and there was no way of establishing exactly where the rendezvous with Angie's kidnapper would be. I walked quickly along the path, which was empty at this early hour, with the river on my right. It was a grey and overcast morning, which lent little cheer to the vista of cranes, industrial units and abandoned warehouses on the other side of the river. After a kilometre or so I saw an old World War Two pillbox coming up on my right.

It was now nearly 7.15 and my phone was still silent, so my anxiety was growing as I walked past the pillbox. Then I heard a voice, seemingly coming from out of the ground.

"Stop. Turn around and walk back," It said. Taken by surprise, I did as instructed and a large man in a leather jacket and jeans emerged from the pillbox. He was bearded, but with a shaven bullet-head, and a teardrop tattoo on his left cheek. A heavy gold chain rested on his barrel chest and his hands were like two hams, the right one dwarfing the handgun he was holding.

"Where's my wife?"

"All in good time," growled Bullet-head, holding the gun steady while looking up and down the path to check for walkers. "Take your clothes off."

"What?" I responded, incredulous.

"If you want to see your missus again with all her bits intact, I'd get on with it. Down to your skivvies."

Realising I had little choice, I obeyed, stripping down to my underpants and standing shivering in the early morning chill.

"Kick the kecks and the hardware over here," instructed Bullet-head. I hooked my toe under my jeans and flicked them towards him, with the gun and holster still attached. Leaving them on the path, he walked over to me and told me to hold my hands above my head while he frisked me, yanking down my briefs and having a good feel around my tackle before he was satisfied that I hadn't been carrying an offensive weapon in my undercrackers. "Put 'em back." He picked up my jeans, removed the holstered gun and, to my relief, shoved it in his pocket before tossing my jeans back to me. He retrieved my phone from the pocket and tossed it in the river.

Fully dressed again and casting surreptitious glances around me in the hope of catching sight of my two companions, I asked again: "Now. Where's my wife?" Bullet-head didn't respond. Instead, he took out a phone, hit a speed-dial button and said simply, "He's clean," before pocketing the phone once more and continuing to point his pistol unwaveringly in my direction. I looked around me, noticing for the first time an overgrown path opposite the pillbox that led into the waste ground beyond. I eyed it expectantly and then, able to contain myself no longer: "For the last time –" I began, but my words were cut short by the sound of a powerful engine.

Disorientated, I looked away from the path towards the sound of the engine, which was coming from the direction of the river. As I looked past Bullet-head to the water, I saw a powerful launch sweep out of the centre of the channel and roar up to the

346

riverbank in a swirl of foam, its driver expertly reversing the prop just as the vessel closed with the bank. Bullet-head waved the gun at me. "Down." I quickly regained my wits and followed as he led the way down two flights of lichen-covered steps to the launch. He clambered aboard and reached for my arm, dragging me roughly over the side, and I sank to my knees in the belly of the boat.

So much for our plan.

The driver was standing at the wheel, his hand feathering the throttle gently to keep the vessel in place. Then up from the small cabin below came a burly figure dressed in a purple wind-cheater and, incongruously, shorts and trainers. His wispy grey-white hair was lifting from his head in the gentle breeze and, despite his ruddy and pockmarked face, he looked every inch the kindly grandfather. Except for the eyes. The eyes were dark pools where no light penetrated. They were like black holes in the cratered cosmos of his face.

"Hello Mr Carter," he said with a genial smile. "It's good to meet you at last. My name's Jack Braddock."

CHAPTER 66

THE LAUNCH SWEPT out into the river and quickly crossed to the other side. I had no idea what Havelock and Omar would do now, with five hundred metres of water between us, but I had little time to ponder this as the boat pulled up alongside the opposite bank next to another set of steps. Braddock, Bullet-head and I all disembarked and the driver immediately rammed the throttle forward and tore off downriver. We ascended the steps and walked down a narrow path between a concrete plant and a brickyard to a service road, where a Land Rover Discovery was idling. Braddock had refused to say a word while we transited the river. Bullet-head pushed me into the back seat, squeezing in beside me.

Now I understood what this was all about. Jack Braddock. Jimmy's father. I knew that without Vanguard's support, I was as good as dead. And so was Angie, if she wasn't already. With this creeping realisation, came a determination not to show weakness before this man.

"OK, I'm here, you fucker. Now where's my wife?!" Braddock turned around from the front seat as the driver pulled away. "She's having a nice chat with some friends of mine. Just a few minutes away. Please be patient, Mr Carter."

His calm, patronising demeanour was infuriating me. "If you've hurt her, I swear I'll –"

"Yeah, I know, Carter," his voice hardening. "You'll kill me. It's an old line. Like I said, please be patient." He turned back to face front. "Nice pair of tits, by the way."

I lunged forward with my hands ready to seize his throat, but Bullet-head was ahead of me and grabbed my wrists, wrenching them back with bone-crunching force before gripping me by the back of the neck and holding me in an iron grip.

"You need to control that temper of yours, Carter. It'll get you into trouble one day."

I sat trembling with rage, but held back for the next few minutes until the car pulled off the service road into a dishevelled-looking yard, at the rear of which sat a warehouse, in a very poor state of repair. Another Land Rover was already parked in the yard.

"Here we are, then," said Braddock cheerfully, getting out of the car and starting towards the doors of the warehouse. "Time for the lovers' reunion!" he called over his shoulder as Bullet-head pushed me out of the vehicle and nudged me towards the warehouse with his gun.

Braddock gripped the double doors and pulled them apart, opening just enough space for us all to walk through. The space beyond was dark and it took my eyes a few seconds to adjust to the gloom. The place stank of a fetid mix of grease, wet concrete and urine. It was poorly lit by grime-covered windows halfway up the walls. Bullet-head pushed me forward with the muzzle of the gun between my shoulder-blades. I now noticed a low murmuring coming from across the floor of the warehouse, which was littered with old bits of machinery and disused plant. As we walked towards the sound, I finally saw its source.

Angie was suspended from a steel girder, her arms tied together above her head and her feet only just touching the ground. She was stripped to her panties and a gag was tied tightly around her mouth, forcing her teeth apart. She was groaning helplessly, her eyes filled with terror. Seeing her small frame so vilely abused made me finally snap and I whirled around and punched Bullet-head squarely in the stomach before running towards my wife. I managed a couple of steps before my head exploded with pain, the floor unaccountably made a lunge for my face and everything faded fast to black.

As I slowly returned to consciousness, I was immediately aware of two excruciating pains, one in my head and the other in my arms. I swiftly understood the source of the former: I'd been whacked across the skull with something hard. The second was due to virtually my entire body weight being borne by my arms which, like Angie's, were tied above my head, with my toes brushing the ground.

I shook the greyness from my eyes and looked around, my head complaining bitterly at every movement. I was face to face with Angie, who was looking at me with tears streaming down her face. Her long blonde hair was dirty and matted and her eyes, flushed an even deeper green by her tears, seemed at once terrified, confused and accusing. I felt so deeply ashamed seeing her hanging there helplessly, with Braddock's men gawping at her nakedness. I tried to tell her it was all going to be OK, but could do no more than mumble through my gag.

Jack Braddock sat before me on a wooden stool, calmly scrolling through his phone. I became aware of several other men standing around, perhaps half a dozen including Bullet-head. They were all dressed like him, in leather jackets and jeans with heavy work boots.

"Ah, our sleeping beauty's rejoined us," exclaimed Braddock genially, pocketing his phone and standing up. He walked up to us and looked into my face, his eyes glinting, with the ghost of a smile on his mouth.

"No need to worry about your good lady," he said. "No one's touched her. At least not yet. Some of my boys are very keen to show her some proper East End hospitality, though." He chuckled. I spat an expletive at him through the gag and my head protested violently. I realised I had to take it easy – I felt instantly nauseous and knew that if I overdid it, I'd find myself choking on my own vomit.

"Let me tell you a story about my son," said Braddock. "He was a tricky tyke from the off. Always giving his mother grief when I wasn't there to give him a taste of my belt. Never seemed to tame him, though. When he was – what, Gazza," looking over his shoulder at one of the men ranged in a semicircle around our little gathering, "twelve or thirteen?" The man nodded with a smile. "He saw this radio-controlled truck in one of the toy shops. Big bugger, it was. All giant tyres and oversized exhausts. He fell in love with that truck. Begged us to buy it for him. But we said, 'no Jimmy, you wait until your birthday like all the other kids.' He was not happy, I can tell you.

"Anyway, one day I'm away on a spot of business and my Sandra rings me up to tell me that Jimmy had gone down to that toy shop and tried to persuade the owner to give him the truck. Said his dad would pay later. Well, understandably the owner was reluctant to oblige. In fact, I gather he became quite heated. So Jimmy, being a determined little so-and-so, even at that age, grabs a screwdriver that's lying on the counter and stabs the guy in the leg. Well, you can imagine. Much wailing and squealing and a lot of blood. But my boy, he has his eye on the prize. So he grabs the truck and legs it out the door.

"You can guess what happened next. Police, ambulance, hysteria all round. The rozzers are round at my gaff within the hour and Jimmy's in the frame. I mean, talk about an overreaction. It was only a tickle – a few stitches and a tetanus jab and the bloke was back on his feet in no time. But he refuses to let it go. I'd already given the police a drink and they were happy, but that old man, he just couldn't leave it alone. Came round to my house – to my home, mind – threatening all sorts. So, my Jimmy, being the enterprising lad he was, he nips round there one night with a can of petrol from my garage and a box of matches and – hey presto – no toy shop.

"That fixed the bloke, I can tell you, especially when I told him that if he didn't shut the fuck up with his whining I'd burn his house down as well with him and his wife in it.

"Anyway, the point of the story is that my Jimmy wouldn't take shit from anyone. If anyone crossed him, he would deal with them personally and head-on. And do you know why? Because he was my son. And because that's the way I do things." And, saying this, Braddock walked over to a work-bench against the wall and began to rummage around among a selection of power tools. His entourage watched him attentively.

Angie was still moaning through her gag, her eyes looking as if they would pop out of her head at any moment. I didn't think it was possible for her to look any more fearful, but when Braddock returned from the bench with a portable angle grinder in his hand, I saw her begin to shake violently and her face turned scarlet with terror.

"So, as I was saying, I like to deal with unpleasantness personally and head-on. If a job's worth doing, and all that." At which point he flicked a switch on the angle grinder and it sprang to life, its silicon carbide disc spinning at 12,000 rpm. "Amazing piece of kit, this," observed Braddock. "Do you know, you can cut stone with it?"

He walked casually towards Angie, whose face had turned from red to white and her forehead was slick with sweat. She was squirming against her bonds, trying to pull up her legs and protect herself.

"I love all those films where the villain says to the helpless hero, 'It's nothing personal'. Well, I want you to know, Carter, that this is very personal."

By now I was swinging from the beam, kicking out with my

legs towards Braddock as he drew closer to my wife, holding the spinning grinder in front of him with both hands.

"What do you think, Carter? Shall we start with a foot and work our way up? Shouldn't take too long to get to her knees, and then we can get started up top," he leered.

I was frantic, swivelling back and forth, kicking for all I was worth, but it was no good. Angie had stopped struggling and seemed to have lapsed into a kind of trance.

"Then when we've finished with wifey here, we'll have a bit of fun with you. I think we'll start with your balls and work our way up. You can watch your guts spill out on the floor." With this, he crouched down in front of Angie and lowered the grinder to her left foot. At which point there was a loud crack and the grinder literally flew out of his hand, landing a good couple of metres away and slowing to a stop. There was a moment's silence and no one moved. Then there were two more sharp cracks a second apart and two of Braddock's henchmen flew backwards, their heads a mess of red and grey matter.

Now Braddock recovered. He pulled a revolver out of his waistband with his left hand and whirled towards where he thought the shots had originated, firing blindly until the cylinder was empty and the trigger produced nothing more than empty clicks.

I could see that his right wrist was bent at an unnatural angle, presumably from when the grinder had been torn from his hand. He waved the gun at the empty warehouse and screamed, "Do you know who you're dealing with?! Do you??! I'm gonna gut you like I'm going to gut these two!! Do you hear?? I'm gonna fucking gut you like fish." Then there was silence and stillness once again, as Braddock frantically swept the walls and windows for signs of the gunman.

Gazza and Braddock's other men had all taken cover. I could see two of them crouched behind an old machine tool with weapons raised. Of the other two there was no sign. Then there were two more cracks in quick succession and the men behind the machine were lifted off their feet and landed sprawling on the filthy floor.

Braddock at last regained his senses and ran for the doors, which one of his associates had closed after he entered. He yanked them open, dashed through the gap and was gone.

Meanwhile, his remaining men had regrouped and were firing wildly at the windows, which were showering glass into the warehouse. Bullet-head was lumbering across the open space to the door when a round took him in the back and he arched like a salmon on the fly before slamming backwards onto the concrete floor, his spine severed. I heard the sound of running footsteps as the remaining men made off in the other direction to what I assumed was a rear door at the back of the warehouse.

As silence fell once again, I saw two black-clad figures in balaclavas and helmets leap through windows on opposite sides of the warehouse, landing gracefully on the concrete pad. It took them just a few seconds to cut us down and as soon as I was free of my bonds I ran to Angie and lifted her from the floor where she had fallen, supporting her and doing my best to shield her breasts with my left arm as we started for the exit. "Let's get out of here," I shouted. Havelock pulled the Sig from his hip holster and tossed it to me. I caught it with my free hand, flipped off the safety and followed him towards the half-open warehouse doors. He was speaking slowly and clearly into the integrated comms unit in his helmet, while Omar walked backward behind me, covering our departure. Havelock exited cautiously, sweeping the yard before calling us to follow him.

It was an easy mistake to make. While sweeping the yard for Braddock and his men, we had neglected the Range Rover parked near the gates, the door of which now flew open and Braddock sprang out armed with a large-calibre pump-action shotgun, held in his undamaged left hand. He wasted no time in loosing off a shot, quickly racking the gun and firing a second. He remained calmly standing beside the open car door, his legs planted firmly apart, racking and firing in a controlled volley. I was amazed at his insouciance, given what he was up against.

As soon as he'd emerged from the car, we'd all moved fast, Omar, Angie and I ducking back inside the warehouse and Havelock rolling behind a low wall running from the side of the building to the perimeter fence. We were fortunate that Braddock was armed with a shotgun, with its limited range and accuracy, and he wasn't shooting with his dominant hand, but the wide spread of heavy-gauge shot was still a lethal threat and the sound of hundreds of pellets slamming into the metal doors was deafening in the echoing space.

"I'll fucking have you all!" screamed Braddock, loosing another shot in Havelock's direction, the shot peppering the brickwork of the low wall. "This is my fucking manor, you cunts and no one fucks with me on my fucking manor!" At which point he clearly regained his perspective on the odds facing him and turned back towards the car.

Angie was crying quietly into my shoulder, which filled me with renewed rage. I noticed for the first time that there was blood running from her left foot. I assumed that Braddock's grinder had nicked her when the shooting had started and it flew from his hand. I saw that the cut was deep, but didn't have time to give it more attention. Still supporting her with my left arm, I raised Havelock's Sig and pointed it through the narrow gap between the giant warehouse door and its wall-mounted hinge. There was just enough space to give me a sightline and I fired a quick double-tap at Braddock as he was climbing back into his car. I saw the fabric of his right trouser leg twitch just above the knee and he let out an animal howl as he collapsed into the driver's seat, yanking the door closed behind him. A couple of seconds later the powerful car was slaloming through the open gates and disappearing up the road in a cloud of splintered gravel.

Havelock emerged from behind the wall and we met in the middle of the yard. Two minutes later, the black people carrier screeched to a halt and we all piled inside. I lay Angie on one of the rows of seats and Havelock passed me a blanket and a first-aid kit. I pulled out a bandage and quickly wrapped her foot, knotting it tightly around her ankle to slow the bleeding. She was clearly in shock and was muttering incoherently, her eyes flitting listlessly around the interior of the vehicle, which was now powering away from the warehouse.

"You were right," I gasped to Havelock. "They'd have found the tracker if I'd had it on me. Smart move to put it in the gun holster. Thank God the bastard kept it on him instead of tossing it in the river!"

Havelock pulled off his helmet and balaclava and smiled. "Well, the launch was a surprise. But chopper trumps boat every time! How is she?"

"A cut on her foot," I replied. "But it could have been much, much worse. Thank you."

"Don't thank me, thank Omar here. I told you he was a crack shot."

"All part of the service," grinned Havelock's accomplice.

"I just wish I'd been as good a shot when I had Braddock in my sights," I said ruefully. "Bloody pop gun. Where was my rifle when I needed it?" Both men shrugged. "Now has anyone got a spare pair of trousers? I'm bloody freezing in just my drawers!"

Ten minutes later Angie and I were dressed in the pilot's and co-pilot's spare flight suits and we were back in the air climbing fast across the Thames flats towards the North Sea.

CHAPTER 67

IT WAS a sombre group that reconvened around the conference table on *Triton* that afternoon. Although we had managed to extract Angie from Braddock's predations, we all knew that with him and his crew still out there I would be under constant threat whenever I returned to the mainland. I was only partially reassured by the resources that Vanguard had at its disposal, because I appreciated that they could not protect me forever. At some point Braddock's and my paths would cross again – and I could in no way be certain about the outcome next time.

Angie was gradually recovering. Within a couple of hours of landing on the ship, her foot had been treated by the medics, a fresh bandage had been applied and she was demanding a full explanation of what had happened. I'd forgotten how tough she could be, but I also knew that she would still be in shock and that she needed time to process things, especially my part in it all.

"I'm sorry, Angie. There's no way I could have foreseen that you'd get dragged into this. I still don't know how they found you. But I can promise you this. When Braddock and I next meet, I won't miss again."

"You were always so damned impulsive," she said, without

357

smiling. "And stubborn. It was stubbornness that put you in the Army, stubbornness that nearly got you killed and stubbornness that stopped you getting the help you needed when you came home. No wonder our marriage fell apart."

I bridled, feeling the same old resentment rising in me. But she was right, of course. All the mistakes had been mine – and she had very nearly become a victim of them.

We had talked a while longer in the ship's hospital, after the medics had completed all their tests. She was physically unharmed apart from her foot and a few bruises. I didn't tell her yet about the putative job offer I'd received from Vanguard, but privately I knew that that was almost certainly the best way for me to put the traumas of Afghanistan behind me, deal with my PTSD once and for all, and build a new life for myself. Which in the end would also be the best way to save my relationship with Angie.

I was jolted out of my reverie by Lowell, who opened the proceedings once again. "We're glad to have you back safe, Charlie. And your wife. Nice work, Bruce," he fist-bumped Havelock, who was sitting beside him, now dressed in chinos and a check button-down shirt. "But now we have two problems. Braddock and Al-Shammari. It'll take Braddock time to regroup and we can think later about how to handle him, but we don't have that luxury with the Iraqi. Charlie, I know you've had a tough day, but we really need to crack on. No problem if you want to sit this one out and rejoin us when you've had a chance to rest."

I shook my head emphatically. "No way. As far as I'm concerned, Braddock and Al-Shammari are two sides of the same coin. I want in on this."

"Okay. Well, Charlene has made some more progress since we last met and I think we're in a good place on Al-Shammari. Charlene, why don't you bring us up to date?"

The redhead leaned forward, her elbows on the table. She

was dressed in a white polo neck and her hair was tied back in a ponytail.

"As I explained yesterday, the second copper scroll may well hold the key to the first – and so to the treasure." She picked up the remote and an image of the palimpsest appeared on the screen, with its translation beside it. "I think the critical point is in the penultimate paragraph," she said, highlighting the same paragraph we'd seen earlier.

And to your care, Master, I entrust the resting place of the burnished scroll. Its unearthing has brought me an unaccustomed sadness I cannot comprehend and I know it is best left to the secret places and to the will of God. Its treasures will bring no peace to the world. I have returned it to the earth whence it came, to the place of worship of the cursed ones upon whose heads be the blood of our Lord.

"The writer refers to 'secret places' and returning it 'to the earth whence it came', so we can be pretty sure it's somewhere underground. But the kicker is the final line: 'the place of worship of the cursed ones upon whose heads be the blood of our Lord.' Anyone any idea what that might mean?" Everyone shook their heads.

"Okay, so here's a verse from the New Testament: Matthew 27:24." Another piece of text appeared on the screen.

So when Pilate saw that he was gaining nothing, but rather that a riot was beginning, he took water and washed his hands before the crowd, saying, 'I am innocent of this man's blood; see to it yourselves.' And all the people answered, 'His blood be on us and on our children.'

. . .

"Many people call this the 'blood libel'. It's regularly used by right-wing extremists, anti-Semites and even some Christians to justify their persecution of the Jews. Their argument is that the Jews took full responsibility for the death of Jesus Christ and so they and all their descendants deserve everything that's coming to them."

"So, this monk, whoever he was, was referring to the Jews in his letter," said Rebecca. "But where does that get us?"

"Well, look at the words before," resumed Charlene. 'The place of worship of the cursed ones'. That can really only mean one thing –"

"A synagogue!" I exclaimed. "It means a synagogue. The scroll is buried in a synagogue!"

Charlene smiled at me, as she would no doubt at one of her students who suddenly grasped a tricky concept in class. "Exactly. Now look at this," and, pressing the remote again, she threw a map up on the screen. She was clearly getting into her stride. She stood, picked up a ruler and walked to the screen, pointing out the landmarks she was describing.

"So, this is Jericho, one of the oldest cities in the world. Archaeologists reckon it's been inhabited since 9,000 BC. Here," pointing to a spot a few miles south-west of the city, "is St George's Monastery in Wadi Qelt, where the palimpsest was found. And here at the lower end of the wadi," pointing her ruler, "is the site of the old winter palace of the Hasmonaeans, the Jewish dynasty that governed Palestine a couple of centuries before Christ. It was the Hasmonaeans who built the aqueducts you can still see the remains of in the valley, bringing water from the wadi down to the Plain of Jericho.

"But most important of all is this," and she screened a picture of what looked to me like a featureless mound of rock and earth. "This is the remains of the Wadi Qelt Synagogue, in the ruins of the Hasmonaean Palace. It's believed to be one of the oldest synagogues in the world, dating from 60 or 70 years before Christ. It was excavated by an Israeli archaeologist called Ehud Netzer in the 1970s.

"And it's only a couple of kilometres from the monastery."

There was a sharp intake of breath around the room. "But how can you be sure that this is *the* synagogue the monk talks about?" asked Rebecca, her scepticism evident. "It could be any one of the synagogues in the area."

"Yes, that's true," replied Charlene patiently. "But remember that this probably has to be a synagogue that was already in ruins by the fifth century, when our monk unearthed and later reburied the scroll. More importantly, it had to be a synagogue that was functioning at the time of the siege of Jerusalem in AD70, so that something could be safely transported to and buried there. There are simply no other archaeological sites within easy reach of the monastery that come close to meeting those criteria."

Rebecca still looked sceptical, but kept her counsel.

"This is good work, Charlene," said Lowell. "I think it's certainly worth checking out. Bruce, Rolf, how easy do you think it will be to get the Israeli Defence Force to help us on this, without giving away what we're doing?"

The head of security and the analyst looked at one another and Rolf answered first. "I have one or two contacts I can talk to in Jerusalem," he said. "Leave it with me for a couple of hours."

"Right," said Lowell. "It's been a long day – longer for some than others," looking in my direction. "Let's meet back here first thing in the morning and put together a plan of action."

As he finished speaking, a young Asian woman rushed through the door and placed a sheet of paper in front of Lowell. He read it quickly and then looked up, eyeing us all gravely. "It seems we may have less time than we thought."

This produced quizzical expressions around the table. In

answer Lowell said, "This is a transcript of a call between Al-Shammari and an unidentified individual on the West Bank about an hour ago. Much of the discussion is obviously in code, but at one point there is a clear reference to *kanis 'aw mujamae yahudiun.*"

"And what's that?" I asked.

"It's Arabic," answered Rebecca. "It means 'synagogue'."

"Oh fuck," I said.

CHAPTER 68

"I NEED A FULL TASKFORCE," said Al-Shammari to the group of men assembled on his terrace, Mahmoud standing at the forefront. "Men, trucks, equipment, weapons. A complete inventory ready by the end of tomorrow, on standby to move on my instruction."

"Yes, sir," responded Mahmoud.

"And I want our passage smoothed in the Territories. No obstacles. Talk to our brothers on the West Bank and in Gaza, Mahmoud. And you, Faisal," turning to a smartly dressed man standing slightly apart from the others, "you are to ensure that there are no problems with your countrymen in Jordan. I will take care of things here in Lebanon.

"Make no mistake that what we are about to embark upon will change the world. We have within our grasp the means to liberate our brothers from the yoke of the American and Israeli filth. They will feel our resolve. They will feel our wrath. They will feel our power. Nothing will be the same again. The days of our enslavement and our humiliation will soon be behind us." Al-Shammari felt slightly embarrassed at the platitudes, but believed the essential truth of every word he uttered.

"But remember this. The infidels are cunning. They are

stubborn and single-minded, like dogs on the scent. We will bring them to heel, but we must remain vigilant and be careful and clever."

There were nods and murmurs of agreement from the men.

"Now go, prepare, with the blessings of Allah."

As the men filed from the room, Al-Shammari's phone rang. He looked at the caller display, which showed no caller ID, and after hesitating for a moment he accepted the call.

He listened to the voice on the other end. "Well, this is a surprise," he said in English. "How can I help you?" He listened for a full minute. "I understand. In person then. I will make the arrangements," and he ended the call.

"Mahmoud, we need to make another trip to London."

CHAPTER 69

WE RECONVENED the following morning in the ops room, where the day shift were busy trying to track down Al-Shammari. They knew about his villa in the vineyard in Lebanon and his apartment in London, but at present he was in neither place and there was growing concern that he may be ahead of us and on his way to Israel, even though there had been nothing in the transcript of his recent call to indicate that he knew the exact whereabouts of the burial site. Nevertheless, in the absence of any clear intelligence on our adversary, and recognising the need for haste, we concentrated on our plans for the upcoming expedition to the suspected location of the scroll.

Rolf had had several conversations with his contacts in the Israeli army, the IDF, and Shin Bet, Israel's feared internal security service. He had fed them both a plausible story that they were in pursuit of a senior Hezbollah strategist posing as an archaeologist who they believed was in the process of planning an attack on one of Israel's settlements in the West Bank. It was a measure of the trust between Vanguard and Israel's intelligence agencies that Rolf was able to secure access for the team to the Palestinian territory with the minimum of fuss. It was obvious to me, reading between the lines, that Vanguard had collaborated more than once with Israeli intelligence and had perhaps even operated as its proxy in past operations. Whatever the truth of this, we had evidently been given carte blanche to carry out our planned intervention without interference.

For my part, I felt queasy about this mysterious relationship with the shadowy Israeli agencies. Despite my experiences in Afghanistan and Iraq, I had an abiding respect for the many Arabs who, at the civilian level, had shown me nothing but kindness, courtesy and hospitality during my years in the Middle East. I also had deep sympathy for the plight of the Palestinians, who I believed had been repeatedly betrayed – by the British, the United States, Europe and most of their Arab neighbours – and whose displacement to overcrowded refugee camps, coupled with the appropriation of their lands in Palestine, I found hard to condone.

But at this point I was in no position to argue geopolitical niceties. I understood that what was at stake here was the stability of a region in which many of the players were itching for a fight and that once it got started that fight would most likely end in an apocalyptic conflict. So I fought back my nausea and bit my tongue.

By late morning, Lowell was summing up our plan. Rebecca, Charlene, Havelock, Omar and I were to return to London, where Havelock was to assemble a team and have it ready to ship out within twenty-four hours. The two women and I were scheduled to meet with an archaeologist friend of Charlene's from the British Museum who had worked on the excavation of the Hasmonaean winter palace and might be able to help us narrow down our search once we arrived at the site of the synagogue. The entire operation was to be coordinated by Lowell, Rolf and Aleysha back on *Triton*, which would be in 24/7 contact with our team.

After a brief lunch, for which few of us had much of an appetite, especially after the litres of coffee we'd all consumed, we gathered on the helideck with our gear and prepared to set off. Havelock was business-like and efficient, Omar laughing and joking with Charlene, who seemed to have taken a fancy to him. Rebecca was unusually quiet and I inferred that she was not altogether sold on our plan, but it was too late to change anything now and we had evidently both reached the unspoken conclusion that there was no point in further discussion.

I had left Angie in her stateroom, surrounded by books borrowed from the ship's copious library. She was still in pain from her damaged foot and I suspected that even more damage had been done inside her head. She was quiet and introspective, unwilling for now to engage with the events of the past few days. She was mortified at having to desert her charges at school but she agreed, somewhat reluctantly, that it was wise to remain on board for the time being, until we had dealt with Braddock. This would also allow her foot to heal properly. I was also hoping that some serious rest might do her good - and go some way towards healing the trauma she had suffered.

The chopper lifted off on a clear, bright March afternoon, with a duck-egg sky and calm aquamarine sea, and powered up to full speed as it made once again for the English coast. The journey passed mostly in silence, as we all contemplated our roles in the mission ahead of us. At one point in the flight I was surprised by a cool hand slipping into mine and I turned to find Rebecca gazing at me with an expression I couldn't identify. I held her eyes for a few moments, trying to fathom the meaning they held, but then, after giving my hand a small squeeze, she smiled wanly and turned back to the window.

We landed at London heliport in Battersea just over an hour later. Havelock and Omar immediately took off in a waiting Land Rover, while Rebecca, Charlene and I grabbed a taxi and headed straight for the British Museum.

Professor Raj Sarma was a diminutive, bespectacled Indonesian in his early 70s with incongruously jet-black hair and a round smiling face. We immediately warmed to him. He kissed Charlene on both cheeks, greeted us all cheerfully and led us to a room on the second floor of the museum where he offered us tea, before pulling out a large-scale plan of some form of building compound.

"This is the winter palace of the Hasmonaeans, on a hill overlooking Jericho just to the north of Wadi Qelt. It was built in the early second century BC and is an extraordinary place," said Sarma, excitedly. We were looking at a large complex of buildings constructed along the wadi we had recently learnt so much about. "It was a sizeable estate, the main part covering around four hectares, but 120 hectares in all, and it had orchards, formal gardens, ritual baths and even a collection of swimming pools. Its plantation produced date wine, perfumes, medicines, persimmon resin, palm oil and a host of different crops. When the Hasmonaeans died out, it eventually became Herod the Great's winter palace in the late first century BC.

"The remains of the palace were first discovered in the 19th century by Charles Warren, an officer in the British Royal Engineers, but it was only properly excavated from the 1970s, by Ehud Netzer, the Israeli archaeologist, and I was with him there as a student. What an exciting time that was! Would you like me to talk you through the excavation?"

"Perhaps you could tell us about the synagogue," interrupted Charlene gently.

"Ah, yes. Now there's a real find! We didn't discover that until the late 1990s." He pointed to a spot just to the north and west of a long line of buildings in the upper part of the palace. "This is the synagogue, on the fringe of the palace grounds. It was destroyed in an earthquake back in Herod's time –"

"Earthquake?" interrupted Charlene.

"Yes, the palace was destroyed in 31 BC and the synagogue along with it. That's when Herod took the opportunity to rebuild the palace for his own use."

We all looked at one another, instantly crestfallen.

"So – there would have been nothing there by the time of the Jewish War in AD70," asked Charlene, who clearly couldn't keep the disappointment from her voice.

"Well, there would've been ruins, of course," answered Sarma, who seemed unnecessarily cheerful under the circumstances, "and they might have been quite substantial, but I doubt it would still have functioned as a place of worship. In fact, part of the synagogue had been covered over when Herod constructed his new palace, so not all of it would have been usable anyway."

"Then I was wrong," said Charlene quietly, almost to herself.

"About what, my dear?"

"Oh, it was a long shot, professor, but my recent researches suggested that the synagogue may have been used as a repository for some of the scrolls rescued from Jerusalem during the Jewish War." She was choosing her words carefully. "I rather thought we might have another Dead Sea Scrolls on our hands," she laughed half-heartedly.

"Ah, I see," said Sarma coyly, cocking his head and looking askance at her with a slight smile. "Buried treasure, eh?"

"Only for us scroll nuts," responded Charlene.

"Well, what if I were to tell you that you may be right after all?" he grinned, raising his eyebrows conspiratorially.

"What do you mean?" asked Rebecca.

"You need to remember that this was quite probably the oldest synagogue in Israel – certainly in Judaea. It would have had great historical and cultural significance, even if it had been partially destroyed. And the palace would have been occupied, so it was far from an abandoned site."

"So?" asked Rebecca.

"So, things have changed a lot in archaeology in the past fifty years. You wouldn't believe how much technology has advanced. And do you know what the biggest advance of all is?" he asked with a twinkle.

We all shook our heads, impatient to find out whether we were completely wasting our time.

Sarma walked over to a filing cabinet and pulled out a sheaf of photographs. "This is the ancient city of Falerii Novi in Italy, about 50 kilometres north of Rome, which dates back several centuries before Christ. It was first excavated in the 1820s, but it was only fully mapped in the last year or so." We looked over his shoulder at a series of 3-D images showing in elaborate detail the walls, towers, gates, buildings, markets, baths and open spaces of a large Roman settlement.

"Impressive," I said, unimpressed. "But what does a bit of clever computer imagery of a Roman town have to do with us?"

"Oh, it's not just clever computer imagery," said Sarma with a violent shake of his head. "These are one hundred per cent accurate pictures of Falerii Novi from nearly two and a half thousand years ago. Today, the entire city is several metres underground and these images were obtained by archaeologists from Cambridge and Ghent universities during a recent detailed survey of the site." He paused and reclined in his chair, before adding with a flourish, "and they did it without putting a single spade in the ground."

Silence. Then: "Ground penetrating radar," said Charlene.

"Exactly, my dear," he replied, turning to the rest of us. "GPR has revolutionised our job. It enables us to see entire cities buried beneath the ground without removing an inch of soil. It works by transmitting high frequency microwaves into the ground and recording the reflected pulses from objects under the surface. The amplitudes and arrival times of the returning pulses are measured and analysed, enabling us to build an extremely accurate picture of exactly what's down below and what it's made of."

"And the relevance to us?" I asked again, becoming increasingly impatient.

"Well, young man, it just so happens that one of my students recently returned from a dig in Israel during which he spent some time GPR-mapping the winter palaces. And guess what?" Professor Sarma obviously had a taste for the dramatic.

"What?" we all said in unison.

"Well, it appears that we still have some way to go before we've exhausted the mysteries of the site," he responded. "It seems that there is another level below that which has been excavated. More than fifteen metres further down, to be precise. And," he added with a flourish, "a tunnel. Linking a basement level below the old synagogue to cellars under the palace.

"And frankly, I can think of no better purpose for a basement below the synagogue than a scriptorium."

CHAPTER 70

THERE WAS a palpable air of excitement in the room now. Professor Sarma's flourish had effectively given weight to Charlene's theory, sufficient for us now to make the trip. He readily offered to provide us with the raw GPR scans of the site, which he said he could have couriered over from his student that evening, but he had one condition.

"I want to come with you," he said, a bright light in his eyes.

We conferred, but it didn't take long for us to reach the conclusion that he would be a valuable complement to the team. He was familiar with the site, he had the scans and he knew how to read them. Sarma left the room to talk to one of his colleagues about taking over his classes for the next few days and spirits were high as we contemplated our next moves. At last we felt that we might have a real head-start on Al-Shammari – at least, we did until Havelock reported on his most recent call with Lowell back on *Triton*.

"Aleysha's team has monitored another call from Al-Shammari," he said in a subdued tone. "He's chartered a jet for tonight. Flight plan is to Amman in Jordan."

"Well, at least it's not Tel Aviv," responded Charlene brightly.

"No, but it seems Amman isn't his final destination," countered Havelock.

We all waited, anticipating his next words.

"He's heading for the West Bank."

We left the museum and made our way to a hotel near Marylebone Station, agreeing to meet the professor later that evening for dinner. Charlene was more excited than I had seen her and her enthusiasm was infectious. She jabbered away in the cab about the prospects for our expedition and I was caught up in her anticipation. But Rebecca was still unnaturally taciturn and as soon as we had checked in she said she had a headache and went straight to her room. Charlene did the same. I was too full of nervous energy to incarcerate myself in a hotel room, so instead I made for the bar and ordered a coffee, then telephoned Angie.

She demanded to know what was happening and where I was going. I demurred on the detail, not wanting to worry her any more than she already was, and promised to call again the following day. I could tell that her earlier shock and introspection were giving way to anger. I wasn't sure whether it was directed primarily at Braddock, at me, or at both of us. For sure I was feeling guilty at having dragged her into all this and put her life in danger, and that was something I was going to have to make up for. But for the first time I also felt a flutter of anticipation: perhaps recent events had provided Angie and me with the catalyst we needed to give it another go? That was something to think about.

I retired to a seat near the window and started leafing through a newspaper I found on the table.

It was just as I was shaking my head in annoyance at some provocative headline, that I saw her through the window. Rebecca had left the hotel, barely ten minutes since making her excuses, and was now running across Marylebone Road, dodging the traffic, evidently in quite some hurry. I don't really know why I decided to follow her. Something in her demeanour worried me, perhaps a subconscious desire to protect her, as I had so conspicuously failed to do with my own wife. Whatever the reason, I found myself walking quickly through the lobby and out of the hotel, dashing across the road, catching sight of her just as she disappeared around the corner into Marylebone Lane.

As I rounded the same corner, I saw her look quickly behind and around her before hailing a black cab and jumping into it. Slipping into the cinematic cliché of a hundred movies, I flagged down a taxi of my own and told the driver to 'follow that cab.' We wound our way through the streets of London's West End, heading south across Oxford Street, rounding Grosvenor Square and on into Berkeley Square, where Rebecca jumped out of her cab, again cast a furtive glance behind her, and disappeared into a boutique hotel. I paid my driver and followed.

I was cautious as I approached the door of the hotel. It was evidently a small and intimate establishment, so there would be no crowded lobby where I could mingle with the guests. I entered, nodding to the doorman, and walked across a small lobby to the reception desk, where I asked the pretty French receptionist whether she had a tourist map of London, all the while looking around for a sign of Rebecca. There were doors off the lobby, marked 'dining room' and 'bar' and, after grabbing my map and thanking the receptionist, I chose the bar. The door led into a short corridor which opened into the bar on the left, and as I walked along the corridor I heard murmured voices.

I stopped just before the corner and listened. One of the voices was Rebecca's. The other I didn't recognise, but was heavily accented. I couldn't hear what they were saying because they were speaking in low voices, so I chanced a look around the corner, hoping that no guests or staff walked by and wondered why I was skulking there. My worries were soon extinguished when I saw the two people sitting at a corner table in the bar.

One was Rebecca. The other, readily recognisable from the photo Aleysha had shown on *Triton*, was Aariz Al-Shammari.

Driven by reflex, I rounded the corner and just stared at them. Rebecca, becoming aware that someone was watching, turned and saw me. The blood drained from her face and she shot out of her chair. Al-Shammari slowly rose to his feet and regarded me coolly. Those few seconds became elastic, and I remember every detail of what happened next as if it were a slow-motion replay. Rebecca grabbed her handbag and made for a side door out of the bar. I immediately made to follow her, but was instantly restrained by a strong arm which encircled my neck and I felt the prick of a sharp knife in the soft flesh under my chin.

Rebecca disappeared through the door. Al-Shammari stood for a moment, still seemingly unconcerned by the turn of events, then nodded slightly to me, turned and followed her. I wriggled against the powerful arm that held me, calculating that there was no way my captor was going to stab me in the throat in broad daylight in a public place. But then I thought of my brother, standing outside another hotel, and relaxed my struggles. The arm relaxed correspondingly and the knife was removed, to be replaced by the muzzle of a silenced automatic placed against my head.

"You move now," whispered the voice behind me, switching the gun from my head to the base of my spine and prodding me into the bar, keeping my body between him and the barman and making for the door through which Rebecca and Al-Shammari had left. The barman looked up briefly and saw only two men walking closely together across the room. He returned to polishing his glasses. The man pressed the gun into the soft flesh below my ribs and continued to push me towards the door. He nudged it open with his foot before shoving me through into a short corridor with another door about thirty feet away.

My time with special forces had taught me many things, and

disarming an attacker with a handgun at close range was one of the simpler lessons I'd learnt. As soon as the door had closed behind us, I pivoted on my left foot, grabbing the weapon with my left hand and twisting it hard to the right. I actually heard his trigger-finger snap as I wrenched the gun downwards, holding his wrist with my other hand while I pushed the gun away from me. I hearing a muffled crack as the weapon discharged into the thick carpet before I managed to yank it from his hand. My assailant had not made a sound, even when I'd broken his finger, but he was turning fast, bringing his left fist to bear on my unprotected chin. Acting on instinct, I brought the butt of the gun up and drove it into the underside of his chin, momentarily disorientating him, before applying a crushing roundhouse blow to the side of his head. He crumpled to the floor, dazed.

At that moment the door to the bar began to open. I dashed for the door at the other end of the corridor and was through it in seconds, running across an empty hospitality room to the rear entrance of the hotel. On reaching the street, I shoved the captured gun into my coat pocket and pulled out the compact satellite phone that I had been given after my own was thrown into the Thames. I hit a speed-dial button and after a single unbroken ring, Lowell picked up. "Nathaniel. We have a big problem," I said.

CHAPTER 71

WITHIN MINUTES of getting back to the hotel on Marylebone Road I received a call from Havelock. The full team were to meet in three hours at a private airfield just outside London. A car was on its way to collect us. The same instruction had been given to Charlene, who duly appeared in reception just after I'd ended the call, her overnight bag already packed. A car was apparently also on its way to collect Professor Sarma.

I was still in shock. I couldn't quite believe what had just happened, especially after the intimacies Rebecca and I had so recently shared. I felt that my moorings had come adrift and all the old uncertainties that had plagued me during the worst days of my PTSD threatened to return with a vengeance.

Oddly, the Vanguard team were remarkably sanguine about the whole thing. Everyone seemed so busy preparing for the days ahead that they were reluctant even to talk about it. Lowell appeared subdued, but pragmatic. "There's nothing we can do about it at the moment. We have other priorities. We have to assume that what we know, Al-Shammari now knows. If you'll forgive the cliché, we're in a race against time. We'll have plenty of opportunity to deal with the Rebecca issue later, but for now, there is one objective and one objective only: to get our hands on that scroll before Al-Shammari does."

Once again I was surprised and impressed by how quickly Vanguard could move. It was only half an hour since my encounter with Rebecca and Al-Shammari and already our plans had been adapted and accelerated. In spite of my sombre mood, I admitted to myself once more that it felt good to be part of a team of efficient professionals who knew what they were doing. It reminded me of the best of the days I'd spent in special forces, before the disaster in Afghanistan.

I picked up my bag from behind the reception desk, where I'd left it before going to the bar for my coffee an hour earlier, and Charlene and I headed outside. Five minutes later a Mercedes 4x4 pulled to the kerb and we jumped into the back seat. The driver was a no-nonsense woman who issued a terse welcome and the moment we'd secured our seat belts, the powerful car pulled away into the traffic.

Despite heavy early-afternoon congestion, it took us just ninety minutes to cover the twelve miles to Biggin Hill Airport on the outskirts of London. I spent part of the journey on the phone to Lowell, catching up on our next steps. We had to assume that Al-Shammari would be moving equally fast to get ahead of us and secure the site. It was now simply a question of who had the best resources and acted with the greatest efficiency.

On arrival at the airport, we were driven directly to the Signature terminal, which was located at the end of the Bombardier hangar and had direct ramp access. As we entered the plush reception area, we were met by Havelock, who immediately turned us around and led us out onto the apron, where I saw a Gulfstream G3 executive jet being fuelled on the tarmac. As the three of us approached the aircraft, another car pulled up and disgorged a clearly over-excited Professor Sarma, his arms bulging with bags and briefcases. We reached the steps just as the fuel truck was disengaging and immediately we heard and felt the engines spool up.

The cabin was roomier than I'd imagined. It seated thirteen passengers in considerable comfort and the space was already occupied by four men in desert camouflage, one of whom was Omar. This time the men were unencumbered by equipment and weaponry, which I assumed was in the hold. They nodded as we entered, then returned to talking quietly among themselves.

The plane was taxiing even as we fastened our seatbelts. Havelock, Charlene, the professor and I were seated around a four-person table out of earshot of Havelock's men and immediately fell to discussing our predicament as the plane rose into the air, circled round to the south-east and headed for its cruising altitude of 45,000 feet.

"Professor, what you're about to hear must go no further," began Havelock. "I cannot stress to you how important it is that this mission is accomplished quietly and with minimum involvement of outside parties. If you do disclose anything of what you learn in the coming days, I'm afraid there will be consequences."

Sarma nodded enthusiastically, seemingly undeterred by the veiled threat. "Yes, yes, of course. And tell me, who are you, exactly?" he asked naively.

"Bruce and his companions are with us to protect us," I answered quickly. "The West Bank can be an unpredictable place and we need to be certain of our safety while we investigate the site."

The professor looked dubious. "Well, I suppose you know best," he said eventually.

Havelock, Charlene and I had separately agreed that we would make no mention of the scroll in the professor's presence. What he didn't know couldn't hurt him.

I turned to Havelock. "Did any of you have any inkling that

379

Rebecca was working with Al-Shammari?" I finally returned to the elephant in the room.

"She was as thoroughly vetted as everyone else in Vanguard," he replied vaguely. There's absolutely no indication that she was anything other than a loyal member of the team." I thought Havelock looked sheepish. He was, after all, responsible for Vanguard's security and had just been betrayed by one of his own people, the worst of all possible security breaches. But there seemed no point in continuing the speculation. As Lowell had said, there would be plenty of time to bottom the conundrum later.

"Now professor, can we take a look at those scans?" asked Charlene.

Sarma rummaged around in one of his three briefcases and withdrew a stack of A2 sheets, which he laid out on the small table. Unlike the 3-D images of the Roman city, these were the original raw GPR scans and required an expert to interpret them. Sarma began to explain what we were looking at, cross-referencing a separate simpler plan of the synagogue itself, and gradually we began to form a clearer impression of the site within the palace complex and the location of the underground rooms beneath them.

"So this is the main entrance to the synagogue," explained Sarma, pointing to an aperture in the south-east corner of the plan. "It leads through a vestibule, here, into this small courtyard – the rooms to the north were probably guest suites or a hostel of some sort. But the heart of the synagogue was here." He pointed to a large hall to the left of the courtyard, accessed by a narrow doorway, which was lined by columns with a wide space between. "This is where worshippers would gather and where the Torah would have been read and studied. It was probably also used as a law court and as a venue for social and political gatherings, perhaps even for banquets.

"What's interesting about this synagogue is that it was built outside the palace boundary. Scholars have always wondered why, but that probably means that it wasn't necessarily regularly used by members of the royal family or their guests, but was mainly there to serve employees and people who lived nearby. I'll come back to that, because it's important for our understanding of the underground facilities."

Sarma paused and asked for a drink of water, which Havelock fetched from a small refrigerator at the rear of the cabin. Sarma then resumed. "But this is what will interest you most," he said, pointing to a niche in the north-eastern corner of the main hall. "We puzzled about this when we first excavated the site. It's only about two-and-a-half metres square, about the size of a cupboard, and the entrance is very narrow and low – about half a metre high and a third of a metre wide. The consensus among scholars is that it was a geniza, a repository for worn-out manuscripts."

Our ears pricked up. This sounded promising.

"But the ground penetrating radar suggests something else," and now he turned back to the scans. "You can see here that there's what appears to be a large room directly beneath and about fifteen metres below the courtyard, which is the oldest part of the building. You would never find it without GPR, because there's no obvious access to it – and it's too deep for our original excavations to have touched it."

"So how *was* it accessed?" prompted Charlene.

"Ah, well there's the thing!" said the professor. "I am strongly of the view that it was accessed from this niche," tapping the plan again. "There must be a stairway of some sort, but it's not clear from the scans – there's too much debris clutter. But it's evident to me that at some point the entrance must have been sealed."

"But why?" asked Charlene.

"Well, there you have me," responded the professor, with a shrug. "But I can tell you this. We noticed at the time of our original excavation that the floor of the geniza was rather different to the rest of the synagogue. Most of it was built out of mudbricks on top of fieldstone, with cobblestone foundations, like the palace itself. The bedding of the floors was also made out of cobbles, with beaten earth on top and perhaps originally overlaid with a lime plaster floor in some areas. But the floor of the niche is a solid block of limestone."

We were all craning forward over the plan and scans now. "So you think the entrance was sealed sometime later?" I asked.

"Entirely possible," answered Sarma. "In fact, probable."

"Perhaps even well after the synagogue had fallen into disrepair?" added Charlene hopefully.

"Indeed," said the professor. "Entirely possible."

"But if it had been sealed, how could anyone have got into the underground room later?" I asked, thinking of the fifth-century monk whose letter had prompted this whole enterprise.

"Well, that's where the tunnel comes in," responded the professor, with a self-satisfied smile.

CHAPTER 72

AL-SHAMMARI AND MAHMOUD had moved even faster than
their rivals. Another call from their client and paymaster had
sharpened their sense of urgency and the girl's unexpected
intervention had been a Godsend. Al-Shammari had consulted
a number of experts in London and Palestine on the contents of
the palimpsest, both archaeological and philological, but had got
no further than the vague reference to a synagogue somewhere
in Palestine. Their efforts were hampered by their necessary
reluctance to be specific about the manuscript's provenance –
and their obvious inability to call upon the expertise of Israeli
scholars – so when Rebecca rang and asked to meet, Al-Shammari jumped at the opportunity with unaccustomed haste, his
intuitive scepticism trumped by expediency.

Rebecca, or Rivkah – the Arab equivalent of her name by
which she had introduced herself – had volunteered little about
the organisation she worked for, although if their meeting had
not been so rudely interrupted he felt sure he would have been
able to extract more. But her motive for contacting him had
been a familiar one, and it resonated with him personally. Her
parents had been well-to-do Palestinians from Ramallah, she
had told him, one a doctor, the other a lawyer, who had both

been killed in an Israeli incursion towards the end of the Second Intifada.

When she became aware of the item for which they were all searching, and began to understand the stakes for which they were playing, her visceral loathing of the Zionists had overcome her loyalty to her employer and made her decision to contact Al-Shammari a personal imperative. The information she gave him was decisive.

The sudden appearance of the brother of the inquisitive – now dead – young Carter, reinforced the urgency of moving quickly. He instinctively knew that he now faced a race, not only against time, but against a formidable competitor with considerable resources.

"Is everything prepared, Mahmoud? Have you secured the men we need when we arrive?"

"Yes sir. They will be waiting for us when we land. Our brothers have been most helpful."

"Good. Then let us be on our way."

For the second time that day, a car carrying passengers in pursuit of a priceless artefact picked its way through London's rush-hour traffic towards a private airfield, this time at Denham on the north-western outskirts of London. Also for the second time, a private jet – this time a Cessna Citation XLS+ – was sitting fuelled and ready for departure on the tarmac. Within fifteen minutes of the two men's arrival, the plane was in the air and streaking south-east across London towards the Mediterranean.

CHAPTER 73

ATAROT AIRFIELD HAD ONCE BEEN Jerusalem's
international airport, opened during the British Mandate in
1924 and operating regular flights under various national juris-
dictions until security problems forced its closure in 2001. Since
then, it has been technically under the control of the Israeli
Defence Forces, but in reality has been closed to virtually all
traffic for more than 20 years.

Thanks to a special dispensation from the IDF, the G3 was
given permission to land at Atarot in secrecy early that evening.
It taxied to a disused hangar and we disembarked along with our
luggage and several rucksacks full of equipment, before it
returned to the runway and immediately took off, heading back
westward towards the coast.

Our party was met by three black SUVs, from one of which
emerged two young men in desert fatigues, both carrying the
insignia of the Israeli Defence Forces, but with no rank indicated. Both wore pistols on their hips and saluted Havelock
briskly when he stepped forward to greet them. He did not
introduce us. They returned to the first vehicle, Havelock's four
operatives took the second and the rest of us climbed into the
third after loading our gear into the back. Within seconds we

were rolling across the tarmac and heading for the exit. We saw the runway lights wink out as we passed through the gates, returning the airfield to darkness.

We sped south in convoy on Route 60 and after twenty minutes turned east onto Route 437. We were waved through the Hizma Checkpoint and passed through the West Bank Barrier – otherwise known as The Wall, 700 kilometres long, three metres thick and up to eight metres in height – that separates the Palestinian occupied territory from Israel. After another fifteen minutes we arrived at the entrance to the Ein Prat Nature Reserve at the western end of Wadi Qelt.

"We walk from here," said Havelock, getting out of the car after we'd pulled into the parking area. We were joined by his men, who unloaded the heavy rucksacks from our vehicle and hefted them onto their backs, passing one to Havelock and one to me. It had been a long time since I had carried a 25-kilo pack and this one immediately felt like a lead weight on my back, but I was determined not to show it to the professionals. The two Israelis saluted Havelock once more, then climbed back into their SUV and drove away, leaving the other two vehicles for us.

Havelock explained that we had a 12-kilometre hike ahead of us, some of it over rocky terrain, along the length of the wadi. "It would have been quicker to carry on east to Jericho and double back to the palace ruins from there, but we would've passed through some heavily built-up areas where there are a lot of watchers and we risked drawing attention to ourselves. It's safer this way, but we'll need to be careful." With this, his men switched on powerful torches and set off along the canyon.

The Wadi Qelt is a popular hiking route and during the day we could have expected to regularly run into other people along the way, but it was now nearly midnight and Havelock reassured us that we would easily make it to Tulul Abu al-'Alayiq, the Arabic name for the site of the Hasmonaean Palace ruins, well before daylight, so avoiding contact with hikers and tourists.

With the soldiers lighting our way, the going was relatively easy, although we regularly stumbled over rocky outcroppings and slipped on loose scree. In places there were steep climbs and the professor, despite being fit and unencumbered by his briefcases, which Charlene was now carrying for him, had to be helped up the more challenging slopes and needed to rest periodically. Given how dependent upon him we were – and the fact that we would not even be here had it not been for him – we cut him some slack.

The wadi was in effect a 12-kilometre-long gorge, cut deep into the limestone of the Judaean hills by the Prat River. Had we been walking in daylight, the professor told us that we would have enjoyed some spectacular natural phenomena and, in occasional open areas, some outstanding views. As it was, for the most part we were focused on our feet and on ensuring that we didn't slip or turn an ankle. In the deeper parts of the canyon there were many small waterfalls and pools and from time to time we noticed looming edifices above us silhouetted against the night sky, which Sarma explained were the ruins of ancient aqueducts that once carried water from the Ein Prat spring to Jericho.

About halfway through our journey we saw lights above us on the wall of the wadi and realised we were passing below the St George Monastery, clinging to the limestone cliff. We walked in silence past the floodlit building which looked almost like an organic outcrop from the wall of the wadi, and I'm sure each of us was reflecting on the middle-aged monk whose discovery had brought us to this place, but whose life had been taken from him.

It took us another two hours before we reached the end of the wadi, which opened out onto the flat plain of the Jordan Valley. Havelock explained that we were now very close to the western outskirts of Jericho and just to the south of us was the Aqabat Jabr Palestinian refugee camp, so from now on we needed to be watchful. We were also obviously alert to the appearance of Al-Shammari, whose whereabouts we couldn't be sure of. We had no idea whether he was ahead of us or behind us; all we knew for sure was that, thanks to Rebecca, he was on his way. We took some comfort from the fact that his route was likely to be a little more torturous, given that he clearly could not fly directly to Israel and would have to make his way here via a more circuitous route. But we had no illusions about the strength of his motivation and the urgency it would provoke.

All of which explained why Havelock's men now opened their rucksacks and each took out a Heckler & Koch MP5 short-barreled submachine gun, which they loaded with full magazines and held at high port across their chests as we walked on.

It was now the early hours of the morning and the sky had cleared to reveal a near-full moon, so our guides switched off their torches and we travelled the rest of the way by natural light. Havelock led us slowly and cautiously north-west from the mouth of the wadi for about half a kilometre until we could see ahead of us the fenced off area that marked Tulul Abu Al-Ala'iq, the site of the ruins we were seeking. As we passed through the gate and surveyed the ruins in the moonlight, I was surprised. I guess I had expected more. In fact, there appeared to be little left above ground apart from some low walls and the bases of columns. However, thanks to the shadows thrown by the moon, we could clearly see the rough layout of the old palaces, which extended for some distance in all directions.

There was no sign of life on the site and we assumed that Al-Shammari must still be behind us, but we knew he would be moving just as fast as we were and that there was no time to be lost. The professor now took over and his internal compass took us straight to the site of the synagogue on the far side of the palace complex, across a deep conduit which had presumably once been running with water, sited just beyond the remains of a line of ancient buildings which Sarma explained marked the northern extremity of the palace.

"This is the synagogue," he said, unable to keep the excitement out of his voice. He walked us across what he identified as the original walls of the synagogue hall, now no more than a metre high at most, past the stumps of an ancient row of columns, until we reached the northern boundary. "This is the northern wall of the building," he said, and beyond this are what we think are old tombs, barely marked and empty now." He stepped back over the low wall and paused before a deep depression in the ground. "And here is the niche I told you about on the plane. As you can see, well sealed by this single block of stone." We all peered into the hole, now lit by several torches, but could see nothing more than a piece of flat rock.

"Well, there's no chance of getting through that," I exclaimed. "So where is this tunnel?"

Sarma turned and pointed to the south-west. "According to the GPR, the entrance is beyond the mouth of the wadi on the far side of the palace."

"Well," said Havelock, "I suggest we find it. And fast." He turned and gave instructions to two of his men to remain in the synagogue ruins, ordering Omar and the fourth man to accompany us as we turned and walked back through the remains of the palace and out through the gate once more.

Following the scan, illuminated by torchlight, the professor led us across the open ground back to the entrance to the wadi and continued along it for several hundred metres until we were back between the steep sides of the gorge. "According to the scan, the entrance to the tunnel is here somewhere."

The sky was now brightening with the first hint of dawn and a grey light was beginning to fall over the wadi. But we could see nothing beyond rocks, a few scrubby pieces of vegetation and the Prat River itself, which at this point cascaded over a waterfall about a metre and a half in height. We all started prodding randomly at rocks and crevices with our feet, which predictably produced no evidence of a tunnel or anything like it. We searched for a good hour without success, by which time we were all fatigued and irritable and it didn't take long for the recriminations to begin. I'm ashamed to admit that I was first out of the blocks.

"So where is this sodding tunnel?" I muttered petulantly. "We've come all this way, for what? Some sightseeing and an archaeology lesson!"

The professor looked crestfallen. He was poking about in the ground, comparing his GPR scan with the terrain and trying to make sense of both. "Perhaps it's all collapsed over time," he said quietly. "I never guaranteed that we'd find it. Just that it's here." At which point the stresses of the last few days finally got the better of me and I stalked off down the wadi. "What a complete fucking waste of time," I cried out behind me. "Let's get back to the synagogue and see if there's any way to get through that rock." The group reluctantly turned to follow me, Havelock's men keeping a constant lookout up and down the wadi.

We'd gone no more than a hundred metres when we heard a shout. Charlene had hung back as we turned to go, and was now urging us to return. Reluctantly, we trudged back up the wadi. Charlene was standing up to her knees in the stream in front of the waterfall and as we watched she stepped forward and allowed the water to cascade over her. It must have been ice-cold after coming down off the hills, but this didn't seem to bother her.

Suddenly Charlene was no longer there. She had crouched and moved behind the waterfall and was shouting, although we couldn't hear clearly for the sound of the falling water. Something clicked into place in my head and I jumped into the water and ducked below the cascade. I was right, it was freezing.

Charlene was crouched in front of a deep depression in the rock behind the waterfall – she moved into it, edging clear of the water, and I followed. I took out my torch and played it across the walls of the depression, feeling all over the rough limestone, but there was nothing.

"I thought –" she shouted over the din. "Yes, for a moment there, so did I," I shouted back. And we both turned to make our way back through the torrent, depression once again descending on us. At which point my foot shot sideways on the slippery rock beneath the water and I was suddenly flat on my back lying across the width of the river with my face being battered by the falling water. I quickly moved out of its path and shook my head. Then I realised something odd. I was well over six feet tall and the river at this point was probably only about a metre and a half wide, yet I was lying at full stretch. I quickly understood why.

My entire body was underwater, but my legs, as far as my thighs, were buried in the rock. Or, at least, they seemed to be. Somewhere under the water they had found a space to slip into. I quickly pulled my knees up to my chest and got down on all fours, feeling about beneath the water. There was definitely a gap there.

Nothing ventured, I thought, and dived below the surface, pushing my head through the underwater opening where my legs had been. The ground sloped steeply down for a couple of metres and then I sensed the gap widening above me just as the ground began to rise again and after a few seconds my head broke clear of the surface. I played my torch, thankfully rubberised and waterproof, across the rock walls and found myself in a sizeable cavern. The water was pouring into the gap through which I had entered, then turned through a narrow channel and flowed back into another hole in the rock to presumably rejoin the main body of water further downstream.

Above the waterline, the cavern was dry and the rock floor was covered in fine sand.

I walked up a shallow slope, heading towards the darkness at the back of the cave, shining my torch around me. After a minute or so the walls began to draw together and the ceiling to descend towards me. There, emerging from the gloom, I saw what we had been looking for. Covered with moss and a little over two metres high and a metre wide, was a vertical fissure in the rock. I shone my torch into the opening, but all it revealed was rock walls and total blackness.

CHAPTER 74

IF HAVELOCK'S party had had a relatively easy time of it on their journey to the West Bank, the same could not be said for Al-Shammari. Unable to travel via Israel, he had been forced to fly to neighbouring Jordan and make his way across the border by less conventional means.

Al Shammari was actually a few minutes ahead of his adversaries when he and Mahmoud landed at Queen Alia International Airport in Amman late that evening. They were met at one of the many private terminals and whisked out of the airport, heading north on Highway 15, better known as Jordan's Desert Highway, before turning west onto Highway 40 towards the Allenby Bridge, one of the main crossing points from Jordan into Israel.

After forty minutes, the driver turned onto King Hussein Bridge Road, which wound its way north past the Kafrein Dam, and drove on past a succession of small villages until they reached Al-Karameh, which had distinguished itself in the 1960s as the political and military headquarters of Yasser Arafat's Fatah movement. Just north of the town, the driver turned off the road onto a little-used dirt track and they bounced over the increasingly rough ground westward towards the River Jordan and the Israeli border.

Sometime after midnight their 4WD Toyota switched off its headlights and drew slowly to a stop in a palm grove beside the river. At a torch signal from the driver, they heard the sound of an outboard motor and the moonlight revealed a four-seater rubber dinghy nestling in a small inlet. Al-Shammari thanked the driver, exhorting him to go with God, and he and Mahmoud climbed into the dinghy. The driver waited for a few minutes until a sizeable cloud obscured the moon and then swung out into the powerful current of the Jordan, tracking north-west to the opposite bank. There they disembarked and were met by a six-seater Land Rover, four of whose seats were already occupied by a driver and three black-garbed, balaclava'd men armed with AK-47 assault rifles. They climbed aboard and the vehicle quickly turned and made its way west, deeper into the West Bank.

As the sun was beginning to brighten the eastern horizon, the Toyota circled the Jericho suburbs and drew up above the ruins, its headlights picking out the barely visible walls of the extensive excavation. Al-Shammari jumped out of the truck, followed by Mahmoud and the armed men, and surveyed the relics of what had once been a thriving ancient community. At first Al-Shammari thought it was deserted, confirmation that they had beaten their rivals to the site. But then in the slowly receding gloom of the pre-dawn he saw an elderly man walking past the site with a pair of goats.

He walked over to the man and asked him in Arabic, "Good father, can you tell me where I would find the synagogue of the cursed Jews?" The old man, his face leathery and lined from the sun, looked baffled. He opened a virtually toothless mouth and responded, "I do not understand, master."

"The worshipping place of the Zionists. We are seeking the ruin of the ancient synagogue here," he explained calmly.

The man's puzzlement deepened in direct proportion to the lines on his face. "No synagogue here, master. Just old ruins. Very old."

Al- Shammari felt a rising anger taking hold of him. "You are sure, good father?" he snapped. "You are absolutely sure there was no ancient synagogue in this place?"

The old man was becoming frightened by his tone, especially now that he had noticed the hooded armed men who accompanied him. He fell to his knees, his hands clasped together. "On the life of my children and my children's children, I speak the truth," he wailed. "No synagogue. No synagogue!"

Al-Shammari turned to Mahmoud, his eyes blazing with fury. "*Ya ibn el sharmouta!* That bitch!"

He wrested his phone from his pocket. "Back in the truck. Now!" he screamed, punching numbers into the phone as they ran back to the vehicle. Thirty seconds later it was swinging away from Ain Ed-Duyuk, five kilometres north of Jericho, fully ten kilometres from Wadi Qelt, notable for nothing more interesting than the few tumbled stones of an ancient ruined cemetery.

CHAPTER 75

BY SHORTLY AFTER dawn there were four of us gathered in the cavern. Myself, Charlene, Havelock and a very bedraggled Professor Sarma who, despite repeated warnings about the difficulty of the passage and the risks to his health, had insisted on crawling through the gap below the waterfall and joining the expedition. I had had to drag him, coughing and spluttering, through the narrow, submerged access and up onto the slope leading to the fissure. Although he was clearly freezing cold, adrenalin from the excitement was keeping him going and his eyes danced in the torchlight as he contemplated our next steps.

Led by Havelock, who had left his two men keeping watch in the wadi, we squeezed through the gap and found ourselves in a narrow tunnel with a sandy floor sloping gently upwards in what I assumed was the direction of the palace ruins. The tunnel seemed partly natural and partly hewn from the solid limestone, and it meandered back and forth as we continued upward. After we had been walking for perhaps ten minutes, our way was partially blocked by a rockfall which it took us a good half-hour to clear. We were still acutely conscious of the fact that Al-Shammari would be hot on our heels and felt the growing need for haste. Havelock had left instructions with the men above ground that if their adversaries were to show up, three of them should do their best to hold them at the ruins while Omar would come to the wadi and enter the tunnel to warn us.

Easing past the rockfall, we next encountered a set of stone steps cut into the rock which led upward into another tunnel. Consulting his scan, Sarma informed us that this must be the access to the palace. Charlene took the initiative and ran up the stairs excitedly, only to return a couple of minutes later with disappointment etched on her face. "It's blocked," she said. "There's some rusted metal, possibly the remains of some kind of gate, but it's half-buried under rock and there's no way past."

"We have to hope that the same isn't true of the entrance to the synagogue's basement," observed the professor unnecessarily.

We continued on our way and a couple of hundred metres further on our worst fears were realised. We came up against a blank wall, unmarked and smooth from top to bottom. I started pressing my hands against it at various points in the vain hope that it might be some kind of secret door which would suddenly slide open on soundless hinges, but Charlene pointed out that that kind of thing only happened in movies. Real life was much more prosaic and if it looked like a solid wall, felt like a solid wall, it probably was just that: a solid wall.

Dejected, we all stood there and looked at one another. I stood with my back to the wall, then slid down onto my haunches, suddenly exhausted by the exertions of the last twenty-four hours. I rested my head against the stone and closed my eyes, while the others milled around wondering what to do next. It was when I reopened my eyes that I saw it: a circular hole in the ceiling of the tunnel about two metres above our heads. "There!" I shouted. "What's that?"

Everyone stared upwards. It was the professor who broke the silence. "There was probably a ladder," he said. "Maybe a wooden one, long gone of course." We all looked at him. "My theory is this. The tunnel was originally built as some kind of emergency exit or escape route for the royals in the palace. Bear in mind that they were under periodic threat from all sorts of factions in their own court, not to mention the rebels and brigands who eventually took Palestine into all-out war. The summer palace was a long way from Jerusalem and they probably felt sufficiently vulnerable to make contingency plans for a quick escape if the palace were ever overrun. I'm sure this isn't the only tunnel. There are almost certainly others leading from different parts of the palace that we haven't discovered yet."

"But why does it extend to here, assuming the synagogue is above us?" asked Charlene.

"I suspect the answer to that lies in what we find in the room, if we manage to get into it. If, as I suspect, it's a scriptorium, then it could be that all sorts of valuable manuscripts were stored there and the palace authorities thought it worth the relatively modest extra effort to extend the tunnel to the synagogue, so that they had a means of getting them out if they ever needed to. That would explain why it doesn't lead directly to the basement room – they just continued the tunnel until they thought they'd reached the right place, then stopped and punched a hole in the ceiling."

"Well, I wouldn't have fancied their chances of getting a whole load of parchment out through that submerged tunnel," I pointed out.

"Well," countered the professor, "remember we're talking about over two thousand years ago. The wadi may well have taken a slightly different route. The hole is in the side of the gorge, so perhaps at one point it was more readily accessible. Anyway, don't you think we should try and take a look at what's up there?" he asked, pointing at the hole in the ceiling.

We snapped out of our temporary torpor and Havelock bent to his knees with his fingers interlaced. I stepped into the cradle of his hands and he hoisted me upward until my head and shoulders were through the hole. I heaved myself up and rolled onto my side before reaching down through the hole for the torch Havelock offered me.

I swept the torchbeam around me and found myself in a circular chamber about three metres in diameter and three metres in height. Part of the continuous wall was occupied by the rusted remains of what looked like an iron door, about one and a half metres in height and full of jagged holes of various sizes produced by corrosion. I pushed against the heavily oxidised metal and was surprised when it bent inward, as if it were only millimetres thick. I smelt the acrid odour of metal decay in my nostrils as I wiped my hands on my jeans.

"I've got something up here," I shouted to my companions. "Can the professor make it up?" Try stopping him, I thought, as I heard him demanding a leg-up from Havelock. Soon his head and shoulders were poking through the hole and I grabbed him under the arms and lifted his surprisingly solid body through the opening. We both shone our torches at what was left of the metal door, through the holes in which we could see only darkness beyond.

"Well, professor, this is it. Are you ready?"

"I was born ready!" he said, laughing at his own cliché. We faced the door, put our hands against it, and pushed.

CHAPTER 76

AL-SHAMMARI WAS INCANDESCENT WITH RAGE. He and his men had driven fast deep into the heart of the city of Jericho to the house of a sympathiser whose name and address had just been given to him by his contacts in Lebanon. Mahmoud had hammered on the entrance of the dwelling in the old city and a bleary-eyed retainer had been thrust out of the way as the door burst open and Al-Shammari and his men entered. The house's owner appeared moments later, half-dressed, and bowed to his uninvited guests.

"Get me a map," ordered Al-Shammari. "Jericho and the surrounding area. I want to know where all the archaeological remains are." The man hesitated, unsure how to comply. "Now!" shouted Al-Shammari. The man reversed out of the room, still bowing, while the retainer brought them all hot, sweet tea. They heard the front door open and close.

"That whore of a sow will pay for this," spat Al Shammari.

"I shall enjoy teaching her a lesson," replied Mahmoud with a sneer. "But first, sir, the scroll."

"Yes, Mahmoud. I know where the priority lies." Mahmoud held up his hands in a concilliatory gesture. He knew better than to provoke his master in this mood. They waited and drank tea, Al-Shammari pacing the room, the three armed men standing silently in three corners, their rifles at the ready.

It was half an hour before their host returned, his arms full of maps and guides. He dropped them all on the table in the centre of the room and spread them out. Al-Shammari and Mahmoud pored over them. After flipping through several tourist guides, each one tossed onto the floor as it was discarded, Al-Shammari stabbed a finger at a page in one of the books, this one an American publication in English.

"What is this?" he demanded of his host. The man, quivering, leaned over his shoulder and replied in a querulous voice, "That is the palace of the old Jews. It is more than two thousand years old. It is said that –"

"I don't need a fucking history lesson!" retorted Al-Shammari, glaring at the man over his shoulder. "Is there a synagogue there?"

"I – I – "

"It's a simple enough question," shouted Al-Shammari, his face centimetres from the quaking man. "Is. There. A. Synagogue?" This last at an almost hysterical pitch.

"I – I don't know, sir," bleated the man. "I –" He got no further. Al-Shammari slapped him hard on the side of the head and the man fell to the floor, whimpering.

"There is a Jew church there," proffered a quiet voice. It was the old retainer. "The archaeologists discovered it only twenty years ago. But there is nothing there, only stones."

Al-Shammari regarded him for a moment, then summoned him to the table. "Show me where, good father." The old man considered the map for a moment, then pointed. "There," he said.

"Good," said Al-Shammari. "Mahmoud, please give the good father some reward for his help."

Mahmoud drew a wallet from his jacket pocket and withdrew some notes, handing them to the old man, who bowed and

401

retired to the unoccupied corner of the room. His master still crouched on the floor, shaking with fear.

"Come," said Al-Shammari, his voice cold as ice. "It is time to teach these infidels a lesson they will never forget." And he swept from the room, followed by his armed companions.

CHAPTER 77

IT TOOK ONLY a couple of heaves for the ironwork to give way, crumbling from the sides and showering us both with rust. Brushing it from our clothes and hair, we pushed through the gap in the centre of the door, followed by Havelock, and shone our torches around the room. I'm not sure what I had been expecting, given the professor's talk of a scriptorium, perhaps shelves stuffed with scrolls, but this was far from what I expected. It was a space about 30 metres square, lined on three sides with a shallow bench cut out of the rock. On each bench was a row of sealed jars, which looked to my untrained eye like baked clay. There was nothing else. The room was completely empty but for the vessels.

If I seemed a little disappointed, the professor was ecstatic, as was Charlene, who had also been helped up into the circular room and had followed us into the basement. As I shone my torch around the walls, I spotted the small square aperture in the ceiling which opened into darkness and which I presumed led to the niche in the synagogue hall several metres above our heads. I walked over and shone my torch upward and could see rungs cut into the wall of a narrow chute, at the top of which I could just about make out what looked like a flat piece of stone.

Havelock, meanwhile, had also entered the room and cracked half-a-dozen powerful glow sticks, which he distributed around the shelves and on the floor, providing more than enough light for our purposes.

Sarma and Charlene were clucking away over the jars, debating what might be inside them and talking excitedly about what a furore they would cause back in London. I, on the other hand, was looking for one thing and one thing only. I walked along each of the stone shelves, examining the jars one by one, but they all looked almost identical. They were all plain with no markings that I could discern, and I began to despair of finding what we were looking for. And then I saw it.

"Professor? Charlene?" I beckoned them over to the wall opposite the entrance and pointed to the last jar on the right, which was pushed back into the corner. The two antiquarians crouched down and examined the jar, which – unlike all the others – appeared to have some kind of emblem etched into the clay.

"My God," exclaimed Charlene. "It's a menorah. The symbol of the Temple." We all stood and looked at it in silence. Like all the others, it was about 40 centimetres in height, but now that we examined it more closely, we could see that it was a slightly different colour, darker and more polished than its companions.

"You know we have to open this, don't you?" I asked quietly.

The professor threw up his hands in horror. "But you can't! It needs to be opened under controlled conditions, in a laboratory. There need to be air filters. We need gloves. It needs to be photographed in situ before we touch it. It –"

"Charlie's right," interrupted Charlene. "This particular jar, we need to open. I'm sorry, professor, but that's the way it has to be."

"But, but –" spluttered Sarma. We were not to be dissuaded and he eventually subsided, his shoulders slumped. While

Charlene directed her torch at my hands, I picked up the jar and tried to unplug it, but it was sealed tight. I tried repeatedly to pull it open, then tried to prise it open with my penknife, but to no avail. Eventually, I gave up. "I'm really sorry, professor," I said, and I tapped the mouth of the jar smartly against the edge of the bench. The entire top simply popped off, leaving a serrated clay edge.

I looked at Charlene and she shrugged, raising her eyebrows. What else were we to do? I returned the jar to the bench. I reached in and felt around inside it, grasping the contents firmly and slowly withdrawing a metal scroll, about thirty centimetres long. It was green with oxidation, but even with my untrained eye I could tell that it was remarkably well preserved. We all three of us looked at one another. The professor, of course, had no idea what we had been seeking and so was in the dark about what we'd found, but Charlene and I were both awestruck.

"This is it," I whispered.

"I think you're right," she replied. "Let me see," and I carefully handed the scroll to her. It was light, but I could tell it was tightly rolled and probably of a good length when fully extended. Charlene sat in the middle of the room, the scroll illuminated by my torch and Sarma's, and began to examine the ancient document.

"Definitely copper, definitely inscribed. I won't be able to unroll it completely – it's too fragile – but let me see what I *can* see." She held the scroll by its ends and carefully drew out the end of the copper sheet, exposing about thirty-five centimetres of text. She scrutinised it closely, following the lines of ancient script. After a few minutes, she began to read.

"'*Herein is a copy of the writing placed in the caves of the Essaioi to the north of the Yam HaMelah*' – that's the 'Salt Sea', the

Dead Sea," explained Charlene, "so definitely Qumran, where the Dead Sea Scrolls were discovered – including the original Copper Scroll!" She went on, slightly breathless: "*together with its explanation and the measurements and the details of each item contained therein, and the cities, towns, villages and places of worship wherein they shall be found.*'" She paused and asked for our torches to be brought closer.

"This is more difficult to read. It's heavily oxidised." She peered more closely under the powerful torch beams, then continued, "*If thou wilt restore the Temple in all its glory, go in faith and find herein the places of those treasures that are Yahweh's.*'

She continued to read. "My God," she breathed, "it's all here. The towns and villages and other locations where you'll find all the places mentioned in the original scroll. This is unbelievable! Here they are, the old Washer's House, the courtyard of the House of Logs, the hill of Kohlit... the entire key to the puzzle!"

"So it's true. This scroll is intended to be read alongside the other," I said quietly.

Sarma, unnoticed, had approached and was looking over our shoulders. "I am beginning to understand why you were so eager to get here and the importance of what you've found," he said, his voice barely above a whisper.

"Yes," answered Charlene in an equally hushed tone. We were silent as the ramifications of our discovery sank in. This was the closest any of us were ever likely to get to a treasure map - and it lead to a hoard worth billions or even trillions of dollars. Even if only a fraction of the treasure were unearthed, the political implications would be enormous.

But the more immediate risk was the scroll falling into the wrong hands.

Havelock spoke for the first time. "We need to move. Now." He turned and led the way.

We were all reluctant to leave this extraordinary repository, especially Charlene and the professor, but we also understood the urgency of getting the scroll to a safe place as soon as possible – and there would be plenty of time for the new find to be properly investigated and catalogued. Charlene passed me the scarf she had been wearing and I carefully wrapped the scroll and placed it in an inside pocket of my soaking-wet fleece.

"Wait," I said, a sudden thought striking me. I unwrapped the scroll and put it on the floor, opening out as much of it as the corrosion would allow. I took out my phone, engaged the flash and took photos of both sides of the manuscript. Then I rewrapped the scroll and returned it to my pocket. Charlene was looking at me curiously, her eyebrows arched in the torch-light. I just nodded.

After a last wistful look around the room, the two academics finally made their way back through the door and lowered themselves through the hole into Havelock's waiting arms. I dropped through last and we all started to make our way back down the tunnel.

Our return journey was quicker than our original trek and within twenty minutes we were back in the cavern and Have-lock was leading the way through the shallow underwater depression to the waterfall, helping the professor through after him. Charlene and I followed.

We scrambled out from behind the cascade into the wadi. The sun was now just above the horizon and the sky was a pale blue dotted with clouds, while the shadows from the wadi walls were sharpening. We were relieved that our clothes would dry quickly with the impending rise in temperature and, with one of Havelock's men in front and one behind, we started walking quickly towards the mouth of the canyon.

We were about a hundred metres from the end of the wadi when there was a deafening roar and the man leading our group pitched forward, the back of his camo fatigues stitched with red.

Instinctively, I grabbed Charlene and Havelock slammed us all against the rock wall, directly beneath the line of fire from the clifftop. Havelock and Omar immediately began loosing short bursts in the direction from which the shots had come.

"Stay where you are!" shouted Havelock, as he ran forward to check on the downed man, while the other gave covering fire with his MP5. A quick check of his companion's pulse obviously confirmed his fears and Havelock joined us against the wall. 'Shit!" he exclaimed. "How fucking stupid was I to get caught in a rat trap like this!" At which another volley of automatic fire rained down from the cliff above us, scattering splinters of rock in all directions. I felt wetness on my cheek and realised that one of the limestone chips had struck me. I pressed myself harder against the wall, as did the others.

Then there was silence, before a calm voice echoed down the wadi. "Lady and gentlemen, I would strongly urge you to lay down your weapons and come out peacefully. We really do not want any more unpleasantness. There are enough ghosts in this place – I would not want to add further to their number."

Havelock whispered for us to shimmy along the wall upstream away from the entrance to the wadi, obviously hoping to find a better firing position, but there was an immediate burst of gunfire from the top of the opposite wadi wall, which until now had been empty. We were now pinned down and it didn't take a military expert to conclude that we had nowhere to go. Charlene was shivering, and not just from her wet clothes, while the professor was crouched against the wall with shaking hands over his head.

"Please," said the voice again, pleasantly, "be sensible. No one else has to suffer."

We looked at Havelock and after a long pause, he nodded. I put my gun down on the ground, as did he and his remaining companion.

"Splendid," said the voice. "Now, if you would be so good as to exit the wadi the way you came in, we can all become better acquainted."

Having no other choice but to comply, we all began to shuffle down the gorge, still apprehensive about the gunmen on the tops of the wadi walls. I paused for just a moment to stuff the wrapped scroll and my phone into a narrow crevice in the rock, then followed the others. It took us another ten minutes to get onto the open ground at the mouth of the wadi, where we were met by Al-Shammari, his henchman Mahmoud and four hooded men armed with AK-47s, two on each side, their weapons held steadily on us. One of them stepped forward and, quickly and efficiently, frisked us for weapons, taking both the handguns that Havelock and his companion had holstered on their hips, together with all our phones, which they dropped into one of their rucksacks.

"My men?" asked Havelock, referring to the two he had left at the palace ruins. "I'm afraid I had to dispense with their services once they had pointed us in your direction." Havelock's jaw tightened and I saw beneath his usually calm and controlled demeanour a cold rage building.

"Now, I see you have been for a swim," observed Al-Shammari with a genial smile. "I hope it was a productive immersion." His smile vanished. "Now, I believe we all know why we are here. I really am most grateful to you all for undertaking – how do you say in English? – the heavy lifting, in our common endeavour. It has saved me much time and effort. But now the time has come to give me what I came for."

We all looked at him in silence. He returned our gaze for a few beats and then nodded to Mahmoud, who moved towards Charlene. Havelock and I simultaneously made to step in front of her, but two of the gunmen cocked their weapons, put them to their shoulders and sighted on us both. Charlene screamed and swore at Mahmoud as he grabbed her by the arm and dragged her over to his boss.

"I have to tell you all that I do not have much liking for Americans, particularly American women who have yet to learn the meaning of modesty," said Al-Shammari, looking pointedly at Charlene, who was squirming in Mahmoud's grip. Mahmoud took out a wickedly curved blade and held it to Charlene's throat. "Now, the scroll, please, or Mahmoud will be forced to demonstrate our aversion to Americans more graphically."

"We don't have it!" I shouted. "It's still where we found it. Now let her go!"

"Such a pretty face," mused Al-Shammari, regarding Charlene almost with affection. Then, in a single fluid movement the blade flashed and a large lock of her hair fell to the ground. Charlene became quite still, her face set in a mask of terror. My breath caught in my throat. "The next time I suspect Mahmoud will be less careful with his knife and we shall see how well the lady reads her manuscripts with one eye. Now, please, the scroll."

The old familiar fury was beginning to take hold. Havelock could see this and whispered to me to calm down. As a former soldier I knew he was right. Don't act on impulse; be patient and wait for your opportunity.

"Okay," I said. "Let her go and I'll fetch it." Mahmoud released Charlene, who ran back to the professor and they hugged one another in mutual reassurance. I began to walk back up the wadi, followed by one of the masked men, his rifle trained on me all the way. I retrieved the scroll, leaving my phone, and returned to the group.

Al-Shammari looked hungrily at the wrapped bundle. "Bring it to me, please." I began to slowly walk towards him. When I was about ten metres away, the sand and scree beneath my feet gave way to an area of solid rock and I stopped. I looked down at the bundle, then at Al-Shammari. After a moment's hesitation I let my arm fall to my side, the scarf fell open and the scroll fell gently to the ground at my feet. I immediately placed my boot over it. Charlene and Sarma gasped. The armed men took a step forward. Al-Shammari waved them off and glared at me.

"This is over two thousand years old, Al-Shammari. It's fragile. How well do you think it would survive my boot?"

"No!" shouted Sarma. "It's too delicate – it will crumble to dust!"

"That would be a very foolish thing to do," responded Al-Shammari hoarsely. "Because then I would have no further use for any of you. Now, please, be sensible, bring me the scroll and we can all go about our business." In reply, I lowered my boot a little further until it was just resting on the scroll. Al-Shammari's eyes blazed. "Tell your goons to drop their weapons and then perhaps we can talk man to man," I said, my gaze locked on his.

In answer, Al-Shammari calmly drew a Makarov pistol from beneath his jacket, pointed it at Havelock and shot him in the leg. Vanguard's head of security crumpled to the ground with a loud gasp. I was so shocked by this sudden turn of events that I reflexively took a step back, momentarily removing my foot from the scroll. In the second or two that it took me to recover, Al-Shammari dashed forward and grabbed the scroll, before screaming, "Kill them all!"

What happened next happened so fast that I barely remember more than a cacophony of shouting, shooting and screaming. It began with the head of one of Al-Shammari's men exploding in a red blur, followed a moment later by a second, his jaw literally blown out of his face. The remaining two men, confused and unable to identify where the shooting was coming from, were firing blindly in the direction of the wadi. Charlene and the professor had thrown themselves to the ground with their hands over their heads. Omar shot forward, rolled and came up with one of the dead men's AK-47s, his finger on the trigger as he rose to his knees.

The hooded men were slow to react. One took a round in the throat from the AK and was thrown backwards. The other swung his gun wildly in my direction, but it was torn from his hands in mid-arc as a hole the size of a tennis ball appeared in his chest. He fell to his knees and slumped forward. Mahmoud had run back to the safety of the wadi and disappeared.

In the silence that followed, we all looked at one another in shock and surprise, stunned by a turn of events that from start to finish had lasted no more than thirty seconds. But before we had a chance to entirely gather our wits, we caught sight of Al-Shammari running fast back towards the palace ruins, the scroll held tightly to his chest, followed by Mahmoud. I shouted to Havelock's man to keep watch over our party and dashed after the Iraqi, stopping only to scoop up one of the discarded AK-47s.

Al-Shammari was surprisingly fit and covered the half-kilo-metre back to the ruins in less than two minutes. I realised how out of shape I was as I struggled to keep up. He was making for a Toyota Land Cruiser which was parked just beside the gate, but just as he reached it he turned, crouched and fired three shots in quick succession. I felt two of the rounds thud into the ground inches from my feet and felt the third tug at my hair. Then my instincts at last kicked in and I ducked, rolled and came back to my feet again in a full sprint.

The Iraqi had made it to the vehicle and was in the driver's seat. The engine roared to life and all four wheels spun as the truck reversed hard away from the gate. At this point, time appeared to slow down and I felt my training take hold, as though a switch had been flicked, setting me on automatic pilot. I knelt on one knee, calmly flipped the gun to semi-automatic, sighted on the truck and smoothly blew out the two front tyres. The vehicle sashayed across the gravel, describing a lazy circle, before attempting to push itself on its rear wheels along the road away from the site.

I watched as the Toyota lumbered forward, its front sliding from side to side, then slowly brought the rifle up to my shoulder again, taking careful aim. The red-hot round passed through the skin of the vehicle and penetrated the fuel tank at 700 metres per second, instantly igniting the petrol fumes, which a split-second later fired the fuel itself and the rear of the vehicle lifted clear of the ground as the tank exploded with a dull whump.

Al-Shammari threw open the door and tumbled to the ground, his clothes alight. I could see that he was still holding the scroll to his chest as he rolled over and over in an effort to put out the flames. He scrambled to his feet and attempted to continue running along the road away from the site, but his legs wouldn't cooperate and he kept slipping to the ground. As he pulled himself painfully to his feet for the third or fourth time, a figure in desert camouflage walked calmly out on to the road ahead and turned to face him, a heavy weapon pointed at his head.

"You!" I heard Al-Shammari cry as I ran towards them.

CHAPTER 78

REBECCA HELD the enormous gun steady, pointed at the Iraqi's head, as I arrived, panting, beside him. "Hello Charlie," she said. I looked at her in amazement for a few seconds, then for some reason my astonishment faded away to be replaced by an instinctive understanding.

"So, no betrayal after all," I said simply.

She smiled, the rifle still rock-steady in her hands. I recognised it as a favoured weapon of Israeli Special Forces: an IWI Dan bolt-action sniper rifle, its powerful .338 Lapua Magnum cartridges capable of inflicting devastating damage to targets more than a kilometre away.

"Just needed to buy you some time," she replied. "This piece of shit was so stupid and so blind to his own hubris that he swallowed my story whole."

Al-Shammari was kneeling on the ground, his clothes still smoking and half his hair and beard singed away. The left side of his face was raw where the flames had caught it. He still clutched the scroll in his left hand and his right was lying on the ground, gripping his pistol. At Rebecca's taunt his face twisted with hatred and he raised the gun. The weapon never made it more than a couple of inches from the ground. In a barely perceptible movement, Rebecca lowered her rifle, pulled the trigger and Al-Shammari's right hand disappeared in a bloody mist, his pistol skittering across the gravel.

The Iraqi screamed, dropped the scroll and pulled the stump of his ruined hand to his chest. His blood was pumping freely onto the ground.

"You traitorous bitch," he snarled. "God will roast you in hell. How could you betray our people like this? My brothers will hunt you down and kill you. They will tear you limb from limb. They will flay you alive and feed you to pigs. They –"

"I get the message, you dog," said Rebecca calmly. "But let me set you straight. You are not 'my people'. You are filth. My father was a proud Israeli, a general and a patriot. Until your 'people' blew him away with one of their fucking suicide bombs – along with my mother and baby sister. You and your 'brothers'," she spat the word, "are nothing more than vermin. You do *nothing* for the cause of the Palestinians. You are self-serving doom-mongers, a pathetic death-cult. You are nothing!"

At which Al-Shammari summoned up some last reserve of strength and surged towards her, the stump of his hand spraying blood in an arc through the air.

Rebecca raised the rifle once more. "You're finished, Al-Shammari," she said, and shot him in the chest.

She let the rifle fall to her side and we both stood and looked at our broken adversary, who looked so much smaller in death. Then we regarded one another in silence for a few moments, before I walked to her and threw my arms around her. She did the same, both of us holding our rifles awkwardly behind each other's backs as we hugged.

"I shouldn't have doubted you," I said.

"Well," she laughed, "I wouldn't have been doing a very good job if you hadn't."

I stepped back and laughed too. "Was that true? About your family?"

"A suicide bomber in Tel Aviv, yes. They were celebrating my sister's twelfth birthday in a restaurant. The bomber took out twenty-five people. My mother and father were killed instantly. Leah survived for two days."

"I'm sorry," I said, painfully aware of the inadequacy of my words.

"Well, thankfully I speak fluent Arabic and these assholes can't tell the difference between us. That's the irony at the heart of the entire conflict. In essence, we're all Palestinians."

"And you're a hell of a shot," I said admiringly. Rebecca looked at her weapon, appearing almost surprised that she was still holding it. "I had good teachers," she said. I cocked my head questioningly. "You don't remember? A training course on the range in Camp Tzrifin five years ago? I was one of the students. Although, as I recall, there were two groups and I was in the one being trained by one of your colleagues, rather than you. But I remember seeing you in the mess hall." I didn't remember, there had been so many training exercises over the years. But I was deeply grateful that we had trained this woman so well.

I heard shouts from behind me and saw our group walking slowly towards us, Havelock supported by his man on one side and Charlene on the other. Havelock didn't seem the least surprised to see his former colleague.

"Good job, Rebecca," gasped Havelock, obviously in great pain from his leg, which was tourniqueted with Charlene's scarf. Sarma and Charlene simply looked baffled. Then Charlene spotted the scroll lying on the ground and, exclaiming "Thank God!", she made to pick it up. Rebecca intercepted her, retrieved the scroll and studied it for a few moments. "So this is what it was all about," she murmured, almost to herself.

She gently blew on the surface of the scroll, dislodging some of the soot, then sighed and walked over to the burning Land Cruiser. Before anyone had time to react, she tossed the scroll through the open window of the truck. We all rushed forward as one, Sarma and Charlene shouting in unison, "Nooooo!" But it was too late. As we stood and looked through the window, the paint on its frame burning freely, we watched as the scroll turned black on the driver's seat before it began to disintegrate and disappeared in the roiling smoke.

We all stood in silence, stupefied. "It's better this way," said Rebecca simply, and walked away towards the palace ruins. We all stood for a minute staring at the burning truck, then turned and followed her.

CHAPTER 79

THE SUN WAS CLIMBING towards mid-morning as we gathered our belongings and prepared to leave. We had retrieved a first aid kit from one of our rucksacks and dressed Havelock's wound, which proved not to be too serious – no broken bone and no artery damaged, the bullet having passed straight through. Recovering his phone from the dead Arab, he made a call and forty minutes later two large people carriers appeared, driven by taciturn Israelis who, if they were military, wore no insignia to indicate as much. While we waited for our escorts to arrive, I jogged back to the wadi and retrieved my phone.

The bodies, friend and foe, were loaded into one of the vehicles, along with the weaponry, and we all piled into the other with our gear. As we were leaving, we saw the first of the crowds from Jericho descending on the site, drawn by the sound of gunfire and the sight of smoke from the burning Land Cruiser.

An hour later we were in Jerusalem, checking into the Orient Hotel just south of Liberty Bell Park. After freshening up, we met in the restaurant, a sombre group, our heads still spinning from the events of the last few hours. Charlene and the professor were still mortified by the destruction of the scroll, but somewhat mollified by the prospect of a thorough professional excavation of the chamber below the synagogue. Rebecca was quiet and reflective. Havelock was the last to join us. He had had his wound redressed by a doctor and now limped towards our table as we ordered the first proper meal we'd had since the day before.

"I have a confession to make, Charlie," he said as he sat down. He glanced over at Rebecca and they shared a look. Before Havelock could continue, Rebecca broke in. "I'm sorry, Charlie."

"For what?" I asked, mystified.

"For deceiving you." I was completely lost.

She took a deep breath and continued. "Nathaniel, Bruce and I talked about it as we were preparing to leave for Israel. We knew we had to slow Al-Shammari down – and we knew I was probably the person best placed to do it, but – "

"Wait a goddamned minute!" I spluttered. "Are you telling me you knew about this all along, Havelock?"

Vanguard's head of security nodded gravely. "Rebecca told us you'd – uh – become close." I looked at her in disbelief. "And we all felt that your feelings might – well – compromise the mission, shall we say? Given that she was going to put herself in harm's way. We felt you might object. Added to which, it was best that as few people as possible knew what was going on."

I sat there stupefied, looking from one to the other. Charlene and the professor wisely stood up and walked off to the bar, leaving the three of us alone. I couldn't think of a word to say. And then, in a sudden release of tension, I began to laugh. Rebecca and Bruce joined in.

"Don't ever do that again," I said, still laughing.

"No chance of that, Charlie," smiled Rebecca, putting her hand on mine. "You're one of us now. No more secrets."

Just as we were settling down to eat and engaging in an earnest discussion of our experiences, a well-dressed man approached our table and introduced himself. "Good afternoon, ladies and gentlemen," he said politely, with a heavy Hebrew accent. "My name is Chaim Mizrahi. Can you spare me a few moments?"

It transpired that our new guest represented whichever shady arm of the military had been despatched to help us. The Israelis had apparently taken on trust much of what they had been told by Lowell prior to our expedition, and it was sufficient for them that they had recovered the body of an Iraqi terrorist they had long had tabs on but been unable to apprehend. This went a long way towards placating them for the disruption we had caused on the West Bank, the fallout from which they were still dealing with. A call between Mizrahi and Lowell shortly before his arrival had seemingly sealed the deal and the Israeli was here to thank us for, as far as they were concerned, a job well done. Then he took his leave, and we were left to celebrate with a lobster salad and a well-chilled bottle of Moet & Chandon.

As our celebratory meal was drawing to a close and the others were chatting animatedly, I took out my phone, swiped to the photo app and discreetly held it out to Rebecca, who was sitting next to me. She looked at the last two photos I'd taken for a long moment, then handed the phone back to me. She didn't say a word – just looked at me, her head cocked on one side, her eyebrows raised questioningly. I looked back at her and smiled, nodded. Then hit delete.

EPILOGUE

I HAD BEEN BACK from Israel for two weeks. A few days of that had been spent on *Triton*, debriefing and watching over Angie as she inched towards recovery. Lowell had been ecstatic with the results of our mission and believed that Rebecca had done exactly the right thing when she destroyed the scroll.

"It would have brought nothing but misery and grief," he observed. "We have enough problems in the Middle East and it would just have inflamed an already toxic situation. Let the treasures stay hidden."

I looked at him in surprise. "Do you think they really existed?"

"Who knows?" he answered. "They've been lying there for more than two thousand years, but you'd have thought someone would have dug up something by now, no matter how well hidden it was. In the event, it doesn't really matter. The very fact that the treasure might have existed – and that the bad guys in the region knew about it – would have been enough to cause mayhem. We'll never know. But," he had leaned back in his chair expansively, taking a sip of the fine malt we were sharing after dinner, "the point is that we took it off the table. One less thing for them to fight over."

I couldn't help but agree.

Lowell had gone on to formalise his offer of a job. Vanguard always needed expertise and people with field experience, he said, and I had proven myself. I told him I would think about it, but I'd already decided to accept. I needed a job, but I also needed the excitement. I hadn't appreciated how much I'd missed it since I left the army and the prospect of working with this exceptional team of talented people thrilled me.

An archaeological expedition had already been mounted to the ruins of the synagogue, led by an overjoyed Professor Sarma and his eager accomplice, Charlene Ramirez. The stone at the base of the niche in the hall had been lifted, the access opened up and all the scrolls retrieved. They were now safely in the care of Charlene and a team of conservators in Jerusalem and there was huge excitement in academic circles about what they would contain. Time would reveal all.

Israeli intelligence services were still looking for Mahmoud, who had slipped away during the melee and vanished without trace, but I had a feeling we would be seeing him again. A lengthy search of Al-Shammari's homes in London and Lebanon had yielded a treasure trove of valuable intelligence, some of which would be used in the months to come to identify and eliminate a number of terrorists who posed a threat both to Israel and its neighbours. Among the items in his Beka'a villa was a large airtight container in which was discovered both the original copy of the palimpsest and the ancient document from which it had been extracted. There was now feverish excitement in theological circles over what the manuscript signified and the Church was wrestling with the implications of a potential new gospel written, not only by one of Jesus's own family, but by a woman. Many experts thought that nothing less than a rewriting of the Christian story was on the cards. But that was all for another day.

Angie and I had parted on better terms than we'd enjoyed for a long time and now she was back home in Hampshire, with the promise of a visit from me very soon to map out our respective futures. Two of Havelock's men had been watching over her until we could figure out what to do about Braddock.

I had moved out of my bedsit and into a Vanguard safe house in South Kensington, where one evening in early April, Angie and I were sitting in the small rear garden, reflecting on everything that had happened and talking about what we would do next. The air was balmy with early spring sunshine and the scent of hyacinths drifting up from the herbaceous border. We had decided to take a short holiday together, as a way of finding out whether we could realistically repair our marriage, and were chatting quietly about where we might go.

I was still a little confused by my experience with Rebecca. I understood that we had been drawn to one another, not only by recent events, but also by our past – and by a shared love of my dead brother. We had both succumbed to an urgent need, but I knew that it had been no more than that: a fleeting need. I sensed that Rebecca knew it too, and we had parted friends in Israel, recognising that if we were to be working together, it was best from then on to keep things professional. It had also helped me gain some perspective on my relationship with Angie. As my confidence grew and the effects of my PTSD gradually receded, I realised that the gulf between us was narrowing and perhaps there was a way back for us after all.

We were talking quietly, looking down the length of the west-facing garden as the sun moved towards the horizon. I had just refilled Angie's glass with the Sauvignon we'd been sharing when a genial voice sounded behind us.

"Well, this is very nice, I must say. Very romantic."

We both turned and leaped to our feet as we took in the two men standing in front of the kitchen patio doors. Both were armed with single-barrel shotguns, both were pointed at us, both were instantly familiar.

"Jack Braddock," I mouthed. "I wondered what rock you'd crawled under."

"Well, that's very nice, I'm sure," replied Braddock sarcastically. "After all we've been through together, I'd have expected a warmer welcome. We have some unfinished business, don't we, Charlie? Now, how about a drink?" He nudged his accomplice, who I recognised from the warehouse as Gazza, towards the table where the bottle and two glasses were standing. "I brought my own glasses, see?" and he held out two goblets he'd taken from the kitchen.

Gazza approached us and Braddock followed. "Sit down, both of you. We're going to have a cosy chat." Both shotguns were still pointed at us as they crossed the ten metres or so between us. I noticed that Braddock was limping badly, clearly the result of my bullet, fired as he ran from the warehouse. He was holding the shotgun in his left hand and his right wrist was in plaster, another legacy of our last encounter.

Angie was wide-eyed, confronted once again with the tormenter who had so nearly ended her life. But she did not cower. Instead, glaring at Braddock, she backed towards the table alongside me, lowering herself into one of the chairs as I took another. Braddock and Gazza pulled the remaining two out from the table and sat back with a comfortable distance between them and us, still pointing the weapons in our direction.

"Why don't you pour us a couple of glasses, love?" said Braddock to Angie. She rose unsteadily to her feet and grasped the bottle with shaking hands, walking around the table towards Gazza, who had taken one of the glasses from his boss. Gazza held out his glass with his left hand, a mirthless grin suffusing his face, whilst holding the shotgun one-handed in the other.

As she leaned down to pour wine into his glass, she deftly switched the bottle from her left hand to her right, grabbing it by the neck, and slammed it into the side of Gazza's head with all her might. He fell off his chair and sprawled on the ground, out for the count.

It took a split second for Braddock to react which gave me the opportunity to upend the table and send it crashing into Braddock's body. His shotgun was driven upward by the impact and when he pulled the trigger the shot blew harmlessly into the air as he toppled over backwards, pinned beneath the table. Angie stepped behind him and, with surprising calmness, twisted the weapon out of his hands. He scrambled backwards, trying to get clear of the table, and I picked up the half-full bottle of wine.

I was suddenly filled with an ice-cold fury. All those years of loss – the pain, the humiliation, the fear – coalesced into one concentrated moment of total, focused hatred. Walking over to the struggling figure on the ground, I put my foot on his chest and looked down at him. "You want a drink, Jack? I'll give you a drink. And I dropped to my knees astride his chest and rammed the neck of the wine bottle into his mouth. I felt teeth crack and snap as I forced the bottle between his lips and then down his throat, pushing as hard as I could, half the liquid running down his throat, the rest spilling out from his lips. Braddock's hands were scrabbling at my chest, his face turning puce and then blue as he struggled to breathe, but I kept pushing and pushing, his mouth widening in a growing rictus as I began hammering on the base of the bottle.

"That's enough, Charlie," said Angie quietly. "That's enough."

I looked up at her and the rage dissipated. I stood up and Braddock gasped as the bottle fell from this mouth, a mixture of blood, wine and broken teeth running down his cheeks.

"Perhaps," I said. "For now, at least."

The shots had brought the neighbours out and we could hear excited shouts coming from the gardens next door, mingled with the sound of distant sirens, which drew gradually closer as Braddock pulled himself upright and regarded me with a dazed expression.

To say the police were surprised when they arrived was an understatement. They knew Braddock by reputation and when they'd taken our statements they looked at us with undisguised admiration.

Gazza had come round while we were waiting for the police van to take them away. Both men were now cuffed and left sitting against the garden fence. The police showed little sympathy with their injuries. Braddock just glared at me. Gazza sat with his head down.

Ten minutes later the van arrived and four police constables came to escort the men through the house and out the front door. As he passed me, Braddock spat, "This isn't over, you cunt. I'll have you *and* your fucking dolly. Keep a good lookout, Charlie Carter. You're a marked man." The two policemen on either side of him pulled him away and they walked off into the kitchen. I followed.

As they reached the police van and the rear doors were being opened, I walked up to Braddock. "A quick word?" I asked the two constables. They nodded. I leaned in close to Braddock and whispered in his ear, then backed away. There was a moment's pause, then Braddock erupted, his face puce, spittle flying from his broken mouth, struggling against the two policemen. He thrashed from side to side, kicking out at the officers as they manhandled him into the back of the van, screaming at the top of this voice that he would find me and kill me.

Angie came up behind me and quietly asked, "What on earth did you say to him?"

"I told him we had it all on film from the security cameras. I told him that at the end his son cried like a baby, whimpering for mercy. But most importantly, I told him what his son said."

"And what was that?"

"He told me he hated his father. That he was ashamed of him and what he'd made him do. That he wished he'd never been born."

Angie said nothing. There was nothing to say.

"So, it's over at last? Can you put it behind you now?"

"Yes. It's over."

As the police shut the doors of the van behind the two men, Braddock still screaming threats and obscenities from inside, Angie and I turned and walked back into the house. And closed the door.

———

More than 2,000 miles to the south-east, an elderly man was walking home from a long day tending his modest date palm orchard. He was readying his crop for harvest and as he walked he pondered how he was going to persuade his two lazy sons to help him. It was the same every year. They would rather pass their days sitting with their friends in the local cafés drinking sweet tea and smoking the hookah. He despaired of them ever doing a proper day's work. Perhaps it was his fault. Ever since their mother died, too young, more than 20 years before, he had struggled to provide them with the parental care they needed. There had been one or two flirtations, but no one to match his Martha, so he had never remarried and his boys had suffered the lack of a mother in their lives.

He sighed and resolved to confront them once more in the morning, as he turned off the road and followed one of the ancient irrigation channels, long since dried up, which led from the river into the olive groves which encircled his village deep in the Palestinian Territories. It was as he was about to turn onto the track which led to his home on the outskirts of the village that he noticed the hollow just below a stand of acacias. It was a deep depression in the ground which he had never noticed before. In fact, he had walked this path a thousand times and would swear that it had not been there until today.

Curious, he walked over to the cavity and peered into it in the fading light. The ground appeared to have collapsed and there was a large vertical fissure on one side of the depression beyond which was total blackness. He edged down into the hollow, his knees complaining, and examined the cleft, which he now realised was a large crack in what seemed to be a solid stone wall, long hidden by the earth. He drew his phone from his pocket and switched on the torch, shining it inside.

His torch illuminated a rectangular room, about 25 metres square. He quickly identified it as an ancient cistern, used to collect and store water from the irrigation channels which once linked the river to the olive groves. It appeared to be empty, except for what looked like a piece of rotted wooden flooring in the centre of the space. Squeezing through the gap, he crawled inside, his knees complaining even more loudly, and walked over to the decaying platform. As he went to lift one of the planks, it splintered and collapsed in his hands, swiftly followed by the rest of the panels. He realised now that it was a large box, obviously very old. Clearing away the debris, he unearthed a large bundle, wrapped in rotting oilcloth.

Separating the folds of the fabric, which had evidently once been bound tightly by some form of twine, he was astonished to find his torchlight reflected off a tightly packed collection of bright metal bars. There were hundreds of them, extending several feet in each direction. Every one the same yellow metal. Kilogram after kilogram of solid gold.

THE END

© Stephen Jacobs, March 2022

ABOUT THE AUTHOR

Stephen Jacobs has spent most of his life in the public relations and communications consultancy industry. During a career break he studied for a degree in Theology at the University of Oxford, where he acquired a keen interest in Judaic and Biblical history and archaeology. 'The Apocalypse Scroll' is his first novel.

Printed in Great Britain
by Amazon

26352286R00245